beijing comrades

beijing comrades

By Bei Tong
Translated by Scott E. Myers
Afterword by Petrus Liu

THE FEMINIST PRESS
AT THE CITY UNIVERSITY OF NEW YORK
NEW YORK CITY

Published in 2016 by the Feminist Press
at the City University of New York
The Graduate Center
365 Fifth Avenue, Suite 5406
New York, NY 10016

feministpress.org

First Feminist Press edition 2016

First English-language edition
Text copyright © 2001 by Bei Tong
A shorter version of this novel was first published in Chinese in 2001 by Tohan
Taiwan Limited Liability Company under the title 蓝宇 (北京故事)—*Lan Yu*
(*Beijing gushi*)
Translation copyright © 2016 by Scott E. Myers
Afterword copyright © 2016 by Petrus Liu

 This book was made possible thanks to a grant from New York State
Council on the Arts with the support of Governor Andrew Cuomo and the
NYSCA New York State Legislature.

First printing March 2016

Cover design by Isaac Tobin
Text design by Suki Boynton

Library of Congress Cataloging-in-Publication Data
Names: Bei Tong. | Myers, Scott E., translator.
Title: Beijing comrades / by Bei Tong ; translated by Scott E. Myers.
Other titles: Beijing gushi. English
Description: New York : The Feminist Press, [2016]
Identifiers: LCCN 2015019785| ISBN 9781558619074 (paperback) | ISBN
9781558619081 (ebook)
Subjects: LCSH: Gay men--China--Fiction. | BISAC: FICTION / Gay. |
HISTORY /
Asia / China. | HISTORY / Modern / 20th Century. | POLITICAL SCIENCE /
Censorship.
Classification: LCC PL2833.5.E49 B4513 2016 | DDC 895.13/52--dc23
LC record available at http://lccn.loc.gov/2015019785

Table of Contents

Translator's Note*

To English-language readers who know it, *Beijing Comrades* by Bei Tong is more likely to be known as *Beijing Story* by Beijing Comrade. Others may know the contemporary Chinese novel as *Lan Yu*, or *Someone Likes Lan*, or *Beijing gushi*.[1] The pseudonymous author, whose real-world identity has been a matter of speculation since the story was first published online in 1998, is known variously as Beijing Tongzhi, Beijing Comrade, Xiao He, Miss Wang, and Linghui. Given the dearth of information about Bei Tong, it is not surprising that there are a number of popular theories about her or his gender identity, sexual orientation, and life story. There are those who believe that she is a *tongqi*, a heterosexual woman with the misfortune of unknowingly marrying a gay man. Others suggest that he is novelist and essayist Wang Xiaobo, late husband of prominent sociologist, queer activist, and public intellectual Li Yinhe.[2] Finally, there are those who insist that

*An earlier version of this essay appeared as "*Beijing Comrades*: A Gay Chinese Love Story." *Amerasia Journal* 37, no. 2 (2011): 75–94.

Beijing Comrades was written by a sympathetic female friend at the behest of the male lovers whose story the novel tells. But while chatroom critics and patrons of gay bars from Beijing to New York City have long debated the identity of the author, other less elusive figures, such as Stanley Kwan, director of the 2001 film adaptation of the novel, speak unequivocally of Bei Tong using feminine pronouns. In this essay I follow Kwan's example, though I also think it is worth asking what bearing, if any, the extratextual identity of an author has on the way we read a story. Would greater knowledge of Bei Tong impact the way we read *Beijing Comrades*—the set of assumptions, expectations, and desires we bring to it? Would it guide our affective response to the novel or influence our conclusions about the "authenticity" of the characters or of Bei Tong's authorial voice? These are questions I leave for the reader to answer.

Beijing Comrades is among mainland China's earliest, best known, and most influential contemporary gay novels. It is also a pathbreaking work of what may be called *tongzhi* or gay fiction from the People's Republic of China (PRC). It came into being when a young Chinese person living in New York City—absorbed by the world of the Internet, lacking direction in life, and bored by the titillating but artistically vapid Chinese-language gay erotica available at the time—decided she would try and write her own homoerotic fiction.[3] Originally titled *Dalu gushi* (A story from the mainland), the novel was serialized on a mainland website, now defunct, called *Zhongguo nanren nanhai tiantang* (Chinese men's and boys' paradise), beginning on September 22, 1998,[4] giving it the additional status of being one of mainland China's earliest e-novels. It remains thematically sensitive today, not only because it includes explicit scenes of lovemaking between men (and between women and men), but also because it makes direct reference to government repression during the Tian'anmen Massacre of 1989.

The story opens in autumn 1987 during China's first decade of reform and eleven years after the death of Mao Zedong. It chronicles the ten-year relationship between Chen Handong and Lan Yu,[5] two men from very different social classes. Handong is a wealthy businessman in his late twenties, the spoiled offspring of elite Communist Party officials with a string of male and female lovers whose affections he secures through a generous stream of money and gifts. Lan Yu is a university student from a working-class background who has just arrived in Beijing from China's far northwest. Naive but by no means dim, he finds himself in Handong's bed when he is alone in the capital and presumably unable to make ends meet.[6] Narrated by Handong, the story chronicles the joys, hardships, and no small amount of sexual bliss the men share as they navigate the uncharted terrain of a same-sex relationship in the time and place where they live. A series of life-changing events propels the relationship into on-again, off-again status. In the central narrative of the story, Handong comes to confront and accept his internal awareness of himself as a gay man—shedding much of his appalling misogyny in the process—while also learning to have a relationship that is rooted neither in domination nor in an understanding of love as a system of investment and return.[7] In this respect, it is quite possible to read *Beijing Comrades* as a critique of the new economic policies that began to take hold in China under Deng Xiaoping's program of reform, first launched in late 1978. The novel may be seen as a response to a moment when money was rapidly becoming a disruptive and mediating force in interpersonal relationships, a dynamic further impacted by

China's pursuit of a mixed and globalized economy. As if to highlight these changes, Handong and other characters in the novel calculate their transactions not only in Chinese yuan but also in US dollars.

The author's choice of pen name, Beijing Tongzhi (literally, Beijing Comrade),[8] may have been an auspicious one, for it likely helped to attract an intended audience while escaping notice of those who would wish to impede the novel's circulation. Consisting of the Chinese characters for *tong* (same) and *zhi* (will, aspiration, or ideal), the word *tongzhi* was widely used in the socialist era (and earlier[9]) as a signifier of revolutionary camaraderie,[10] equivalent to the English word *comrade* or Russian word *tovarisch*. In recent years, the word *tongzhi* has been adopted and resignified by LGBTQ activists seeking a new vocabulary to describe themselves.[11] The new usage was first proposed in 1989 by playwright Edward Lam, who used it in the Chinese title of the Hong Kong Lesbian and Gay Film Festival. Since then, it has come to designate a subaltern sexual identity, similar in some ways to the English word *gay*.[12] Like gayness, tongzhiness has been a catalyst for the emergence of a personal and collective identity capable of challenging the archaic and pathologizing pseudoscientific term *homosexuality* (*tongxinglian*). Today, the use of *tongzhi* is so widespread—for some, the word carries primarily or only this "secondary" meaning—that it would be inaccurate to describe it as a form of gay slang. Indeed, the term has emerged as a site of culture wars in recent years, as evinced by editorial struggles over whether or not to include the additional meaning in new editions of Chinese dictionaries.[13]

Beijing Comrades is full of many twists and turns, but none are as complex as the genesis of the text—or texts—itself. There are, in fact, three separate and quite distinct versions of *Beijing*

Comrades, each with its own tone, length, subplots, intended audience, and publishing platform. The first version is the one written and posted online by Bei Tong in 1998, when the author was living in New York City.[14] Hastily executed and with no shortage of typos, this sexually graphic e-novel bursts with an exuberant and spirited amateurism that, far from blemishing the novel, is precisely a part of what makes it a pleasure to read. In the postscript accompanying the revised Taiwanese version that would be published in print more than three years later, Bei Tong reflects on her decision to write:

> The days of autumn 1998 were the grayest I'd had since coming to the United States. I had no idea where my life was headed. . . . I immersed myself in the world of the Internet: playing chess, chatting online, surfing porn sites.
>
> After reading all the pornographic stories that were out there, I cursed: FXXX![15]. . . I knew I could write something better.
>
> And so I threw myself furiously into writing, then posted my writing online. . . . Had I created a story, or stepped into one? Was this a dream or was it the real world?[16]

The intermingling of dreamworld and reality that Bei Tong describes in the novel's postscript is discernible in Beijing Comrades itself, where the boundaries dividing truth from falsehood, deception from certainty, and this life from the next are porous and flexible. Throughout the novel, Handong's path to greater self-awareness is paved with stumbling blocks of misrecognition, whereby class, gender, and other anchors of identity are turned upside down. Even the urban topography of China's capital city is hazy and elusive; an underground gay quanzi (circle) is hinted at but never directly shown. Indeed, most of the place names in Beijing Comrades are fictitious, including the names of universities. In the present translation, I preserve these imaginary names, even when clues in the text point suggestively to specific locations.17 Why Bei Tong chose to fictionalize place names can only be a matter of speculation, but the novel remains a response to a very real time, the late 1980s and early 1990s, when Beijing's gay community was at an early stage of formation.

The 2002 print book edition, published by Tohan Taiwan as *Lan Yu*, presented an edited version of the novel. Significantly polished in its language, this second version of Bei Tong's book arrived on the heels of Hong Kong filmmaker Stanley Kwan's 2001 Mandarin-language film, *Lan Yu*, which was based on the e-novel and shot without permits in Beijing. Kwan had learned of the story from film producer Zhang Yongning, who had personally hunted down Bei Tong after reading the story online and would later become the film's producer. The movie differs in significant ways from the novel and won a number of awards in Hong Kong and Taiwan. It also made history by being shown at China's first LGBTQ film festival, the China Homosexual Film Festival (now the Beijing Queer Film Festival) in 2001. The film strips away much of the novel's depiction of Handong's work and family life in order to focus in a quiet and restrained way on the closed, intimate world that he and Lan Yu share.

The cover of the Tohan book is a still from Kwan's film, depicting a steamy encounter between Handong (played by Hu Jun) and Lan Yu (played by Liu Ye), accompanied by a stern warning that the book was not to be read by anyone under the age of eighteen. Even with the warning, graphic sexual content was largely removed from the book. Whether one considers the Tohan version "graphic," of course, depends on the standard one is using, but in most cases, the explicit sex of the e-novel is replaced by sensual pleasures confined to kissing, caressing, and holding, aided by a liberal use of euphemism. In the first erotic encounter between Handong and Lan Yu, for example, what were once orgasm and ejaculation are alluded to by means of associated physiological responses such as heavy breathing and clenched fists, and direct references to genitalia are deleted entirely.[18]

Soon after the Tohan publication,[19] a greatly expanded version of the novel was drafted by Bei Tong in the hope that official (*guanfang*) publication[20] in mainland China would be possible. This hope was not realized, as Bei Tong was not able to find a publishing house that would accept the manuscript. The expanded version adds nine new chapters to the original thirty-two[21] and was given to me directly by Bei Tong for translation and inclusion in this edition; it has never been seen by readers in any language. Since Bei Tong prepared the manuscript in anticipation of publishing through official PRC channels, graphic sexual content was also absent in this third version. In the expanded, forty-one chapter version, new characters and subplots are introduced beginning with chapter four, but it is only from chapter twenty-six onward that significant new content is added.

The present edition represents an attempt to synthesize these three distinct versions into a single English translation. It uses the third and final version as the basis, but restores in full the erotic sections of the original e-novel and also takes into consideration many of the edits that the author made for the Tohan version.[22] Often, it was necessary to choose between two or even three versions of a single line or paragraph, and in some cases entire sections would jump about from one version to the next. In each case, the decision to go with one version over another was a subjective one, always made with a view to what I believed would be the best contribution to this translation. In the long course of our communication, Bei Tong also sent me numerous fragments of text—paragraphs, sentences, words, ideas—for me to translate on an ad hoc basis and include in this volume. *Beijing Comrades* is thus very much a hybrid text. It is an experiment in translation and could not have been otherwise. As such, it has the potential to raise practical and theoretical questions about the relationship between a translation and its source text(s), for the paradox of *Beijing Comrades* is that it is a translation for which there is no unified original. I am grateful to Bei Tong for reading and enthusiastically voicing support for this translation.

I first came into contact with Beijing's gay quanzi in 1998 when I was a foreign student in that city. There, I frequented Beijing's newly established gay bars, eventually working at one of them part-time and meeting a young Chinese man with whom I entered into a romantic relationship. I could not, of course, have known that Bei Tong was in New York City at precisely the same time I was in Beijing. Her postscript suggests that there can be something productive about cultural distance and the experience of displacement. It is this displacement—not only in space, but in time—that compelled Bei Tong to write a story about Beijing, just as my experience as a foreign student in the formative years of Beijing's still-emergent gay culture and community planted the seeds for my later fascination with this project. It is something of this sense of displacement that I hope the English-language reader might experience in encountering this most unusual work.

Notes

1. The original Chinese title of *Beijing Comrades* is *Beijing gushi*, which may be translated as *Beijing Story*.
2. Wang Xiaobo died in April 1997, more than a year before *Beijing Comrades* was written, but I have spoken with several readers who, unaware either of his passing or of the novel's publication date, believe that he is the author of the book. Part of the basis for the belief is that Wang cowrote the screenplay for Zhang Yuan's 1996 film *East Palace, West Palace*, widely cited as China's first queer movie. Wang's involvement with Zhang's film, in addition to his personal relationship with Li Yinhe, has led some to the conclusion that he may have penned *Beijing Comrades*.
3. Bei Tong 2002.
4. A number of English-language online sources state erroneously that *Beijing Comrades* was published in 1996. The inaccuracy originated with an error that appeared on the English-language website of Stanley Kwan's film *Lan Yu*, which was based on the novel. In a personal correspondence, Bei Tong confirmed that she posted the first instalment of *Beijing Comrades* online on September 22, 1998.
5. In this essay and throughout *Beijing Comrades*, I preserve the Chinese convention of placing family name before given name.
6. Numerous online sources debate whether or not Lan Yu should be seen as an "MB" ("money boy" or gay male sex worker). This is not surprising, for *Beijing Comrades* skillfully crafts ambiguity precisely around this question to build narrative tension in a story that is centrally concerned with the uneasy relationship between love and money. On the one hand, Lan Yu's entrance into the story is facilitated by Handong's assistant, Liu Zheng, who picks the young man up to feed his boss's insatiable appetite for new sexual adventures. And yet, we learn almost nothing of the circumstances surrounding this procurement, nor do we find out what Liu Zheng and Lan Yu might have said to each other when they met. This narrative lacuna lends itself to varied speculations about Lan Yu's motives for going with Liu Zheng and pursuing a relationship with Handong. For a discussion of Chinese gay men's views about money boys, see Rofel 2010.
7. Michael Berry makes a similar point when he writes that the novel

"gradually interweaves the characters' material and sexual desires in a complex web of exchange and symbolic ownership" (2008, 315).

8. In the present English translation, *Beijing Comrades* is a pluralization of the author's original pseudonym, Beijing Comrade. Many thanks are due to Clarence Coo for first suggesting this title. The author herself suggested Bei Tong as her nom de plume for this translation. It was created by combining the first syllables of the disyllabic words *Beijing* (literally, northern capital) and *tongzhi* (comrade or gay). Bei Tong, the Gay of the North.

9. The word was already in use during the Xinhai Revolution (1911) to describe Sun Yat-sen's followers.

10. It is still used this way in the mixed economy milieu of the current day PRC, though primarily in the context of government and Communist Party rhetoric, and cautiously divorced from explicit revolutionary connotations. A review of the state-owned newspaper *People's Daily* shows that one should not underestimate the extent to which the "official" sense of the word remains in use today. Of the more than 230,000 articles in which the word has appeared since 1946, over 40,000 of these appeared after the year 2000. For the full texts of *People's Daily* articles from 1946 to 2012, see the online database *Renmin shuju* (People data), accessible with log-in through the *People's Daily* website (http://www.people.com.cn).

11. In some respects, this resignification was similar to the way LGBTQ communities have appropriated the word *queer* in the US context, but with the obvious difference that the Chinese term *tongzhi* had (and continues to have) positive connotations, whereas *queer* had (and, for some, still has) negative ones. More recently, the term *queer* (*ku'er*) has gained currency in Chinese, though primarily as a critical term used in academic discourse and among LGBTQ activists. For greater discussion of the use of the term *tongzhi*, see the introduction to Leung 2008.

12. The idea that *tongzhi* and *gay* should be seen as equivalent is not without its detractors. Chou Wah-shan, for example, has argued that terms such as *gay* and *lesbian* are culturally specific and cannot be used to represent the specificity of same-sex relations in Chinese societies. Others find *tongzhi* to be an unsatisfying term because of its narrow emphasis on gayness, as opposed to a more expansive notion of queerness. See Chou 2000.

13. See Marsh 2012.

14. At the time of writing this note, the original e-novel was available at the following website, among others: http://www.shuku.net/novels/beijing/beijing.html.

15. "XXde," unambiguous code for "*ta made*," a common curse.

16. Bei Tong 2002.

17. For example, I believe there is sufficient textual evidence to conclude that the university Lan Yu attends, Huada, is probably a stand-in for Tsinghua University, and that, in an inversion of north and south, the university from which Handong graduated, Nanda ("South University"), is likely a stand-in for Peking University (also known as Beida, "North University"). To begin with, Huada's founding anniversary is May Day, just two days after Tsinghua's founding anniversary of April 29. Secondly, Peking University is famous for its classical gardens and architecture, and Handong states unequivocally that Huada is not "nearly as beautiful" as Nanda. Finally, Peking University is geographically southwest of Tsinghua, lending further support to the idea of a correlation with Nanda. It is also possible that One Two Three, the fictitious gay bar featured in the novel, is modeled after Half Bar (*Yiban yiban jiuba*, literally "One Half One Half Bar"). Now closed, Half Bar was one of Beijing's earliest gay bars, and one where I worked part-time when I was a foreign student in that city.

18. Bei Tong 2002, 18–19.

19. One indication of the success of the Tohan Taiwan edition is that it was translated into Japanese and published by Japan's largest publisher, Kodansha. Capitalizing on the sentimental and melancholic attachment to autumn one finds in the novel, the cover of the Japanese edition identifies the translator as "September." See Pekin Dōshi 2003.

20. An official or *guanfang* publication is one that successfully passes through state censorship procedures and is thus able to enter into the state-sponsored literary arena.

21. The e-novel and Tohan Taiwan versions both consist of thirty-one chapters and an epilogue (*weisheng*); the expanded version consists of forty chapters and an epilogue. In this translation, I treat the epilogue as a final chapter.

22. In an epigraph at the beginning of the Tohan version, Bei Tong writes, "All edits to this book were made by the author."

Bibliography

Bei Tong. 2002. *Lan Yu*. Taipei: Tohan Taiwan.

Berry, Michael. 2008. *A History of Pain: Trauma in Chinese Literature and Film*. New York: Columbia University Press.

Chou Wah-shan. 2000. *Tongzhi: Politics of Same-Sex Eroticism in Chinese Societies*. New York: Haworth Press.

Leung, Helen Hok-sze. 2008. *Undercurrents: Queer Culture and Postcolonial Hong Kong*. Vancouver: UBC Press.

Marsh, Viv. 2012. "New Chinese Dictionary in Row over 'Gay' Omission." *BBC*, July 21. http://www.bbc.com/news/world-asia-china-18920096.

Pekin Dōshi. 2003. *Pekin Koji Ranyū*. Translated by Kugatsu. Tokyo: Kodansha.

Rofel, Lisa. 2010. "The Traffic in Money Boys." *positions* 18 (2): 425–58.

beijing comrades

One

He's been gone three years now. A thousand days and nights, and each time I close my eyes there he is before me, the person I see in dreams. But you're dead, I say, reaching out in astonished euphoria to grab a hand or elbow or shoulder. My fingers move toward him, toward the white shirt he wore the day he left, but the image is illusory and like a puff of smoke he's gone. Three years and I still have this dream. The only difference today is that now I know it's a dream even as it's happening, all the way until I open my eyes and the moon floats back silently to the other side of the world.

It's all warm blue sunshine here in Vancouver—so different from Beijing with its brutal sandstorms and stifling heat. They say there are four seasons here, but each one dances with the same radiant sunshine, soft breeze, and gentle, teasing moisture that always seems to linger in the air.

In my dream I am laughing and drinking with the friends of my youth. I am in a car, darting through an endless maze of streets and alleyways. I am outside on a bleak autumn day; I pull him into my arms and kiss him.

When morning comes, the dense mosaic of maple leaves suspended outside my window reminds me where I am. In time I become aware of the young woman sleeping next to me—my new wife. I close my eyes and there he is, calling me back to my dreams, my memories.

My life in China couldn't have been more different from what it is today. Born and raised the spoiled offspring of high-ranking cadres, I spent my early years encased in and protected by the bureaucratic structures of power by which I was surrounded. I was different from the children of other government and Communist Party officials, though, for I was neither ignorant nor incompetent.

After high school I entered the Chinese Literature department of an elite university, but soon discovered that I didn't care for stories and by my second year had begun devoting most of my time to the business venture I'd undertaken with a motley crew of friends. A sizable loan after graduation allowed me to launch my own trading company. Whatever it took to make money, I did; whatever people would buy, I sold: food, clothes, anything I could get my hands on short of human beings and weapons. I would have sold plastic bags of shit if I had thought people would buy them. That was the early 1980s. Trade with Eastern Europe was booming in those days.

My life wasn't as extraordinary as it might seem. There were plenty of others in Beijing with family backgrounds similar to, if not more powerful than, my own. But not everyone played the game as well as I. Five years after graduation, relying on my father's connections and my own wisdom and talent, I had built a company with assets worth millions.

I never thought about getting married back then. I didn't

even have a regular sex partner—woman or man—though I did start dating girls my first year of college. I still remember clearly the first girl I slept with. I was crazy about her, with her long, black eyelashes that fluttered around her tiny eyes when she spoke and dimples that formed in the corners of her mouth when she laughed. She was the most beautiful thing I'd ever seen.

The first time I saw her was in the university library, sitting with some shifty-eyed kid who thought he was hot shit. I pretended to read a book, but couldn't take my eyes off her. For a full hour I sat there, imagining what her tits looked like under her blouse and thinking about what my roommate had told me. He said she was two years ahead of us and that all the guys in her department wanted to bang her. That was exactly what I wanted: older girls. To me, that meant they were real women, not little girls. A real woman was what I was after—not just to have fun with, but to tame, control.

When the guys in my dorm found out I liked her, they started giving me a hard time, saying I was in love and all that. She and I played courtship games for a while, but things weren't moving as quickly as I wanted. It wasn't easy for college students to get laid in those days, with their sex-segregated dormitories and half-dozen or more roommates. Each time I got together with that girl, I was so horny my nuts would be on the verge of exploding, but after one or two timid kisses she would bashfully push me away. This went on until one day we skipped class and went to my parents' house in the Chaoyang District where I'd grown up. That's when I fucked her.

She was bubbling over with excitement when we got there. Neither of my parents was home and I came up with some excuse to get rid of the maid. At first we just sat there on the bed, hugging each other and wondering what to do next. Then we kissed for what seemed like an eternity. When I put my hand under her blouse to see how far she would let me go, she threw herself into me, kissing me frantically until finally I was holding her tits. Only then did she screw up her face in protest, pushing me away halfheartedly, whimpering no, and saying she had never done it before. My heart pounded violently. The rejection was like a stimulus pushing me forward and I couldn't have controlled myself if I had wanted to. Clumsily, the words fell out of my mouth—I love you, I'm going to marry you—that kind of bullshit. Ineptly, I pulled off her clothes but left mine on except for my pants, which I pulled down. I lifted her legs and tried sticking it in the way I'd learned from friends and porn videos, but after three or four tries I still couldn't get it right. Finally, she grabbed it and guided it in, but I had no idea what to do once inside and came immediately. Then she started crying—from pain or happiness, who knows? I figured all girls cry when they do it for the first time.

When it was over we lay next to each other in bed and talked about getting married. I was so grateful to her for giving herself to me, so puffed up with masculine pride, that even I was close to tears. When she asked me if I would ever love another woman, of course I said no. But secretly I told myself that even if we got married, she would never be the only woman I slept with. I thought I had found love.

A year later I found out that I wasn't her first. Who knows what number I was? Her being a slut was apparently common knowledge throughout my department. I was the only one who didn't know.

Eventually we broke up. From then on I had a different girl on my arm every week and the inventory of notches on my bedpost grew. I quickly learned that there was nothing particularly difficult about getting girls. The hard part was getting rid of them.

It's not that I wanted to be the kind of guy who fucks and dumps girls. It's just that each girl I met wanted the same thing. It didn't matter if they were rich, snobby bitches or nice, humble girls; it didn't matter if they were outgoing or shy; and it didn't matter if they were bookworms or idiots. At the end of the day, each girl I met had one thing and one thing only on her mind: how to catch a man.

In many ways I loathed these girls who pestered me constantly about getting married, schemed in secrecy about the future, and were generally determined to keep me in chains until my death. These kinds of ill-fated relationships continued until there came a period of time when the mere sight of a woman filled me with terror. It was right around then that an older buddy of mine in the gay circle introduced me to a younger guy, a singer at a karaoke bar. That's when I discovered a new kind of play.

He was the first guy I hooked up with. It's been a long time and I don't remember his name, but the episode is firmly etched in my memory. Light skinned, clean, and pretty, his only defect was the rash of zits spotting his face. Someone had mentioned he was in his early twenties—older than me—but he only looked around eighteen. I didn't ask. It was hard to ask guys like that their age, even more taboo than asking girls.

I went to the bar where he worked and paid for him to do a couple of numbers from his song menu. He belted the songs out like he thought he was some kind of Hong Kong pop star, then sat down for a while. He was shy but not altogether incapable of conversation, and we chatted on and off throughout the night until he got off work and took me back to his place.

The moment we stepped out of the bar his entire personality changed. He suddenly became animated, talking incessantly about who knows what until we got to his apartment. I, on the other hand, remained passive, observing that, despite the nonstop chatter, he was being somewhat cautious about what he said. He was trying to figure out if I was interested.

We went to the one-bedroom apartment where he lived. It was a decent place, well furnished and very tidy. I couldn't help but compare it to the filthy college dormitory I lived in at the time. Eight students to a room, each with his own chaotic, disorganized little corner. We called it "The Kennel."

"My parents bought it for me for when I get married one day," he said, looking me up and down with a smile. "Anyway, I'm gonna take a shower. I probably smell like those people in the bar! You gonna take one?"

"Later," I said, sounding aloof and even rude. I was trying to conceal my inner panic. I had always assumed it would be easier with a guy, but I was wrong. The first time with a girl had been much easier.

He took a shower, then came out of the bathroom wearing nothing but a pair of underwear. He had a hot body: short, but lean and muscular. I sat on the couch looking up at him with a combination of fear and desire as he made his way toward me. Everything about him looked different from when I'd first seen him at the bar. Only his hair was the same: dry despite the shower he had taken. He came to a standstill after reaching the couch and looked down at me, hands on his hips, showing me the goods. Then he sat down. Wordlessly, he began slowly taking off my shirt, kissing my neck, and rubbing my crotch while I sat in petrified silence, so desperate to conceal my excitement that I hardly breathed for fear of him noticing.

He kissed my neck for a few moments, then moved his lips

down to my chest and began kissing my nipples. Seeing that I was still unresponsive, he stopped what he was doing and looked up at me with a vague look of indignation. He had no idea of the intensity and feverish desire by which I had been gripped. He ignited everything in me: love and tenderness, yes—but also the urge to dominate, even abuse him. I grabbed him by the arm and dragged him to the bedroom, where I pushed him onto the bed, then put my hands on his body: young, male flesh. Smooth and hard, completely different from the soft curves of a woman's body. He stood up from the bed, taking me with him. We stood facing each other for a moment, then he got on his knees in front of me. He lowered my pants, then my underwear, and my thick, engorged cock popped out. He laughed.

"It's huge!" His mouth ran up and down the shaft as he spoke. I couldn't believe what I was seeing. He was sucking me off like a girl!

Panting unevenly, I closed my eyes and leaned my head back. I had asked girls to do this in the past. Some of them would comply, but there was always something forced about it. Most of the time they would either give up after two or three strokes or their teeth would scrape incessantly along my shaft until even I wanted them to stop. But he was doing it because he liked it, and he did it with studied expertise. His lips moved along my cock while he used his hand to play with his own dick.

"I'm coming!" I practically yelled. His mouth came off me, and with one hand he masturbated me to climax, leaning closer so I could come on his eager face. Never in my life had I experienced such a thing. No sense of obligation. Just pleasure.

It took me a few minutes to pull myself together. When

I did, I looked down at him and saw that he was still hard. Pulsing there before me, his erection was somewhat of an embarrassment for me, a visible indictment of my own lack of interest in going down on him. He didn't seem to mind in the slightest though. He just pulled me down to the floor and placed my hand on his cock, guiding it with his own hand to make me jerk him off while using his other hand to play with his asshole. His body trembled all over and he moaned in a way I'd only ever heard from girls. Suddenly, and with a consuming desire that surprised me, I became exceedingly turned on by the idea of seeing him in pleasure. The amateur singer with the pimply face shook frantically and his breath became heavy. Then he came.

It's okay, I consoled myself. It's good to have a variety of experiences. Thoughts like these raced through my mind as I tried to make myself feel better about what had happened. I had long known it was possible for two men to do this sort of thing, but I had no idea how much I would like it.

Lying on the floor together afterward, he told me he was famous in the gay circle and that countless guys were after him. As if reading from a cue card, he added that I was the cutest guy he'd ever done it with, carefully pointing out that while other guys may have had superior technical skills, sex was, overall, better with me. I knew he meant this as a compliment, but hearing this annoyed me. There I was, giving up my virginity twice—first to a girl then to a guy—and both times it was with some used-up slut!

Still, I liked it. Not just the sex but the simplicity of the relationship. To think that two people could have sex within just a few hours of meeting each other. And when you got out of bed there were no guarantees about the future: no expectations, no demands. The next day you could be lovers, you could be friends, or you could pass each other on the street without so much as a word. When I left that spotty-faced singer's apartment, I decided right then and there that it was only fair that I should be able to make up for lost time: I was going to have lots of sex! I embraced the adventurous side of my personality and, relying on the ever-growing stack of banknotes at my disposal, bought and kept any boy or girl I wanted—all the way until I met Lan Yu.

Five years after college I was twenty-seven. Financially successful and well-known in the business world, my arrogance was insufferable. Never one to spend much time alone, if I wasn't in my office working I was hanging out with friends or whomever I happened to be sleeping with at the time.

The day I met Lan Yu, I had been in the office most of the day working on various projects. Just as I started mulling over what I was going to be doing that evening, Liu Zheng walked in. He worked at my company; we had been friends since childhood.

"That Russian guy didn't look too happy when he was leaving the office!" Liu Zheng said with a laugh.

"Fuck," I grumbled. "That guy's really testing my limits. I'm sick of him trying to take advantage of me. As far as I'm concerned, he can stay here and work or he can get the hell out. It's not like he's that good at his job anyway." I thumbed through the stack of paperwork in front of me then looked up again. "Oh, right. We're going bowling at the Imperial tonight. You coming?"

Liu Zheng smiled. "Did you ask Hao Mei to come? I meant to tell you she called this morning to say hi."

"She's not coming," I replied. "I don't want to see her tonight. Listen, do me a favor and get her a present, a little pocketbook or something. I need to figure out how to get her to stop calling me every day."

"Ha!" Liu Zheng laughed. "Had enough of your own girlfriend, huh? Well, listen. A few days ago I went over to Di Street to pick up a few workers. I met this kid. He says he just started university here in Beijing. You interested?"

"Excuse me," I said blithely, "I'm not interested in anyone right now, male or female! How do you always manage to get involved with these sketchy people? They could be full of diseases, you know? It's fuckin' disgusting!" I laughed.

"No, no, no," Liu Zheng assured me. "This one's totally naive: sixteen, just started school, looking for a job. He doesn't talk much, but he obviously needs to make a little money. You should go for it!"

"And you believe what he says?" I laughed. "He's probably just some migrant worker. Beijing is full of those kinds of swindlers these days. He'll probably mug your ass the second he gets in your car!"

Instead of arguing about it, Liu Zheng continued tallying his grievances against the newly hired Russian interpreter, whom he suspected of being more on the Russian negotiator's side than ours.

Liu Zheng was two years older than me, but we had graduated from university the same year. From primary to middle school we were in the same homeroom, but in high school we were in different classes—me in the humanities, him in hard sciences. After high school he didn't have much luck getting into a good university; he was only accepted by a local teachers' college. Not wanting to be a poverty-stricken middle school teacher after graduation, he came to me looking to fill his stomach. I couldn't turn away an old friend, so although I had no need for a physicist, I let him work at my company as

10

associate director of management. He had no real job description. He was just sort of my eyes and ears, an exalted company gopher. I liked him because he was smart, honest, sincere, and not particularly competitive or jealous. But he also had another important function: arranging my tricks. A married man, Liu Zheng was remarkably restrained when it came to his own personal life, but fully tolerated and even encouraged my hedonism. Well worth the price of a sinecure.

"All right, so I'll see you at the Imperial tonight," he said before standing up to leave.

"Great," I replied. "Hey, by the way, if you really think that kid's legit, go ahead and bring him." I must have been bored and looking for a distraction.

"Very well." Liu Zheng smiled.

"What are you going to tell him?"

"I'll tell him it's an interview."

I laughed. "I've never heard of a company where the boss has to interview a migrant worker just to do some heavy lifting. You know, you're a fucking sneaky guy, Liu Zheng, deceiving an innocent youth like this!"

"Hey, if you suddenly find a conscience buried deep in that soul of yours, we'll just forget about it. I know the guilt would be unbearable." His smile was angelic, but he was fucking with me.

"What are you talking about? The only thing that would be unbearable to me is not meeting him!"

"Fuck!" Liu Zheng rolled his eyes in feigned exasperation.

"Anyway," I continued, "as long as he's clean."

"Relax. He's definitely a *virgin*," Liu Zheng replied, stressing the final word in English. "My only worry is he'll think *you're* the one who's dirty!"

"Go fuck your granddad!" I said with a laugh.

11

Two

With the prospect of getting laid dangling seductively before me, I was no longer able to focus on my work. Instead, I spent the rest of the day slacking off and looking forward to the Imperial. It wasn't even the bowling I cared about. I had always loved that place, with its dramatic lighting and vaguely futuristic interior design; it was spacious and never got too crowded. Best of all, it was refreshingly free of riffraff and troublemakers from off the street.

Wei Guo and Zhang Jie were meeting me there. Zhang Jie, tall and lanky with glasses and smooth, almost mannish black hair pushed up behind her ears, was typical of the new elite that had cropped up in the nine years of reform since 1978. A close personal friend, she had powerful connections that I worked as much as possible. She and Wei Guo walked in.

"Hi, hi, have you eaten?" we all asked each other. "Yes, yes, good, good."

Zhang Jie noticed me glancing toward the door.

"Who are you waiting for?" she asked.

"Liu Zheng," I replied. "He's bringing the son of a friend of mine from out of town. The kid just started university here in Beijing and my buddy wants me to keep an eye on him."

"You've certainly got a lot of projects!" Zhang Jie said with a laugh.

Liu Zheng showed up around six or seven. Trailing behind him was a short and not particularly good-looking kid gazing around absentmindedly as he walked in. This can't be him! I thought. Liu Zheng had been vague when telling me where he'd met him so I wasn't expecting someone sleek and urbane, but this kid? This was your typical Communist Youth League hopeful from the provinces. I felt the stabbing annoyance of disappointment. Fucking Liu Zheng.

"Director Chen, Zhang Jie, Wei Guo." Liu Zheng greeted us with smile and a nod. He never called me "Director Chen" when we were alone but kept up appearances when others were around.

The kid stood off to the side, staring fixedly at Liu Zheng. He seemed to be waiting for an order.

"Right," Liu Zheng said, as if remembering why he was there. "Lan Yu, this is Director Chen. Director Chen, this is Lan Yu. The surname's Lan. It's rare."

My left eye twitched involuntarily as I listened to the introduction. I was annoyed at Liu Zheng for bringing me this stray puppy but resolved to be nice.

"Hi!" I grinned and stuck out my hand.

"Hello." Lan Yu reached out timidly. He was visibly nervous, and probably surprised a company director would want to shake his hand.

What happened next can only be described as one of the greatest mysteries I have ever experienced. It's something I've gone over a thousand times in my mind, playing and replaying it in a series of failed attempts to revisit the immediacy of the experience. It's true I was utterly indifferent to Lan Yu when I first saw him walk into the Imperial looking like a child lost at an outdoor market. But all this changed the moment our hands touched and his eyes met mine. It was something about the eyes: uneasy, sorrowful, and deeply suspicious of everything around him. A distant, even haunted expression lingered in his eyes and there was none of the fake, sycophantic smile I was so used to seeing in both my personal and professional life. His skin was dark but clean, his features pretty and delicate, lips clenched together emotionlessly. My heart pounded. I couldn't remember the last time I'd felt that way.

I quickly averted my eyes, telling myself, You're not some kind of fucking schoolboy! I looked beyond Lan Yu's shoulder and saw Zhang Jie and the others bowling.

"You like bowling?" I asked nonchalantly.

"I don't know how." He had a northern accent.

"You from the North?"

"Uh-huh."

I didn't like his curt responses. Deciding to play cavalier, I walked over to the rest of the group to join the game. Everyone was gathered near the base of the bowling lane except Lan Yu, who remained rooted to the carpeted side of the room where I'd left him. Nobody seemed to notice his absence.

I leaned against the shining metal table near the opening of lane number three. A few paces ahead of me, Liu Zheng and Zhang Jie were standing, arms folded, on either side of the lane. They were watching Wei Guo, who had struck an ambitious pose, left arm akimbo, right arm held high with a bowling ball perched on his fingertips. Knees slightly bent, he stared in fixed concentration at the pins before him. It was an impressive sight, but evidently not enough to hold the attention of Liu Zheng, who suddenly turned on his heel and

14

walked toward me. He leaned against the table next to me then moved his head toward mine until our cheeks were parallel and our ears almost touched.

"You eaten yet?" he asked in a quiet, almost furtive voice, eyes fixed on Wei Guo as he spoke. Our earlier greetings of "Hi, hi, have you eaten?" were just customary; now Liu Zheng wanted to know.

"No, why? You wanna go somewhere?" My voice was much louder than it needed to be. I was trying to sound annoyed to hide my emotions. Liu Zheng didn't know it, but my heart palpitated violently in my chest. I was consumed by the desire to know what Lan Yu was doing behind us. Was he still standing there? Was he trying to decide whether to join us? Had he gone to buy a drink, or to the bathroom, or simply left the building altogether? I wanted to know, but couldn't bear the thought of losing face by turning around to find out.

"No, you guys go ahead. I just ate," Liu Zheng said, his voice sounding unnaturally remote. He stared straight ahead at Wei Guo, who had just knocked down all but one of the bowling pins and was excitedly giving the thumbs-up sign to nobody in particular. I studied Liu Zheng's face carefully. He was making arrangements for me.

"No, really. You and Lan Yu go ahead," he repeated nonchalantly.

Just then, and with a synchronized motion that was so precise it must have looked timed, Liu Zheng and I craned our heads like two owls to look at Lan Yu. He was still standing at the back of the room, staring at us with a dull expression on his face.

"We'll just grab a bite to eat," I yelled over my shoulder, as if Lan Yu had been involved in the conversation the whole time. "Walk and talk, yeah?"

He nodded obediently.

"Zhang Jie, Wei Guo," I called out, getting up from the table and walking toward them. "I gotta go. I gotta feed my bro's kid or I'm going to get accused of neglect! You guys coming? My treat." For some reason I was still speaking very loudly. I suppose I thought making a spectacle would create the illusion of normalcy.

"You guys go ahead. Have fun," Zhang Jie said, eyeing me with a smile. She seemed to be insinuating something, as if she knew more than she was letting on. Under the circumstances, I didn't care. I had bigger things to worry about.

With Lan Yu seated next to me, I drove through the city where the cement-colored buildings and narrow, winding alleyways of old Beijing seemed to blend into one another. There were few private cars in China in those days, and it was still early enough in the evening to see the endless rows of workers on bicycles surging forward like swarms of locusts. I glanced to my right as we passed Beijing Railway Station. It was a chaotic scene: hundreds of new arrivals, mostly migrants from the countryside, sitting or sleeping on bags stuffed with clothes or cheap goods they wanted to hawk. Others wandered through the terminal with lost expressions on their sunbaked faces.

Lan Yu sat in the passenger seat next to me surveying the people outside. He seemed completely indifferent to me despite the effort I'd made to talk to him at the Imperial. I glanced over at him repeatedly, noticing the way he folded his hands in his lap while looking out the window. A group of pedestrians darted into the street; I almost hit the car in front of me. I gripped the steering wheel tightly and accelerated. He was so hard to read.

Twenty minutes later we arrived at our destination: the

Country Brothers Hotel. It was in the Chaoyang District, not far from where Liu Zheng had found Lan Yu to begin with. I kept a long-term rental there, a luxury residential suite, for personal use any time of the day or night. I parked the car and walked speedily toward the monumental building at the northern end of the parking lot. Lan Yu straggled a dozen paces behind. Reaching the front entrance, I walked through the lobby without even checking to see if he was still with me. I didn't want to be spotted by hotel employees who might have recognized me or, worse, by any professional associates who might have been there.

We took the elevator to the Cantonese-style restaurant on the tenth floor. Standing there in the cold metal box of the elevator, I stared at Lan Yu's blurred image reflected in the tall, silver doors in front of us. It was bad enough that we had barely exchanged a word in the car. Now, standing shoulder to shoulder and hemmed in by the four walls of the elevator, the silence was killing me. I fought the urge to turn my head and look at him.

The dining room of the restaurant was enormous and very well lit, and a vast collection of window lattices, carved lacquer screens, and miniature pavilions conspired to create a spectacularly classical ambience. The food they served was nothing special, but it was better than the overpriced garbage they served at the French and Italian restaurants next door. I hated European food. To me it was nothing but piles of cheese and tomato.

When we were seated, I started in with the questions:

"How old are you?"

"Sixteen. Almost seventeen."

"Why are you starting college so early? I was almost nineteen when I started."

"I started school a year early, then skipped a grade."

"Where are you from?" I continued my line of questioning.

"Xinjiang."

This surprised me. Bordering Soviet Central Asia, Xinjiang Province was China's far west. The Uyghur population there spoke a different language. Practically another world as far as I was concerned. Since Lan Yu was ethnically Chinese, I wondered how long his family had been there.

I examined him carefully as he spoke. Still no trace of a smile, but he stared at me with an attentiveness I couldn't fail to notice. His mannerisms were delicate but natural, unaffected, and for a moment he had a vague air of intellectuality about him. This was alluring in itself but wasn't even the chief provocation of my desire. What really tortured me was the excruciating air of anxiety that gripped him. I didn't care what the reason was. All I could think about was getting him into bed.

"S'ow's Beijing?" I spoke very rapidly. "So how" came out as one word.

"Huh?" His face turned red. He didn't understand my Beijing accent.

I laughed. "When I first got here, I couldn't understand what these people were saying either. Especially the guys. They really mumble. It's ridiculous!" I was repeating something Fang Jian, my old college roommate, used to say. He was from a small town and hated the way Beijingers spoke. I was born and raised in Beijing, but Lan Yu didn't have to know that. I didn't want him thinking I had the superiority complex typical of so many city people.

Lan Yu's lips moved a fraction. This I accepted as a smile, even if it was forced.

When our food came, he barely touched any vegetables but

eagerly devoured two full plates of fried rice. He was clearly famished. I tried making conversation.

"You study architecture? That's smart. You can make a lot of money with that. When I was in college I had two good friends who studied architecture. During our third year they helped some guy at a big firm work on a design and made a ton of money. Humanities majors like me were chronically broke, so the rest of us were jealous as hell!"

My efforts were met with monosyllables. I sighed and looked out the window at the sprawling city below, wondering if I should just give up. The restaurant was high up enough that out in the distance I could see the faint silhouette of the Forbidden City, an ancient black square framed by long rows of streetlights. I settled the bill and we left.

Stepping onto the cold marble floor outside the restaurant, I tried again. "Which university are you at?" I pushed the elevator button. "Don't your parents give you money for school?"

If my earlier questions had triggered reserve, this one resulted in total silence. Lan Yu stared at the elevator door in front of us, and I couldn't tell if he was reluctant to answer the question or if he just hadn't decided what to say yet. During dinner I had noticed the way he fidgeted; now I couldn't help but wonder if the things he had told Liu Zheng were true. Based on what I knew about guys like him—out of luck and more than happy to accept a meal from an older guy with cash and a reputation—probably not. The more I thought about it, the more his story about being a student seemed like bullshit.

When the elevator came we descended the building toward the second floor where my room was located. Surrounded by the quiet hum of the elevator, my mind wandered to six months earlier when I'd brought some girl from the School of Foreign Languages back to my room there. She was no virgin, but it was the first time she had sold herself. I wondered whether Lan Yu's story was similar to hers.

I looked across the elevator at Lan Yu. He wore a pair of dark blue trousers and a plain white T-shirt. Simple and clean, though the trousers were too short at the ankles and somewhat tattered at the seams. He eyed me cautiously from the corner of the elevator where he stood. Subtle but constant. He didn't seem to think I noticed.

When we got to my room he became even more reserved than he had been in the restaurant. He stepped across the threshold but halted abruptly, making it difficult for me to shut the door. He was waiting for an invitation to come inside.

"Have a seat," I said. "This is the living room. The dining area's over there, and the bedroom's in there."

Lan Yu remained near the doorway.

I turned on the television and handed him the remote control. "Here. They have a ton of stations. Cable."

Lan Yu looked unimpressed, but took the remote from me.

"I'm gonna go take a shower," I said. "I've been running around all day. I probably smell like those people in the restaurant!" For some reason, the zit-covered singer had popped into my mind.

Still Lan Yu remained frozen near the door. Making my way toward the bathroom, I glanced back to smile at him. Suddenly I heard a voice.

"Director? Um . . . Director Chen?"

The words came out abruptly. Lan Yu's face was red and he appeared to be gathering courage to say something. "Can I work at your company?"

"Um . . . What did Liu Zheng tell you?" I was afraid of saying something different from Liu Zheng. I didn't want to screw up the plan, but at the same time wasn't sure what the plan was. I had forgotten to discuss with Liu Zheng whether giving the kid a job really was part of the deal.

"He said . . . I mean, 'cause your company doesn't usually hire people to work half days. But I have class during the day, so I can only work in the evenings. So Liu Zheng wanted me to ask you." He quickly added, "I can work until eleven." Surely he must have known our office closed before then.

He was so earnest I suddenly felt guilty. Maybe he was just a nice, innocent kid after all.

"Come to work tomorrow," I said with a halfhearted smile.

Lan Yu beamed. It was the first time I really saw him smile. Sweet, radiant, beautiful.

It was September, but the heat was still in the air and the days were incredibly long. In that part of China, autumn days burned with sunshine until well past eight o'clock, when the last rays of deep-orange sunlight filtered through the burning red carpet of leaves stretching from the Summer Palace to the foot of the Great Wall. I sat on the couch draped in a loosely tied bathrobe, stroking my cock and thinking about how to get Lan Yu into bed.

He was very upbeat now that I'd offered him a job and a monthly salary of ¥150. When I asked him if he wanted to take a shower, he hesitated at first but quickly agreed after poking his head into the luxurious hotel bathroom. "This shower's awesome!" he called out before jumping in. I leaned back into the couch, listening to the sound of the water splashing against his naked body while spreading my thick, toned legs until the bathrobe fell open around my thighs. Watching the steam drift out of the cracked-open door, I smiled, wondering what was going to happen next.

There's no doubt about it: it's a hell of a lot easier to seduce a man than a woman. If I had asked a girl to take a shower there she would think I was hatching some sinister plot. But Lan Yu went willingly. While he was gone I called room service to order a bottle, something sweet but with a kick to it. I asked for a bottle of red wine, then changed my mind and asked for white. Next, I slid a porn video into the VCR. Everything was set. I sat back down on the couch, my heart pounding in my chest as I waited.

A few minutes later, Lan Yu came out of the bathroom wearing the light blue pajamas I'd stuffed into his arms before he went in. I always kept a new set of pajamas in the room as well as an extra bathrobe. The pajamas were far too big for him. They hung off his shoulders with long, pendulous sleeves that made him look like some kind of Han dynasty official. His hair stuck to his forehead in a wet, clumpy mess.

"Relax. Have a drink." I handed him a glass of wine.

Lan Yu took the glass, but remained standing, seemingly unsure of what to do.

"Have a seat." I could tell from his breathing that he was more relaxed than when he had gotten into the shower.

Lan Yu sat down and looked up at the television, where he saw a naked white girl licking another girl's pussy as she squeezed her tits and moaned. A panicked look swept across his face. Frozen in shock, he remained seated in front of the TV, gripping his glass tightly. I knew this would have been his first time seeing a porn video.

"Have you ever seen one of these?" I asked.

He shook his head, eyes glued to the TV set.

"Do you have a girlfriend?"

Silence.

"Do you have a girlfriend?" I repeated.

"No." There was alarm in his voice. His face was red and

22

his dick pulsed visibly through the fabric of the pajamas. I turned off the TV and moved toward him, gently placing a hand between his thighs. He pushed the hand away. I put it back.

When I placed my hand between his legs a third time, he tore his gaze from the TV and looked up at me with a timid expression.

"Here, let me help you," I said with a grin as I leaned into him. Nervously, he took a sip of wine while I pulled the pajama bottoms down. His dick wasn't especially large, but it wasn't small either. He had the thick constitution of a northerner, but his legs were thin because of his youth. It occurred to me that, at sixteen, he wasn't even fully developed yet.

Lan Yu looked at me again, but this time with a face flushed with desire and even a kind of feeble imploring. I peeled off the pajama top and gently pushed against his chest to make him lean back into the couch. With one hand still firmly wedged between his thighs, I placed my other hand across his shoulder, then bent down to run my tongue along his chest, kissing his nipples and massaging the back of his neck. He gripped the couch and looked down at me, utterly transfixed by what I was doing.

"If you're uncomfortable, just say so," I said. He continued staring at me in silence.

If there's one thing I've learned, it's that it doesn't matter if it's a guy or a girl: When you sleep with a virgin, you've got to be gentle. This is the moment they're going to remember for the rest of their lives. Do it right and they'll obey you forever.

I moved back up to Lan Yu's lips, licking them gently with my tongue. His mouth was rigid and unyielding at first, but then he started kissing back, sinking deeper into the couch and wrapping his arms around my neck. What turned me on about him wasn't so much his physique but rather his unspoiled boyishness, so clean and virginal. I don't know. Maybe it was nostalgia for my own lost youth. But that couldn't have been everything. There was also something about his eyes. Unforgettable.

I began kissing him frantically, clutching at every inch of his body until his cock was in my hands. By the time I stretched my hand farther and started rubbing the velvety patch of skin under his balls, he was overwhelmed with excitement. He closed his eyes and his breathing got heavier. His face remained tense, as if he was trying to restrain himself from showing too much pleasure. Then he grabbed my arms and without any warning let out a soft groan and came.

I almost laughed. I didn't think he would come so fast.

We fooled around two more times that night. Things eventually progressed to oral sex—I went down on him, then he did the same to me—but I didn't ask him to let me fuck his ass. It wasn't the right time yet.

I don't know if it was the effect of the alcohol or because he was tired or because of his age, but Lan Yu fell asleep almost instantly after the third time. Looking down at his handsome, youthful face while he slept, I thought to myself: I have to treat Liu Zheng to dinner.

The next morning I got up early. I had an 8:00 a.m. appointment with the credit manager of China Construction Bank to discuss a ¥10 million loan. Lan Yu was still sleeping heavily and I didn't want to wake him, so I had breakfast sent up to the room and wrote him a note. *Forget about the job. Focus on your studies. If you need anything, contact Liu Zheng.* I put down the pen, then picked it up again. *Let yourself out after breakfast.* Then I put ¥1,000 next to the note. I wanted to leave more than that but fought the urge because I didn't want him getting greedy. This, I knew, would only make it harder for me to say no if he had any unreasonable demands further down the road.

Later in the day, I wrapped up the loan deal, then took my colleagues to lunch at a Hunanese restaurant. We were barely seated when the manager pulled me aside to tell me Liu Zheng was on the phone. I got up from the table and went to the service desk at the front of the restaurant.

"Was the kid still asleep when you left this morning?"

"Yeah, why?"

"The hotel called to say you left ¥500 in the room with a note."

"What note?"

"He said he was only taking half of what you left him and that it was only a loan. He said he'll pay you back when he has the money."

I was perplexed for a moment and didn't know what to say. "Okay. I'm busy right now. We'll talk about it later." I hung up the phone and smiled. Perhaps I would be seeing Lan Yu more than I had originally thought.

I made my way back through the smoky, crowded restaurant, unable to get the image of Lan Yu out of my mind. I entered the private dining room where my colleagues were seated, and my senses were hit by the rich, heavy aroma of Hunanese chili peppers. I pictured Lan Yu's lips—rigid and unyielding at first, then with the faintest trace of a smile, then kissing me—and my heart began beating rapidly. Laughing cheerfully, I sat down and raised a glass to the company, just in time to hide the erection growing in my trousers.

Three

Hao Mei worked in sales management at a joint-venture company. She was my girlfriend. I liked her because she embodied a particular type: the beautiful, professional woman.

When it came to women, there were two kinds that I went for: The first was the college girl. The second was a girl like Hao Mei. I couldn't stand bitchy supermodel types. They wanted it all, but the goods were secondhand and they had shitty dispositions to boot. When it came to guys, I tended to go for creative types: painters, musicians, that sort of thing. Guys like that usually only wanted a one-time thing; often they did it for the money or just to try something new and exciting. But a college guy? I had never slept with one of those, not because I didn't want to, but because I'd never had the opportunity.

The truth is, it was a lot harder to find guys than girls, especially quality guys. A guy would go to bed with you faster than a girl, but a decent guy who was into that kind of stuff? Few and far between. I suppose that's why I liked quality guys best: the thrill of the hunt.

Hao Mei was from the South, from Guangdong Province. By her own admission, she only came to Beijing for a guy, "a mistake of a guy," as she put it. I believed whatever she told me, and didn't care much anyway.

What I liked most about Hao Mei wasn't her good looks or her wit or her sharp and sensitive mind. What I liked about Hao Mei was her big, round ass. She didn't have the typical flat ass of most Asian girls. Hers was full and curved, fat and plump, and stuck out gallantly like a peacock's feathers when she walked. We only fucked in two positions: Me seated with her on top, riding me while I juggled her ass in my hands. Or, her on all fours, hands and knees anchored to the bed while I plowed her doggy style. I was particularly fond of this second position because of the way she would thrust back into me while I knocked her thick, meaty ass around in my hands like a bag of dough. Obviously, I couldn't tell her it was mainly her ass I was into or she would think I was a jerk. The day I met Lan Yu, I had been dating Hao Mei for half a year and had spent eight or nine thousand yuan on her, and that was on crap gifts alone.

One bright but chilly Sunday morning, I was wrapped in a blanket, deep in sleep, my arm stretched out lazily across Hao Mei's big ass. November was just around the corner and the leaves would be falling off the trees soon. It had been two months since the day I met Lan Yu.

The radiator hummed softly in the corner, and the empty bottle of pinot noir we had drunk the night before was lying on the floor. On the dresser, a Teresa Teng cassette sat mute in the tape deck next to a cheap imitation of some Tang dynasty glazed pottery, a dragon that stared vacantly across the room with a grimace on its face. Hao Mei had picked these things up while visiting her cousin in Shanghai the weekend before—the

27

tape for herself, the figurine for me, a peace offering for the argument we'd had because I didn't want to accompany her on the trip.

The brash sound of the telephone jarred me out of sleep. Hao Mei picked up the receiver and passed it to me. It was Liu Zheng.

"What the hell are you calling me this early for?" I mumbled, half-asleep.

"What do you mean, early? Have you looked at the clock? It's almost noon!"

"Anyway, what is it?" I asked impatiently.

Liu Zheng wasn't in a great mood, either. Whatever it was, he couldn't have been thrilled about dealing with it on his day off.

"Lan Yu called this morning. He said he just finished his midterms. I guess he wants to see you."

For a moment I was silent. By this point I had more or less given up hope of seeing Lan Yu again. I wasn't expecting him to contact me and had actually forgotten that I'd given him Liu Zheng's number to begin with.

"You do remember him, don't you? He's that kid who—"

"I know, I know," I interrupted, rubbing my eyes. "Just have him—" I looked at the clock on the wall. "Tell him to meet me at Country Brothers at two."

I hung up the phone and a sudden surge of excitement rushed through me. I climbed out of bed, tripping slightly over the telephone cord, and pulled on a pair of pants.

"Who was that? Are you going out?" Hao Mei sat up in bed, casting an alarmed look my way. She wanted to know more but stopped short of probing for details, undoubtedly because of what I had told her on our third date: "Whether work related or personal," I had said, "if I don't freely offer the information, it's a private affair and you would do well not to ask." Hao Mei broke up with me at least once a week because of this thoroughly unreasonable demand, but always came back to me like a well-trained house cat, moaning and groaning about how she had fallen in love with "a little devil."

"Come on, get up," I said, tossing her clothes to her. "We can have breakfast first, but I have some important things to do in the afternoon."

"What's the hurry?" she protested, slipping on a shirt.

"Nothing," I replied. "It's just work, but I have to go."

Hao Mei didn't ask any more questions. She knew when to keep her mouth shut.

It was two o'clock in the afternoon and the lobby of Country Brothers was dead, nothing but a few tables occupied by small groups of people engaged in conversation. At two twenty, Lan Yu walked in looking completely different from the last time I'd seen him. His eyes darted around the room as he entered. I stood up and waved.

"Sorry I'm late," he said, stopping short of offering an explanation.

"How did you get here?"

"By bus." His Mandarin had improved. "I'm not very familiar with Beijing yet. I just screwed up one of my transfers."

Studying him as he spoke, I did my best to take it all in. In just a few short months, he actually seemed to have grown taller. Still he offered no smile, but the aura of gutted despair that had enveloped him the first time we'd met was gone and there was almost a look of contentedness on his face. That faint anxiety in his eyes, though—that hadn't changed.

"Next time take a taxi," I said, tearing myself away from his eyes and refocusing my attention on the conversation. "Or, if

I have time, I'll pick you up." I started toward the elevator to take him up to my room.

Lan Yu started to follow, but then hesitated. "Do we have to go up?" he asked.

"Um, would you prefer to go somewhere else?" I didn't know what he was getting at.

"I don't know. Anywhere. Outside?"

"Right now?" The idea was ridiculous. "Aren't you going to be cold?" It was already late autumn, but he wore only a thin white jacket, hardly enough to ward off the chilly fall wind.

"It's still early in the day. It's not too cold out yet."

"Okay, fine," I said, the words sounding a little more acerbic than I had intended. "Why don't we go sit over there for a while?" I motioned toward a small café on the west side of the lobby. If this kid was planning on blackmailing me or wanted some kind of heavy relationship or something, he was definitely fucking with the wrong guy.

We sat down at a little table. Lan Yu was silent as we waited for the waitress to bring us our drinks. I lit a Chunghwa cigarette. That was my brand.

"Aren't you in school right now?" Peals of smoke poured out of my mouth and I stared at him with a clinical gaze. "What made you call me?"

Lan Yu squirmed in his seat. "I guess I just wanted to get out of the dorm for a while," he said, trying to sound nonchalant but clearly troubled by something. Nervously, he took a sip of his soda. A long silence ensued, followed by more silence. I was growing tired of the game.

"Listen," I said, placing my cup of coffee on the table. "If you have something to say, say it. I need to be out of here by three."

"Oh, no, it's nothing," he replied. "I just wanted to talk. I'll go back to campus now." He stood up to leave and I, still seated, looked up at him. He might have been overly sensitive, but his self-respect was undeniable. He wasn't going to just sit there looking like an idiot.

I remained seated. "Let me drive you home."

"Oh, that's okay," he said, throwing me a polite little smile. What the fuck? I laughed in disbelief. It was bad enough that he was rejecting me, but he didn't have to be so nonchalant about it. Besides, where had a small-town kid like him picked up a genteel affectation like that?

"Have I offended you, old man?" I asked, still looking up at him as he gathered his jacket to leave.

"Huh?" He looked at me in confusion. Apparently, he wasn't used to Beijing humor.

It took some finagling, but I eventually got Lan Yu to stay awhile. The way I did it was this: First, I insisted on driving him back to his dorm. When he agreed, I asked him to come with me to my room to get my car keys. He told me he'd wait in the lobby, but I insisted, protesting that he wasn't going to make me go traipsing around the hotel on my own. After some back and forth about it, he finally caved in and we went upstairs.

When we got to my room I wasted no time getting down to business. I followed Lan Yu inside, then locked my arms around his torso from behind, pulling him with me as I backed up against the wall of the entryway. He didn't resist, but he didn't exactly respond with the erotic delight I'd hoped for either. It was only when I began planting kisses across his neck that he started to get turned on.

That's right, I thought, twirling him around to kiss his lips roughly. Quit acting so fucking naive.

31

I looked down at Lan Yu's cherubic face and watched him nod off to sleep. Completely covered in sweat, even his eyelashes glistened with tiny pearls of watery moisture. His youthful cheeks flushed with warm shades of red. Waking suddenly, he smiled when he saw me, but in an instant his heavy, sleepy eyelids closed again.

"You really worked up a sweat," I laughed softly as I ran my tongue gently along his chest. "The next time you cook you won't need salt. Just lean over the wok and let it drip!"

Lan Yu opened his eyes and smiled weakly.

"Seriously," I continued with a jocular tone entirely out of step with his drowsiness, "the next time you need to get some, just give me a call. Don't wait so long! Four out of five experts agree: it's not healthy for a young man to go so long without getting laid."

That woke him up. His smile disappeared and he looked at me with an injured expression. "I didn't come here to . . . *get some.*"

"Then what did you come here for?" I asked cavalierly. I got up from the bed under the pretense of going to take a leak. The truth was, prolonged eye contact with Lan Yu was making me a bit uncomfortable.

"Nothing," he faltered. "It's just that . . . I mean . . . one of the guys in my class died yesterday. He was in the bunk right below me. I just don't want to be in the dorm right now."

"Oh man!" I exclaimed, poking my head out of the bathroom. "How did he die?"

"He broke his spine doing a roll in gym class," he replied, pointing to his neck. "The top part, up here. He was the only guy in our class from the countryside. They hardly have any PE classes in their schools, so he never learned how. He was afraid he wasn't going to pass the tumbling exercise, so he asked me to go with him to practice. His parents came this morning. I heard his mom was crying so hard at the hospital that she passed out. He was an only child. Just last week he was saying he didn't know how he was going to survive all this time away from home." Lan Yu looked up at me. "He shouldn't have said he wasn't going to survive. It's bad luck to say something like that."

"Oh well," I said bitterly as I returned from the bathroom. "Dying is nothing. It's the living I feel sorry for." Lan Yu became quiet at this, and I suddenly felt guilty for making such a flippant comment.

"Hey," I said tenderly, sitting next to him and placing my hand on his arm. "Don't think about it too much." I stood up again, grabbing his arm so I could pull him with me. "Why don't we get cleaned up and go to the nightclub downstairs?"

Lan Yu raised his arms over his head in a disinterested stretch, then paused as if remembering something. "Didn't you say you had to leave at three?" he asked. I looked at the clock on the wall. It was five.

"I decided not to go," I said, returning to the bathroom to take a shower. "Anyway, it wasn't that important."

We sat at a small corner table in the nightclub, watching the other patrons as they reveled on the dance floor. When I asked him if he was having a good time, Lan Yu said it was the wildest nightlife he had ever seen. I ordered him a drink—a martini—which he said was okay but a little too bitter. Then I got us a private karaoke room. After carefully inspecting the song list, Lan Yu said there wasn't a single number he knew. So we ended up singing "I Love Beijing Tian'anmen." Everyone knows that song.

It was past midnight when Lan Yu finally insisted on going

back to campus. He also insisted that I not drive him. "I'm not a girl," he said, putting down his drink and standing up to leave. Somehow that impressed me, but I was also annoyed that he was leaving so early. Whatever. The whole night had been a waste of time.

Four

Not long after we started dating, Hao Mei began to pester me to let her introduce me to Yang Youfu, some distant cousin who wanted to get in on a business deal with me. When I asked her what kind of kickback she would be getting for the introduction, she spat out a loud *humph* and stuck her nose in the air. "That," she replied righteously, "is a private affair. You would do well not to ask."

"Oh, really?" I teased, impressed by her witty comeback. "Well, maybe you don't want to tell me because you're hoping he'll pay you with rolls of fat. I bet you love that short, stubby body and big fat stomach!"

"*Eeeeeew!*" she squealed, pouncing on me as if to devour me whole.

I planted a perfunctory kiss on her nose, then sighed. I was becoming less and less interested in this girl. She was just another transplant from the provinces.

Like Hao Mei, Yang Youfu hadn't been knocking around the capital for long. He was only a bit over thirty but looked older than his age—Probably, I thought, because of all the fat piled up in his face. The first few times I met him, I wrote him off as a pathetic and impotent ass-kisser. Each time I saw him, he would scuttle up to me, a fawning grin glued to his face, and holler, "Hey, Brother Chen!" Still, when he asked me to help him make some connections, I did what I could—it was no skin off my ass. I introduced him to a couple of reporters who gave him ad space in their newspapers, thereby allowing him to put the word out for some horseshit product that didn't even exist yet. I thought he was a tool.

After getting to know Yang Youfu better, though, I grew to like him. He had the forthright character of a northeasterner. There was no bullshit about him, no pretense. He was generous and had a big heart. If he had one of something, he'd find a way to give you five. If there were ten, he'd make it twenty.

Yang Youfu had a high tolerance for alcohol—so high, in fact, that in all the time I knew him I never saw him hit his ceiling. One Saturday afternoon I went with him and Wei Guo to Ming Palace, a huge, multistoried spa where men sat around in fleecy white robes watching TV, chain-smoking, and doing nothing. Almost as soon as we walked through the door, Yang Youfu put back a few drinks. Before long he was wasted.

"Whatever you want, Brother Chen! Just let me know and I can hook you up. You want to try a luxury delicacy from the Northeast? Manchurian tiger? *Very* rare, *very* valuable. Don't worry, Brother Chen, I can get it for you!" When he was drunk Yang Youfu would tell you anything. Who knew if it was true or not?

"Fuck, I don't need *that*!" I replied, slapping my knee. "Get me the Emperor's youngest daughter—a virgin—wait, make it *two* virgins, one girl, one boy. Get me *that* and we'll start talking!"

36

"Fuck!" he shouted, slamming his shot glass on the table. "I thought you wanted something *hard* to get! How old do you want 'em?" Yang Youfu looked at me intently, and for a moment it almost seemed like a serious question.

"Ha!" I exclaimed, pouring him another drink, but getting more alcohol on the table than into his glass. "What do you think I am—some kind of monster? You want to be a child rapist? Go ahead, but sooner or later you'll pay with your life!" *Ha ha ha ha!* We laughed in unison.

The Ming was one of the many distractions ushered in by the so-called age of reform, the era of primitive accumulation that had promised to transform China from an impoverished nation into a powerful one. The Cultural Revolution had died with Mao, but lack of order was just as much a defining feature of the new era as it had been of the old. In principle, even those without powerful family backgrounds could jockey for successes never before thought possible. All you needed was some guts and determination, and entry into the get-rich-quick class was yours for the taking. A little luck didn't hurt either. Yang Youfu was the epitome of those who had managed to make it big overnight. I don't know if luck had anything to do with it, but he definitely had balls.

That night at the Ming, I gambled, drank, and played pool with Yang Youfu and Wei Guo late into the night, stopping only at three in the morning when the three of us got a room on the second floor and crashed for a while. We had barely closed our eyes, though, when the deafening sound of construction outside woke us up. By the time we finished breakfast and rolled out of there, it was ten in the morning and we'd been at the Ming for nearly twenty hours. I said goodbye to the guys and stepped into the street.

There were few cars outside, just the familiar sea of bicycles everywhere you turned. It was nearly December and the snow fell in thick, heavy flakes as I drove my car through the narrow alleyways, competing with bicycles and pedestrians for tiny spaces while making my way back to the main road. Through my tinted windshield I watched a cyclist as he sped up and squeezed the brakes just in time to prevent himself from crashing into a pedestrian.

Inside the cold, dark interior of my BMW, I felt suffocated. I needed some mental purification after the thick, dense smoke of the Ming, but had no idea where I was going to get it.

I drove aimlessly, listening to music on the tape deck and observing with wonder the endless stream of bicycles in the streets around me. The entire nation, it seemed, was trying to get somewhere. Where were they going? A family rolled past the front of my car. A little girl sat in a basket attached to the front of the bicycle, which was being ridden by her father; unable to fit completely inside, her legs hung out the front of the basket and dangled there. Mom sat on a small makeshift seat behind the father, hovering precariously above the back tire; her hands were planted firmly on her husband's waist. They were perilously close to slipping and falling into the snow, but to me it seemed a vision of perfect happiness: the happiness of a life enjoyed together. Other people would still be in bed at this hour, sleeping late with the sun on their faces and their arm stretched out lazily across someone's ass. They were enjoying their happiness. Liu Zheng would be with his family, enjoying his happiness. Where was my happiness?

I considered visiting my parents, but that wasn't happiness. That was being a good son. I thought about Hao Mei, but being with her would have been even less gratifying. Then I thought of Lan Yu.

The last time I had seen him he had given me a phone number for what he said was his dormitory. But what was the point of calling? To begin with, he was probably lying and wasn't in school at all. But even if he was, I knew from experience that university dorm receptionists were grumpy old men who didn't even bother notifying students that they had phone calls. And how did I know the number was even real?

It didn't matter anyway. The slip of paper Lan Yu had written the number on had probably been swept away by the maids at Country Brothers. Besides, until that moment I hadn't given serious thought to calling him anyway. Sooner or later, I figured, he would contact me through Liu Zheng.

And yet, he hadn't contacted me through Liu Zheng and as a consequence I hadn't seen him since the night he quietly drank his martini in the hotel disco before standing up to leave. On his own. Because he wasn't a girl.

Just thinking about sex with him made my palms sweat.

On and on I drove, determined to find a distraction, but not knowing what it would be. I considered calling a girl I knew who was in business school and had said with a wink that she wanted to "study business" with me. Or perhaps I'd go hang out with some of the guys I knew in the gay circle. Maybe a new face had shown up, someone I could get to know. I felt frustrated knowing I had no way of getting in touch with Lan Yu.

Then it crossed my mind: Maybe Liu Zheng has his number.

I picked up the Big Boss on the passenger seat next to me and dialed Liu Zheng's home number. Big Boss was China's first cell phone and I, of course, was among the first to have one. A primitive piece of technology, it was as big and clunky as it was expensive. I balanced the phone against my ear with one hand while steering with the other.

"Liu Zheng!" I hollered. "That kid—you know, Lan Yu. Do you have his number?"

"Yeah," he replied. "You gave it to me to hold on to, remember?" A surge of relief rushed through me.

"Call him and ask him if he can meet me at Country Brothers in twenty minutes."

A few minutes later Liu Zheng called back. Lan Yu wanted to know if I'd be available at seven.

"That's too late!" I shouted. "If he wants to see me, fine, but he has to come to Country Brothers right now." If I was going to get gratification, it had to be instant.

"Okay, okay, I'll tell him," Liu Zheng replied, sounding somewhat thrown off by the unreasonable rancor in my voice.

The instant I hung up I regretted what I had said. The idea of seeing Lan Yu was so much more appealing than the alternatives. Waiting half the day until seven o'clock would have been more than worth it.

I didn't have to regret my brash impatience for long. A few minutes later Liu Zheng called back to say Lan Yu would be able to make it by six. "Will that work?" he asked. The answer was yes.

At six o'clock I stood outside the main entrance of Country Brothers to wait. This time Lan Yu was extremely punctual. At six on the dot he showed up wearing the same white jacket he had been wearing the last time I'd seen him. If it had been cold then, it was freezing now. I couldn't understand why he was wearing so little. I watched in distress as the snow piled up on his shoulders, eyelashes, and hair.

"You need to dress more warmly!" I said sternly. "Otherwise, you're going to catch a cold. Here, wear this." I took off my scarf and put it around his neck, fully aware that I was making a bigger fuss than the situation warranted.

Lan Yu smiled awkwardly and looked around nervously as I wrapped the long white scarf around his neck. Evidently he was uncomfortable with the idea of another man dressing him in public.

"So, how's school going?" I continued, walking through the front door of Country Brothers and into the lobby.

"Oh man!" he said with sudden enthusiasm. "Everyone's terrified of falling behind, even the people who were at the top of their class in high school. Everyone's competing against everyone else, but no one will come out and say it." His lips formed a smile as he spoke and two dimples danced at the corners of his mouth. He was just as beautiful as before.

"Don't put too much pressure on yourself," I said. "Just keep up with it and you'll do fine."

"That's what I think," he said, then paused. "You know what? I heard that one year there was a student who killed himself because he failed a midterm!"

"Wow," I laughed. "Only a nutcase would do that! You wouldn't do something like that, would you?"

The grave look on Lan Yu's face made it clear he didn't like the question. "No," he said curtly, "I wouldn't." I changed the subject.

"How's the food in the dining hall?" I asked.

Whatever my shortcomings, I'd always had one strong point: I was good at showing people my concern. This was why I had so many friends, not to mention lovers.

"Pretty good," Lan Yu replied. "It's all northern-style cuisine. The steamed buns are huge! The only bad part is the noodles."

"Ha!" I laughed. "Never eat noodles at a school cafeteria. They weigh them down with a ton of water. There was this one time I ordered half a kilo of noodles for lunch. They'd been soaked in water for so long I ended up pissing five times in a row and was still hungry two hours later! I've eaten at a million campuses. Nanda University is pretty good. That's where I went to school. Huada is the worst."

"That's where I'm going—Huada University!" Lan Yu beamed with pride. I studied his face closely. I still wasn't entirely convinced that he was a student, but something about the way he spoke told me it might be true. I wanted to know for sure, though, so I probed for details.

"Where did you come from just now? Did you have dinner yet?"

"No, not yet," he said, looking somewhat embarrassed about it. "I had to work this afternoon, a tutoring session. I didn't want to be late so I came straight here."

I fought back a smile. I couldn't put my finger on it, but there was something so wonderfully unexpected about him.

We had dinner in one of the hotel restaurants. All through the meal we kept looking at each other, eager to get back to my room. If Lan Yu had been a girl, I would have caressed his neck or shoulder or held his hand while we ate. But he was a guy, so we just stared at each other, stifling our mutual desire from across the table. The moment we finished eating we rushed back to my room. I pinned him against the wall and pressed my body against his, kissing his face and running my fingers through his hair.

"Why haven't you been in touch with me?" I asked, kissing him through the words. "I've thought about you every day."

"I've been so busy with my classes . . . I wanted to call, but I was afraid that . . ." His hands ascended to the back of my head and his voice trembled. I buried my face in his neck, still holding him firmly against the wall.

The intensity of two men making love can never be matched by straight sex. I fumbled with the buttons on his shirt, then gave up and tore it open, revealing two broad shoulders and a narrow waist covered by a canvas of skin that seemed to glow as if on fire. I kissed him with feverish excitement, pressing my body against his and traveling the length of his back with my hands. Gripping his shoulders then his arms, I slowly lowered myself to the floor, pausing to kiss his chest, his stomach, his hands and fingers, until finally I was on my knees and his cock was in my mouth. I squeezed his ass, so firm and compact compared to Hao Mei's, then tried to put a finger inside. He trembled slightly but didn't stop me. When I went in a little deeper he pulled back and hunched over, holding the back of my head for balance as if he was about to fall. He gazed down at me and stroked my hair, a look of breathless expectation stretched across his face.

I stood up to kiss him again, then pulled in close to his ear and whispered, "I'm crazy about you. Whatever you want to do . . ."

These words worked. All at once Lan Yu's demeanor changed and I could feel the tension melting away from his body. Then he did something that surprised me. Slowly and somewhat awkwardly, he fell to his knees and began sucking me off. I grabbed the back of his head and pushed in deeper, slow but firm, then winced in discomfort when his teeth scraped against me. He didn't seem to know exactly what he was doing but I didn't care. I was just happy that we were together. He blew me for a while, then stood up again, completely out of breath. Kissing me feebly, he wrapped his arms around my neck once more.

We took a shower after we came, then lay back down on the bed. Unlike the first time we had made love, this time he stayed awake after sex and we started talking. We were under the blankets, me on my back, him propped up on an elbow so he could look at me. I told him to stop calling me Director Chen and to use my given name, Handong. It means "Defend Mao Zedong Thought." I began to tell him some things about myself. He listened intently, looking cheerful and relaxed and periodically asking questions.

"When you do business do you lose money sometimes?" he asked. It struck me as a naive question, but I didn't mind.

"Of course," I replied patiently. "But as long as you make more money than you lose, it's okay."

The mention of money made me recall a story I thought Lan Yu would find amusing. "This one time I ordered a big batch of lollipops from some guy in Spain for the Lunar New Year. His shipment was late—I mean, it came way after New Year's, so none of my buyers wanted it anymore. But it was a huge order, and after a few weeks we had a couple hundred kilos of candy that would be melting soon. So after a week or so I decided I might as well just give it to my employees. My god, there was a period of time when every single employee had a lollipop sticking out of their mouth!"

"You can eat candy at work?" Lan Yu's eyes widened. He seemed to have missed the point of the anecdote.

"If it doesn't interfere with your work performance, sure."

He sat in silence for a few moments, apparently pondering what I'd just told him. "Does it bother you that you don't use what you studied in college?" he finally asked.

"No. I knew I picked the wrong major," I said. "I hated literature. I should have pursued a business major—management or something like that."

"But even though you didn't, you still get to be the boss now," he said cheerfully.

"Oh, I'm pretty much just muddling along," I said, trying to sound modest. I got up from the bed and walked to the other side of the room to grab a Chunghwa from the pack on the table. I lit it and turned around to face Lan Yu. He was still lying in bed, naked under the blankets and watching my every move. When I looked at him he averted his eyes, laughing softly as if he had been caught doing something he wasn't supposed to. I took a deep drag off the cigarette. I needed to clarify a few things before we went any further.

"Look," I began. "You and I were brought together by fate. The only problem is that you're so young I feel guilty for even getting to know you. In the West this kind of thing isn't a big deal, but in China we can be prosecuted for hooliganism. What I'm trying to say is you have to be discreet. This is between you and me. Don't go talking to other people about it. Also, there are no strings attached, okay? With this kind of thing, if we want to be together, fine. But if it doesn't feel right for either of us, then it's time to move on."

Lan Yu listened with absolute concentration. I was trying to figure out how much I needed to spell out and how much he would be able to figure out on his own. I continued.

"The truth is, if two people get to know each other too well, the whole thing starts to get embarrassing. I mean, two guys!" I laughed. I was trying to give him the hint that I didn't want him taking the whole thing too seriously. He continued staring at me like some kind of schoolgirl in love for the first time, but said nothing.

Lan Yu and I saw each other a few more times after that conversation, but it never progressed to anal sex. I didn't want to pressure him, and besides, I knew that it would only be good if we both wanted it. I'm patient by nature and, in fact, the suspense only compounded my interest in him. He never asked for money or talked about his financial situation, and I never inquired. One time, though, I asked Liu Zheng to give him a call to find out if he had enough money for the semester. Liu Zheng reported that between financial aid and tutoring gigs, Lan Yu was fine.

He really was stunning to look at. Rapidly acquiring the seductive charm of a young man, his only shortcoming was his appalling attire. His clothes weren't even up to speed with what Beijing guys were wearing in those days, and that wasn't saying much. So when my ex-lover Min went to Hong Kong— we had stayed friends—I asked him to pick up a dozen or so articles of clothing in a specialty store that carried designs for young men. Beijing didn't have those kinds of boutiques yet.

It was after Min came back to Beijing that things with Lan Yu got ugly. One night when Lan Yu was over I told him to go look in the closet where I'd hidden the clothes from Hong Kong. He opened the bags and looked inside, then mumbled something I couldn't make out. That was it—not so much as a thank you. The following morning he got up at six, saying he had class at eight. I offered to give him a ride, but he said not to bother, that taking the bus was just as fast. When I asked him to take the clothes with him, he hesitated for a moment, then briefly rummaged through the bags before pulling out a pair of jeans and a bluish-gray jacket. "I'll get the rest later," he mumbled. He seemed to be speaking more to the closet than to me.

I sat up in bed watching this scene in amazement, asking myself whether Lan Yu was turning out to be more trouble than he was worth. This was only the fifth or sixth time I'd seen him but already I was beginning to notice a kind of aloofness about him. Something fastidious, difficult to please. An irritating indifference, not just with the clothes, but in general.

Most of all, I was bothered by his failure to appreciate me. I began wondering whether I wanted to see him again.

I tried falling back to sleep after Lan Yu left but couldn't. When I finally got out of bed at nine, I went to the office, where I told Liu Zheng and my secretary that if Lan Yu called I wasn't in. Fortunately, I hadn't given him my cell phone number.

Days passed and we had no contact. I thought about calling him, especially when I was horny—which was often—but I always resisted.

In December I had to go to Czechoslovakia for business. I wasn't eager for the trip because I hated flying—my friends used to joke that I was an old man who needed to catch up with the times—but I ended up going through with it, in part because I was going stir-crazy in Beijing. Before leaving for the trip, I finally broke up with Hao Mei, whose big ass was getting to be like candy to a child: eat too much of it and you get sick. When I told her it was over she said little in response. She had never been the kind of girl who liked to argue. Ironically, her silence only made it that much more difficult to dump her.

I stayed in Czechoslovakia for six days, signing contracts, meeting with associates, and handling some goods that had been detained in customs. I had planned on staying a couple of extra days to see if I could meet some Czech guys, but I was terrified of diseases, which I knew were so common in Europe, and ended up getting cold feet at the last minute. That's when I decided to do something bold. I saw my associates off when they returned to China, then flew to Hong Kong, where I spent a few weeks. I was more comfortable there than in Europe. In Hong Kong I was adept at navigating the city's pleasure-seeking underbelly.

In mid-January I flew back to Beijing. I hadn't forgotten about Lan Yu, but I didn't mention him to Liu Zheng or to anybody else.

The New Year came unusually late that year. By the end of January, my employees were getting antsy and counting the days before the weeklong holiday, which wasn't due to arrive for almost three more weeks. Business was slow, and I often sat at my window watching the festive atmosphere outside.

Beijing. A city of contrasts. Clean and orderly but always with a pervasive bustle of activity. Children bundled up in scarves and thick padded gloves stomped through the snow carrying hot, steaming rows of candied hawthorn fruit on wooden sticks. Grown-ups rushed headlong into the wind, clutching at their collars to cover their throats. Everywhere you looked, students and migrant workers bustled in the street, carrying little bags or struggling with big ones as they traveled here and there for China's most important holiday.

I shut my office door and returned to the window, where I looked outside and saw two tiny snowmen perched on the hood of a car. They were about as high as a ruler and had little eyes and mouths made out of twigs and rocks. A smashed up cigarette butt stuck out of one of their faces; the other had a little red ribbon tied around its neck. It was hard to tell if they were supposed to be two men or a man and a woman. I leaned back into my chair, absorbing the serene snowy scene outside and thinking: Lan Yu must be getting ready to go home right now.

Five

"I saw Lan Yu this morning," Liu Zheng said matter-of-factly as he handed me a stack of paperwork. I had returned from Hong Kong just the day before. The announcement came out of nowhere.

"What? Where?" My heart jumped.

"You know the company Fan Haiguo started up near Zhongguan Village? He's working over there." Zhongguan Village was Beijing's hi-tech district. Everyone called it China's Silicon Valley.

"That's strange," I said. "Wouldn't he have gone home to celebrate the New Year with his family?"

"Apparently not."

"Did he see you?"

"No," he replied. "I was driving past Fan's shop and saw Lan Yu carrying a box inside. I think he's doing computer installation or something. I'm not sure."

"Has he called here?"

"Are you fucking kidding me? He's called at least twenty times. I didn't mention it because I didn't think you wanted to know."

I leaned back in my chair and laughed, my eyes narrowing impishly. "What does he say when he calls?"

When Liu Zheng saw I wasn't rankled by his news, he laughed too. "He just asks if you're here and that's it. Hey, wait a minute. I thought you were through with him! Are you playing some kind of game or what?"

"Now, *there's* an idea!" I said, laughing. "A game! Why don't I swing by Fan Haiguo's shop to see if any of his employees want to play a game?" I was laughing even harder at this point, but didn't tell Liu Zheng what game I would be playing. I wasn't sure myself.

Fan Haiguo was working in the back of his shop when I entered. I was curious to know where he had found the smuggled computer parts he would have needed to get his business off the ground. But at the same time I didn't particularly feel like wasting time chatting with him, so my eyes darted around the room the instant I walked through the door. I was looking for Lan Yu.

"Do you need a computer, sir?" A young shop attendant greeted me.

"I'm just—I have some business to talk with the owner about."

When the attendant realized I was there for his boss he didn't ask any more questions.

Just as I was about to send the attendant off to look for Fan Haiguo, I heard the foul language of some typical Beijing punk bellowing in the back room.

"What the fuck are you doing with that monitor? Open your fucking eyes and learn how to do your job!"

"The boss told me to put it here." It was Lan Yu. His voice was calm and steady, but very firm. This was the first time I'd ever heard him argue with someone.

"Just put it over there. And move this box." Now it was Fan Haiguo himself, intervening in the quarrel.

"Stupid cunt," the punk muttered under his breath.

Lan Yu looked at the repugnant coworker, but didn't say anything. He placed the monitor on a table and was about to pick up a box when he saw me. He froze, then smiled.

Fan Haiguo was still spitting out orders to his employees.

"You two," he said to Lan Yu and another employee with wire-rimmed glasses, "move these boxes. How am I supposed to get through here when they're piled up like this?" When Fan Haiguo turned around and saw me standing in the doorway he broke into a wide smile. "Brother Chen! What are you doing here? I haven't seen *you* in a while!"

"I come with business," I said in a mock serious voice. "You interested?" I peered over at Lan Yu out of the corner of my eye. Obediently he carried out Fan Haiguo's orders, but threw excited glances in my direction every few seconds. He was happy to see me!

Fan Haiguo and I talked for a while about some Japanese computer components I pretended to be interested in buying. Then I said goodbye and turned around, noting with amusement the bewilderment on Fan Haiguo's face. He must have been surprised I'd gone all that way just to talk about a purchase, especially when I could have called. Just before stepping outside, I threw Lan Yu a look that said "meet me outside" and gestured toward the door. His eyes followed my finger and he saw my dark blue Bimmer parked on the opposite side of the street.

I sat in the car waiting. Waiting, and excited. Ten minutes later, Lan Yu came running out of the shop and jumped into my car.

"I was afraid you'd already left!" I heard joy in his voice.

"I was just passing by," I lied. "I had some work to do in

the area but I'm finished now." Even I thought it sounded like bullshit. "Hey, so you work at Fan Haiguo's," I continued. "Aren't you going home for the holiday?"

"This year me and another guy from school are staying in the dorm," he replied. "He's from Hainan Island. Our vacation isn't even long enough for him to make the trip there and back, so he's not going home to visit. Being from Xinjiang, it's the same with me."

We sat in the car quietly for a few minutes before I broke the silence.

"Did your boss say you could leave work?"

"I asked him but he said no," he laughed. "I told him I had something important to do, but he went into a tirade, so I told him I quit!" Lan Yu paused for a moment. "You know, Beijingers have such bad tempers. They're so arrogant, and they really bully people from other parts of the country."

"Hey, what are you trying to say?" I laughed. "I'm from Beijing!"

"Yeah, *right!*" he laughed. "You told me you came here for college!" He had a good memory.

I burst out laughing. I wasn't going to confirm or deny a thing. The old saying crossed my mind: You can't fool youth! I started the car and we drove out of Zhongguan Village.

"Hey, can we swing by campus for a minute?" Lan Yu asked as I turned at an intersection. "I want to get out of these dirty work clothes."

I looked at the cheap cotton-padded black jacket he wore. He had a point. It was filthy.

"Cars can only enter through the south gate," he continued. "You know where that is?"

"Nanda and Huada are practically next door to each other. How could I not know?" Although I hadn't attended

Huada, I had been there a number of times and was familiar with the area.

The Huada University campus was quite large, but it wasn't nearly as beautiful as Nanda. I entered the south gate and drove toward Lan Yu's dormitory building. If it had been any other time of year, there would have been students coming and going, carrying backpacks and laughing and chatting as they walked or rode their bicycles to class. But it was time for the New Year, and the entire campus was deep in the slumber of the weeklong vacation.

I pulled up to the entrance of building number eight, and Lan Yu jumped out of the car and ran inside. When he and I had first met, I thought he was making everything up, that he was just some migrant worker from a small town who'd concocted a story about being in college. And yet there I was, parked outside his dorm room at one of China's top universities. This was the final confirmation I needed to see that he was definitely telling the truth. Meanwhile, if there was anything he chose not to share with me, rather than lie about it he just kept his mouth shut. There weren't a lot of people like that. I thought about myself and my own behavior. Of every ten sentences that came out of my mouth, nine were bullshit. Then again I'm in business, I rationalized. You've got to screw people if you want to get ahead.

When Lan Yu came out of the building he was a completely different person. A pair of jeans hugged his thighs and he wore the same bluish-gray jacket he'd pulled from my closet the last time I had seen him. The jacket was open, causing the zipper pull tab to sway back and forth, revealing a dark brown interior lining, as he quickly made his way back toward me. I watched him from the car, vaguely wondering what had happened to the white jacket he wore the first few times I had seen him. I could tell from the tiny beads of water clinging to his forehead and eyebrows that he had washed his face. I gripped the steering wheel and my dick got hard.

"I can't wear this on campus," he said, jumping into the car. "Students here don't dress this way. Some Japanese exchange students actually came up to me the other day and spoke to me in Japanese!" There was a vague sound of embarrassment in his voice, but also an unmistakable hint of pride.

Forty-five minutes later Lan Yu was naked in my bed, lying on his side and watching a couple of gay porn videos I had recently brought back from the United States. Two good-looking, muscular guys fucked riotously on the TV screen. I went into the kitchen to grab a beer, then returned to the bedroom and handed Lan Yu a glass of orange juice. He raised his eyes apologetically. "Are you mad at me for leaving the clothes here?"

"Of course not," I replied, tousling his hair. "Come on, I'm a big boy. I'm not going to get upset over a little thing like that."

"I didn't mean anything by it," he continued. "I just didn't want you to think I was after your money."

"I would never think that." He was so pure. I didn't know what else to say.

Lan Yu's eyes returned to the video, and I turned down the headboard light and got into bed to hold him from behind. I kissed the nape of his neck while running my hand firmly up his back, over his shoulder, and down his chest. Wrapping my right arm around his torso, I gently squeezed his left pec, wondering if he had actually grown bigger since the last time I had seen him. Perhaps I was only imagining it, but he seemed stronger now, sexier.

Hooking my chin over his shoulder, I riveted my gaze to his profile. I could only see the outline of his face, but it was enough to see that his eyes were closed. Whatever I was doing, he was apparently enjoying it more than the video. With my chin still pressed against his shoulder, I ran one hand down the front of his body—his chest, his stomach, the silky trail of hair leading down his belly—until his balls were in my hand. That's when I decided to go for my target. I pulled my hand back, then stuck two fingers into my mouth to moisten them before returning them to where they had just been, this time from behind. Gasping quietly, he reached back to grip my forearm. His body stiffened. Slowly, I entered him with one finger, then two, then moved my lips to his ear. "Does it hurt?"

Lan Yu shook his head to say no, but I couldn't see his face.

I pulled my fingers out and reached toward the other side of the bed where I'd put a tube of lubricant under the pillow before surprising Lan Yu at work. Wrapping my arms around him in a bear hug, I rolled our bodies downward until we were lying on our sides. I smeared a thick glob of lube on my cock. When the lube met his skin, he trembled.

"Is it cold?" I asked. He ignored the question and backed into me.

Slowly I entered him. I wanted him to raise his leg because we were lying on our sides, but at the same time I didn't want to give him orders, so things were a little awkward until I got the head in. It popped out immediately. The guy getting fucked in the video moaned loudly.

At last Lan Yu turned to look at me. One look at his face, so overflowing with tension and excitement, was all it took for me to abandon the ridiculous spoon position, lift him up roughly, and put him down on his hands and knees. Taking hold of his waist with my left hand, I used my other hand to push his torso against the bed. This is the best angle for sex, especially if it's their first time.

When I entered him, he gripped the pillow and moaned. It was explosive. The sexual pleasure was only part of it; the real high was his unswerving commitment to endure this for me. I tried to exercise self-control, to go slowly, to ease what I knew would be the searing pain of the first time. But I was in a daze at that point and gentle lovemaking rapidly turned into coarse and rough sex. Each time he took it, my desire for him grew a little more.

"I can't stop thinking about you. I think about you every day. I just . . . it's just so fucking . . ." I had no idea what I was saying or what was going on around me. He was very tight despite the amount of lube I had used. Without thinking, I reached under him to jerk him off.

"Oh . . . ," he moaned, and in an instant my hand was wet. I couldn't believe it. He actually came before me!

We didn't shower but lay in bed together, a sweaty, cum-drenched mess. I held Lan Yu close, caressing him as I had only done with girls in the past.

"Did it hurt?" I asked quietly.

"A little." He turned his back to me as if to tell me he was ready for sleep.

"If you didn't like it we don't have to do it again."

"No, I liked it. Let's get some sleep." He kissed me and I turned off the light.

I could tell that he liked it. With men the only problem is that getting fucked is damaging to their self-respect. Girls go through something similar when they lose their virginity, but it might be worse for a guy.

The truth was, I was becoming attached to Lan Yu. I cared

about him. Anal sex was just a way of expressing that, especially between men. I wondered if he could understand that.

He was so pure, so quiet, and, yes, introverted. I figured I would never know.

All of this transpired in February. My employees were restless for the New Year vacation, set to begin in a matter of days, and I, the boss, didn't much feel like working either. It was six months since I had met Lan Yu, and we were together nearly every day at that point. I no longer took him to Country Brothers because it would have aroused too much suspicion to have a regular male companion, so he stayed with me almost every night at Ephemeros Village, where I had a large two-bedroom apartment. Lan Yu loved it, saying it was much more comfortable than the hotel.

There weren't many entertainment spots in Beijing back then, but I still managed to take him out often. Most of the time we went to hotel nightclubs, but we also did karaoke, bowling, that sort of thing. Sometimes we would go for a swim or to the sauna.

What Lan Yu didn't know was that I also had a second, slightly more nefarious agenda, albeit one that was largely unconscious at the time: to make him shake off the cultural and intellectual arrogance of the old world and learn to enjoy the material pleasures of the new one. Lifestyles of the wealthy were unimaginable to the vast majority of the population, who barely had the luxury of schlepping off to a public bath for a weekly shower, let alone lounging beside sun-drenched swimming pools. I wanted Lan Yu to enjoy this life and to appreciate that it was I who was giving it to him. Besides, he was an architecture student. I didn't want his research on Ming dynasty quadrangles and other obscure themes making him think he was better than me.

I wasn't wild about the idea of Lan Yu working, but he still had the two home-tutoring gigs. He said his pupils were the kids of Huada University professors, that the jobs were already in place, and that he couldn't back out now. This, I thought, was reasonable, but I was adamant about his not taking on a third student. When I asked him about it, however, he became quiet, not wanting to answer the question. What was he so worried about? Next semester's living expenses?

One night after a tutoring session with a high school student, Lan Yu got home late. All throughout Beijing you could hear the celebratory sound of fireworks exploding; New Year's Eve was just two days away. He had gone to China Telecom to call his family after work, but the line was long and he had had to wait forty-five minutes. I told him to stop going there to make calls, that he could make as many long-distance phone calls as he wanted from Country Brothers or from Ephemeros.

Still, the call home made me curious about Lan Yu's family, whom I knew nothing about.

"I was beginning to think you were raised by wolves," I joked. "You're like the Monkey King: born by jumping out of a stone!" I was referring to Sun Wukong, the popular character in *Journey to the West*.

Lan Yu gave a resigned laugh but quickly became serious. "My mom died a few years ago. I still have my dad but I don't want to go back to visit. That woman—the one my dad married—doesn't want me to either."

"So your dad's still alive?" I pressed to find out more.

"Yeah, alive and well. I have a three-year-old half sister too." His eyes burned with the deep distress he had, not always, but often. It was as if he was lost in some memory, but he would never say what it was.

On New Year's Eve I insisted that Lan Yu come with me to my parents' house, where I always spent the holiday. It was risky bringing home a lover, but I couldn't bear the idea of him being on his own. As I had expected, my family treated "my friend's little brother" very well. Especially my mother. She had always been the warm and loving one in the family— in this respect I liked to think that I took after her. My two younger sisters, Aidong and Jingdong—"Love Mao Zedong Thought" and "Respect Mao Zedong Thought"—were more like my father: cold, distant, fake. Later Lan Yu would tell me that he never knew a family of high-ranking cadres could be so kind. It was gratifying to hear, but I knew it was only because my aging father had long since lost his iron-fisted control over the family. When I told Lan Yu this, he told me I should be grateful for the family I had.

It was nearly midnight and the Beijing night sky was saturated with the sound of exploding fireworks. Standing on the sidelines of the action, I watched Lan Yu as he lit fuses with Jingdong, the younger of my two sisters, and Aidong's husband. I watched my mother as she walked toward me, a big smile on her face, and thought: if they knew the truth about my relationship with Lan Yu, I'd be dead to them.

Six

Spring had arrived and everything was perfect. I had made an enormous sum of money from a recent deal and had a new associate—a major player in the industry—with whom I'd be collaborating. And I had met a new guy, a drummer in a band.

Things were in full swing for Lan Yu, too. The new semester had long since begun and his schedule left him only enough time to see me once every two weeks or so. A few days before his classes started, I sat him down on the living room couch and gave him a bankbook, an account with ¥20,000 in it. He opened it up and timidly peeked inside, then set it down on the rosewood tea table before us. "I still have two hundred left from that five hundred you gave me back in September," he said, staring at me blankly. There was the faintest tone of protest in his voice.

"Quit worrying so much about saving money," I insisted. "If you need to spend it, spend it."

"Well, what I was thinking was . . ." He gave an uncomfortable smile. "I was thinking I would pay you back when I have the money."

"Don't be ridiculous!" I said. "What kind of person do you think I am? Besides," I joked, "if you were to pay me back, I'd have to charge you interest. That five hundred you took from me? I'm gonna need a thousand for that!" Lan Yu looked at me with a smile, but stopped short of laughing. I didn't like to see him worry.

"Listen, really," I said, looking at him gravely. "Don't worry about it. One day when you graduate and start working, you can pay it back. But," I continued to jest, "don't say I didn't warn you about my high interest rate!"

Lan Yu remained seated on the couch, the bankbook resting in his lap like a rejected lover. Somehow, inexplicably, he was reluctant to take it. My temples throbbed in irritation. What the fuck is wrong with this guy?

The drummer's name was Huang Jian. He was only okay looking, but he was great in bed and we had fantastic sex. He was more than a little willing to cozy up to me—so willing, in fact, that he agreed to my altogether unreasonable demand that he get, not just an STD screening, but a complete physical before I slept with him.

The thing about Huang Jian was that he liked to put on a little makeup before sex. I don't know why, it was just this thing he was into. He especially liked purple eye shadow, which he would apply with great care while gazing at his reflection in the mirror. I myself wasn't so keen on the whole thing. After all, I liked men because of their masculinity and women because of their femininity. Somehow, though, Huang Jian managed to pull it off in a way that didn't entirely disgust me, and besides, he liked having sex with the lights dimmed so I couldn't really see it anyway.

Huang Jian had two personalities, and sex with him always proceeded in one of two directions. When he wanted to be my dirty little whore, he would sit at the foot of the bed and gaze at me with a teasing, slutty look. Then he would crawl toward me on his hands and knees until reaching his target—my cock—which he would tease with his tongue before moving downward to lick my balls. His tongue was so tender, like a thousand ripples of water gently massaging me. Meticulous and considerate, he would roll my nuts around in his mouth, taking great pains to ensure his teeth didn't get in the way. Finally, he would dive back onto my cock, swallowing the entire thick length all at once. He was a very patient cocksucker, extremely focused on his work, and never tiring or, worse, complaining. I had to push him off of me periodically to keep from coming too soon.

When Huang Jian was in his other mood he was like a man possessed. Full of aggressive energy, he would rapidly change positions while sweating bullets and yelling out obscenities. I would kiss his body all over sometimes, but rarely gave him head and never let him fuck me. I had always refused to be penetrated; my stubborn nonreciprocity disappointed no small number of my lovers. Huang Jian didn't mind, though: he was truly submissive and loved serving men. When I fucked him, it was always with him on his knees, ass perched up high, begging me to pound him harder and harder as he reached back to grab my forearm and pull me in deeper.

Huang Jian conjured up from within me a powerful urge to conquer. It was only after meeting him that I realized just how easy it is to dominate a woman. Dominating men is much harder, and only some of us can do it right. I can't deny that when he climaxed, it left me with a strong feeling of triumph.

Early one morning, I woke up feeling unusually groggy. There was Huang Jian, hovering over me and giggling at the red streaks he'd left all over my body the night before. That was one of his favorite things to do: put on heavy red lipstick, then kiss me from head to toe.

"You're fuckin' twisted," I said with a yawn.

He nuzzled into my chest like a spoiled child.

"You fuck me so great!" he said. "I'm not kidding—the more you fuck me, the better my drumming gets. Sometimes I think sex is the only thing that helps musicians get better."

"That's the most ridiculous thing I've ever heard," I mumbled, still half-asleep.

Huang Jian and I joked around for a while, then he took a shower and headed home.

It was the end of April and I had wanted to call Lan Yu for some time. With Huang Jian out of the apartment I couldn't resist the temptation any longer. I picked up the phone and called Lan Yu's dorm building. I had been encouraging him to let me get him a cell phone or at least a pager, but he said there was no way he could be that flashy at school; it would just be too awkward.

The phone rang for a full five minutes before someone picked up. When I finally got Lan Yu on the phone, he said he had midterms that week but would be able to see me on Saturday after he was finished. I said okay and hung up, disappointed. I wanted instant gratification. And I wasn't used to being rejected.

When Saturday came around, Huang Jian gave me a call saying he wanted to come over in the evening. That makeup-wearing drummer must have put some kind of spell on me because I had completely forgotten that I had plans with Lan Yu.

When Huang Jian arrived, I went into the kitchen wearing

nothing but a pair of underwear and poured a glass of wine. He sat on the couch and popped a porn video into the VCR.

"Look at that position!" he yelled, pointing at the screen as I returned to the living room. "We're *definitely* trying that later." I looked at the TV. One guy was lying on his back while the other guy sat on his dick and rode him. But instead of facing each other, the guy on top turned around so they were facing the same direction. As Huang Jian had suggested, it was an impressive stunt.

"Hey, by the way," he said excitedly. "I went and saw that drum set today. It's awesome! It's from West Germany." In addition to everything else I had bought him, Huang Jian now wanted a $4,000 drum set. He had also made it more than clear he wanted a car, but I hadn't agreed to that one yet.

Out of nowhere the doorbell rang. I figured it was probably the delivery that Huang Jian had ordered: some kind of American food, unclear to me exactly what. All I knew was that Huang Jian absolutely worshipped the West and ate nothing but Western food, sometimes Japanese. Japanese I liked, but the other stuff? I had no idea what he saw in it.

"I'll get it!" Huang Jian shouted. Wearing the bathrobe he had changed into, he got up from the couch and swaggered toward the door in his typically pompous way.

"Chen Handong, please." It was Lan Yu's voice.

"Fuck!" I muttered under my breath as I jumped to my feet. I darted into the bedroom to throw on some clothes, then rushed toward the door.

The look on Lan Yu's face when he saw me wasn't so much anger as bewilderment. This reaction wasn't the least bit lost on Huang Jian, who threw his competitor a bitchy look before sneering at me and walking into the bedroom.

I considered pushing Lan Yu back into the hallway so we

could talk, but I didn't want to lose face by seeming too eager to placate him, so we continued standing there, facing each other in the doorway.

"What are you doing here? Why didn't you call first?" I sounded like I was lecturing a child.

"I told you I was coming over today after I finished my midterm examinations," he replied, enunciating each syllable as if to make sure I understood what he was saying.

"Okay, but you should still call first." I had completely forgotten about our rendezvous, but was determined to make it sound like it was his fault.

"I didn't know you—anyway, you're busy. I'll just go back to campus." Lan Yu hesitated for a moment, then turned around and left.

I wanted to stop him, but didn't. That night, I didn't feel like having sex and wouldn't have been able to get hard anyway. Huang Jian, for his part, took the opportunity to deride me for being so inept at planning my affairs. He didn't care that I was fucking someone else; he just wanted me to do a better job juggling all the pieces.

I didn't have any contact with Lan Yu for a month after that. Again and again I thought about calling him, but each time I persuaded myself to hold out. Nor did I ask Liu Zheng to contact him for me. For some reason, I no longer felt that he or anyone else should be involved in what we had. Finally, it was Lan Yu who called me first.

"How are you?" I was determined not to lose my chance to get him back.

"Okay," he replied in perfect Beijing Mandarin.

"How've you been?"

"Okay."

"How are your classes?"

"Fine."

"I've been worried sick about you, Lan Yu!" This was true, but I only said it because I wanted him to hear it; I needed verbal ammunition if I was going to win him over.

Silence.

"Your summer vacation is coming soon."

"Yeah."

I needed the conversation to move forward. "Hold on," I said. I put the phone receiver down on my desk and got up to shut my office door. I returned to the phone and lowered my voice.

"I've missed you so much, Lan Yu," I said in a desperate whisper. "I've never been like this before. Remember how I said that with this kind of thing, if we want to be together—I mean, maybe you hate me, but—" I took a deep breath and continued. "Listen, if you only want to be friends, that's fine. But you don't have family here in Beijing and I took you home to meet mine and—I mean, I really regard you as my little brother." At this point I was beginning to sound a little dramatic. But it was real.

Lan Yu remained silent, but at least he hadn't hung up.

"Look," I said. "I've been staying at Ephemeros. Just me, no one else." That was a lie, since Huang Jian was sleeping there almost every night at that point. But if Lan Yu was going to be coming over, I'd make sure Huang Jian was gone, purple eye shadow and all.

I told Lan Yu I'd wait for him at Ephemeros at six. He didn't say whether he would be coming, but before I had the chance to ask him, I heard one of his dorm mates in the background saying he needed to use the phone. Lan Yu hung up, and at five thirty I left the office to go home and wait for him.

A little before seven, Lan Yu showed up at my sixth-floor

apartment looking just as vexed as the day we had met. When I opened the front door, he walked inside without so much as a greeting and sat down on the couch. A period of awkward silence ensued, until I realized I had to do something to make him feel at ease. I sat next to him and tried to think of something to say.

"I didn't think you would come."

In lieu of a reply he stared at the floor.

"Why did you run off like that the other day?"

I was stalling. I needed time to figure out what I would do in the event that he started throwing accusations at me. Far from condemning me, however, what Lan Yu did next caught me so completely off guard that it took me a moment to realize what was happening. Without removing his eyes from the floor, he reached across the empty space between us and took my hand in his. He moved closer to me and embraced me, kissing my lips, my cheeks, my forehead. I was so stunned by what he was doing that I had almost no reaction.

Wordlessly, he began peeling away my clothes. Wherever his hands went, his lips followed closely behind, planting kisses on my skin where the clothes had been. He got on his knees and was about to pull off my shoes when he stopped and looked up at me, eyes full of expectation. It was like he was waiting for me to answer a question he couldn't articulate, no matter how urgent. Unable to bear the tension any longer, I lifted him back up to the couch, wrapped my arms around him tightly, and began frantically kissing his mouth, his cheeks, his eyelids. Never had a kiss infused me with so much passion. We kissed endlessly, stopping only when we were both exhausted, out of breath even. I felt as though the world around me had gone black; there was nothing else, only us.

He had the clean, soapy smell typical of young men. Taking

my hand, he stood up from the couch, pulling me with him, and it occurred to me that he was exhibiting dominant behavior for the first time since we'd met. I wanted to run my hands along his body, but my fingers shook uncontrollably, leaving me no choice but to anchor them forcefully to his shoulders. Lowering myself, I unbuttoned his pants, pulling at his underwear and kissing his abdomen. Reaching up, I tried grasping at his chin with my thumb and forefinger. I fumbled; he was too far away. Lan Yu looked down at me with yearning in his eyes. My body burned. "Handong!" he called out in a heavy, trembling voice.

Sex with Huang Jian and with Lan Yu was equally intense, but they were intensities of very different kinds. With Huang Jian, it was raw physical intensity. With Lan Yu it was this as well, but my body wasn't the only thing that was engaged. My psyche was, too.

After making love, Lan Yu said he was exhausted and wanted to sleep. He rested his head in my lap and I tousled his hair.

"Your hair is so stiff," I said.

"Is that a good thing or a bad thing?" he mumbled, eyes closed.

"It's terrible," I said with a smile he couldn't see. "It's so hard to tame that way!"

He laughed faintly. "Well, so what? I'm not your horse."

I looked down at him. Only then did I notice how worn-out he looked. His features were drenched with a kind of fatigue that nobody his age should have. Slowly he drifted into sleep, mumbling something about feeling like a zombie, neither dead nor alive, as I studied his cherubic features. I remember wishing he didn't feel that way.

The following day I stayed home from work and Lan Yu skipped class. That's when we had our first fight.

"How many times do I have to tell you, Lan Yu? Messing around with this kind of thing isn't that serious! It isn't serious and it can't be!" I slammed the newspaper I was reading on the living room tea table and sat on the couch, arms folded in a defiant posture.

"What *is* serious to you, then?" He entered the living room and scowled at me. He hadn't raised his voice, but his words were razor sharp.

"Listen," I said, raising my hands in exasperation. "I feel exactly the same as the day we met. If we're having a good time we stay together. Otherwise, forget it!" I was trying to shift the focus away from me, and I also knew that this would sound like a threat. These words, I knew, would tap into his insecurities.

"What do you think I am, Handong? Some kind of . . ." He faltered, unable to find the right word.

"I think of you as my friend, my little brother. Stop acting like a woman. Every little thing makes you so damn suspicious."

After our argument, Lan Yu went to campus and I was in a bad mood for the rest of the day. What right did he have to place demands on me? Who did he think he was, anyway? He was just some kid! A kid who had apparently forgotten that I was the one supporting him.

I didn't feel like going to the office after that so I called up a friend and asked him to meet me at a karaoke bar for a drink. We even found a couple of girls to hang out with us while we sang shitty pop songs and pounded back beers. Then I won ¥4,000 playing cards. I didn't get home until three in the morning and, for a while at least, was able to completely forget about the fight with Lan Yu.

Lan Yu and I continued seeing each other after the fight, sometimes often, and always at Ephemeros. He never mentioned the argument again and we kept sleeping together as usual. We didn't have anal sex every time, but once in a while I would ask and he never refused me.

And that, I think, is the difference between men and women. When a woman has sex with you, it's because of something you have—genius, money, or whatever—or because they want to find someone who will let them be a parasite forever. After they get what they want, they use sex as a way of rewarding men. But when men have sex there's no rhyme or reason. They're just satisfying a primitive need.

Seven

Another sweltering Beijing summer had arrived, and no matter where you turned the city was alive with action. Young lovebirds strolled side by side. Middle-aged ladies ambled through the Wangfujing shopping district in search of fabric and housewares. For three solid months there wasn't a bicycle lot in sight that wasn't jam packed. Each day before dawn, the parks teemed with retirees in various postures of tai chi. By afternoon they were full of opera singers, chess enthusiasts, and old men carrying little birds in bamboo cages. When evening came, throngs of middle-aged dancers with portable cassette players squeezed into public squares to twirl beneath the stars. And sometimes when darkness fell, hidden deeper in the tall clusters of trees, solitary men with furtive looks on their faces moved silently through the park, searching for sex, love, or some combination of the two.

In my world, however, it was just another long and tedious summer. At least it started out that way. Business was at a standstill, and I spent my days inventing petty tasks for my employees to execute. Just as I was about to give up even making an effort to do business until the arrival of fall, a contact advised me that the apparel industry was nearly always unaffected by the summertime blues. China's textile trade was closely linked to Southeast Asia, and there were plenty of opportunities to make money. I dove in enthusiastically, calling associates from Bangkok to Singapore until finally I drummed up enough of a buzz to warrant a trip.

Originally, I had the wild yet feasible idea of making love and money at the same time by taking Lan Yu with me. I even contacted a border-control official who, after two conversations and one bottle of Chivas Regal, told me not only that he could get Lan Yu a passport within three days but also that it could be done without going through Lan Yu's university administration. This impressed me, since getting permission from one's school or work unit was always required to go abroad. That's why, after all the hard work and pulling of strings, I was angry when Lan Yu told me he couldn't make the trip because he had landed a summer job at a construction site.

To me, the idea of working at a construction site sounded like a living hell, especially in the summer heat. During the first weeks of summer, nearly all my days were spent indoors listening to the radio announce temperatures reaching thirty-eight degrees Celsius, though it felt more like forty. Lan Yu finished his finals and started his job, where he stayed each day from ten in the morning until ten at night. He said it was a time-sensitive project with two work crews on rotating twelve-hour shifts. His was the day shift. Lan Yu wasn't particularly light skinned to begin with, and by the end of his first week his skin turned so dark you would have mistaken him for a black man. The whole thing was getting to be more than I could bear. We had another fight—a significant one this time.

"What exactly is the point of you taking this job?" I asked him, turning off the TV and standing up from the couch. "You want to be a construction worker for the rest of your life?"

"I just want to get a little hands-on experience," he replied evenly. He seemed taken aback by the question. "I think it's good for me to spend time at a construction site so I can learn more."

"How much are they paying you?"

"Five hundred yuan a month."

"Five hundred yuan a month!" I repeated with a derisive laugh. "A motel hooker's asking price is four times that!" I crossed the room and stood in front of the window, where I folded my arms and looked outside in defiance. "Besides," I continued, turning to face him again. "What the hell kind of job is that? Standing outside in the blistering heat for twelve hours a day?" Lan Yu had no response to this, so I kept pushing. "What about the ¥20,000 I gave you? Isn't that enough?"

"You know I'm paying you back for that," he retorted angrily, tapping the remote control against the palm of his hand in agitation. "Or maybe you just thought you were buying me for a few months!" He was so goddamn sensitive.

The way Lan Yu was acting left me with an uncontrollable urge to sock him in the face. He just didn't get it!

"You want to get hit?" I asked impulsively, though I knew I wouldn't do it and didn't have to in order to get my point across. "If ¥20,000 is all it takes to buy you, you've got low self-esteem. Pretty good price if you ask me."

Lan Yu was silent for a while, then got up from the couch and walked toward me. "You would know about motel hookers. You have a lot of them at Country Brothers, don't you?" With that, he turned on his heel and walked to the kitchen.

"That's none of your fucking business!" I yelled after him,

so full of rage that specks of spit flew out of my mouth. The truth was I hadn't seen Huang Jian in over a month.

"Then don't mind my business, either!" he yelled from the kitchen.

There was no reconciliation after that. No fiery makeup sex, nothing. A few hours later he announced that he wanted to go stay at the workers' dormitory at the construction site.

"Fine with me," I said. "But if you leave, don't bother coming back." This was all it took to make him change his mind. Lan Yu remained with me at Ephemeros, coming home close to eleven each night looking like a wreck. I derived a kind of sick pleasure from this, so great was my resentment.

Still, each night after he came home and took a shower and got into bed, I would cuddle up next to him to kiss his neck and rub his shoulders, doing my best to excite him and, I hoped, fool around. He always resisted at first, explaining how tired he was. But he was a young man, after all, and exhaustion eventually submitted to libido. Even then, though, he often just went through the motions, trying to get it over with as quickly as possible. When he finally came—if he came at all—it was only a matter of seconds before he fell asleep, leaving me alone in the world of the wakeful to watch him and wonder which emotion was stronger, my affection or my resentment.

One evening I had just returned from a business trip to Shenzhen, where a friend of mine invited me to tour a Hong Kong–invested factory as part of my new interest in the apparel industry. Returning home, images of workers hunched over piles of clothing—black sweaters, gray trousers, and, in one case, an odd-looking fuchsia garment with a frilly neckline controlled by a blue drawstring—swirled about my mind. When I entered the apartment, I noticed the bankbook I'd given Lan Yu wedged among the stack of course books he'd read the previous semester. I pulled it out and opened it up only to discover there was no record of him having made a single withdrawal.

Fine! I thought, slamming the bankbook down on the table. If Lan Yu wanted to believe I'd think more highly of him if he didn't take my money, fine. I wasn't some noble and virtuous gentleman. He could take my money or not, but he was still mine to play with. If he rejected it I would just be playing for free. Never had I been so furious at one of my lovers—or, I thought bitterly, should I just call them my playthings?

That same night Lan Yu came home past ten looking like shit. Dirt smudges streaked his haggard face, and one of his fingers was wrapped in a thick mass of gauze and medical tape. He said he had cut it on a piece of glass. I couldn't bear to look at him, let alone talk to him, until he came out of the bathroom and got into bed. That's when I put my arms around him and kissed him. Then I put my hand between his legs and started to rub his crotch.

"Handong," he said imploringly. "I'm exhausted. Let's do it tomorrow."

"But I've been thinking about you all day!" I whined, ignoring his plea and continuing to kiss him. Despite my provocations, he remained prostrate with his eyes closed until I heard his breathing get heavier. He was falling asleep.

"Wake up. Hey, wake up!" I said, pushing him. "You're no fun."

Wordlessly, I crawled on top of him and kissed him. He reciprocated, reluctantly at first, but soon became aroused, and when he did he jumped up from the bed, laid me down on my back, and started to give me a blow job with a surprising degree of enthusiasm. I looked down at him, mesmerized by what he was doing, while stroking his cheeks, tugging at his hair, and gently slapping him across the face. When he looked up at me hungrily, almost desperately, I grabbed the back of his head and pushed him down roughly until I hit the back of his throat. He gripped my thighs frantically; it was hard to tell if he was trying to push me away or pull me in deeper. My balls tightened with pressure. I knew I was about to climax, so I pulled him off of me. When I came, it was to the sound of him gasping for air. He was playing with himself and came almost at the same time.

It took Lan Yu a few minutes to catch his breath and come down from the high. He stayed between my legs for a long time, looking up at me now and again through the kisses he planted on my inner thighs. I reached for a towel to wipe his face, then pulled him up to me so he could collapse in my arms while I stroked his hair. We lay like that for some time until finally he fell asleep in my arms. I pulled the blanket over us and turned off the light.

At some point in the middle of the night I got up to use the toilet. Pulling myself out of bed, I glanced at the alarm clock: just past two. I pissed, then splashed water on my face and went back to bed. Lan Yu was fast asleep, lying on his side facing the wall. I put my hand on his shoulder and rolled him onto his back. Then I laid my entire body directly on top of him. He woke up.

"What are you doing?" he mumbled, sounding annoyed.

"I can't sleep. Come on, stay up with me for a while."

"Go back to sleep! I have to work in the morning."

"It's almost seven," I lied. "You have to get up soon anyway."

"It can't be seven. It's still dark out!" He pulled a pillow over his head, then pushed me off of him and rolled onto his stomach to go back to sleep.

I turned on the small TV I kept in the bedroom and put a

tape in the VCR. It was a bisexual porn video Min had picked up in Hong Kong when buying Lan Yu the bluish-gray jacket and other clothing. I glued my eyes to the image on the screen: a girl and a guy, both on their knees, taking turns sucking a second guy's dick. I turned the volume all the way up and lit a Chunghwa cigarette. Even I thought I was acting weird.

Lan Yu tossed and turned a few times, then finally sat up and stared blankly at the TV screen. To me, he paid no attention whatsoever.

"The problem with you," I said, "is you're too young. You can't even keep up with *this* old comrade." I put the cigarette out. "Keep rejecting me like this and my dick is gonna fall off!"

Lan Yu yawned, then gave a sleepy laugh. I leaned over and kissed him, fully expecting him to resist me, but he surprised me by slowly wrapping his arms around my neck and gently biting at my lips, nose, and chin.

When I had woken him up a few minutes earlier, it was mostly just to be an annoying brat. But now that he was awake, I was getting turned on again for real. I pulled him closer and made him lean against me so we could watch the TV together. He started to get hard and I put my hand down the front of his pajamas, thinking about how unlikely it would be for a girl to have sex with you if you woke her up like this. I was turned on by the idea of waking someone up in the middle of the night, having hot and frantic sex, then going back to sleep.

I turned him around so we were both facing the TV and my dick pressed into him. I returned my gaze to the TV, where the bisexual three-way had evolved into an even hotter scene. The girl was on her back, legs spread wide, getting fucked by the first guy while the second guy kneeled beside them, playing with her tits and muttering a string of obscenities. I spit into my hand and smeared the saliva on Lan Yu's hole while wrapping my other hand gently around his throat. I came soon after entering him, but stayed inside afterward, kissing his neck as he jerked himself off. Just before he came, he twisted his torso around until his lips met mine and his hand reached behind my neck to pull me closer. "Oh . . . ," he moaned, moving his tongue across my lips and chin as he came.

Neither of us was able to fall asleep after that. Lan Yu took a shower, then lay back down on the bed and looked out the window.

"How can it still be so dark out?" he asked.

"It's only three. Go back to sleep. I'll wake you when it's time to get up."

"You fucker!" he laughed. "You told me it was seven!" Lan Yu never would have said "fucker" when I first met him. But he'd been in Beijing for almost a year now, more than enough time to master the local vernacular, which was so legendarily vulgar it had its own title: Beijing Bitching.

We stayed up talking and laughing and watching TV until five in the morning, when we finally snuggled up and went to sleep. Just two short hours later, however, the alarm went off and Lan Yu headed to the bathroom to get ready for work. He shut the door, perhaps because he was afraid of waking me up, but I could still hear the quiet sound of him washing his hands and face, getting dressed, and quietly slipping out the door.

Ever since the night at the Imperial when we first met, there had been periods of days, weeks, even months, when Lan Yu and I didn't see each other. But what happened the following day was the first time we formalized our separation by breaking up.

He didn't get home from the construction site until eleven

thirty that night. His face, once so handsome, was dark and emaciated. I was sitting up in bed reading when he got home. He threw his bag on the bedroom floor, then told me he had fallen asleep on the bus and didn't wake up until it pulled into the terminus. The bus driver had to nudge his shoulder to wake him up. By the time he was standing in the parking lot of the terminal, the bus lines had stopped running and he had no choice but to take a taxi home. It had also started raining, not heavily, but just enough to leave him with a clammy dampness from head to toe. I remained in bed, trying to act cool but cringing at every word he said. I didn't even know he had been taking the bus to work. I had always assumed he took a taxi with the money I gave him. I loathed his obstinacy.

Lan Yu peeled off his clothes and collapsed onto the bed, covered in dirt and sweat. A feeling of revulsion rose in me.

"Oh, come on!" I said. "Get up, Lan Yu. What are you, some kind of migrant worker? Go take a shower." I pushed his shoulder a few times.

Dutifully, he got up and went to the bathroom, half-asleep and muttering something I couldn't make out. No more than five minutes later, he came out of the bathroom and plopped back down, head first, onto the bed. Beads of water clung to his forehead, but his hair was dry and clumped together with a white material that looked like plaster or maybe paint. Staring at the back of his head while he slept, I seethed with anger and my veins pulsed with a sadistic desire for revenge. That's when it happened.

"Lan Yu." I poked his shoulder again, this time much harder. He woke up, startled and confused, evidently puzzled by my unwillingness to back off after his compliance with my request.

"This is getting old," I said. "Let's just end it. You can focus on your studies and live a normal life. Go find a girlfriend at your school and . . . and that's it."

He looked at me but showed no reaction. Everything about him was numb.

"If you need money, talk to Liu Zheng. He'll get you some."

I wanted to provoke him, to piss him off as much as I could. And yet, what his expression revealed was not the devastation I'd hoped for, but perplexity. He sat up in bed, but didn't say a word.

"I told you a long time ago. When I mess around with this kind of stuff, it's usually for a year, max. You and I have been together long enough. I'm sick of this. Sick of you."

How gratifying it would have been if he had responded like a woman, bursting into tears or arguing with me hysterically. But he was silent.

"I'm going out tonight. Tomorrow you can just get all your stuff out of here and don't come back. Just go to your dorm or whatever." I had the weird feeling I was about to laugh. I couldn't even look at him.

By the time I finished my speech, I was already out of bed, fully dressed, standing at the foot of the bed with my back to him. I pushed open the door and walked out.

The muggy summer air felt good compared with the air-conditioned nightmare of my bedroom. I was enormously pleased with myself. All my resentment against Lan Yu—his tedious world of construction-site materials and extended work hours—had finally come out.

I got into my car and drove aimlessly. Turning onto Third Ring Road, I passed an international hotel I had been to on more than a few occasions. For some reason, I had never noticed that its rooftop was trimmed with long rows of bright, shimmering lights, a riot of color and twinkling stars. On the other side of the street, a crew of street cleaners in dark, drab clothing traveled briskly in the opposite direction. Riding three-wheeled pedal carts that looked like miniature tractors, they paused periodically to collect trash from off the street. They talked and laughed as they worked, and for a brief moment I found solace in this simple, unaffected scene. But the longer I drove, the worse I felt.

The next morning, I asked Liu Zheng to stop by Lan Yu's construction site to find out whether or not Lan Yu had gone to work that day.

"Yep," he reported when he returned to the office. "He's there at the construction site."

"What the fuck?" I sulked. "He acts like nothing's happened!"

"Listen, Handong, I could understand you being upset if he were a woman, but he's not, okay? Don't waste your emotions on him." I had never told Liu Zheng anything about my feelings for Lan Yu, but he was a smart guy. He could figure things out on his own.

"I'm not wasting anything," I said, shifting into a light and cavalier tone. "It's just that I don't know what to do with him. He's not exactly prone to being controlled, you know!"

"You want to control him? First give him a car, then take him on a big vacation to the US. If that doesn't work, go hire a thug to knock him to the ground. Then you'll see how prone he is!" Liu Zheng laughed, greatly amused by his own pun.

With Lan Yu gone, I didn't want to stay at Ephemeros, nor was I especially keen to go to Country Brothers, so I decided to camp out at my parents' place for a few days. On my first night there, my father went out drinking with his old army buddies and my youngest sister had a date. My other sister was married by then and lived with her husband and his parents. It was just my mother and I alone in the house.

I sat at the dining room table, munching on a plate of stir-fried cucumbers, my mother's specialty. She could tell there was something wrong.

"Little Dong, what made you want to come home right now?" she asked, pouring me a cup of tea.

"Nothing special. I guess I missed you and Dad," I said facetiously.

Ever since reaching adulthood I had always joked around with my mother. I couldn't stand that formal way of speaking to parents typical of most Chinese children. My mother enjoyed my playful irreverence. It gave her a laugh.

"Did you break up with your girlfriend?" She sat down at the table and looked at me.

"Believe me, I'm trying, but she won't let me!"

She laughed again. She knew her handsome, well-heeled son had no trouble finding women.

"Little Zheng told me your girlfriend—oh, what's her name—Hao Ming? Anyway, he says she's real nice. When am I going to meet her?" "Little Zheng" was what my mother called Liu Zheng.

"Yeah, she's great, Ma. She's like a boa constrictor squeezing me to death. Anyway, I can't promise you'll meet her since I'm doing my best to dump her."

"Well," my mother said, standing up to inspect a dishcloth hanging on the clothesline, "if that is true, then I must inform you that your father's associate Xu Haihong came by again yesterday to ask about you. He still wants to introduce you to his daughter. She seems real nice, Handong. And her father is getting a promotion this year—he's in foreign trade! I'm sure the Xu girl would just love it if you asked her out on a date. If you want, I can talk to her dad again and set it up for you."

"Come on, Ma!" I pleaded. "Can we please just drop the subject? I'm not going to prostitute myself to a dog like her just because her daddy's getting a promotion. There are lots of other girls out there, you know."

In a flash my mother went from cheerful to annoyed. She poured me another cup of tea with a petulant look on her face, then plunked the ceramic pot on the table, put her hand on her hip, and looked right at me.

"Well, at this point, anyone will do, Handong. Just don't put it off any longer. You need to focus on finding somebody and settling down." Having gotten this out of her system, she went back to her normal, gentle voice. "Just look at Little Zheng. Isn't it wonderful how he has his own family? And a son!"

With that, my mother turned on her heel and walked into the kitchen to ask the maid to do something. I remained at the table, silently repeating the words she had just said. *Anyone will do*. If that "anyone" was Lan Yu, she'd be beside herself with anger.

For the rest of the night I sat in the bedroom my mother still kept for me at the family house, obsessing. Again and again, I considered the ways in which Lan Yu and I being together was absurd, abnormal, and ultimately impossible. I even thought of a ridiculous word: *love*.

I put a cassette in the tape player, hoping to get my mind off of it. It was some Chinese rock group that had just put out a new recording. One of Lan Yu's classmates had told him about it excitedly, so I'd picked it up in the university district, the only area of Beijing where one could find such things. The jarring guitar rhythms irritated me. I turned it off.

I am not, I reasoned, going to get sucked into this so deeply that I fall in love with a man! I knew I was normal. I just liked a good adventure, not to mention the fact that I was way too horny for my own good. Anyway, it didn't matter. I had already ended things with Lan Yu before they spiraled out of control. I had made sure it wasn't too late for either of us to return to a normal life. Breaking up was good for him, and it was good for me.

And yet, I couldn't stop thinking about him.

I threw the tape into the trash, then pulled it back out. Maybe Lan Yu would like it.

Eight

Predictably enough, my visit to my parents' became stifling after a few days, so I packed up my things and went back to Ephemeros. Just before getting in the car, my mother and I had yet another conflict about "the Xu girl." I had made it more than clear that I wasn't interested, and yet she wouldn't leave it alone. The argument wasn't that big and we even managed to laugh about it as we said goodbye, but we both demonstrated how stubborn we could be.

The fight with Lan Yu, however, weighed heavily on my mind, and I found myself worrying about our relationship more and more with each passing day. Truth be told, though, even more vexing than this was the troublesome business affair I'd recently landed in. I had created a serious dilemma by screwing up a major deal involving a batch of imported Volkswagens. Due to some petty regulation I hadn't complied with, I had to rid myself of the cars before January, even if it meant selling them at a loss.

Late one Saturday afternoon as I was gathering my things to leave the office, Liu Zheng walked in. He told me Lan Yu's foreman had called to report that Lan Yu hadn't been to work in eight days.

It had been almost two weeks since we had broken up. At first I had been outraged that he kept going to work, as if my sudden disappearance ought to have made him fall apart completely. I resented his apparent ability to recover so speedily from what should have been the earth-shattering disaster of losing me. But now, learning from Liu Zheng that he had suddenly stopped going to work a full two weeks later, I was confused. And worried.

When I got home that evening I couldn't stop thinking about it, so I finally broke down and called his dorm at Huada. Nearly all of the students were gone for summer vacation and the phone rang no less than fifty times before someone finally picked it up.

"Room 815, please."

"Okay, wait a minute."

Ten minutes later, he returned to the phone. He said no one was in 815 and everyone had gone home for the summer.

I had plans to meet with clients that evening—a couple of guys who were interested in purchasing the Volkswagens—but called them to reschedule. I had to go to Huada.

I hadn't been to Lan Yu's dormitory in nearly six months, since the previous January when he wanted to change out of his work clothes after I hunted him down at Fan Haiguo's computer shop. Parking in front of building number eight, I noticed how gutted and desolate everything appeared during the summer vacation. Everything looked exactly the same as six months earlier, apart from the snow. The memory of Lan Yu exiting the building flashed before my eyes. Bright winter sunshine bounced off his glistening hair and he wore the bluish-gray jacket with the brown lining.

I entered the building and my senses were hit by the heavy stench of urine. It was the smell of a men's dormitory restroom, something I hadn't been anywhere near since my own graduation. The Public Security station in the lobby was unmanned and a single lightbulb hung dimly from the ceiling—hardly enough to illuminate the hallways, which were enveloped in stygian darkness. I could barely read the numbers on the doors, and in some spots had to run a hand along the wall just to avoid bumping into it. Eventually, however, I managed to reach 815. I knocked a few times then waited. Nobody answered so I knocked again. This went on for some time until I finally accepted that Lan Yu wasn't there. Still, I couldn't bear the idea of giving up and walking away, so just as I was about to turn around and leave, I twisted the doorknob. It was unlocked.

Lan Yu's room was as silent as Mao's mausoleum, and if it hadn't been for the moonlight shining through the window I wouldn't have been able to see a thing. It was your typical dorm room. Eight twin beds distributed along four bunks, two bunks to the left, two to the right, with a long, narrow table in the middle. Diminutive study desks lined the walls, and chairs were scattered about the room. The deathlike silence was so engulfing that it was some time before I noticed what appeared to be a human body lying on the lower berth near the window. Panic gripped me. I was almost unable to move.

"Lan Yu!" I called out in a loud whisper. Though I didn't know if the person was him, I hoped he would respond. But my call was met with silence.

My heart pounded in terror. Was he dead? I stepped forward, my eyes drilling holes in the figure on the lower bunk. Only when I stood over the body was I able to make out the face. It was him! I squatted down and put my hand against his forehead. Somehow, I had expected him to feel icy cold, but it was just the opposite: he was burning up. I grabbed his hand and checked for a pulse. Faint and rapid. I moved my ear closer to his face and heard him breathing. He was alive!

I wanted to carry him out on my shoulders, but he was heavier than I expected and I couldn't lift him. I darted into the hallway and called out to the darkness.

"Is anyone here? Somebody, help!"

Two guys popped their heads out of the room next door. "What is it?" they asked. They were the only other people on the floor.

"One of your classmates has to get to the hospital immediately. Please, come help me!"

The taller of the two helped me lift Lan Yu, and we carried him into the hallway. All I wanted was to get him into the car as quickly as possible, but the two guys started prattling on just as casually as if they'd been discussing their coursework.

"What department and year is he?" the shorter one asked.

"Architecture, 87. Name's Lan Yu. He didn't go home for the summer."

"Oh, right! That guy who dresses like a Jap! I think he has relatives here in Beijing."

"I don't know. He doesn't talk much. I've never had any contact with him."

The tall guy turned to me, almost dropping Lan Yu in the process. "Are you a relative?" I fought back the urge to punch him in the face.

"I'm his big brother," I replied icily.

We got outside and put Lan Yu in the passenger seat. I looked at my watch and turned the key in the ignition. It was nine o'clock. Lan Yu was seated next to me, breathing lightly and leaning against the door with his eyes closed. I stepped on the accelerator.

I registered at the front desk of No. 3 Hospital then sat down with Lan Yu to wait. The emergency room was much more crowded than I had expected. A steady stream of nurses wearing surgical masks rolled patients here and there, while in the adjacent corridor a middle-aged woman made a scene at the prescription window. "It's his liver!" she screamed at the pharmacist, who stood on the other side of the counter staring at her skeptically. On the other side of the waiting room, a foreigner—a Russian, perhaps, though it was hard to tell—sat on a wooden bench, gazing into space, a heavy anxiety carved into the deep, dark pockets of his eyes.

Despite the bustle of activity, we didn't have to wait long, and soon enough a young, petite nursing intern wearing glasses brought Lan Yu to the inspection room.

"Why did you wait this long to bring him in?" she asked. She was soft spoken but stern. This long? She made it sound like there was no hope.

The young intern put Lan Yu into bed then popped a thermometer into his mouth and pulled the bedsheet up to the middle of his chest. I hovered over him, sweeping my eyes across his face and searching for signs of life. His eyes were sealed shut, lips parched and split. My stomach felt queasy. I desperately wanted to hold his hand, to find some way of showing him that I was there for him, but I was also frightened of what the medical staff would think. Finally, unable to control myself any longer, I grabbed his hand. My eyes welled up with tears.

The intern looked at me with a strange expression on her face, leaving me no choice but to fabricate an explanation.

"This is my little brother!" I told her in despair. "If he dies, how am I going to tell our parents?"

The intern nodded sympathetically then took me by the elbow and ushered me out of the room. In the hallway, she tenderly explained that a severe tonsil infection had caused Lan Yu to fall into a coma. She also said that he had a high temperature and was dangerously dehydrated. She gazed into the room as she spoke, her words pulsing with genuine concern for her feeble patient who lay in the hospital bed, his still-handsome face plagued by the thin, haggard air of sickness.

I remained at Lan Yu's side throughout the night, rubbing him down with alcohol to break the fever and bring his temperature down. For hours I watched the IV as it dripped, standing over him to study his expression in meticulous detail. By four in the morning, his breathing had changed. This alarmed me at first: it was so quick and uneven. But I also realized this could mean he was regaining consciousness.

The intern was a miracle worker. From the moment we arrived until five in the morning, she took Lan Yu's temperature every half hour until at last she removed the thermometer for the last time and announced with a smile that he was down to thirty-eight degrees Celsius. Lan Yu was going to be fine. The young nursing intern left the room and shut the door behind her, leaving me alone to bury my face in my hands, close to tears, breathing deeply, and wondering whether I was going to pass out from exhaustion.

It was a testament to Lan Yu's youthful resilience that on his second day of treatment, he sat up in his hospital bed, stretched his arms, and said he was hungry. A big smile broke out on my face when I heard this. That afternoon I took him home.

When we got back to Ephemeros, I turned down the air conditioner, poured a big glass of water, and quickly put him under the covers. Propped up with a pillow, Lan Yu sat in bed, quietly observing me as I flitted about the apartment.

"You know, you are too much!" I called from the living room. "Here you are, almost eighteen years old and you still have no idea how to take care of yourself. You had a fever for a week and you didn't even go to the doctor!" My paternal instinct had been goading me to say this ever since Lan Yu had regained consciousness, but I had held off until now.

"What are you talking about?" Lan Yu retorted cheerfully. "I *did* go to the doctor—he gave me a huge pile of medicine. When I got back to campus I took almost all of it!"

"I thought you were going to die!" I said, returning to the bedroom. Lowering myself to one knee, I scanned his face for leftover signs of illness. Lan Yu closed his eyes and leaned back into the pillow with a pensive look. "What are you thinking about?" I asked with concern.

"Oh, it's just that—you know, when I was a kid, the one good thing about getting sick was you didn't have to go to school. My mom would sit with me all day. She always made my favorite dishes." He smiled weakly.

"Look at you!" I laughed. "You probably weren't even really sick. Deceiving your poor old mom like that!" I kissed his forehead and ran my hand across the top of his head. Pulling the blanket up tightly under his chin, I instructed him to get some rest, reminding him that he could still have traces of fever. With his hand in mine, I sat in a chair beside the bed and began to leaf through a stack of paperwork that one of my assistants had dropped off. It was a preliminary agreement for the sale of the imported cars—the hard-earned product of the intense round of negotiations that had taken place the night before. I knew it was going to be a major battle, but hadn't participated because Lan Yu needed me.

After I put him to bed, Lan Yu lay quietly on his back for a few minutes. Then he got into the fetal position, eyes poking out of the blanket to watch me as I read. Pretty soon he disappeared under the blankets completely. But no sooner had this happened when a hand popped out from the side and began squeezing my leg. I swatted at it lightly while doing my best to hide my smile, but before I could reprimand him for his bad behavior, he rolled onto his stomach and dangled his right leg off the bed. I looked down. A single black-socked foot loitered shamelessly near my calf.

"Don't do that! Go to sleep!" I said with feigned exasperation as I returned the offending limb to the bed.

Not only did he fail to stop, he stepped up the harassment by reaching for my crotch. I looked up from my document to find half a face peering out of the blankets. Lan Yu was trying—not very hard—to hide his smile.

"Excuse me, sir, but are you engaging in hooliganism?" I laughed.

By way of an answer, Lan Yu rubbed even more at the bulge in my trousers, which was now just as hard as the thermometer the girl intern had been poking into his mouth.

Fuck it! I thought, jumping on top of him and grabbing his wrists more roughly than I meant to. I raised his arms, pinning them one by one above his head. He was totally overpowered by me. In this position, I thought excitedly, it was almost like I was raping him.

"You're really asking for it." I stared into his eyes menacingly. "You brought this on yourself, you know, so don't blame me if I get rough!" Lan Yu squirmed beneath me as if trying to escape, but his inviting smile told me he loved it. Before I could escalate the assault, however, he abruptly stopped moving around and looked up at me with an absurd tough-guy look on his face.

"So I brought this on myself, huh? What are you gonna do about it?" he sneered, trying to sound manly and threatening, as though he were picking a fight.

"I'm gonna fuck you is what I'm gonna do!" I replied, pinning his arms down harder and bending down to kiss him aggressively.

I wasn't really planning to fuck him, at least not at first. We were only playing and, besides, I thought he would still be too weak for sex. But the more I kissed him the more I wanted him. I hadn't seen Lan Yu in a couple of weeks. I missed him. I missed his lips, his body, his scent. He must have missed me, too, because when I finally released his hands he immediately moved them to my face, kissing my lips and wrapping his legs around me. He had never been particularly verbal during sex, but at that moment his silence carried a special kind of intensity. The quiet serenity emanating from his person was broken only by the sound of his breathing: short, frantic, rapid. Was it sexual arousal or was he not yet fully recovered?

Lan Yu opened his mouth and stuck his tongue out slightly to meet my lips as I pushed them against his. Our tongues met, entwined, teeth bumping together carelessly. I kissed his face, then his neck. He had a scar on his upper arm, a large circular dent from a childhood inoculation. I kissed the scar then lifted his arm to kiss his armpit, nipples, chest, stomach, navel. When I got to his waist, I buried my face in his pubic hair then kissed his cock. I didn't suck it, just gently kissed it while looking up at him. His eyes were shut but his mouth was open, and the glowing rays of sunlight cast by the setting sun created a halo around him. For a moment he looked unfamiliar, almost unreal, like a gold-plated mannequin shimmering in the sun.

I opened his legs roughly and buried my face between his thighs. He gasped loudly, gripping the back of my head and tugging at my hair as if to pull me closer. I loved how that felt: pleasure and pain. When I moved back up to kiss him again, I ground my pelvis into him, cradling his lower back with one hand to pull him into me, while my other hand gently grabbed a fistful of hair and slowly pulled his head back, giving me full access to his neck, which I dove into with a series of bites and kisses while he clutched at my shoulders and gasped. I held him there, arms and legs wrapped around me, pinned to the bed as securely as if he had been handcuffed. Rays of light filtered through the window and into the bedroom, shedding a blanket of warmth across a bed set ablaze by the fire of two men making love.

Without any warning I sat up on my knees and made a twirling motion with my hand. This, he knew, meant I wanted him on his side, the only position he liked getting fucked in because, I figured, it was the only one that didn't hurt. When we first started having sex I didn't like that position, but grew to love it over time. It made his ass stick out lewdly, giving me an invitation to pull up beside him, lift his leg, and enter him.

I wrapped my arms around Lan Yu's chest. He grabbed my forearms with both hands, pulling me into him tighter. He ran his tongue against my skin. It crossed my mind that perhaps I shouldn't penetrate him while he was recuperating, but I couldn't control myself. Desire flooded out reason— and, besides, the way he pushed back into my hand while I played with his ass told me he wanted it. I spit into my hand, and slowly entered him. Before long, he was banging against each thrust with a moan. "Don't come," I whispered in his ear. "You don't have the energy."

"Oh . . . ," he moaned, then turned back to look at me. He placed an arm around the back of my head and pulled me closer until his pouting lips pressed against mine. I cupped my hand around one of his pecs, so thick and hard now compared to when we first met, and fucked him hard and steady while our tongues became tangled in each other's mouths. The last moan to fall from his lips was the satisfying sound of him collapsing next to me. In the past I wanted only to take pleasure. Now I wanted to give it to him.

Between his body's struggle to heal and the sex we'd just had, Lan Yu was completely worn out. He lay on the bed beside me covered in blankets, breathing heavily and gazing at the ceiling with a look of contentment. Then he turned to give me a big, beautiful, happy smile. I got out of bed to draw him a bath and quickly jumped back into bed to cuddle with him while we listened to the water filling the tub. When his bath was ready, I put him in the tub and gently washed him. That's when we started talking about his stay at the hospital.

"Did you see the way the nurse was looking at you?" I teased. "She was totally into you."

"No, she wasn't! She was so old," he protested. He paused for a moment, then added, "You know, right before we left, she told me that when I was in the coma my big brother was so upset he almost started crying." Lan Yu looked greatly satisfied as he told me this, but it wasn't smug satisfaction. It was, rather, the kind of excitement a child has when he tells you something he's proud of and can't wait to see your response.

I averted my eyes and gave a self-deprecating laugh. Lan Yu's words touched me, but they also provoked a vague feeling of guilt. He was so easy to satisfy, so easy to make happy. The reality was, he wanted very little from me. But the one thing I increasingly felt he wanted, that one precious yet utterly elusive thing . . . it was this that I was most afraid to give.

After Lan Yu's illness, our relationship entered a new stage. A better stage. The summer came to an end, and he was going to be starting his second year of university in a little over a week. My situation with the Volkswagens wasn't improving—the potential buyer backed out at the last minute—but I always made an effort to spend as much time with Lan Yu as I could. In this respect, I had changed for the better.

He changed in some ways, too. For one thing, he finally stopped talking about paying me back. He even began accepting my money and my gifts much more willingly than before. Still, there was a part of me that wondered whether he was only doing these things to make me happy.

We never talked about the time I broke up with him and kicked him out of the house. It was a dark chapter in our history. I knew it left him with scars, but we never talked about it.

Six months later, I finally found a sucker—a vague acquaintance of mine—who swallowed the bait and bought the entire wretched lot of cars from me. I wasn't normally in the habit of taking advantage of personal acquaintances, but in the business world, I rationalized, you have to do what you have to do. One evening when Lan Yu and I were chatting in bed, I made the mistake of sharing this information with him. He came back with the simple, yet cutting reply: "Money can make people crazy."

On February 5 Lan Yu and I spent New Year's Eve reveling in the joy of the bed we shared. When the clock struck midnight and the Year of the Snake arrived, I looked into his eyes and kissed his lips, promising myself that from this moment on, it was only going to be the two of us. Me and him, nobody else. But I wasn't able to keep that promise, at least not then.

Nineteen eighty-nine turned out to be an extraordinary year—for me, for us, and for the entire nation.

Nine

One morning in mid-February my youngest sister called. She still lived at home.

"Big brother!" her sobs crackled through the phone. "Come home! It's Dad—he's really bad!"

"What? What happened?" I stammered out. Just two days earlier I had endured a twenty-minute lecture from the old man, who felt the need to berate me about some expectation of his that I had apparently failed to live up to.

"He was fine last night!" Jingdong cried even more loudly, as if the sound of my voice had somehow exacerbated her grief. "But then at around two or three in the morning Ma woke up and saw there was something . . . I don't know . . . something was wrong with him . . ." Her voice trailed off, replaced by the sound of crying.

Forty-eight hours later my dad died of a brain hemorrhage. His departure left me, the legitimate son of his lawfully wedded wife, with no other choice but to dive without delay into arrangements.

There was no time to mourn. My father was a powerful man with a vast network of social and political connections. The phone calls, the telegrams, the endless condolences, and the visits from neighbors—one after another they poured in. Then there was the funeral itself with all the arrangements this entailed. In addition to contacting the local funeral committee, we had to procure the casket, the black armbands, the flowers, and all the other things used in the ceremony. The whole thing was exhausting, not just for me, but especially for my poor mother, who was twenty years younger than my father but who aged very quickly in just a few days. She had loved my dad very much, and the large banner with the words "Let Us Deeply Mourn Comrade Chen Fumao" hanging over his portrait in the mourning hall was devastating for her to see. There was nothing for me to do but go home and help her get through the difficult period.

On the second Saturday of my visit, Lan Yu called to find out when I'd be coming back to Ephemeros. I had been with my mother and sisters for twelve days at that point. Surely, I thought, that was enough time to fulfill my filial duty. By the time Lan Yu called, I was ready to say goodbye to the gloomy environment and get back to my normal life, so I told him I'd come back to Ephemeros that evening.

I didn't realize how happy I would be turning the key to my own front door. There was Lan Yu, curled up on the couch with a book. When he saw me enter, he jumped up and gave me a kiss. "Is our Ma doing better these last couple of days?" he asked with concern.

When Lan Yu first met my mother, he called her Auntie, but then I told him that in Beijing, guys always referred to each other's mothers as "our Ma."

"She's getting by," I said listlessly before suddenly brightening up. "Come on, let's go grab a bite to eat!"

"How about staying in?" he asked, gently brushing my hair back from my forehead. "I didn't think you'd feel like going out, so I picked up some takeout."

I looked over Lan Yu's shoulder and peered into the kitchen, where a stack of paper bags was piled up high on the table. On the floor next to the table there was a case of Yanjing beer. It occurred to me how incredibly thoughtful this guy was.

"A case of beer on the floor!" I laughed, walking into the kitchen to grab a couple of bottles and two glasses. "That's how we did it in college."

"Well," he said with a laugh, "I guess tonight is like college, too!"

We moved into the living room and rapidly devoured the takeout meal he had picked up. He knew I loved Shanghai cuisine, and the mouthwatering assembly of drunken chicken, simmered fish halves, and stir-fried eel with chives was the best homecoming surprise I could have asked for.

When we were done eating, I scooped everything up from the living room table and threw it on the kitchen countertop. I collapsed back onto the couch and Lan Yu snuggled into my arms, which I wrapped tightly around his shoulders and chest. I thought back to eighteen months earlier, when I had first met him. It seemed like a lifetime ago. Before I had time to think too much about the strange fate Lan Yu and I shared, however, the alcohol kicked in and my mind turned to recent events. I just couldn't believe how sudden my dad's death had been.

"We were never close," I sighed. "He was always angry

about something, and when I was younger I hated it when he was at home. But just now when I was there, the house felt so empty without him." I held Lan Yu tighter as I spoke, but gazed straight ahead as if I'd been talking to myself.

"From the time I was little, I never liked him. He was always yelling at me, and he used to beat the crap out of me too. He did get better as I grew older. There even came a point when he would try to talk to me about things going on in my life or in his life, or about current affairs or hobbies or whatever. But by then I didn't even want to be close to him. I remember the year I got into Nanda, he was so happy that he got drunk and went door to door throughout the neighborhood. He wanted to tell everyone that, unlike all his friends' sons, his son got into university by passing the exams, not by relying on connections." I took a big swig of beer. "You know, I always hated the way he treated me, but now that I think about it, the old man actually helped me quite a bit when my career was getting off the ground."

I pushed my head forward and looked down at Lan Yu, who lay quietly against my chest. His eyes were open and he was listening carefully. He was always a good listener.

"Just before he died," I continued, "he opened his eyes and looked around at everyone sitting in the room. He knew he was about to die, I could just tell. Then, right before he closed his eyes for the very last time, he looked me straight in the eye. I was the last person he saw in this lifetime. I could tell he wanted to say something, but he couldn't speak. I had the feeling he wanted to tell me that he really—that he really cared about me, you know? I thought maybe he wanted to tell me something, that he thought—that he thought I had turned out okay . . ."

My eyes filled with tears. I couldn't continue. A long period of silence passed before Lan Yu spoke.

"It seems like he was in a good place when he passed," he said. "Our Ma was there, you were there, your two little sisters. You were all there, right by his side. I bet he felt really happy." His voice got quieter. "My mom was alone when she died. Just her and a bottle of sleeping pills."

In a year and a half, this was only the second time he had mentioned his mother's death. I had no idea she had killed herself. Now I knew why he never talked about it.

Lan Yu suddenly unlocked himself from my embrace and sat up on the couch. He turned to face me. The way he looked at me . . . I couldn't pinpoint exactly what it was. Sad, hurt, but there was also something cold and detached about the way his eyes burned into me. There was something he didn't want to share with me, or didn't know how to. "My family—" he started to say, then hesitated.

"Yeah?"

"Well, for as long as I can remember, we always lived in the northern part of Xinjiang, near Ürümqi, but even farther, near the border with the Soviet Union. But my parents weren't from there originally. My mom was born in the South, in Hangzhou, and my dad is from the Northeast, from Harbin."

I looked at Lan Yu's thick hands and fingers, which he rubbed together anxiously as he spoke. Now I knew why he had the strong and sturdy physique of the North, but the delicate countenance of the South.

"My parents were both professors at the local polytechnic university," he continued. "When I was a kid growing up, everything was perfect. I always had so much fun with my dad. He used to take me and my mom out all the time; he was always trying to find fun things for me to do. I had this stamp collection he helped me with. He taught me how to play the Chinese fiddle and a few other instruments. He would help me with my math homework—everything. By the time I finished primary school I had an eighth grade education. It was all from him.

"My mom didn't talk much, but I remember she was so sweet and loving to everyone she met. She and my dad never fought. The only time I remember them ever getting in an argument was this one time when my mom accused him of being sexist because he wouldn't help with the housework. But even then she was laughing about it the whole time. I remember her walking out of my dad's study, yelling, 'Fine! Don't help! But I'm not talking to you anymore!' She was annoyed, but she had this big smile on her face. And that was the end of the argument." He gulped down a mouthful of beer.

"When economic reform started in the late seventies, my father was among the first group of intellectuals to dive into the business world. He did something with some kind of industrial ventilator—invented it or developed it or something—then got hired by a township enterprise to work on it. My mom continued teaching at the university, so we were still able to live in the campus apartment provided by the work unit, but my dad left campus every day to go to work. His job paid well and before long we were the most prosperous family on campus. We were the first to get a refrigerator, a color TV, stuff like that. I remember the neighbors coming over to look at my dad's electric typewriter. Everyone on campus admired us."

I had the vague feeling I knew where Lan Yu's story was going. Fortunes were lost as quickly as they were made in those days.

"My father was never like *you* businessmen." He looked at

me with sudden reproach and I realized how much he had drunk. "He wasn't the kind of guy who had lots of indiscriminate affairs, but it didn't matter. It only took one affair for him to decide he loved the other woman more than my mom, and when my mom died, he remarried almost immediately." Lan Yu paused, twisting his shirttail between his fingers and staring into space.

"I had seen that woman before," he continued. "People always talked about her like she was some kind of beauty queen. But to me she was the ugliest woman in the world. I was only a kid and didn't fully understand what was going on, but . . ." He interrupted his own sentence by pouring the contents of his glass down his throat and immediately poured himself another drink. "But it was the affair that caused my mom's stroke. She was so young! I remember the doctor saying it was a tragedy, that forty was far too young for something like that to happen. I remember going to the hospital every day after school to visit her. But my dad hardly went at all."

I didn't want Lan Yu to get too drunk, but I didn't want to interrupt him. He had never told me this much about himself. It was a rare opportunity to find out more about this person who was such a big part of my life, but about whom I knew so little.

"Actually," he continued, "she was fine when she got out of the hospital. Well, sort of fine. The stroke left her partially paralyzed, but at least she was alive." He wiped his eyes with the back of his hand. "Two days later she killed herself, in part because of the paralysis, but mainly because of the affair. Before she did it, she wrote a long letter to me and my dad. She said she hated money—that money can make people cold, selfish, unfeeling. She said the truly precious things in life weren't silver or gold, but passion, conviction. She was the kind of person who would rather die in glory than live in dishonor. That's what she said at the end of the letter: *I'd rather be a shattered vessel of jade than an intact but worthless piece of clay.*"

Lan Yu buried his face in his hands and took a deep breath. I could see it was getting hard for him to tell the story. I was feeling it too; my own heart weighed heavily in my chest. I wanted to touch him, to find some way of comforting him, but he gave me no indication that he wanted me to, so I remained on my side of the couch, staring at him quietly and wondering what he was going to say next.

"She wanted me to study hard." His speech was slurred at that point. "She wanted me to get out, to get away from that tiny campus and into a good university. She wanted me to stand on my own two feet. She wanted me to be an honorable man with"—he hit his knee with a clenched fist—"an honorable man with an invincible spirit. A man who would inspire awe in everyone he meets. That's what she wanted me to be!"

Lan Yu suddenly fell silent and looked up at me with eyes that were, by now, completely red and swollen. For a moment I thought I saw hatred in them.

"I can't do it!" he continued. "I can't be the man she wanted me to be!" He lowered his head and stared at the floor, seemingly dissociated from the conversation. He held his glass against his knee at an angle that caused beer to splash to the floor. With his other hand he fiddled with a bottle cap.

"She never would have guessed that less than a year after she died, my dad's entire arrangement with the township enterprise would collapse." He sat up straight and looked at me again, but more lucidly this time, as if trying to sober up. "When he lost his job he lost everything, even his own savings. But by then he was already married again, and he and that woman had a daughter, so he had to make a living somehow. He had no choice but to go back to teaching. Everywhere he went people laughed at him, saying first he drove his wife to the grave, then he became a pauper. I always felt they were laughing at me, too.

"That woman, his new wife, treated me decently for a while, but then she changed. When I was in my third year of high school, we had to do these simulated exams to prepare for the National College Entrance Examination. Each student was supposed to give the teacher a few yuan for the printing cost, but that woman argued with my father about it. She said they didn't have the money. It was three yuan! By the time I got into Huada the following year, she could barely stand the sight of me. She said the family was facing hardship and she and my dad's salaries were barely enough to put food on the table. My dad just stayed out of it. All he wanted to do was play chess." Lan Yu paused and looked at me with eyes that were glazed over. "By the time I left he was an amateur level six." He reached for the half-empty bottle at the foot of the couch.

"Hey you," I said tenderly. "Slow down with the drinking."

Lan Yu ignored me. "So when I got accepted to Huada, I borrowed a hundred yuan from one of my uncles in Hangzhou. Then I came to Beijing and met Liu Zheng. Then I met you."

Lan Yu looked up at me with an abject smile. It didn't last long. "Fuck!" he shouted, slamming his glass on the table. "Why do I have such fucking bad luck all the time?" The explosion came out of nowhere. I couldn't help but wonder whether the bad luck he was referring to was his relationship with his father or with me.

"Stop drinking. You're going to get drunk." I took the glass away from him.

"I'm fine. I'm not drunk," he said, standing up and stumbling to the bathroom. He leaned against the wall for support as he walked.

A few minutes later he came out of the bathroom and collapsed back onto the couch. He yawned loudly while reaching down to the floor to pick up his glass. He must have forgotten he was looking for it, though, because he immediately sunk back into the couch empty-handed and gazed at me with a dreamy look. "Wanna fool around?" he asked.

I shook my head. "I'm not in the mood."

He closed his eyes as if he hadn't heard what I said. "No one's ever been this good to me since my mom died," he muttered.

If someone had told me just a few months earlier how deeply those words would impact me, I wouldn't have believed them. He was talking about me!

Bright morning sunshine penetrated the window curtain and shot into the bedroom. It was well past eleven the following morning. We'd just woken up.

"My head . . . ," Lan Yu groaned, clutching his skull. "I drank so much last night."

"You seemed okay to me," I lied.

"I picked up all that beer for you, but I was the one who drank it all," he said sheepishly, still rubbing his head. On the nightstand a steamed bun filled with red-bean paste sat, half-eaten, on a plate of crumbs. I had bought a dozen or so at the bakery in my mother's neighborhood. Lan Yu loved the way they made them. He had wanted one before bed, but passed out before finishing it.

I turned onto my side and looked at him, examining every inch of his face. His thick, dark eyebrows; his deep, pitch-black eyes; his long, sexy eyelashes. A speck of sleep was caked in the corner of one eye. I pretended it was a crumb from the steamed bun.

Lan Yu didn't fail to notice the sweet and loving look I was giving him. He turned onto his side to face me and our fingers intertwined in the narrow space between us. "What?" he asked, kissing my hand.

"Nothing. Just looking at you." I smiled.

"You're nuts!" he laughed, sounding like a true Beijinger.

"Yes, I'm nuts. I am truly nuts!" I pulled him close to me and kissed him gently on the lips. He smiled and pushed his nose against mine.

If there was one thing about Lan Yu, it's that he never failed to surprise me. Just as I was about to scoop him up and bombard his neck with kisses, he pulled away from me, shimmied down my body, and, without any warning whatsoever, took my flaccid dick in his mouth. It didn't take me long to get hard. Looking down, I took him in with my eyes, stroking his face and enjoying the dizzying feeling of his tongue rolling around under my foreskin. Unexpectedly, he pulled me out of his mouth and looked up at me with a peculiar expression.

"Handong . . . ," he said quietly.

I didn't realize it at the time, but Lan Yu had seen something strange in my eyes.

"Keep going, baby," I said nonchalantly, as I sunk the back of my head deeper into the pillow. I closed my eyes and a battle raged inside. I wanted to show him what I felt, but I myself wasn't sure what it was.

It was rare for me to orally pleasure Lan Yu. But at that moment I wanted to, needed to. Perhaps it was the only way I knew how to express my feelings at the time. Perhaps it was because of the way he had exposed so much of himself the night before. Whatever the reason, I pulled him upward until his waist hovered above me, then I guided him into my mouth. I pulled him out just before he came and his cum splashed across my lips.

After he came, Lan Yu began traveling back down to the lower half of my body. He wanted to suck me again, but I stopped him, pulling him back up to kiss my cum-covered lips. I looked into his eyes and saw a vague air of guilt, probably because I hadn't climaxed yet. He changed positions once more, this time getting on his knees. He was trying to tell me I could fuck him.

"I don't have to come," I whispered into his ear. "I just want to hold you."

It was rare for me not to feel like having sex. But I couldn't stop thinking about everything he'd told me the night before. Not just the stuff about his family. He also said he was afraid he was turning into a degenerate. That he couldn't change. He said he was terrified that his professors and classmates would be able to see who or what he really was, that it was only with me that he could truly be himself. He said there was nothing that could save him now, nothing that could make him return to his old life.

Lan Yu couldn't blame me for what was happening. If it was I who had dragged him into the water to begin with, now it was he who was pulling me in deeper. I looked down at his angelic face as he fell asleep in my arms. Pull me in! I thought. I'm the one who started this; this is what I get.

But then I thought about my dead father and grieving mother. How could I be their son and be with Lan Yu at the same time?

Ten

By May that year, social tensions were escalating. The democracy movement swept through universities and surrounding neighborhoods like wildfire, not only in Beijing, but in hundreds of cities across China. At the height of the protests, students and workers were erecting barricades to hold back People's Liberation Army troops. The army circled the city to beat back demonstrators, who had come together to express their dissatisfaction with the slow pace of reform and quickly numbered in the hundreds of thousands.

On April 27 Lan Yu abruptly announced that he and his classmates were planning a student walkout. On May 13 he informed me that there was going to be a hunger strike. He bubbled over with excitement as he spoke.

"Are you guys out of your fucking minds?" I asked, turning a corner near Xuanwumen Station. We were in the car on the way to dinner. "Just not happy with things being okay the way they are, huh?" I looked to my right and saw Lan Yu in the passenger seat, scowling at me like a kid who'd just been scolded by his dad.

"You used to be a student, Handong. You of all people should appreciate the urgency of this!"

I couldn't believe his naïveté. "Listen," I said, suppressing my laughter. "If students are as concerned about the nation as they say they are, they should just keep studying. And us businessmen? We should just keep doing business." I meant this and he knew it, but I deliberately adopted a blithe tone because I didn't feel like getting into an argument.

Lan Yu raised his hands in exasperation. "People like you are parasites of the nation!" he shouted. He meant this, too, but there was also the faintest hint of irony in his voice, as if he knew he was parodying an outdated revolutionary language. Like me, he was adept at saying what he meant while softening the delivery. That's how we avoided fights.

"Well, fortunately for me," I replied, "this isn't the Cultural Revolution. If we were back in those days, you'd probably ferret me out and parade me through the streets for a public denunciation. Sorry, mister, this is 1989, not 69!" I laughed.

He smiled and kissed my right hand, which he'd been holding in his lap since the beginning of the conversation. My eyes were glued to the road in front of me, but I could feel his gaze on my face.

"Listen," he continued, suddenly sounding serious, "if this movement continues to grow, could it have a negative impact on you?"

"Yes, as a matter of fact, it could," I clowned, unwilling to dignify his sober question with a sober answer. "If my company collapses because of this, I could end up a street beggar. I don't have any other skills!"

"Don't worry," he said, grinning from ear to ear. "If anything happens to you, I'll take care of you!" The idea of taking care of me seemed to please him immensely.

"Hell no," I said. "I'd *rather* be a beggar!"

Up until that point, Lan Yu had been a good sport and had readily gone along with my playful banter. But now he stared out the window, a worried look on his face.

"Hey," I said, dispensing with my silliness once and for all. "Just don't get sucked in too deep, okay? Something bad could happen. I mean, really, look at the Cultural Revolution. What good came of that?"

"I know," he said, pulling his gaze from the window and looking at me again. "I won't, I promise. I'm not even participating in the hunger strike. I'm just a sympathizer." He lifted my hand and pressed it against his cheek.

And so it was that all across Beijing students were "making revolution." According to Lan Yu, however, some students were less interested in making revolution than in taking advantage of other people's revolution so they could skip class and do their own thing. He told me there were three distinct "parties" on campus that benefited from the student walkout.

The first were the "Trotskyites." They weren't really Trotskyites. They were just called that because, in Chinese, "Trotsky Party" sounded like "TOEFL Party." Those were the TOEFL maniacs, the students who spent all their free time studying for the Test of English as a Foreign Language, usually to get into a good study-abroad or graduate program. Relieved of their class duties, members of the Trotsky Party were free to spend the duration of the student walkout studying for their impending English exams.

The second group of opportunists was the "Mahjong Party"—the students who, if given the chance, would be happy to do nothing but play mahjong all day. So when the revolution came, that was what they did.

And finally there was the "Butterfly and Mandarin Duck

Party." Those were the couples, the students in love, who were not likely to complain about having additional time to gaze into each other's eyes.

I tried to make Lan Yu confess he was part of the Butterfly and Mandarin Duck Party, but he insisted he wasn't. That party, he told me, was strictly for "serious" couples. I didn't say anything, but it wasn't lost on me that he obviously felt that what we had was nothing more than an illicit affair, a secret pleasure stolen in the night.

The truth was that what we called ourselves—what we called this thing we had—didn't matter anymore. The only thing that mattered was that we were together nearly every day at this point. Classes at universities across Beijing were effectively suspended, and Lan Yu had a great deal of free time on his hands. When we weren't in bed, most of our time was spent dining in restaurants. I was cautious about this latter activity, though, frequently changing locations so we wouldn't be seen together often.

I knew a few gay spots, but never took him to any. There were no real gay bars in Beijing in those days, just private parties and a few hotels whose bars were known to be gay meeting points. None of the bars openly called themselves gay, nor could they, but it was common knowledge that many of the patrons were. In some cases management knew this, but turned a blind eye as long as things stayed discreet. It didn't matter anyway, because taking Lan Yu to these places was out of the question. To me he was like a perfect piece of jade: flawless, absolutely unblemished. Taking him out to enjoy Beijing's incipient gay nightlife would have been tantamount to inviting other guys to go after him.

Although I never took Lan Yu to gay places, I took him to plenty of straight ones. One night we went to a karaoke bar where the working girls provided the "three accompaniments." The first accompaniment referred to chatting, the second to singing, and the third to drinking or fucking, depending on the girl's character and which bar you happened to be at. I deliberately chose a young and very innocent looking girl to accompany Lan Yu, and she spent the evening chatting, singing, and drinking with him. She was a nice girl and I thought we were having a great time, but Lan Yu looked uncomfortable the whole night. When we stepped out of the bar and into the street, I smiled and poked him in the ribcage.

"What's the matter? Did she scare you?"

"No, I just wasn't into her."

"You need to practice being with girls!" I said with a laugh, placing emphasis on the word *girls* as if this would somehow make him see the patent obviousness of what I was saying. "Otherwise, how are you going to find a wife?"

Lan Yu shoved his hands in his pockets and pinned his gaze to the sidewalk before us. I knew him well enough to know what silence meant. He was upset.

"Look," I continued, "you're young now, but pretty soon you're going to have to start thinking about these things."

This only aggravated him further. Abruptly, he halted on the sidewalk and gripped my shoulder to make me slow down. "Why do we have to get married?" he asked in a fraught voice. "Aren't things fine the way they are now? What's wrong with what we have?"

I gave him a conciliatory smile but didn't say anything in response. It wasn't that I didn't know the answer to his question. I did. I knew exactly what was wrong with what we had. But I didn't tell him because I didn't want to fight about it, especially not in public.

Lan Yu continued brooding about it as we walked toward

113

the car. Ahead of us a young Uyghur was selling lamb kebabs at a grill parked on the sidewalk. The rich smell of mutton and spice after so much beer was too great a temptation to pass up, so we stopped and bought thirty wooden sticks. The Uyghur's Mandarin wasn't great, but he was friendly and chatted with us as we stood eating under the stars. Lan Yu didn't feel like small talk, though. The instant we left he asked me in a deep whisper, as if afraid the street vendor might overhear, "Do you want to get married?"

"Of course I do!" I laughed. "Maybe I'll go out and find me a nice little lady this weekend!" He was visibly hurt by my flippant comment, which I'd made for no reason but to avoid the subject. But I just didn't feel like getting into it with him. It was my fault for having brought up marriage to begin with.

It was past midnight when we got to the car, which I'd parked in an open lot on the roof of a building. It was dark and quiet, and our footsteps knocked loudly on the concrete rooftop, which was empty except for a handful of lonely cars waiting patiently for their owners. Aside from the moonlight, the only visible light was a flickering glow emanating from the window of a tiny Public Security booth perched near the top of the staircase. Inside, a guard sat fast asleep in front of a small black-and-white TV. A comedic performance was playing, and soft peals of audience laughter erupted periodically and floated into the night sky. Apart from the three of us, there wasn't a soul around.

I couldn't see Lan Yu's face clearly in the dark, but I could sense that there was something wrong. He stopped abruptly and turned to face me.

"Handong," he said after taking a deep breath. "I'm not getting married. There's no turning back for me."

He stood close to me, so close that I could smell the familiar scent of his breath when he spoke. I felt the tension rise in my chest as I fought the urge to throw myself into his arms. I never would have thought I could have done this in public, but in one rapid motion I grabbed him and held him tight. The words raced through my mind—There's no turning back for me either!—though I couldn't bring myself to say them. I knew in my heart Lan Yu was becoming my world.

I pulled him closer and pressed my lips against his, and I suddenly realized that this was the first time we had ever kissed in public. I remember thinking we should have been on a tropical beach, on the highest mountaintop, or in a beautiful clearing of trees. We should have been surrounded by a halo of sunshine. But there was only darkness.

On the morning of June 3 I had barely stepped into my office and had my first sip of tea when I received a call from Cai Ming, a professor friend who informed me in intonations befitting a radio crime drama that tonight was the night the students were going to act. I asked him how he knew for sure.

"Believe me," he said. "It's 99 percent accurate."

The announcement didn't come as a surprise. Given the way tensions had been brewing the past couple of days, I was actually shocked the students hadn't acted sooner.

A few hours later, my mother called to tell me that under no circumstances was I to go outside that night. She was distressed about activities taking place in the streets, so I tried playing it down by assuring her that nothing was going to happen.

"Besides," I said, "what would I go out for? I'm not interested in stirring up any trouble."

I hung up the phone and immediately called Ephemeros.

When Lan Yu picked up the phone I told him he was not to even think about going outside. We argued about it for a while before he finally agreed. But two hours later, at around 5:30 p.m., he called to say something big was happening. He and a classmate were heading to Tian'anmen Square.

I lost my temper when I heard this. "You are not going out tonight!" I shouted, stretching the phone cord so I could close my office door for privacy.

"We're just going to check it out! I'll be home later tonight."

"No! I'm telling you, Lan Yu, something bad is going to happen!"

"How do you know?"

"Believe me. It's 100 percent accurate," I said, deliberately inflating Cai Ming's initial assessment.

"Well, I'm going."

"What's gotten into you, Lan Yu?" I was angry. But I was also worried.

"I'll be back before ten, Handong! I'll be careful, I promise." He had clearly made up his mind. Why was he suddenly being so goddamn stubborn? I hung up the phone and rushed out of the office, telling my secretary to cancel my six o'clock.

There were very few people outside and most of the shops had closed earlier than usual. An eerie silence hung in the air as I soared past one of the many clusters of apartment buildings that had popped up in recent years. An old man in a beige cardigan stood on a balcony. With a cigarette in his mouth and a wire clothesline above him, he tended to a potted flower while a girl stood at his side watching attentively. It was a vision of normalcy in a city on the verge of chaos.

I was home in fifteen minutes, but it was too late. Lan Yu was gone. This, I thought angrily, is the so-called "benefit" of being with a guy. They just do whatever they want!

With Lan Yu nowhere in sight, I had no choice but to return to the streets and look for him there. I drove aimlessly at first, passing large groups of people one moment and empty streets the next, hoping that by the grace of some miracle I would see him. The mood outside was tense. After what felt like an eternity, I finally parked the car and sat down, exhausted, near the main gate of Tianda University, which was kilometers from Tian'anmen but not one bit lacking in demonstrators. Rubbing my temples, I told myself that I had been stupid to imagine I would just magically stumble across Lan Yu in a city of this size. I glanced at my watch. A quarter past eleven. I'd been driving for five hours.

The atmosphere around Tianda was carnivalesque. Large groups of students walked together, some waving flags, others playing guitars and singing folk songs. A portable cassette player blared out "The Internationale" and the Chinese national anthem. I heard the shrill but commanding voice of a female student screaming into a bullhorn: "Support Tian'anmen! Support Tian'anmen!"

The nighttime June air was humid and oppressive. The city seemed darker than usual and there wasn't a star in the sky. Again and again, I used a pay phone to call home, cursing myself for having forgotten my cell and Lan Yu for refusing to have one. But Lan Yu wasn't there.

Exhausted and despondent, I eventually felt I had no choice but to go home and wait. It was before dawn and I was tired, but I only went into the house for a brief moment to see if Lan Yu was there. When he wasn't, I went back outside and squatted at the side of the road. I wanted to wait along the main artery leading to Ephemeros Village because I knew Lan Yu would have to use it to get home. There I sat, chain-smoking and going over all the various possibilities of what might

117

have happened. I hadn't eaten in nearly eighteen hours, since lunchtime the previous day, but wasn't at all hungry. A soft red glow rose in the east, and I started to lose hope, wondering if something bad had happened. Lan Yu! I thought to myself. Lan Yu, Lan Yu, Lan Yu! I held my head in my hands and looked down at the ground, repeating his name over and over.

Finally, I pulled myself together and started thinking about what to do next. I decided that I had to go back out and look for him again. Even if I myself had to go to Tian'anmen, even if I got killed, I had to go back out. I stood up to get into the car.

Just as I was standing, I saw a figure in the distance moving toward me. I didn't even have to see his face to know that the person limping in my direction was him. When he got closer I saw that his white shirt was covered in bloodstains. Even his face was smeared with streaks of blood. I was stunned into silence.

"Those people are fascists! Animals!" he seethed as he approached me.

"My god!" I grabbed him by the shoulders. "Lan Yu, what happened?"

He looked down at the blood splattered across his chest. "It's not mine," he said. "Other people's blood got all over me." I knew I was supposed to be consoled by these words, but seeing him drenched in the blood of others was just as horrifying as if it had been his own.

He told me he had hiked all the way from Beiheyan Street. When we entered the house, I wanted to get him out of his clothes and into a hot bath immediately, but he refused, saying he just wanted to sit down for a minute. I made him some tea, then we sat at the kitchen table and he told me what had happened.

"The first time they started shooting at us, everybody ran

in the opposite direction and I fell to the ground and started crawling. When they finally stopped, I looked up ahead and saw someone just lying there—not moving at all. I reached out to grab him because I wanted him to keep moving, but when I took hold of his hand it was covered in blood! Everywhere around us people were yelling and throwing things at military vehicles. There was this girl on the ground next to me—I tried grabbing her shoulder to make her come with me, but she just kept lying there—I mean, she couldn't even move, she was so scared! Then they started shooting at us again, but she still wouldn't move so I crawled on top of her and covered her head with my arm. I crushed her hand by accident and she started crying, but . . . ," he stammered and looked up at me in despair. "What else could I do?"

I shuddered as I listened. My mind filled with gruesome and bloody images of what had happened.

Lan Yu grew quiet for a while as he sat at the kitchen table and carefully examined his forearms and elbows, which were dotted with tiny cuts and the occasional big red scuff mark. It was hard for me to imagine him—so meek and full of tenderness—braving a hailstorm of bullets to save the lives of others.

"There were more and more injured people lying on the ground," he continued. "We just started dragging everyone toward any pedicab we could find and putting them in. We carried this one guy who was completely covered in blood . . . We carried him for so long, Handong! We wanted to find someone with a flatbed tricycle, the kind used for transporting goods, so we could put him on it. We finally found one, but the old man riding it said the guy we were carrying wasn't even breathing. That's when I realized the whole time we'd been carrying a dead man . . ."

On and on he went. Lan Yu had never been a very verbal

person, and this was the first time I'd ever heard him talk this much. Finally, his stuttering voice faded off and he became quiet.

"You must have been scared to death," I said, stroking his hair. We had moved to the couch, where Lan Yu rested his head in my lap.

"Sort of, not really," he said, looking up at me and clutching the cloth of my trousers at the knee. "Everything was happening so fast you didn't even know you were supposed to be scared. But now—yeah, I realize I was scared, especially when I saw how the streets were full of tanks and military vehicles. Some of the people were able to hide in the narrower lanes. There were also a few people who tried to pull me into their houses, but I just wanted to get home as soon as possible."

He looked up at me again. I kissed his forehead, then stood up to draw a hot bath and help him take off his clothes. The most important thing, I knew, was to get him warm and in bed. After that I was going to wash his shirt. It was his favorite, the white one he loved so much, and I didn't want it getting ruined.

After his bath, we got into bed, exhausted from the long night's events but too agitated to sleep.

"I really thought I was going to die," he said as I held him in my arms. "I thought I was never going to see you again." I kissed his forehead. He felt so good, so warm and clean and perfect after the nightmare of what had happened.

My eyes suddenly brightened into a playful smile. "I can't believe how selfish you are!" I exclaimed. "I was about to go to Tian'anmen Square to look for you. I might have gotten killed. Did you ever think about that?"

"You were really going to go there?" he asked in wonder. "You mean, you really—you really care for me that much?"

The word *care* came out very quietly, as if he was somehow afraid to say it.

Afraid of showing my true feelings, I squeezed him tight and adopted a blithe tone. "No," I said, "I hate you! In fact, now that you're not dead, I'm gonna kill you!"

With the fear of death behind us, our bodies came together, each man taking the other's flesh as proof that he was alive. I loved Lan Yu's body. I loved holding him, feeling him next to me, his warmth. He was so full of life. I pressed my lips against his neck and held my cheek against his chest and listened to his heartbeat. He was mine! He was here!

Lan Yu fell into my arms, alternating between kissing the curve of my neck and looking up at me. His beautiful dark eyes were full of something—what was it? Fervor, a fervor that was as passionate as it was intoxicating. His lips touched mine and my head swirled with one thought: I cannot, will not, lose you!

I fell to the floor and Lan Yu cascaded with me. We collapsed into each other's arms and the words came out. Those three nauseating words I had never said before, not even to a girl.

"I love you!" My heart pounded in my chest. I cradled his cheeks in the palms of my hands and my eyes burned into his. I would have liked to dive headlong into his body if I could. I couldn't believe I had said it, but at the same time it felt so natural coming out. It was the only thing I felt at that moment, the only thing I could think of to say.

I love you, I had said. And it was love. It wasn't just sex. Whatever other people might have thought, whoever other people thought we were, I knew we were in love. When I think about it today, the bittersweet pain is almost too much to bear.

Eleven

From that fateful June day until the beginning of September, Lan Yu was on summer vacation and had very little to keep himself busy. He wouldn't be working at the construction site again that summer, so he asked me to help him find a job—not, he said, for the money, but to gain more experience. Of course, I was willing to help, but I had one condition. I wanted him to learn to drive and get a driver's license. He agreed and I found him a job doing design work at a friend's architecture firm. Almost overnight his days were busier than mine.

The day he got his license I surprised him with a car, a white Lexus. When he saw the car parked in front of the house, he laughed and said, "Wow, cool!" and that was it.

The post-Tian'anmen political environment was hard on business. Everywhere you turned there were "sanctions" imposed by Western governments. It was a royal pain in the ass, but everyone else was in the same boat and, I knew, it would only be temporary. Unexpectedly, however, things went from bad to worse. One of my warehouses caught fire and more than ¥7 million in small household appliances was gone

122

overnight. Blame lay squarely on the shoulders of Liu Zheng, who was supposed to have found an electrician to repair a badly damaged circuit. What could I do? I had no choice but to fire him.

"Is it really worth losing your friendship over?" Lan Yu asked, scrutinizing a design he had just finished. "You and Liu Zheng have been friends forever!"

"I know, Lan Yu, but this is more than I can take. He knows business is bad right now. He knows this is a crappy political environment. And yet he goes ahead and does the worst possible thing he could have done. Liu Zheng is becoming a major liability for me. One more fuckup and he'll destroy everything I've built!"

"It wasn't directly his fault," Lan Yu said, ironing out the corners of his drawing with the palm of his hand. It was an architectural design he had drawn with pastel-colored fountain pens.

"He knew he was supposed to get that goddamn circuit fixed," I fumed.

"Yes, but didn't you say that his kid has been sick recently? He must have been so stressed out about it that he forgot." Lan Yu wasn't going to stop finding excuses for him.

"That's his problem," I said stubbornly. "Who's going to compensate me for my losses? He's lucky I'm not suing him!"

Lan Yu smiled with a kind of calm resignation. "You businessmen don't know a thing about friendship."

"Wake up, Lan Yu! Business isn't about friendship, it's about profits."

"What if it's someone from outside the business world? What if it's a friend?"

For the first time in my life I didn't have an answer. Lan Yu must have sensed this because he kept going.

"Listen, Handong. Firing him is not going to bring the

money back. Liu Zheng is a good man. If you just show him a little mercy, think of how grateful he'll be." He waved his hand as he spoke, accidentally knocking over a bowl of paint. "Fuck! I fucked it up!" Lan Yu didn't swear often.

I dropped the subject. I needed more time to decide what to do.

With each passing day, I realized more deeply the impact Lan Yu had on me. He, on the other hand, hadn't changed a bit. Other than the fact that he was taller and more handsome now—not to mention considerably more skilled in bed—he was exactly the same as the day I'd met him.

The next day Liu Zheng knocked on my door and entered my office. It was the first time he'd ever knocked before entering. After a few moments of awkward silence he spoke.

"Handong, you don't even have to say anything. I know it was my fault, and I just want to say that in the time that I've worked here I've saved up a pretty good bundle, about ¥3 million. It's yours, take it for the company as compensation." He paused for a moment. "There's just one thing though, Handong. Please. Please don't kick us out of the apartment, at least not yet. You know my younger brother is living at my parents' house. We can't go there."

Liu Zheng and his family also lived at Ephemeros, in an apartment identical to mine. Both were under the company name. I watched him carefully as he struggled to get the words out. In all the years we'd known each other, this was the most difficult conversation we had ever had.

"Just wait until I find a new place," he continued. "Otherwise, my wife and son—"

"Listen," I interrupted him abruptly. "You know this is the most difficult period the company has ever gone through.

Business has never been easy, but now with this fire it's going to be even worse." I was exaggerating somewhat, but I wanted to impress on him the severity of the situation.

"I just sent out a memo firing two of your coworkers. They were responsible for this as well. As for you, you'll be working without pay for the next three months. I don't want to make a big deal about it by telling everyone, so I'm just going to let the finance department know and they'll take care of it. I want you to learn a lesson from this."

Liu Zheng appeared to be trying to maintain a poker face, but he wasn't doing a very good job. A look of surprised gratitude showed in his eyes. He had fully expected me to fire him.

"How's Little Wu?" I asked.

Liu Zheng sighed. "His fever hasn't gone down yet. It's been almost two weeks."

"Well, I had someone contact the medical director of the children's hospital. You can transfer him there later today. The hospital he's at is no good."

Liu Zheng was more distressed than happy upon hearing this news. "My wife's work unit has a contract with the hospital he's at. They won't pay for him to go anywhere else."

"Listen, Zheng. It doesn't matter. The company will pay for whatever costs are incurred at the children's hospital. Just do it. If Little Wu's fever gets worse and something happens, you're going to regret it."

Liu Zheng lowered his head.

"I know you've got a lot on your mind right now," I continued. "You don't have to work a full day's shift. You can come in at eight and leave at two. When you're here, just help me keep things in order, and when you're not here I'll do the rest. Everyone's shaken up about the fire and everything else. You're the only person I can trust to get things done."

Liu Zheng kept his head lowered for some time, then finally raised it to look at me with eyes that were puffy and red. He couldn't speak.

"Okay . . . ," he finally said. "Okay . . . I'm going now." He left my office.

I guess you could say I earned a debt of gratitude that day. Showing this kind of compassion was something taught to me by Lan Yu. Little did I know that nearly five years down the road, Liu Zheng would do me a kindness so great, so huge, that the debt would be returned with more "interest" than I ever could have imagined.

Another winter had arrived, bringing a huge snowfall with it. One evening, Liu Zheng and his wife invited me to their home for Sichuan-style hot pot. Liu Zheng told me to bring Lan Yu with me. It was an extraordinary night. And not just because of the food.

I don't know what it was, but Lan Yu had a way with kids. They loved him. Little Wu warmed up to Lan Yu the moment we arrived. He grabbed Lan Yu by the hand and led him into his bedroom to show him the red paper flower his teacher had given him for being a good student.

Liu Zheng and I watched as the two of them disappeared into Little Wu's room. Then Liu Zheng turned to me. "God, Handong. If only Lan Yu were a girl. It would be so perfect!" I knew he meant well, so I couldn't resent him for saying it, but it still hurt. I laughed it off.

"If Lan Yu were a girl, I wouldn't want him," I said, trying to sound lighthearted. "I think he's pretty okay the way he is!"

"Well," Liu Zheng replied, "I suppose it's only normal for you to feel like that. Stay with anyone long enough and you'll feel that way—even with a dog or a cat!"

My heart sank. I knew Liu Zheng's intentions were pure, but he would never be able to understand my feelings for Lan Yu or our relationship. And yet, there we were at his house, having dinner with him and his wife.

"Then again," Liu Zheng added, "you always have been the sentimental type."

Like her homemade hot pot, Liu Zheng's wife, Shi Ling, was from Sichuan Province. She had been considered the prettiest girl in college, and her parents had hauled her over the coals more than once for "marrying down" to Liu Zheng, who had a pristine family background but wasn't much to look at. Sometimes when I looked at the two of them, I was envious of that unique kind of love and affection between a husband and wife.

Ling had had a good upbringing. She was full of life and energy and was a decent person. I'm sure she knew about my relationship with Lan Yu, but she didn't have that prying, meddlesome personality so many people are cursed with. She never treated us like an oddity, or as if we somehow needed her pity. Whatever she might have thought privately, she never treated Lan Yu as anything but a close friend of mine.

We finished dinner and nighttime fell. Little Wu had long since gone to bed, and the four grown-ups stayed up, sitting at the small dining room table, Lan Yu and I on one side, Liu Zheng and Ling on the other, chatting and drinking distilled sorghum spirits. The dishes had been cleared away, but the postdinner refuse clung to the table in drips and spots. Like everyone else, I was getting tipsy.

Liu Zheng and Lan Yu entered into a heated debate about the corruption plaguing China's primary education system. Liu Zheng ranted and raved like a madman, but it was clear he knew a great deal about the subject, at least from a theoretical perspective. Lan Yu, meanwhile, illustrated the problem by raising issues he had experienced firsthand as a child at school. While this went on, Ling and I talked about national affairs. I struggled to hear Ling's voice over the stentorian intonations of her husband, but was also trying to listen in on the other conversation taking place. My solution? Interrupt all three of them.

"Hey, Liu Zheng!" I called out. "The way you're talking right now, you should have given your life to the cause of education."

"What do you mean, given my life?" Liu Zheng hollered back. "Don't jinx me! If I had given my life, my wife and kid would be going hungry right about now!"

"You see that?" I laughed, turning to Ling. "All he thinks about are his wife and kid. Truly a model husband!"

"Who, him?" she said with a smile. "He's all talk!" Ling laughed, casting her husband a knowing look that made it clear her words were just a playful expression of spousal humility. This spirited gesture, however, passed unnoticed by Liu Zheng.

"Hey, wait a minute!" he protested, dropping the smile and riveting an offended look on his wife. "Tell the truth, now, Ling. You know everything I do is for the two of you!" Liu Zheng's speech was slightly slurred and his face flushed red as he pouted in Ling's direction. He had had a lot to drink and was unable to tell the difference between a joke and an insult. By way of a response, Ling ignored him. She grabbed the bottle in the middle of the table and stood up to pour Lan Yu and me another round of baijiu.

"So, how did Big Sister manage to get herself caught, anyway?" Lan Yu jumped in, looking at Ling with a smile. He was good at diffusing tense situations.

Ling recovered swiftly from the upset. "I was tricked, that's how!" She laughed. "He said we looked like husband and wife and I believed him!" We all laughed, and she leaned back in her chair, gazing softly at Lan Yu and me across the table. She looked like she wanted to say something.

"But if you ask me," she continued in a gentle voice, "it's the two of you who look like a married couple." She smiled.

Never in my wildest dreams could I have imagined that she—or anyone—would say something like that. I turned to look at Lan Yu, whose eyes were fixed on the empty metal pot at the center of the table. Was it happiness he was feeling, or awkwardness? Or, like me, a little bit of both?

Out of habit and without thinking, I grabbed Lan Yu's hand from the table and moved it to my knee, where I held it tightly as the four of us continued to chat. Liu Zheng and Ling surely saw it, but acted as if they hadn't even noticed. It was an incredible feeling of acceptance, something I had never experienced before. For the first time since Lan Yu and I met, we didn't have to hide. Everything felt right, as natural as the snow falling outside.

It was May Day, which also happened to be the founding anniversary of Lan Yu's university. He had an entire week of vacation; it was finally our chance to take the long-awaited trip to Southeast Asia. On the way back we stopped for a few days in Hong Kong. Lan Yu had always wanted to go there.

It was a fantastic trip. Everywhere we went we just blended into the crowd. No one knew us there and my constant worries about being spotted together dissolved. Southeast Asian culture is different from China's, and for the first time since we had met, Lan Yu and I could actually express a little affection in public. Nothing major, just simple things like touching an arm or shoulder while walking down the street. Something so simple, yet so precious.

Before I knew Lan Yu, I always thought that one had to change partners periodically in order to keep from getting bored. I never knew having a stable partner could bring such happiness. Even the negative aspects of being in a relationship—jealousy, possessiveness—could be a turn-on. On the third day of our trip, we were in Singapore having dinner at an upscale restaurant on Orchard Road. I went to the restroom and when I returned to the table, I found Lan Yu checking out some cute Singaporean guy at another table. I marched right up behind him and whacked him on the back of the head. Sitting back down at the table, I told him I wouldn't tolerate him liking anyone else. "One look at another guy and I'll kill you!" I said. Lan Yu just looked at me sheepishly and didn't say a word. For the rest of the night he kept trying to make up for it by being even more attentive than usual.

The truth was, Lan Yu was much more sensitive than I. He was certainly more fastidious, picky even—this was an aspect of his personality that intensified more and more each day. If I so much as spoke to an attractive young man or woman, he would become so sullen and quiet that I couldn't help but tease him a little bit. Anytime I fooled around on the side, I was always cautious to make sure he didn't find out.

Although Lan Yu and I entered into a new period of stability in our relationship, I didn't completely stop sleeping with women. I went to bed with them not because of any physiological need, nor even because I liked them, but because of a need that was entirely psychological: I wanted to prove to myself that I was a normal man.

One night we went to a drag show in Bangkok. Lan Yu asked me to explain the difference between the performers and women. I told him that drag queens were men, and that while most of them had kept their male parts, some of them had cut them off. Lan Yu said he thought it was disgusting. When I asked him if he wanted to hook up with one of them, he gave me a shocked look. "Are you sick in the head?" he asked.

In many respects, Lan Yu was actually a very conservative and traditional person. What I didn't know was whether or not he struggled with internal battles over his relationship with me. We never had a conversation about it, but my gut feeling was that he and I felt the same way: that what we were doing was ultimately abnormal.

China was much more closed off in those days, and its people were much less aware than they are today. On the one hand, we lacked the knowledge and information we needed to understand what we were feeling. And at the same time each of us was unconsciously doing his best not to understand.

Twelve

Soon after returning to Beijing from Southeast Asia, I was invited to accompany a government business delegation on a trip to the United States. We were supposed to go in August. At first I was adamant about not going—to Lan Yu, at least, who patiently listened to my long list of objections to the impending trip. The biggest issue was that I had virtually no business ties with America, so my participation in the group was largely symbolic. But there was also the fact that I was exhausted from the trip to Southeast Asia—which had, incidentally, done little to dispel my fear of flying.

In late July, however, I unexpectedly picked up a new buyer, a major American importer, to whom I began exporting textiles. All at once I was eager to join the delegation. I was determined to win the American over and develop what promised to be a lucrative relationship. When the Yankee asked me about quotas at our meeting in Seattle, I told him I would more than meet his expectations.

"Quotas are the easy part, a side dish compared to the

main course," I said to the interpreter with confidence. "I'll take care of it."

I had only the most rudimentary English, but knew enough to laugh when the interpreter turned to the American and said, "Quotas are peanuts!"

When the business leg of the trip was over, I considered staying on a few days to visit Los Angeles and Las Vegas with the rest of the delegation for the fun part of the trip. But I decided not to, in part because I had already been to both of those places, but mainly because I missed Lan Yu. So I ended the trip and returned to China on my own.

Stepping out of the gate at Beijing Capital International Airport, I saw Lan Yu in the distance. As always, the summer sun had darkened his skin, but by that point in our relationship I thought he was even sexier that way. There he stood at the arrivals gate next to a grumpy-looking female quarantine officer in drab military garb. His face bubbled over with excitement and shone through the sea of dark heads bobbing in front of me. He wore dark blue shorts and a loose-fitting gray T-shirt with a short vertical slit at the neck. The slit was unbuttoned, forcing the flaps of cotton to fall open so that the golden glisten of his chest was revealed. A single glimpse of his radiant, smooth body, so healthy and full of youthful vitality, and my heart began pounding hot and violent in my chest. His hair was longer than usual, but it was the same haircut I always asked him to get. Parted in the middle, it fell against his forehead loose and disheveled. He hated it—he said it made him look Taiwanese—but with these sorts of things, he had always more or less done what I asked.

I wasn't the only person in the terminal who thought he

was gorgeous. Two teenage girls exiting the plane cast googly eyes at him as all the passengers made their way toward the waiting area. Their four eyes stared fixedly at him, but it was me he was waiting for. Just seeing him was enough to make my heart pound and my dick get hard. He saw me and waved.

I was barely able to hide my excitement as we walked out of the glass door and into the parking lot. Since we were in public I was unable to grab him the way I would have liked to, so I compensated by glancing at him again and again, flashing him my dreamiest bedroom eyes and going over in my mind what I was going to do to him the minute we were alone. I stood next to him as close as possible while putting my suitcase in the car, at one point intentionally and playfully rubbing my cheek against his arm then looking up at him lovingly. I could hear his breathing getting heavier; he was getting turned on. In the car, he gripped the steering wheel firmly and looked straight ahead in silence, but I knew his heart was racing out of control. My eyes darted from his face to his crotch and back again. I put my hand on his thigh, but only for a moment. My real target was the bulge swelling between his legs, which I soon began rubbing through his shorts.

"Don't, Handong. I'm driving!" he pleaded in frustration. I responded by rubbing even more at the rapidly growing oval-shaped tent. Lan Yu commanded a great deal of self-control, and I knew he would have no trouble driving. But I wanted to torture him until he couldn't take it anymore. Finally, he exited the highway and turned into a hotel parking lot.

"What are you doing?" I asked.

He parked the car. "How am I supposed to drive with you grabbing me everywhere?" he pouted, leaning back into the seat and pulling the key out of the ignition before looking at me with an impish grin. "Wanna go in?" This was all I needed.

We went into the lobby of the hotel and got a room. The guy at the registration desk, I knew, would think nothing of two men getting a room together. It was common enough among businessmen, even if only to nap for a few hours.

Lan Yu grabbed me the instant the door shut and pressed his lips against mine in a long, deep kiss. I put my hand under his shirt to feel his broad chest, his neck, and both of his nipples, but quickly lost patience with the idea of foreplay and threw him onto the bed to literally rip off his clothes, or at least his T-shirt, which I actually did tear apart. Starting at the little slit at the neckline of his T-shirt that had been taunting me since I saw him at the airport, I ripped the entire thing straight down the middle until it fell open around him. He was surprised by this, but had little time to protest since I immediately pulled him into my arms, holding him around the waist with my left arm while using my right hand to unbuckle his belt, which lashed against his skin as it tore out of the loops. It was a good thing I had luggage in the car since I would have to give him a shirt to wear afterward.

He was beautiful. His body was that of a grown man, but he still retained so much of the charm and allure of youth with his big, sad eyes, pouty lips, and long locks of hair hanging in his eyes. I looked at his face, but only for a moment before continuing to undress him, taking off his shoes and socks then pulling his shorts around his feet. He's mine, I thought. All mine. That boy, standing in the airport only an hour ago, now in front of me naked, lying on the bed, raising his arms above his head, leaning his head to one side and looking at me, waiting for me to take him, hold him, kiss him, make love to him. I had given so much and it was all for him. He was mine!

I ravaged Lan Yu's body, kissing and biting him roughly until I pulled him on top of me, gripped his jet-black hair, and pushed the crown of his head downward to make him go down on me. I must have pushed too deeply, though, because he suddenly gagged so hard that for a moment I was afraid he was going to throw up. Still, he kept gazing up at me with that look of blind love I had seen so many times. That's when I grabbed a fistful of hair, lifted his head up, and rolled him onto his stomach. With no foreplay whatsoever, I entered him, making him inhale sharply through his tightly clenched teeth. I came almost immediately.

I collapsed onto the bed and Lan Yu nuzzled into my arms. He hadn't come yet.

"That *hurt!*" he said accusingly. "That hurt more than it's ever hurt before. It hurt so bad I broke into a sweat!" He touched my hand to his forehead, which was in fact quite damp. I drew him closer and kissed him on the nose.

"I'm sorry!" I said. "I just missed you so much that I couldn't control myself."

I had never been penetrated so I couldn't fully understand the experience, but seeing him anguished made me feel terrible.

"I thought you were trying to kill me!" His voice was sulky, but I knew him well enough to know he wasn't actually angry. I kissed his sweaty forehead, then his lips, then pushed him off of me and laid him on his back. I scaled downward with his cock in my hand, kissing every stop along the way until finally he was in my mouth. The whole thing went in until it hit the back of my throat and the soapy smell of his dark pubes crushed against my nose. Then I had an idea.

"*Hoo haha hi huhhee hee?*" I mumbled, his dick still in my mouth.

"What?" Lan Yu looked down at me in confusion.

136

His cock popped out of my mouth. "You wanna try fucking me?"

"What?!" he exclaimed, taken aback by the suggestion. "I've never done that before!"

"Neither have I," I said, before rolling his balls one by one in my mouth. "I want you to be the first." Whatever it took to make him happy, I was willing to do.

I got on my knees and Lan Yu positioned his cock against me. But no sooner was he about to enter me when he hesitated, seemingly unsure of what to do. I had no choice but to reach back and guide it in. It made me recall with amusement the first girl I slept with, who'd done the same thing for me so many years ago. With adequate spit and verbal instruction, he finally entered me, but with so much force that the entire length went in all at once.

"Ow! Fuck!" I cried. "Go slow, it hurts." I winced and bit my arm. I didn't like it, not one bit. I simply couldn't believe anyone could derive pleasure from such a painful onslaught. But I was determined to stick it out. If he could endure it for me, I could endure it for him.

After a while, Lan Yu got the rhythm of things and started to enjoy it.

In addition to being excruciating, it was also a strange experience. Lan Yu was completely different from his usual submissive self. Holding my waist with both hands, he entered me again and again.

"I didn't know you were such a wild little beast!" I said, turning around to look at his blissed-out face. This made him laugh, but within moments the look of concentration returned. I, on the other hand, derived no pleasure whatsoever from what he was doing and didn't even have any desire left at that point. My cock was limp and I felt nauseous. Still, I continued enduring the assault, an alien discomfort so great that Lan Yu may as well have been an oil drill. It was the emotional element that kept me going. The feeling of devotion. Of giving myself to him.

Finally, Lan Yu came. To me the feeling was mainly reminiscent of wanting to take a crap.

"Did you like it?" I asked him after we'd gotten cleaned up.

"It was okay, but I like it better when you blow me or jerk me off."

Perfect! That was the first and only time I'd ever been penetrated. I didn't like it, but I don't regret trying it.

How many times we had sex that night, I myself don't know. All I know is that there came a point in the evening when we both realized we were starving. But we were also gripped by a paralyzing, sex-induced lassitude, and by the time the food we ordered had arrived, we were already asleep.

The textile deal with the American was going exceptionally well. I was planning on buying a luxury home—a "villa," they called it—in the Northern Suburbs, a wealthy residential area on the outskirts of Beijing. I still hadn't decided whether the house would be a home for Lan Yu and myself, or if I would just give the property to him for him to do with it as he pleased. At that point in our relationship, there was nothing I would have hesitated to give him.

Thirteen

One weekend in October Lan Yu and I went to an indoor swimming pool, a recreational place called the Labyrinth. I liked it because only Chinese people went there, and only wealthy ones at that. It wasn't like all the big hotels and restaurants, where you were thrown in with a bunch of foreigners. Being around too many foreigners had always made me uncomfortable.

Bowling wasn't the only thing Lan Yu couldn't do when we first met. He couldn't swim either. Most people from the land-locked part of China he came from couldn't, he explained. But after we started going to the Labyrinth, he gradually learned under my patient coaching.

I was reclining on a bright green-and-yellow lawn chair near the edge of the pool, sipping an iced tea and watching Lan Yu demonstrate his newly acquired aquatic moves, when out of nowhere I heard a voice.

"Hey, Handong! What are you doing here?" It was Cai Ming, the professor friend who had called me the day Lan Yu had acted so heroically at Tian'anmen. Cai Ming walked toward me, his teeth flashing in a wide smile. That's when I noticed a second guy trailing behind him. Fuck, I thought, it's Wang Yonghong.

Yonghong was a real prick. Barely twenty, he had already accumulated enough rottenness for several lifetimes.

"Just getting some R & R," I replied nonchalantly, lifting my glass to my lips. "Been pretty busy lately."

"Busy what? Fucking chicks? Look at you, hanging out here all by yourself. What's up?" Cai Ming may have been a professor, but he had the mouth of a hoodlum. Not your typical scholar type at all.

The two of them sat down. Yonghong flicked his cigarette butt into a puddle next to the pool.

Cai Ming was a good friend and a good guy, but I sometimes questioned the company he kept. Same with Zhang Jie. She had been in the same high school class as Yonghong and knew him well. I had no idea what these friends of mine saw in him.

"Not fucking as many as you are! What's shakin'?" I had the feeling they wanted something.

"You know, I was just thinking about you." Yonghong said before Cai Ming could answer my question, which was largely just for show anyway. Yonghong was apparently speaking to me, but his eyes were fixed on the pool as if he hadn't even noticed I was there. Cai Ming got up to go take a dip and Yonghong turned to me with a confrontational air.

"I got a batch of steel," he said. "And I'm selling it at a damn good price. You interested?"

I never would have said it out loud, but I was impressed. Steel was hard to come by. You'd need a gang of pirates to get that into China.

"Sure," I said with an air of disinterest, "but what am I

going to buy it with? I'm still waiting for this goddamn American to pay me for his shipment." I took a sip of tea and a drag off my cigarette. I was pleased with my story about the American, which I'd come up with off the top of my head to get Yonghong out of my face. Foreigners were easy scapegoats.

Even if I'd really been interested in the steel, I wouldn't have wanted to have any business transactions with Yonghong or anyone else from the Wang family. He was the kind of guy who couldn't tie a shoelace without assistance from the great reserve of personal resources he commanded. His grandfather had political connections reaching into the highest levels of power, his father was a high-ranking military officer, and his older brother was a filthy-rich businessman sleeping in the same rotten bed as his dad and granddad. I did my best to stay out of the entire family's way.

Before Yonghong could counter my move, Lan Yu jumped out of the pool and walked toward us. He ran his towel over his soaking wet hair, shaking his head as he walked. When he got closer and saw that I was talking with someone he had never met before, he threw me a smile and plopped down at a different table.

Lan Yu's skimpy black bathing suit showed off his legs, stomach, and ass generously: dark, sexy, sunbaked skin peppered with tiny beads of water. The way Yonghong devoured him with his eyes hadn't escaped me. He was perceptive, too, as he had clearly noticed Lan Yu smiling in my direction.

"Who's that?" he asked. "How come I've never seen him before?"

"Just someone I'm hanging out with."

"New piece of ass, huh?" Yonghong laughed. "You lucky bastard!"

"No big," I said, dropping my cigarette butt to the ground

and trying to sound like I didn't give a fuck. Until that moment, I hadn't been sure if Yonghong was into guys, too, but I guess I had my answer now. Cai Ming must have said something. Otherwise, how could Yonghong have known about me?

A few minutes later, Lan Yu returned to the water and Yonghong suddenly lost interest in the batch of steel he was trying to peddle. The moment Cai Ming came back to the table and started talking to me, Yonghong stood up and sauntered toward the swimming pool.

"So, I take it Yonghong is into this kind of stuff, too?" I asked Cai Ming. My eyes were glued to Yonghong, who splashed around in the water with Lan Yu, trying to strike up conversation.

"*Into?* Into isn't even the right word. He's addicted to it!" Cai Ming laughed, gesticulating with his hands. "He himself says it's a problem! You didn't know that?" Cai Ming bellowed with laughter. I smiled to act like everything was fine, but it was a weak performance. Given this new revelation about Yonghong, there was something about the way he spoke to Lan Yu that made me more than a little uncomfortable.

Eventually, I managed to ditch Cai Ming and Yonghong by pulling Lan Yu into the massage room. As we lay there getting worked on, I asked him whom he had been talking to in the pool.

"What are you asking me for?" he laughed. "He's your friend, isn't he?"

"Well, what did he say?"

"He said he was a friend of yours. Then he asked me where I worked."

"Did you tell him?"

"I said I was in school."

"Well, don't talk to people like him anymore. You have to

be careful. You don't know what kind of person he is. I know he seems all right, but he's a cad. Believe me."

"Okay, but why are you mad at me about it? What did I do?"

I was annoyed by the whole thing, but decided to drop the subject. I didn't want any drama with Lan Yu, or worse, with Yonghong, who, frankly, I knew had friends I couldn't afford to piss off. A few days later I asked Lan Yu if Yonghong had tried to contact him and he said no. This was good news to me. I was more than happy to let the episode stay in the past.

At that point in our relationship, Lan Yu almost never slept on campus. By the time students hit their third or fourth year, he told me, their personal lives were not regulated so closely by the university administration, and a fair number of his classmates lived off campus. He drove his white Lexus to school every day, but was cautious to make sure nobody found out about it. He always parked either just outside the campus or in the university residential area reserved for professors and their families, then rode his bicycle to his classes or dorm room. Despite his efforts at discretion, however, just about everyone in his department knew about his "rich older brother."

One Wednesday in November, I came home late in the evening because I had been caught up with a pressing business negotiation. It was dark and quiet when I stepped into my place at Ephemeros. Lan Yu wasn't home yet. I recalled that earlier in the day he had said he needed to be in the sketch room of his department until seven and that he would be home by eight. He was usually very punctual, so I paged him—after the events at Tian'anmen, he had finally broken down and allowed me to get him a cell phone and pager—but he didn't reply. I tried calling him, but his cell phone was turned off. I didn't think he could have been in his car. By eleven o'clock I was worried. Then the phone rang.

"Is this Shen—I mean Chen? Chen Handong?" A man with a very heavy Beijing accent hollered into the phone. "You know a Lan Yu?"

I froze. "Yes. What is it?" I felt as though my heart would rise upward and get caught in my throat.

"All right," he said. "I'll take him there. You pay the—" He yelled something I couldn't make out, apparently to someone he was with. "You pay for the cab fare and medicine when I get there."

"What happened?" I asked.

"He got hurt. Mugged. Nothing serious. Just his arm." The man hung up and I sat there in disbelief. How did this guy manage to cause me so much worry?

When the cab driver arrived with Lan Yu, I gave him ¥300—more than enough to cover the cab fare and the bandages and disinfectant he had bought for Lan Yu.

"Hey, thanks brother!" The driver grinned before driving off.

I helped Lan Yu get inside. He looked bad. His color was off and he was extremely weak.

"How on earth did this happen?" I fretted, poring over each scratch and bruise to make sure he was okay. "The Huada campus is usually so safe. Especially that early! It was only eight at night."

"I don't know how it happened, either," he said sullenly, throwing himself onto the bed.

"Listen, Lan Yu, if someone tries to mug you and they want your money or your car or whatever, you just give it to them—it's not worth getting hurt over! You didn't try to fight back, did you?" I was angry at the mugger, but frustrated with Lan Yu, too.

He was silent. I took this to mean yes, he had fought back. "Then you were part of the problem, Lan Yu!" I said imploringly. "You're too attached to money—you should have just given him whatever he wanted. People like that will kill you in a heartbeat. A lot of cab drivers have been killed that way."

"Are you done yet?" he asked. His left arm was tied up in a bandage, hanging in front of his chest, and his right hand was wrapped in gauze. He had obviously tried to fight back or else he wouldn't have gotten hurt this way. I kneeled in front of the bed and gently took his right arm in my hand.

"Does it hurt?"

"It's fine," he said grumpily.

I leaned in and kissed his lips. "Remember. It's not for nothing they say money is the root of all evil. What matters is life! I just worry that if you don't control your temper, something bad is going to happen to you." I sounded like I was lecturing a child.

He gave me a cheerful smile. "Give me another kiss!" He hadn't listened to a word I had said.

A week later, Lan Yu's arm was improving. One afternoon he rushed into the house excitedly to tell me that because of his injury, there were two exams he didn't have to take. "Where there's a loss, there's always a gain," he said, repeating the old adage. He jumped onto the couch and clicked on the TV with a giddy smile on his face, and it suddenly occurred to me that this guy, ten years my junior, really was still a kid.

Two weeks after the mugging incident, my secretary stepped into my office and dropped an envelope onto my desk. It had just arrived in the mail, but there was no return address. In fact, there was nothing inside the envelope at all except a check for ¥100,000 from a company called Wonderland. That, I knew, was the company of Yonghong's older brother, Yongzhuan. Later in the day, Yongzhuan called me. He was nearly fifteen years older than his younger brother.

"Listen, Handong," he said in a conciliatory voice. "You know what Yonghong is like. Don't fight him on this." I had no idea what he was talking about.

"Oh, god, of course not!" I exclaimed, sounding like an idiot but unsure of what else to say. I didn't know what the phone call was about, but it obviously had something to do with Lan Yu. "Besides," I continued, "you and I have our friendship to think about."

"Exactly!" Yongzhuan said. "Anyway, the hundred grand is just a little something to help the kid forget about it."

"Well, that's very kind of you," I said. I had no idea what Lan Yu was supposed to "forget," but I had to play along to save face. "You know, I never really thought much about this anyway," I continued. "Yonghong isn't the kind of guy who gets out of line." This was all I could think of to say.

After we hung up, I started thinking. I remembered the way Yonghong had tried to talk to Lan Yu in the swimming pool. I didn't know the details, but I figured what had probably happened was this: that bastard Yonghong had tried to hook up with Lan Yu on a number of occasions, and finally succeeded. When he saw I wasn't doing anything about it, he got the jitters and asked his older brother to pay me off—just in case I was silently plotting my revenge. Whether or not Yonghong had actually told Yongzhuan all of this, who knows? I suspected that all Yongzhuan knew was that something bad had gone down between Lan Yu and his brother, and that ¥100,000 might help clean up the mess.

I didn't say a word to Lan Yu about the check or the phone call. Instead, I called Zhang Jie. She knew Yonghong well and wasn't averse to a little gossip. If there was anything to know, she would be the one to know it. She answered the phone and I told her I needed to come over to talk.

"You guys are too much!" Zhang Jie jeered with a big smile on her face while pouring me a drink. "Two guys fighting over a guy?" She was shocked, but obviously loved the drama.

"Wait—no, that's not what's going on at all," I protested. "I don't even know what happened!"

"Quit bullshitting me!" she laughed.

"I'm not!" I insisted. "I truly have no idea. I can't read Yonghong's mind, and it's not like Lan Yu's my wife or something. He never told me what happened. Besides, I'm not even into that kind of stuff anymore!"

"Geez!" she exclaimed. "If that's the way you feel about it, then Lan Yu's really wasting his emotions on you, isn't he? I mean, why even bother being faithful? He should have just slept with Yonghong!" Zhang Jie rolled with peals of laughter.

"Well, did he?" I asked.

"No!" she shrieked. "God, I wish I'd been there. Apparently that little guy of yours is tough as nails. I heard he grabbed the knife right out of Yonghong's hand and told him he'd die before he'd sleep with him!"

"*What?* Yonghong is the one who beat him up? I thought Lan Yu got mugged! What a fucking scumbag!" I fumed. I was furious at Yonghong, but I also had to admit that Lan Yu was braver than I. I don't know what I would have done if I had been in that situation. One thing was for sure, though: I was way off in my estimation of what the ¥100,000 was about.

I didn't say a word about my conversation with Zhang Jie to Lan Yu. I felt powerless in the face of the situation and didn't want him to see it. At the same time, however, I was truly puzzled. Why hadn't Lan Yu told me the truth about what had happened?

That evening, I held Lan Yu in my arms like I held him every night. We messed around a bit, but didn't take it very far because of his injuries. When he tried going down on me, I prevented him because of the strain it would have put on his arm.

"Don't you worry," I said with a kiss to his nose. "When you're all better, I'm gonna pound you so hard, it'll be worth the wait!" That brought a smile to his face.

I drew him deeper into my arms. "Hey, Lan Yu, I've been meaning to ask you something."

He looked at me searchingly. I hesitated, not entirely sure what I was about to say. "Do you think gay people can have everlasting love?"

He smiled as if relieved by the question. "I don't know," he replied. "I've never thought about it." Lan Yu had never liked theoreticals. He'd always been the kind of person to go with his gut feeling.

"Well, I think they can," I said confidently. "If straight people can have it, then gay people can, too."

"Are you talking about us?" he asked, and his eyes sparkled.

I grinned sheepishly. "I'm talking about me."

Lan Yu laughed softly, but seemed at a loss for words.

"Lan Yu," I continued. "Do you care about me?" I had never asked anyone such a question. Before meeting Lan Yu, I had never known what it felt like to lack self-confidence.

"Of course I do," he replied quietly.

A long silence followed. "It was Yonghong, wasn't it?" I asked. "You were lying when you said you got mugged."

More silence.

"He's good looking," I said. "And generous."

Lan Yu yanked himself out of my embrace and looked at me angrily. "It makes me sick just looking at him!" he said. "I didn't do anything, Handong. I didn't ask him out, I didn't flirt with him, nothing! That guy has mental problems."

"Why didn't you tell me about it?"

"I just thought the whole thing was so disgusting, I didn't want to tell you about it. I was afraid that—I don't know—I thought it would put you in an awkward position." He averted his eyes and for once it was I who had nothing to say.

Fourteen

I bought the villa in the Northern Suburbs: a huge five-bedroom, two-and-a-half-bath house with two garages and even an indoor swimming pool. Lan Yu enthusiastically agreed to help me with the renovation and design. What I didn't tell him was that it was to be our new home. Instead, I told him I was helping a friend who lived in the United States buy it. When we got to the estate I took Lan Yu from room to room, soliciting ideas.

"Wow!" he said, poking his head into the master bathroom. "That friend of yours has some serious money. He's spending—what, a couple hundred thousand yuan on renovations alone?"

"You like it?"

"Like it? It's amazing!" he said, knocking on a wall. "I love the overall structure. Something about it reminds me of the architectural style of northern Europe. I read this article about a famous amusement park in Copenhagen. Some of the features here remind me of one of the structures they had in their 'Nordic Village.'" Lan Yu stepped into the kitchen. "Oh my god, look at these tiles!"

I couldn't conceal my excitement any longer. "What would you say if I told you this was our new home?"

Lan Yu looked at me in shock. Then he looked at the bedroom again. "Holy . . . fuck! Are you kidding me?" he shouted as he flung his arms around me in delight.

Lan Yu and I moved out of Ephemeros and into the villa, which we christened "Tivoli Gardens" after the Danish amusement park he had read about. I still held on to the old apartment, but almost never went there.

The first time we made love at Tivoli, it was in the bathroom. Lan Yu was in the huge hot tub–style bathtub, his face poking out of a thick swirl of bubbles that made him look like a baby wrapped in an enormous white blanket. I stood outside the tub wearing nothing but a pair of pajama bottoms, inspecting my chin in the mirror to see if I'd sprouted any new stubble.

"You look—at *most*—twenty-five," Lan Yu said, eyeing me up and down from the tub. I was thirty at that point. Lan Yu would soon be turning twenty.

I beamed with pride. It wasn't for nothing that I exercised at least two hours a day and watched what I ate.

"Oh, by the way," he laughed, distracted by some other thought. "You should see our teaching assistant this semester. He's this new graduate student. Not even thirty and he already has a beer belly!" Lan Yu attempted to wipe a thick blob of suds off his forehead, but only succeeded in getting more of them on him.

"Sounds like you've examined him pretty closely!" I said, leaning into the mirror. "You have a thing for him or what?"

"Well," Lan Yu replied without the slightest trace of irony, "he *is* awfully nice to me."

I put the razor down and turned to look at him. Lan Yu

sat motionless in the tub, his arm resting along the outside rim. Crouching like a predatory animal, I moved toward him in playfully exaggerated slow motion, maintaining eye contact the entire time. He clenched his fists as if challenging me to a fight, but when I tried to bite his arm, his reflexes were faster than mine and before I knew it he had plopped a big handful of suds on the top of my head. The whole thing reminded me of the water fights I used to have as a kid.

"Ha!" Lan Yu laughed. Lovingly, I bit his arm a second time, then jumped into the tub to join him, pajama bottoms still on. I sat in his lap, facing him, grabbed his arms, and continued biting: neck, face, whatever I could find. Slowly, so as not to fall, I shifted positions so that I could hold him from behind and kiss the back of his neck while he laughed in delight. By the time I finally stopped biting and kissing him, his upper back was covered with faint teeth marks. Only then was I satisfied enough to settle down and cuddle with him in the bathtub, pants and all.

"Hey," I whispered into his ear. "We may not be able to get married, but I've given you everything I can. Do you understand what I mean?" I didn't know exactly where I was going with this, but I wanted to speak from the heart.

Lan Yu was still laughing from the water escapade we'd just had. I couldn't see his face, but he nodded his head to say yes, he did understand.

"Do you regret having met me?" That was my next question. It was something I had wondered about for a long time.

His laughter quieted. "No," he said, shaking his head, and I hoped it was true.

The next thing I knew, Lan Yu extricated himself from my embrace and sat up in the tub, seemingly startled.

"Hey, what's this?" he asked, reaching back to grab my

rapidly stiffening cock, which pressed against his lower back through the pajamas. I wrapped my arms around his torso to pull him back toward my chest, noticing the way his skin, submerged in the water, felt even silkier than usual. I pressed my chest against his back and strained my face forward to smell his cheek. I had always loved his smell. Then I turned him around so we faced each other. I hooked my hands under his thighs and he wrapped his arms and legs around me. Gently, I lifted him out of the water and laid him on his back on the broad marble platform separating the tub from the wall. Still standing in the water, I lifted his legs and perched his ankles on my shoulders. We made love like that, right there in the tub with the steaming hot air swirling around us.

The days following our move to Tivoli were the happiest and most carefree we had shared. Lan Yu would be graduating soon and spent most of his time working on his thesis, a building design he hoped he would be able to sell further down the road. I, meanwhile, was going to my office two or three days a week. My business pursuits were progressing smoothly, and I was also in the process of planning my next move. A friend of mine had given me the opportunity to invest in and manage a joint-venture cosmetics factory. Running a factory was new territory for me, but I was energized thinking about the possibilities.

Life was so good in those days, I even started to think it might be possible for Lan Yu and me to stay together forever. Our relationship was my nesting ground, a home for my heart. As to whether or not love between two men could ever gain social acceptance, I never gave it much thought. Financial security meant not having to worry about things like that.

I didn't know whether two comrades could be lifelong partners, loving and taking care of each other till the end.

153

There were those who said relationships like ours couldn't survive longer than a year, but I knew this wasn't true because I'd spent several years living contentedly with someone of my own sex. Perhaps it was precisely because our days were full of such joy, so quiet and stable, that the onset of ruin was that much more devastating.

Fifteen

The Bible says there are two kinds of sin. The first is original sin, the kind that Adam and Eve committed before passing it down to us. The second is the sin we commit when we are led into temptation by Satan. When I first met Lin Ping, I thought she was just that: Satan, a bewitching devil luring me to ruin. But I was wrong. The devil was myself.

My professional life was thriving at that juncture. On top of everything else that was going on, yet another rare opportunity had presented itself. I became the director of City Commerce. Not just anyone could enter that world. It was a major coup, an opportunity to penetrate an exclusive stratum of power and rub shoulders with high-ranking public figures. The new arrangement was sure to multiply my business opportunities exponentially. It was at this time that a small American company hoping to strike it rich in China had asked me to be their go-to guy. That's when I met Lin Ping.

When that American devil first walked into my office, I didn't know who the woman beside him was. I didn't even know if she was Chinese. All I knew was that I was transfixed by the stunning Asian woman before me. It wasn't long before I figured out she was the interpreter the American had brought with him to help with our negotiations.

She was phenomenal. Her sapphire-blue suit showed off two long legs, a narrow waist, and perfectly proportioned hips and ass. Her long, curly hair was tied up on top of her head, falling here and there in seductive strands around her neck and shoulders, black as a crow in flight. She had a simple elegance. Her only jewelry was a delicate pair of square-shaped earrings, sapphire blue like her suit, perched on two tiny earlobes and twinkling against a background of snow-white skin. There was something about her face that looked Western: long, narrow, and very modern. A high-bridged nose, thick, full red lips, and eyes much lighter than the average Chinese woman. Her eyes were a lucid hazel that peered into the world as if calling out from a foggy dream.

The way she carried herself with the American was perfect. Not a trace of arrogance, but nor was she self-effacing. Somehow, she managed to walk the fine line between sober earnestness and polished self-confidence. A fucking master-piece, I thought, eating her up with my eyes. I wanted her. And I was going to have her.

The three of us went into the conference room and sat down, me on one side of the table, she on the other side next to the American. She interpreted between English and Mandarin as the American and I exchanged a few obligatory pleasant-ries. Then we got down to business.

If I had been eating her up with my eyes when she first walked into my office, I was now slowly gnawing at the bones, extracting every drop of marrow I could from the exquisite flesh before me. I didn't know whether she had noticed the way my eyes penetrated her, but I felt that she was gazing back at me periodically. Was there more going on than the attentiveness required of an interpreter? Her smiling eyes were as gentle as a doe's. They signaled openness—to what? Not once did she avert her eyes from mine. Not once did she try to hide from my clinging gaze.

When the dialogue with the American was over, we stood up from the table and walked toward the door. I shook the American's hand and said goodbye. Then I turned to her.

"Miss Lin deserves a special thank you for making our negotiations proceed so smoothly today," I said, squeezing her hand. "Your English is exceptional." I had no idea if her English was good or crap.

"Thank you," she fumbled shyly. She didn't interpret my compliment for the American, who patiently waited for us to finish speaking. Her modesty spurred an adrenaline rush.

When I got home that evening, I was still reeling from the experience. Excitedly, I recounted the entire affair to Lan Yu, who laughed at the story, but didn't have much to say in response.

"You really have no interest in women?" I asked him while pouring myself a scotch. Lan Yu was seated on the couch reading a magazine. The glossy cover showed a wrecking ball hovering over a decimated building.

"Women are all a little fake," he replied bluntly.

"So you're telling me you've been at your school for nearly four years and not one girl has gone after a good-looking guy like you?" I teased him.

"Girls? What girls? There are hardly any girls in the architecture department. And the ones that *are* there . . . well . . ." He laughed. "There's even a rhyme about it."

"All right, let's hear it then!"

Lan Yu took a deep breath:

"Huada girls though sweet and proper
To the eye have naught to offer.
Don't bother trying to cast your hook,
Her nose is buried in a book."

"Ha!" I chortled. "Who came up with that?"

"Someone wrote it on one of the desks at school."

"Well, it's a good thing I majored in the humanities. You science types are pathetic when it comes to going after girls."

"So, you still want to go after them? Even now?" Lan Yu put down the magazine and looked at me.

Raising my hands, I made circles out of my thumbs and forefingers and held them to my eyes like glasses. "We are already old, it doesn't matter to us anymore!" I laughed. I was quoting Zhao Ziyang, the general secretary of the Central Committee of the Communist Party. He had been purged and put under house arrest after delivering a sympathetic speech to student demonstrators during the hunger strike the previous year. When Lan Yu heard me imitating Zhao's heavy Henan accent, he burst into laughter. "Anyway, even if I went after the ladies, I couldn't run fast enough to catch them!" I continued, ascending the staircase while Lan Yu remained on the couch, shaking his head and laughing.

The second time I saw Lin Ping was at my company again, but this time in the quiet solitude of my private office—and alone. Her boss had returned to the United States and asked her to come see me face-to-face to go over the details of our agreement. I was more than happy to oblige. When we met, she wore another blue suit, a kind of bluish-green cyan this time, bright and colorful, but with a lingering elegance that made my blood race.

We talked shop for a while then chatted animatedly about this and that for some time until there appeared a brief lull in the conversation. I leaned back in my chair, riveting my gaze on her in a way that was, I thought, polite and professional, but which carried an unmistakable hint of flirtation that she couldn't have missed. She maintained composure at first, and looked me straight in the eye, calm and cool. A few moments later, however, she broke eye contact and looked down at her hands folded in her lap. Damn! I had never met a woman like her.

"Would Miss Lin allow me to thank her by accepting my invitation to dinner?" I asked, leaning forward in my chair and holding her steady in my gaze.

For a brief moment, Lin Ping's face was overcome with a kind of panicked indecision. Looking downward, she fingered the hem of her skirt as if trying quickly to decide what to do. In a flash, her lips formed a smile, and I heard the words I wanted to hear: "I'd love to!"

For dinner I picked a posh French restaurant called Le Ciel Harmonieux. At eight o'clock on the dot, Lin Ping strode into the lobby where I waited, the automatic glass doors unfolding before her like parting seas. My eyes lit up. One hundred seventy centimeters of breathtaking beauty. Her simple but elegant ash-gray evening dress clung to her finely wrought frame. The dress had a little black floral ornament on the right shoulder, perfectly matching the sleek black pocketbook she carried in her left hand. Her hair was up in a loose bun with strands of hair falling over the tiny black earrings she wore.

What a fucking body! Slim, slender, and tight—so different from Hao Mei with her big, clunky ass. She was just the right height for me, the perfect complement to my tall, masculine frame. My mind spiraled with desire as her dainty feet clicked their way toward me in the lobby. I stood up from my chair to greet her with a gentle, lingering handshake. Something was definitely happening between us.

We stepped into the lush, well-lit dining area, my right arm hooked around her waist. Testosterone surged through my veins as we made our way through the maze of tables, lighting up a runway of grandeur as each man we passed, whether Chinese or foreign, turned to drink her in with his eyes. I beamed with a kind of pride I never thought possible. Lan Yu would never be able to give me that.

Lin Ping and I conversed throughout dinner and late into the night. She told me she had graduated from Fifth International Studies University four years earlier and had worked as an English interpreter ever since. The job with the American company was her third since graduation.

Like Hao Mei, Lin Ping was originally from the South. Her father was an official in some government agency or another, and her mother was a typist. I sat across the table from her, more captivated by the way she spoke than by what she was saying. Everything about her was mesmerizing. Her delicate mannerisms, the graceful way she ate, her gentle laugh, her frankness and openness. I was enchanted.

When I got back to Tivoli it was nearly midnight. Lan Yu was still awake, reading the paper in bed.

"How come you're still awake?" I asked.

"I can't sleep," he said with a yawn. "How was work?" He never took any interest in my work. It was just something to ask.

"Okay," I said, turning off the light. "Let's get some sleep."

Lin Ping and I went out a few more times after our first date.

The power her charm and sex appeal held over me grew stronger and stronger, but my desire was frustrated by her apparent unwillingness to consummate the deal by sleeping with me. We only met at night, staying out pretty late each time. With a little logistical help from Liu Zheng, I was able to arrange things so that Lan Yu had no idea what was going on.

One Saturday night I had to attend a social gathering at the Dai household. Donald Dai was the number-two bigwig in the high-flying world of Chinese finance, and he had the English name to prove it. I'd managed to get myself invited through a friend in common. To make everything feel more natural, I asked Lin Ping to accompany me at the last minute. She agreed. Everything was perfect at the party, thanks in no small part to Lin Ping. It was good for me to have a woman by my side, and especially a woman like her. Her beauty and charm won people over wherever she went.

"I want to thank you for coming with me tonight," I said as we left the party and our feet hit the pavement outside the Dai house.

"You'd better," she said with a playful smile. "How do you intend to do it?"

"How about dinner?"

"That doesn't count!" she cried. "Although"—her voice became quiet—"you must have read my mind because I really am starving. Let's get something to eat!" She laughed sweetly. In each of our interactions she had been so professional and restrained. This was the first time I'd seen the cute girly side of her. There was something so tender and loving in her manner—or so I thought at the time.

That night after dinner, I kissed her in the car. I was on the verge of exploding, and the way she draped herself around me like a shawl told me she liked it too. But before I could go any further she pushed me away abruptly.

"Handong!" she cried faintly, clutching at the collar of my shirt as she pinned her eyes to my chest.

"Hmmm?" I cooed.

"There's something I need to know," she continued, turning away from me and resting her folded hands in her lap. "Do you have a wife?"

I laughed. I found it amusing that she would even ask such a question. "What makes you think that?" I asked.

"Let's just call it a woman's intuition," she replied, gazing straight ahead through the windshield.

"Listen," I said. "I'm single. I've never been married." I touched her arm gently to signal that I wanted her to look at me. "You want me to show you the marital status on my household registration card?" Rich or poor, everyone had a household registration card. It said where you were authorized to live and work, as well as whether you were married or single.

Lin Ping smiled bashfully and looked down at her lap. Then she looked up at me again. "Handong," she said. "I'm so scared of this! I'm scared of getting in too deep. I'm scared of hurting you, hurting myself."

I was struck by her words. Few women will demonstrate their love this openly. Especially beautiful women.

It was one o'clock in the morning when I took Lin Ping home, gently kissed her good-night, and went back to Tivoli. Still wound up from the date but ready for some shut-eye, I kicked off my shoes and went straight to the bedroom. Lan Yu was sitting up in bed, watching a movie on the VCR. He didn't even look at me, let alone greet me.

"Up this late!" I said nonchalantly. "Don't you have class

tomorrow?"

"Tomorrow's Sunday," he said coldly.

"Well, I'm going to take a shower and go to bed." I unbuttoned my shirt, hoping that if I didn't say much he wouldn't start asking questions about where I'd been all night. It didn't work.

"You're pretty busy these days," he said abruptly. He was no dummy.

"Yeah, work stuff. What a pain!" I hated it when he started acting suspicious.

Lan Yu turned off the TV and pulled the blanket over his head as if to tell me he was going to sleep. When I returned from the bathroom after my shower, the blanket was pulled down again and he was lying on his stomach with his head turned to one side, almost falling off the edge of the bed. I turned on the headboard light, then stood at the side of the bed and looked down at him. Eyes closed, the contours of his thick black eyebrows and pouting lips were as exquisitely precise as if they'd been carved in stone. His expression when he slept was always so serene, so calm and unperturbed, without the slightest trace of artifice. I squatted next to the bed and gently kissed his lips. This must have roused him out of his sleep, because he rolled onto his back, muttering something. I climbed into bed and lay directly on top of him and kissed him until he woke up.

"Go to sleep," he said sternly, though he was struggling to force back a smile. We were face-to-face, but his eyes remained closed.

"But I *want* some," I said in a saccharine and slightly high-pitched voice.

"*Want* some!" he said as his eyes popped open. "You come

home this late and you *want* some? No way, go to sleep." He looked at me in annoyance, a barely perceptible smile dancing on his lips.

"But I've been so *very* busy," I said in an exaggeratedly sweet voice. Lan Yu groaned and pushed me off of him.

Unable to bear the game any longer, we burst into laughter. We often played with this kind of role reversal, teasing each other until the whole thing became so silly that we had no choice but to start laughing and rolling on the bed together, giggling through the kisses.

"Man, what made *you* so grumpy tonight?" I asked after we had settled down from the fun. I was still on top of him, enjoying the sensation of his fingers running through my hair.

Instead of answering, Lan Yu pulled his hand away from the back of my head and looked at me straight in the eye. "Handong," he began soberly. "Were you out sleeping around tonight?"

"And what if I was?" I quipped cheerfully. "You wouldn't want me anymore?"

Lan Yu sighed. "I just worry that it's *you* who doesn't want *me* anymore," he said, looking wistfully at the ceiling. I studied his face. His smile was gone, and his eyes were full of that kind of anxiety I knew so well, that deep distress that made me want him so badly when we first met and that still ignited my passion even now. At that moment, however, the distress he displayed provoked not desire—or not only desire—but a combination of sadness and guilt. Under the soft glow of the headboard light, my heart was flooded with so much passion for him, so much devotion to what we had, that my eyes filled with tears.

"Are you crazy?" I asked, burying my face in his neck. "How could I not want you?"

I didn't talk to Lin Ping for two months after that. The truth was, I did have some guilty feelings about "sleeping around."

In the end, it was Lin Ping who called me. Twice. The first time, her voice was calm and steady, as if there were nothing at all awkward about the long period of silence that had transpired between us. She was brief, though, saying little more than to ask how I was doing, then hanging up before the conversation went too far. Just enough, I noted with a vague sense of sudden frustration, to give me a taste of what I had been missing. Whether she intended it or not, her manner on the phone did something to me. My blood started racing the moment I heard her voice, and I felt the sharp stab of disappointment when she said goodbye. At twenty-five, she was five years Lan Yu's senior. She had accumulated a kind of feminine maturity that oozed through the telephone. Women were sexiest at that age.

The second time she called, we made plans to get together. I told her I was going to a cocktail party on Friday night and asked her if she would like to come. Her answer—"Sure!"— got me excited, but worried. I hung up the phone, repeatedly telling myself not to do it. It wasn't because Lan Yu and I had legal ties—I knew we didn't. It was because I didn't want to betray him.

And yet, in my gut I knew that when Friday night came it was going to happen. Lin Ping and I were going to sleep together.

Sixteen

The cocktail party was at the home of a boring, pompous, and utterly officious bureaucrat. The setting was informal, but nearly all the attendees were government officials and their spouses, so the social and career stakes were just as high as at any other event. I knew all the major players in attendance and, as expected, the evening went off without a hitch.

When the event was over, Lin Ping said she wanted to get some air, so we hit the streets of Beijing for a walk. Together we strolled through a quiet, dimly lit neighborhood. Arm in arm we passed the occasional shop or restaurant, just as cozy and natural as if we'd been a couple deeply in love for years. No matter where we went or what we did, I always took every opportunity to display my affection for Lin Ping. How much affection I actually felt was beside the point. With women, even the tiniest trace of tenderness could be expressed as if it were the greatest love in the world. But with men—with Lan Yu—it was the exact opposite. No matter how much love I felt for him, I couldn't show even the slightest trace in public.

After our walk I took Lin Ping to Country Brothers. For

the first half hour we sat on opposite sides of the couch, just making small talk. The bellboy brought some champagne and we drank a toast. "To friendship!" we shouted, clinking our glasses together. Her directness excited me. The male desire for conquest raced through my veins as I moved closer to her side of the couch. I had had my suspicions about what was going to transpire that night, but when she held up her champagne and looked me in the eye—that's when I knew for sure: I was going to fuck her.

We kissed. I pushed my tongue into her mouth and she gasped, clutching first my shoulders, then the back of my head. Impatiently I advanced, wrapping my arms around her until finally I grabbed her by the waist and, in one quick motion, lifted her and carried her to the bed, where, item by item, I slowly began removing her clothes. Her demeanor was completely different from what I had observed thus far. She was usually so confident, elegant, self-assured. All this slipped away and in my arms she became shy, submissive, obedient. She untied her hair and it fell to the bed in a heavy cascade. Unable to wait any longer, I tore open her blouse and grabbed her left breast with one hand while prying her legs open with the other. I pressed up against her, kissing her lips, then her neck, then moved down to her chest, sucking her breasts one by one while moving my hand toward her pussy. I fingered her for a while, then pushed down my pants, raised her legs, and entered her in one solid motion.

It had always struck me as odd that I was able to hold out much longer before coming with women than with men. Sex with Lin Ping was enjoyable enough, but the truth was it lacked the magical fireworks I had hoped for. It was exciting, but the excitement I felt was more about psychological conquest than about the physical act itself. It didn't matter though. When I saw the way I made her come again and again—that was exhilarating, intensely so, to the point that I very nearly cried.

"Handong!" she screamed, digging her nails into my back and kissing my neck. "Oh god . . . oh . . . oh . . . oh . . . oh," she moaned as she wrapped her legs around me. It took some time, but I eventually managed to climax too.

With women, you have to hold them for a while after sex or they're not going to get the ultimate satisfaction they're looking for. Lin Ping nuzzled into my chest, clutching one of my thick, strong hands while I stroked her neck with the other.

"I feel so stupid," she said, shaking her head and looking down with a laugh.

"Why?" I asked. "You're the most intelligent woman I've ever known."

She laughed. "I bet you've said that to a million girls!"

"Actually, I used to—" I started to speak, but Lin Ping cut me off by blocking my mouth first with one finger, then with a kiss.

"Handong," she said, turning to look me in the eye. "I don't care about the past. I don't even need to know what's going on with you now. All you have to know is that there's a girl right here named Lin Ping who loves you very much. As long as you know that, everything else is okay."

She shifted her body and sunk into my arms again. Eyes open in a wide stare, her gaze focused on some vague location on the other side of the room. The scent of her shampoo hit my nose. She continued:

"If there ever comes a day when you no longer care for her, just tell her to go away. It will be hard for her because she loves you very much, but she will do it. She'll just quietly disappear." Lin Ping turned to look at me again, a sad smile stretching its way across a face that was by now completely red. No one with a heart could have failed to be moved.

The sudden appearance of Lin Ping in my life forced me to confront a crucial question: whether or not to get married. My mother had been pestering me to do so for some time, particularly after my father's death. I was beginning to feel the heat.

I had no doubt that Lin Ping—an ordinary girl from an ordinary family—would make a suitable wife. Though born poor, she was the kind of woman who strove endlessly to reach greater and greater successes in life. I needed her. For my life and for my career.

And what about Lan Yu? I asked myself. What would I do with him? Let things stay as they are? Retain him as my "kept" boy? Would he even go along with that?

After hours of agonizing over these questions, another option crossed my mind: just call it quits and break up with him. But no matter how many times I imagined this scenario, I didn't think I could do it.

I've always believed there are no coincidences in life. Even if you don't understand it at the time, everything happens for a reason. Thus I felt certain it was no coincidence that at the very moment I started to think about marriage, I met Dr. Shi. Dr. Shi was a psychiatrist, a professor at the university where Cai Ming taught, and he had devoted a good part of his career to the study of homosexuality. He was the first expert on the issue I had ever met. Talking with him was the first time I began to gain knowledge on the subject.

After a lengthy four-hour discussion, Dr. Shi gave me his diagnosis. First, he assured me, I was a completely normal man who just happened to have slight homosexual tendencies. All I needed to do was break things off with Lan Yu and getting married would be no problem at all. The real problem, he said, originated with Lan Yu, who was a true homosexual and who, Dr. Shi suspected, suffered from severe paranoia. With therapy, he reasoned, Lan Yu would be cured of the disorder, thus allowing me to extricate myself from the relationship and move on with my life.

I burst through the door when I got home that night, beside myself with excitement about sharing my big "scientific discovery" with Lan Yu. Armed with the doctor's encouragement, I was determined to convince Lan Yu to take aggressive steps to enter into therapy and get cured. It would be a difficult discussion, but I had to do it. For him. For us.

Neither Lan Yu nor I could cook, so we either ate out or ordered in almost every night. When I told him about the conversation with Dr. Shi, we were in the car coming back from dinner at Beijing's finest Peking roast-duck restaurant. Lan Yu was in the driver's seat talking animatedly about school stuff while trying to concentrate on the road ahead. With great zeal he described everything that was going on in his department: the various activities of the student affairs office, the teachers' office, and the dean's office; where his classmates would be assigned jobs after graduation, including how many would stay and work in Beijing; his recent job interview at the Institute of Design; etc. On and on I listened to him ramble, feeling impatient and increasingly annoyed. When he was finished, I told him that if they tried to make him leave Beijing after graduation, I would buy him a household registration card for Beijing so that he could stay in the capital. Then I quickly changed the subject before he could keep talking.

"Listen, Lan Yu," I began. "Have you ever thought about what we're going to do in the future?"

He turned his gaze from the asphalt and looked at me. "What are you talking about?"

"Don't you think it's abnormal for two men to be together?"

He returned his eyes to the road and fell silent.

"Actually," I continued, "it's a psychological problem. You

see, sometimes people develop a kind of—like, an illusion or misrecognition. People like you—I mean, like us—it's a kind of ... like a sexual perversion." I did my best to parrot the words I had heard Dr. Shi say, but they failed to convey exactly what I meant.

To my great surprise, Lan Yu was more than prepared to tackle the subject. "Well," he began, "I've read a lot of literature about this, and they don't think it's an illness anymore, at least not outside China. It's just—I mean, I can't remember exactly what they call it—it's just, some people like women and some people like men. They're just two different choices. That's all."

His words astonished me. Never would I have imagined he'd read any materials about such matters. "When did you read this stuff?" I asked.

"I've been following this kind of research ever since you and I met. It's all foreign literature."

"Oh, okay, *foreign* literature," I retorted. "So what? They have *pornography* in foreign countries too, don't they? They have *sexual liberation* in foreign countries, don't they?"

"It was a science journal, okay? It was legit."

"Well, whatever you might have read—listen, Lan Yu, this is a psychological disorder!" Though rapidly losing hope of convincing him, I wasn't giving up yet.

"So you're actually saying you think we have a mental illness?" He forced out a fake and deeply unhappy laugh.

"Not *we*! *You*! At least I still like sex with women. What about you?"

"I've never done it before. You know that." His voice was defensive.

"Have you ever even liked a girl? You don't even like magazines like *Playboy*!"

Silence. This was my cue to continue, to cut deeper.

"What I'm trying to say, Lan Yu, is that you basically see yourself as a girl."

"I do not!" he retorted angrily, hands trembling against the steering wheel.

"Be careful, you're driving! Listen, if you don't see yourself as a girl, then why do you like men?"

He didn't have a ready answer to that, but a few minutes later he spoke again. "Handong, I don't . . . what I mean is . . . it's *you* that I like."

By the time we got home we weren't speaking to each other. Unwilling to let the subject drop and die, though, I told Lan Yu about Dr. Shi, adding that I wanted him to go into therapy right away to get cured.

"No!" he said resolutely. "I'm not going!"

"But Lan Yu—you have to get married one day! It's important for you!"

"I'm not getting married!"

"Not getting married!" I scoffed. "Listen, Lan Yu, you're twenty now. What happens when you're thirty, forty? How are you going to establish yourself in a society like this one?" The more I spoke, the more I sounded like a nagging parent, or perhaps like I thought I was Dr. Shi himself.

"Besides," I continued, "don't you want children? Men have a responsibility to continue the family line! You'll have to face this pressure one day!"

"What pressure, Handong? Nobody in my family cares about the family line and I don't care, either! What pressure do I have?" He buried his head in his hands.

I had forgotten that Lan Yu's family situation was different from my own. He didn't have the same obligation to marry and have kids as I did. I needed to work a different angle if I was going to convince him.

"Didn't your mom say—" The words were barely out when Lan Yu glared at me with contempt. This, I knew, was the dagger in his Achilles's heel. "Didn't she say she wanted you to be an honorable man with an invincible spirit? You have to try, Lan Yu!"

For the first time since the conversation began, he had nothing to say. This, I knew, was an admission of defeat. It meant he agreed with me. And yet, just as we were about to go to sleep he returned to the subject.

"Do you want to break up with me, Handong?"

"My god, Lan Yu!" I said. "Why do you take my good intentions and turn them against me?" I pulled him into my arms and held him close. "Can't you see I'm trying to help? If you think I want to break up with you, it's all in your imagination."

Lan Yu was in a bad mood in the weeks that followed, but finally agreed to make an appointment with Dr. Shi. He never vocalized it, but I knew he hated me for pushing him into therapy. He began coming home late every night and even slept periodically at his university dorm. On returning home from his first visit to Dr. Shi's office, he entered the house and proceeded straight upstairs without so much as a greeting.

"Hey!" I stopped him. "How did it go? What did you guys do?"

Lan Yu halted halfway up the stairs and looked at me over the banister. "We talked, okay? He showed me pictures. Tried to make me think about stuff."

"What else?"

"If you're that interested, why don't you go see him yourself!" he said angrily before storming up the stairs.

Life with Lan Yu was difficult during that period. If I wanted sex, he went along with it, but his lack of interest was plain, and most nights he just jerked me off before rolling over and going to sleep. Often, I would wake up in the middle of the night to the restless sound of night talk. I could never make out what he said, though, just inaudible mumbling punctuated by loud, sorrowful moaning.

"Lan Yu, wake up!" I would say, nudging his shoulder. Each time he awoke he would sit up in bed, trying to calm himself before going back to sleep.

Things were even worse in the daytime. Tired and sluggish because of poor sleep, he was also rapidly losing weight because he had lost his appetite.

When I asked him what it felt like to be in treatment, his reply was always the same: "Nothing." He had become empty, hollow.

One Monday morning, I went to Dr. Shi's office to inquire about Lan Yu's progress. Reclining in his black leather swivel chair, the psychiatrist asked me if he could be frank. I told him he could, and with great calmness and patience he gave me his assessment. Not only, he said, was Lan Yu perverted in his psychosexual orientation, but he also suffered from paranoia and severe depression. Most alarming of all, he added, was that the patient was not cooperating with therapy.

"The outcome of the first stage of therapy has been less than ideal. My recommendation moving forward is that we try hormonal injections. This will help him *blah blah blah*," Dr. Shi went on glibly.

"Hormonal injections?" I exclaimed when he finally finished what he had to say. The words came out as a shout. "No, we can't do that." I couldn't accept the idea of injecting hormones into someone who was basically healthy, at least physically.

"Well," the doctor said, crossing his legs authoritatively,

"there *are* other options. For example, we could have him look at images of nude men—perhaps even a picture of you—while applying a . . . um . . . a sort of stimulus. The idea, of course, would be to create a conditioned reflex of pain that would be associated with the image."

"What kind of stimulus?" I asked.

"Well, we would start with a mild electroshock therapy."

"No!" I said resolutely. "Absolutely not!"

I'll never know if it was Dr. Shi's convictions about the dangers posed to society by homosexuality, or simply because he felt guilty about the exorbitant fees he charged me, but he continued to give me other suggestions. One by one, I dismissed them all.

In the days that followed, I puzzled endlessly over Dr. Shi's explanations of Lan Yu's condition. I recalled what the doctor had asked me the first time we met: "Are you in love with him or are you just looking for a little fun?" My reply was full of hems and haws, but I ultimately told him I was only looking for a little fun.

"Then there's nothing to worry about!" he said cheerfully. "You're obviously not a homosexual. You just don't have a serious outlook on life."

On the surface of things, Dr. Shi's words made sense. But then I kept thinking. By his logic, anytime I messed around with a girl without falling in love, it would just be me "not having a serious outlook on life." It would only be if I fell in love with a girl that one could say I was truly heterosexual. But I had never been in love with a woman. So what did this make me?

I also thought about what the doctor said about Lan Yu: that he saw himself as a girl. Without doubt, in some ways Lan Yu's longing for me was like a woman's love. He had always been very sensitive, delicate, loving. But he was also a person with deep self-respect, who always stood on his own two feet, who was strong and tenacious and brave. Those are qualities both men and women can have.

After spending most of the day at the office thinking about Dr. Shi and the therapy, I decided to give Lan Yu a call. I asked him to come to my office so we could go play pool when I got off work. More importantly, I wanted to talk to him about something, though I didn't mention it on the phone. At first he said he was busy and couldn't leave the house. Then he said he felt sick and wanted to go to bed early. When these excuses didn't work, he agreed to come see me.

"Where are we going?" he asked as he walked into my office and plunked down on the couch.

"Where do you want to go?" I asked.

"Wherever." His voice was languid and he eyed me suspiciously from the couch.

"Are you going to see Dr. Shi tomorrow?"

"Day after tomorrow."

"Well, don't go, okay?" I said, mindlessly moving some paperwork around on my desk.

"Why not?"

"Just because. Don't go anymore from now on, either. It's putting you through too much."

A great big smile stretched across Lan Yu's face. He jumped up from the couch and pounced on me, hugging and kissing me with every ounce of energy he had.

"Are you out of your mind?" I said with a laugh as I pushed him off of me. "I'm at work!"

My absurd attempt at curing Lan Yu of his homosexuality died right there in my office. Before long, his original spirit was restored and I finally saw that smile—sweet, radiant, beautiful—that I had come to know and love. He also started eating again. Having weathered this storm, his attachment to me felt even deeper than before. And yet, this was exactly what worried me.

Seventeen

One weekend, business called and I had to head south for a trip. First Hong Kong, then Hainan Island. Lin Ping insisted on seeing me off at the airport.

"You have to be careful in Hong Kong," she exhorted as we said goodbye at the boarding gate. "Anytime you go outside or drive or do anything, just be really careful!"

"I'll be fine," I assured her with a squeeze of the hand. "I go to Hong Kong all the time!"

"I know," she said with an air of resignation. She pulled her hand away from mine and reached into the pocket of her jeans to produce a delicate box made of heavy, decorated paper. "This is jade," she said solemnly. "My grandma gave it to me— my mom's mom. She told me an eminent monk had touched it and that it can ward off evil. Here, take it." Lin Ping placed the box in the palm of my hand.

I opened the box. Inside sat a rectangular, emerald-green stone with a splash of red in the center. It looked like a baby heart gently throbbing in a sea of green. On the back was engraved a single character: *Lin*.

"Thank you," I said, looking into Lin Ping's misty eyes then giving her a big hug. I had no idea whether the piece of jade could chase away evil, but I couldn't deny that I was moved by the gesture.

In Hong Kong I went to a jeweler in Chungking Mansions and had Lin Ping's gift put on a gold chain. On a whim, I also had it appraised: the mild-mannered Cantonese jeweler pulled out a magnifying loupe and after just a few moments told me in heavily accented Mandarin that the jade was of the highest quality. A rush of guilt came over me. I hadn't given a single thing of real value to Lin Ping, and here she was gifting me an exquisite gemstone. Stepping into a bar in Hong Kong's Lan Kwai Fong District, I recalled what Liu Zheng had said about her: she was the kind of woman no man could resist.

Ten days later, I called Lan Yu to tell him I would be returning to Beijing in a week. The truth was, I was coming back from Hainan that very day. Arriving at the airport, I descended the plane to the tarmac. Looking up at the terminal building in front of me, I saw Lin Ping's hazy figure hovering in the window above. She waved and smiled. I opened my shirt collar and held up the jade pendant for her to see.

Inside the building I greeted her with a big hug. She wore a tight white T-shirt with a scandalously low neckline and a pair of jean shorts. All tits and legs. She looked great.

"Let me take you to dinner!" I said once we were settled in the car. "I know a great place."

"Don't you ever go anywhere other than restaurants?" she asked in baffled amazement. It was true that at this point in our relationship, nearly all our time together had been spent in hotels and restaurants. We decided to go to Ephemeros.

Lan Yu and I had long since moved our belongings out of

Ephemeros and into Tivoli. Apart from furniture and a couple of kitchen appliances, the old apartment was basically empty. When Lin Ping and I got there, we were only inside for a few moments before I started to feel uneasy. It was strange for me to be with her in that space.

"All right, you've seen it. Let's go eat!" I said playfully, grabbing her by the hand and pulling her back outside toward the car.

"Hey, not so fast," she protested. "Why don't we just pick up a few things and cook here? We'll have a nicer meal that way—tastier, too!" When I reluctantly agreed, she gave me a shopping list, and I went downstairs to the little vegetable market on the east side of the residential compound. When I came back, she whipped up two dishes and a soup in thirty minutes flat.

She couldn't help but laugh when she saw my uncouth table manners. "How's my cooking?" she asked.

"Nectar for the gods!" I sputtered, chomping on a plate of stir-fried prawns. Her cooking was, in fact, very good—much better than anything one would find at a restaurant.

"Did your mom cook much at home?" she asked.

"The maid did most of the cooking when I was growing up," I replied. "Ma only made a couple of special dishes. Her Beijing-style shredded pork was fantastic. And her stir-fried cucumbers—oh my god, so good!"

"Really?" Lin Ping cooed across the table. "If she has time, I hope the dear old lady will teach me to make stir-fried cucumbers just like she does."

I knew that if I were to take Lin Ping home, the "dear old lady" would leap with joy. Lin Ping was a paragon of womanly virtue. As a son, this would be the greatest happiness I could give my mother.

This woman! I thought, gazing at her from across the table.

Lin Ping: poised and graceful, great in bed, and overflowing with all the virtues a woman should have in the home. Without question, I was going marry her. It was time for Lan Yu and me to have a talk.

A week after returning to Beijing, I removed Lin Ping's necklace and went back to Tivoli. Instead of giving me a hello kiss, Lan Yu grumbled that I hadn't called first.

On the third day of my return, I finally built up enough courage to have the talk I'd been waiting for. Lan Yu was busy at work in the bedroom we had converted into his work studio. When I tiptoed through the door, he briefly turned around to glance at me, then went back to his drawing.

"What's up?" he asked with his back to me. "You scared me."

"Lan Yu, I'd like to talk with you about something."

When I first stepped into Lan Yu's studio, his voice had been neutral, indifferent. But now he turned around in his chair and looked at me attentively. Judging from the earnestness in his eyes, I could tell he knew it was something big. "What is it?" he asked.

I took a deep breath and resolved to be blunt. "Lan Yu, I'm getting married. And I've found the right girl."

Lan Yu stared at me in silence. It was a look I knew all too well, the same one he had given me over two years earlier when I had cruelly told him I was sick of him and didn't want to see him anymore. Fear, despair, hopelessness. These were the emotions written on his face.

I was as hard hit by Lan Yu's reaction as he'd been by the news I'd given him. It was hard for me to see him so immersed in anguish. I myself couldn't believe it, but I suddenly felt I was going to cry.

"You knew this day was coming sooner or later, Lan Yu," I

said, looking down at the floor. He remained silent. I couldn't bear his silence.

"Lan Yu!" I continued. "Things can stay exactly as they are! The only difference will be that I'll have a wife!" I looked up from the floor with a pleading look on my face. This was my promise to him. And it was something that I truly believed could work.

Lan Yu looked at me with eyes full of tears and lips that trembled. He quickly tore his eyes away from me, however, shifting his gaze to the ceiling as he pushed a knuckle under a puffy eyelid to hold back the tears. He had never been the kind of guy who cried easily.

After what seemed like an eternity he looked at me again, this time with firm resolution in his eyes. There was also a trace of bitterness.

"When you made me go into therapy I knew this was the reason," he said, forcing out a laugh to conceal his tears. I couldn't bear seeing him this way, so I took his hand and lifted him out of the chair. I held him close to me.

"I don't like it either, Lan Yu," I said, kissing him with lips that were, by now, as trembling and dripping with tears as his. "But I have no choice!"

Lan Yu gripped the back of my head and pressed his cheek firmly against mine. His tongue touched my face softly, catching tears as they rolled down my cheeks.

We stood this way for a while, holding each other and periodically peppering each other's faces with soft kisses. Unexpectedly, Lan Yu pulled away from me and turned around to grab the box of tissues resting on the mahogany drafting table behind him. With comic incongruity, he blew his nose loudly, then handed me a tissue of my own. I blew my nose too, and we laughed and stood there in his studio, laughing and crying at the same time. A good deal of time passed, and he leaned into me with a kiss.

We stripped off our shirts, slowly, gently, without any sense of urgency. Lan Yu clasped his hands against my shoulders and pushed me downward. Together we descended to the carpeted floor of his studio, where we lay as he gently kissed my neck, my chest, my nipples. I gasped in pleasure, but when he went down farther, there was nothing I could do: my dick hung lifelessly between my legs. Eager to excite me, Lan Yu played with my cock for a while, but no matter what he did the idea of sex just wouldn't move from thought to action. Thinking a new strategy might work, I went down on him, but he was just as limp as I was. Just as I was about to abandon the idea of sex altogether, he suddenly motioned for me to stop. With a look of discomfort, he twisted his arm around and pulled out an eraser that was wedged between his back and the floor. We looked at each other and laughed.

We didn't need to have sex. At least I didn't. All I needed was to know that he was mine, to have the peace of mind of knowing we were going to be together. But peace of mind was nowhere to be found. How could it be, when everything was about to change?

In the middle of the night, we awoke to the sound of the wind blowing outside. Shadows of leaves fluttered through the windows and danced on the curtains like ghosts. In the darkness we started to make love all over again. This time it was beautiful, powerful. We shared something no words could express, but we intimately understood. Our future was uncertain, and our lovemaking was filled with hopelessness and despair.

After we had both climaxed, Lan Yu sat up in bed. I rested my head in his lap, gazing up at him, lazing dreamily in the serenity of the postorgasmic afterglow.

"Well, I guess everything turned out better than I thought it would," Lan Yu said suddenly with a gentle smile.

"What did?"

"I was sure you were going to end things between us."

I looked up at his fluttering black eyelashes and lush red lips. "I could never do that," I said. And yet, we both knew it was far from settled what would happen after I got married. However nice my words might have sounded, even I wasn't convinced.

Eighteen

It took some mental preparation, but I eventually sat my mother down and told her about my new fiancée. At first, she took issue with Lin Ping's family background, saying it was too humble for a family like ours. She said she wanted me to find someone whose family was better matched in socioeconomic status, or perhaps someone from a family of intellectuals. When I heard this I clenched my fists and ground my teeth. If she really wanted me to find a mate from a family of intellectuals, Lan Yu would have more than fit the bill.

I was increasingly worried about my mother's ability to find endless fault with my choice of bride, but the moment Lin Ping stepped over the threshold and into the house, I knew everything was going to be fine. Her warm, charming demeanor and impeccable manners won my mother over instantly; even my sisters pulled me aside to whisper, "Wow, not bad!" Standing in the kitchen doorway, I peered into the living room where I saw my fiancée pour her future mother-in-law a cup of tea. Ma beamed with happiness. Nothing made me happier than seeing her smile.

In the early stages of my relationship with Lin Ping, I thought that Lan Yu and I would be able to go on just as peacefully and contentedly as before, at least for a while. But I was wrong. Arguments became the central feature of our daily life. Our fights weren't even over matters of principle or about substantive issues like my impending marriage or the future of our relationship. We fought over petty trifles: who came home at what hour, who had forgotten to do this or that household chore. We always patched things up quickly, though, and each time it was Lan Yu who initiated the ceasefire.

One afternoon as Lan Yu and I were in his white Lexus on our way to lunch, we made our way past the gates of Tianda University, where a long line of students had formed. "What are all these people waiting for?" I asked.

"They're registering for the TOEFL exam," he replied. "They're trying to study abroad."

"Wow," I laughed. "That's dedication!"

"That's nothing!" he said, turning the car southward in the direction of Houhai Lake. "When I first started at Huada, I heard that an entire section of the biology department's graduating class of 86 left the country after graduation."

"Is that what you want to do?" I asked.

"I can't," he said wistfully. "If you want to go to the United States, you have to prove you have a relative who's a US citizen. Besides, it's tough with architecture. Even if you get into a program, you're not going to get funding unless you know someone who'll go to bat for you."

"Well, if you really do want to go, I can help you arrange it. All we have to do is get you a business visa and you can go with a group. When you get there just switch to a student visa. Easy."

I knew from his silence that I had said something wrong.

He was visibly upset, but instead of saying so, he just kept his eyes on the road ahead of him. I switched on the radio to act like nothing had happened, but the racket of the news announcer's voice was even more uncomfortable than silence. By the time Lan Yu parked in front of the restaurant we were headed to, the whole thing had become unbearable. He pulled the key out of the ignition and turned to me. "Are you really so eager to get rid of me?"

This time I fell silent. If the car had still been running, I would have kept fiddling with the dial on the radio.

"I don't want to go anywhere, okay?" he continued as he opened the car door. "I like it here, I like Beijing."

I got out of the car, slipping on my sunglasses and feeling puzzled. Not long ago Lan Yu had clearly told me he wanted to go to the United States for graduate school. So why was he saying this now? Perhaps he was hinting he would want to stay in Beijing only if the two of us could be together. Whatever was going on inside his head, he didn't want to share it with me.

"Man!" I said as I shut the car door behind me. "Dr. Shi was right. You really are paranoid!"

Lan Yu cast a conciliatory smile in my direction. This was normal for him. When one of our discussions hit a zone of discomfort, he would extend an olive branch by laughing it off or by saying something pleasant. Not always, but most of the time.

After lunch, I went to the office for the rest of the day. When I came home that night, my ears were greeted by the gentle rhythm of Chinese pop music. I was surprised, since Lan Yu had never been a fan of contemporary pop. He was more attuned to traditional folk music, especially the Chinese fiddle.

"Hey! I'm home!" I yelled.

Lan Yu didn't hear me, so I opened a bottle of wine and sat on the living-room couch, where I listened quietly as a couple of songs, both unfamiliar to me, drifted from his studio. I don't remember many of the lyrics from the first one. Something about telling my darling not to say goodbye, about whether a wind should blow or a rain should fall. But the second song I remember clearly:

> *No one loves you more than me.*
> *How can you bear to see my pain?*
> *When I needed you the most,*
> *You just silently walked away.*

Listening to the two songs, I couldn't help but wonder whose feelings they better described, mine or Lan Yu's.

I started spending less and less time at Tivoli in the weeks that followed. I told Lan Yu that I was staying at my mother's house, but the truth was I was almost always at Ephemeros with Lin Ping. Pretty soon, however, I found out Lan Yu wasn't sleeping at Tivoli every night, either. Unless we made specific arrangements to spend the night together, he usually slept in his dormitory. Sometimes I wondered if there was anywhere else he was sleeping, too.

Although I had already asked Lin Ping to marry me, we hadn't set the date yet and I hadn't begun even the most basic preparations. Consciously or otherwise, I was stalling for time. I wanted to resolve things with Lan Yu before moving on.

One August evening, we went to a Korean restaurant called Arirang. Lan Yu had heard about it from a Korean architect friend and had been wanting to try it. I liked it fine, but didn't see what the big deal was since most of the food was pretty similar to Chinese cuisine: rice, noodles, meat, and vegetables. As we were eating, I asked Lan Yu if he wanted to hang out with some of my friends later that night.

"Not really," he replied offhandedly. In a period of great uncertainty in our relationship, one thing was for sure: Lan Yu was no longer the docile, compliant guy he had been when we first met.

I gave a shrewd smile. "Believe me," I said, lowering my voice. "You'll have a good time. They're like us."

He looked puzzled by this remark. "What do you mean, *like us*?"

"I mean, they mess around with this kind of stuff, too," I said with a mischievous grin.

Lan Yu looked at me in confusion. The confusion quickly turned to anger.

"You have got to be kidding me!" he said, raising his voice. "So you've 'messed around' long enough, huh? Is that it?" The group of Korean exchange students at the table next to us turned to look. I don't know whether they understood Chinese, but our voices were more than loud enough to catch their attention.

"You want to pawn me off to someone else before your wedding!" Lan Yu continued, fuming with anger. I had no idea what he was going on about.

"You want us to go hang out with Yonghong, don't you?" he continued. "You fucking piece of shit! Fuck you!" Lan Yu stood up from the table and stormed out. I ran out behind him, but was unable to stop him from getting in the car, which was parked on the street outside. All I could do was open the door on the driver's side and grab him with all my might.

"Don't touch me! Take a fucking cab!" he shouted.

"You can't drive like this!" I yelled. "You're going to crash!" Lan Yu didn't listen. He threw my hand off his arm, shut the door, and started the engine.

"Stop, Lan Yu, please!" I screamed, opening the door and grabbing his shoulder again. "You want to get yourself killed?"

Lan Yu stepped on the accelerator and the car lunged forward, taking me with it. "Okay! I'm a bastard!" My voice quivered and my eyes filled with tears. "I'm a no-good piece of shit, okay? Now stop the car! I'm not going to let you do something reckless!"

Lan Yu stepped on the brakes abruptly. The night air was silent and I heard the unsteady, almost violent sound of his breathing. He gripped the steering wheel in front of him and his head hung low. Soon, the uneven sound of his breath was replaced by soft, choking sobs. He was unable to hold back the tears. I squatted next to the open car door and rested my hand on his leg.

"That's not what I was trying to do, Lan Yu!" I said, looking at him in desperation. "I would never do that. I just wanted to introduce you to some people who—I mean, just some people who are a part of this circle. I just wanted to make you feel better . . ." I, too, was nearly sobbing at this point, but reached up to wipe away his tears. I was desperate to make him understand. Near the entrance to the Korean restaurant, two employees stood in silent amusement, watching the spectacle. I didn't care what they thought. Standing up, I gently nudged Lan Yu, signaling for him to move to the passenger side. When he did, I got in the driver seat and slowly drove us back to Tivoli.

Neither of us said a word on the way home. After I parked and we went inside, I sat on the couch. Lan Yu immediately headed toward the staircase—most likely, I thought, to go to his work studio, the only place in the house he wanted to be lately. I wanted to talk before he vanished into the other room. I didn't want us going to bed without patching things up, at least to the extent possible under the circumstances.

"Lan Yu, hey," I said. He stopped, midstep, and turned around to look at me from the staircase.

"Will you come sit with me for a while?"

He hesitated, but came back downstairs and sat on the sofa opposite me.

"Will you sit next to me?" I wanted him closer. He moved next to me and I put my arm around him. He didn't stop me, but the stiffness of his body told me he wasn't eager to be touched, either.

"Have you been assigned a job yet?" I asked. He had already graduated, but it had been ages since I'd asked him anything about what was going on in his life.

"I've been working for a few months now, Handong," he said coldly.

"Oh, really?" I asked in surprise. "Why didn't you tell me? Which work unit is it?" I had been so preoccupied by my ambitions of becoming a mighty official—not to mention by my relationship with Lin Ping—that I had shown practically no interest in him for months.

"City Construction Number Nine," he said mechanically. "City Nine. It's a construction company. Most of the workers are demobilized soldiers who've been transferred to civilian work."

I knew he couldn't have been happy with this job. During most of his final year at Huada, he had been saying he hoped to be hired at the Institute of Design. He had also told me on a number of occasions that he hoped to attend graduate school in the United States, but anytime I myself raised the subject he became quiet and sullen.

"If you don't like City Nine, you should go work at a foreign enterprise. A friend of mine manages the China division of a construction company. I can contact him."

"I already signed a five-year contract."

"So what? Give them a little cash and they'll let you go."

He scoffed. "You really have a lot of faith in money, don't you?" I didn't want to talk about it, so I changed the subject.

"Hey, did you know there's a place in Beijing called One Two Three? A lot of people like us go there. You know, just *regular* people," I said, intentionally stressing the word *regular*. One Two Three was one of the first gay venues to pop up in the capital.

Lan Yu looked at me in surprise when I told him about the bar. "Why haven't you ever mentioned it?" he asked.

"I don't know . . . I didn't think you'd like it," I said, though this wasn't entirely true. I didn't want him to know the real reason I had never told him about it. The mere thought of him being surrounded by men he might find attractive was enough to make me feel as though my heart had been ripped from my chest.

"And here I've been thinking this whole time that you and I were the only two people in Beijing who were like this!" he managed a laugh.

"No, there's a lot," I said, pulling him into my arms. "But you have to make an effort to find that world or else you would never know about it. I rarely go to those kinds of places. You get a lot of different kinds of people there, some decent guys, some garbage. You have to be careful." Lan Yu lay in my arms, quietly listening.

"I also heard there's a park and some public restrooms where guys go to fool around," I continued. "I've never been there, and don't you go either! It's really dangerous. I've heard some people have even been arrested." Lan Yu nested deeper into my arms.

Out of the blue I remembered something. "Right," I said. "I've transferred ownership of the house and the Lexus. They're yours now. If you don't want the house, sell it. Use the money to start a business or something. Everyone else is going into business these days, so why not you?"

I was accustomed to Lan Yu's silence, but at that moment he was even more quiet than usual. I felt I needed to keep speaking, if for no other reason than to kill the silence.

"You need to drive more carefully," I continued, for lack of anything better to say. "I mean, the state you were in tonight—don't ever drive like that! Life is too precious."

Lan Yu stood up from the couch and looked down at me coldly. "You're very considerate when dumping your lovers," he said bitterly. "Any other instructions?" Without waiting for me to reply, he turned around and went upstairs. "I'm taking a shower and going to bed," he said, then disappeared at the top of the staircase.

That night Lan Yu and I had sex as always, but he was distant, mechanical. When I looked into his face I saw nothing. His eyes were empty. It was as if he had seen me so many times that he was numb to what he was looking at.

"Turn around," I said, slapping his butt. "I wanna do it that way." *That way*, he knew, meant I wanted to fuck him.

He got on his belly and stuck up his ass. "You'll have to pay extra for that, sir," he said coldly. I can't describe how my heart deflated when I heard this. Not to mention my dick.

I looked at Lan Yu's ass perched up high in the air, his face buried in the pillow. I desperately desired to tell him something: *I want you*. But I was too ashamed to say it. How could I when I had just told him I would be getting married? Yes, I wanted to be with him, but there were also times when I felt a kind of hatred for him. And yet, I knew, this was a completely unreasonable impulse on my part: How could I hate him when he had done nothing wrong?

Still feeling hurt by Lan Yu's comment, I turned off the light and lay down to go to sleep. He lay next to me quietly, but there was something about his breath—tense, uneven—that told me he had something on his mind. Suddenly and without warning, he crawled on top of me, kissing my lips, my cheeks, my eyes, searching in the darkness for whatever part of me he could find.

"Please don't be mad, Handong!" he said. "You can do it that way. You can do it any way that you want. I didn't mean what I said."

He couldn't see me in the darkness, but he could touch me, so I turned my head away from him so he couldn't feel the tears as they streamed down my cheeks.

Nineteen

In accordance with my mother's wishes, Lin Ping and I set our wedding date for National Day, the holiday commemorating the founding of the People's Republic of China in 1949. The event was to take place on October 1, 1991, a little more than four years after the day I had met Lan Yu.

I was vehemently opposed to the date. It was too soon and I wasn't adequately prepared. It didn't matter that I had done just about everything I could to get ready. First, I bought a huge apartment at Movement Village, a residential complex in central Beijing, and renovated the spacious, five-room unit to be my and Lin Ping's marital home. When the apartment was ready I took Lin Ping to Hong Kong, where I bought her a two-carat diamond ring, dozens of outfits, and a mountainous hoard of cosmetics, accessories, and other assorted junk. And yet, despite all this, I still didn't feel prepared.

Lan Yu and I had essentially moved out of Tivoli, which now sat vacant in the Northern Suburbs and was little more than a place for us to meet up two or three times a week. He had moved into the employee dormitory provided by

City Nine. He said he liked it because it was right next door to work. I went to Tivoli even less than he did and floated between Ephemeros and Country Brothers, usually with Lin Ping in tow. My fiancée didn't move in with me, but she slept in my bed almost every night and always accompanied me to the many social functions I attended with professional contacts. Everybody knew I was engaged to be married. I basked in the attention.

One evening when Lan Yu and I had a dinner date, I made the mistake of asking him to meet me at Ephemeros. When he rang my apartment door, I stepped into the hallway and led him straight back downstairs without even inviting him inside. But just as the elevator doors opened at the ground floor, in walked Lin Ping through the narrow corridor leading from the outside into the building. She had her own key by then, but almost always told me when she'd be coming over. It was an awkward moment for all of us, but especially for Lan Yu, who knew exactly whom he was looking at. What Lin Ping thought, I couldn't be entirely sure. Fortunately, both of my lovers kept their cool, much more, in fact, than I did. Without skipping a beat, each said something like, "All right, Chen Handong, just stopping by to say hi. See you later!" then exited the building before walking off hastily in opposite directions.

Neither of them said anything about the incident afterward, but they were smart people who could figure things out on their own. That's when things started going bad.

It began when Lin Ping told me her boss had given her an opportunity to go to the United States for a three-month-long advanced-interpretation training program. She wanted to go. When I objected on the grounds that she and I were about to get married—on National Day, I added—she told me we would just have to postpone the wedding. Her sudden lack of enthusiasm made me realize she had probably figured out more from the chance encounter with Lan Yu than she'd let on. Game over. I'd fucked up.

The following morning, things went from bad to worse when Liu Zheng walked into my office and told me my mother had called him the night before. She wanted information about a man named Lan Yu.

"What?" I asked in a panic. "How does she know about him?"

"I have no idea," he said. "But she seems to know a lot about what's going on."

"Did you tell her?"

"I didn't tell her, but I didn't make up a bunch of stories, either. I can't look our Ma in the eye and lie, Handong."

"And you call yourself a friend?" I was pissed.

Liu Zheng threw his hands up in the air. "You can't keep hiding this, Handong. If you don't end things with this guy, if you keep putting things off with Lin Ping, obviously the old woman's going to find out sooner or later!"

"Does Lin Ping know, too?" I asked in sudden alarm.

"I can't say for sure, but I think she does."

"Fuck!" I slammed my pen on my desk, gripped by helplessness.

Before the clock struck ten the following morning, my mother called to tell me to come home. The moment I entered the house and saw her puffy red eyes and the miserable look on her face, I became riddled with guilt.

"How can you be so disgraceful, Little Dong?" she said, standing up from her chair and looking at me with eyes of fury. "What kind of a man are you?" She cried as she spoke. This was the first time she had ever spoken to me in this way.

"Where on earth did you get this crazy idea, Ma?" I asked. "There is absolutely no truth to this! Someone out there is spreading lies about me."

"Hiding this for so many years . . . ," she continued, gripping the arm of her chair and sitting down slowly. "Thank heavens your father is dead. If he knew about this, it would be worse than death." Her gentle tears turned into heavy sobs. She wasn't listening to a word I said.

"From the moment I knew I was pregnant with you," she continued, "I never wanted anything bad to happen to you. When you were little, I knew the other kids at school bullied you. I used to get so mad I would go to your school and argue with your teachers about it. Then you got older, and every day you were more and more a decent young man. You were so good in school. I was so proud! Do you know how proud I was?"

She was crying so hard at that point she could barely get the words out. I didn't show it, but in my heart I wasn't doing much better than she was. The sorrow I felt was unbearable.

"You always did so well in school," she resumed with great ardor. "Then you started doing business, and now you've even become an official—director of City Commerce! You've grown up and gained everyone's respect—you know how happy that's made us? But now, Handong, to look at you and know you've done this disgusting thing . . . If people found out, how would you look them in the eye? Huh? How?"

I looked at the floor. I knew she wasn't done yet.

"When you have a pet, you can't bear to see it get hurt. But when a mother sees her own son looked down on by other people, rejected by the world around him, isn't that worse than death? Isn't it, Handong? I'm just so afraid of what's going to happen . . ." She put her head in her hands and cried softly.

It was excruciating for me to see her like this. Whatever

else I might have been, I was still a man and a son, and seeing my own mother so grieved that she desired her own death was more than I could take. When I looked at her red, swollen eyes, nothing else mattered—neither Lan Yu, nor his love for me, nor my own emotional needs. My eyes burned with tears I struggled to fight back. I needed to clean this up. Fast.

"Listen, Ma. You've misunderstood! What you don't know is that this kind of thing is a big trend for rich people," I chuckled, trying my best to sound calm. "I mean, some people actually compete with one another to see who can have the most fun! But nobody takes it seriously. You just get a guy and go do stuff. Just go hang out at places." I paused like an idiot, unsure of what to say next. I was determined to convince her.

"Anyway, I'm over it now, so it doesn't even matter," I continued. "I'm into horse racing now. I mean, it's kind of the same thing. It's just a hobby."

It took a while, but I eventually managed to convince her. Before long, the tears stopped rolling down her cheeks and she looked at me attentively. I saw my chance to bring it home.

"Actually," I continued with scholarly authority, "ever since the ancients, China has had what they call the 'Southern Style.' Haven't you heard of it? I mean, rich people have just always done that, Ma! You remember Cai Ming? Sometimes he gets into this, too. You just have dinner, conversation, stuff like that—and that's it. There's nothing else going on." Whatever it took to make her feel better.

Eventually, my mother swallowed the story that my relationship with Lan Yu was strictly platonic. I told her Lin Ping and I would be getting married the following month, and at last her tears were replaced with a smile.

I didn't know it at the time, but Lin Ping knew everything about Lan Yu. And she did a good job hiding it.

I began giving serious consideration to how I was going to confront Lan Yu and finally end our relationship once and for all. It had nothing to do with Lin Ping, nor was it entirely for my mother. It was mostly for myself.

I knew I couldn't do with Lan Yu what I had always done with guys in the past: keep them as fuck buddies. Leaving things at the purely physical level would have been impossible, in part because he wouldn't go along with it, but also because each time I saw him I would be drawn anew into the turbulent waters of emotional entanglement. Keeping things as they were but just seeing less of him wasn't the solution either, since the greater the distance between us, the more powerful my longing. My break with Lan Yu had to be permanent, absolute.

The radio weather forecast reported it was going to be windy with low temperatures all night. Sure enough, howling winds beat against the bedroom window, keeping me awake until the early hours of the morning. By the time the sun came up, the wind from the night before had blown away the clouds, leaving clear, bright sunshine in their place. The leaves had been blown off the trees, leaving a kind of desolate beauty in their wake.

It was one of those rare mornings when Lan Yu and I awoke in the same bed. We were at Tivoli. He had told me the previous night that he was looking forward to sleeping in late because he didn't have to be at work until eleven. I woke up before him and got out of bed to look out the window at the beautiful fall scenery. Then I turned back toward the bed to look at Lan Yu, who was still asleep on his stomach. He loved that position. Right cheek pushed up against the bed-sheet-covered mattress, a tiny pool of spit quivered in the lower corner of his mouth. He rolled onto his back, using his foot to push the blanket down to the base of the bed, and I noticed that the underwear he'd put on before going to sleep had somehow disappeared. He was naked now except for the calm serenity that enveloped him after the untamed frenzy of our lovemaking the night before. For a long time I stood there by the window, scrutinizing him and wondering if I was really going to do what I thought I was going to do. Quietly I stepped across the floor back to the side of the bed and gently pulled the blanket up to his chin.

Thoughts raced through my mind as I looked down at him. Did I really want nothing more from him than his body? Was I with him for no other reason than to satisfy my sexual desires? If I ended our relationship, would I be losing anything? I squatted beside the bed and gazed at Lan Yu's angelic face. He woke up.

When he saw me next to him, he gave me a seductive smile. He thought I wanted to have morning sex. How can you be so clueless? I thought. He had no idea what I was about to do.

"Put some clothes on," I said, striding out of the bedroom. I didn't want to break up with him when he was in the nude.

Lan Yu got up, washed his face, and threw on some clothes, then he came into the kitchen to get something to eat.

By now Tivoli had the appearance of an hourly motel, and a cheap one at that. The refrigerator hadn't been touched for months and was completely empty except for a box of crackers and a few cans of soda. Lan Yu had never been especially picky when it came to food, and I was unfazed when he made breakfast out of a dozen crackers and a can of soda. The only thing on my mind at that moment was where to begin.

"I've done you wrong, Lan Yu. I never should have led you down this path. But I'm not going to hurt you anymore." The words sprayed out of my mouth like vomit. I was utterly lacking in shame.

"What are you talking about?" he mumbled, mouth full of crackers.

"I know you've always hated me," I continued. "It's my own fault for doing this to you."

"Seriously, what are you talking about?" he repeated. "I've never hated you." He was usually so sharp. Why was he so slow-witted today?

"Don't lie to me, Lan Yu. It's obvious. You don't listen to me anymore. You don't care about me anymore." Apparently it wasn't enough just to break up with him. I also had to find some lofty excuse for it.

"How can you say I don't listen to you?" he replied, visibly getting upset. "First you wanted me to go into therapy, so I went into therapy. Then you wanted to see less of me, so we're seeing less of each other. Now you want me to date other guys, so I'm trying that, too."

I was blown away. I couldn't believe he was reacting this way.

"But this is for your own good!" I protested. "You need to understand that, Lan Yu." That's when the conversation escalated to a fight.

"Bullshit!" he said, slamming the refrigerator door shut. "You just want to end things because of that whore."

That pissed me off. I wasn't going to let him disrespect me. "Who's a whore?" I shouted. "You're a whore! A little fucking boy whore!"

Lan Yu stood up from the table and walked toward the front door.

I grabbed his arm as he walked past me. "Where do you think you're going?"

"Don't touch me!" He tried to pry my hand off his arm, but I clenched my fist tighter.

"I'm not done yet!" I said, standing up.

"You want to end this for good, Handong? Fine. There are plenty of other guys out there. I figured that out long ago. Don't worry—I won't bother you again!"

I would never have imagined he would react this way!

I let go of Lan Yu's arm, then walked into the living room and sat on the couch. I couldn't remember the last time I'd been so upset. Reaching for the cigarettes on the table next to me, my hand shook so violently I had to use my other hand to steady it.

Lan Yu sat down on the other end of the couch, as far away from me as possible. We both stared straight ahead.

"I don't live in a vacuum, okay?" I said, still avoiding eye contact. "There are things in my life I can't just ignore. I have a career, I have my mother. I have to face up to these things, Lan Yu. I'm just afraid that if you and I are together—" I faltered, unsure of what I was trying to say. Lan Yu stared at the floor in silence.

"Look," I continued. "I'm not going to let you destroy me, okay? I'm not a homosexual. I need to have a normal life."

Lan Yu's reaction to this surprised me. Without even turning to look at me, he reached across the space between us and took my hand. After a few moments we turned to face each other, and for a split second I even saw gentleness in his eyes.

"I knew it would end like this eventually," he said, squeezing my hand. "I've been waiting for this day to come for a long time. I still remember what you told me when we met: 'No strings,' you said; it would be 'embarrassing' for two men to stay together. And now, just as predicted, you're getting married. Who knows? Maybe I'll get married too."

The anguish on Lan Yu's face then was so deep he may as well have had the word itself carved on his forehead. He looked at me with tears in his eyes, but it was I who broke down first. I turned my head in the other direction and started crying—just like a woman, right in front of him.

"Handong, don't . . . ," he said, choking with sobs. "It's not a big deal, really."

What was wrong with me? Here I was dumping him, and he was the one consoling me! I disgusted even myself.

In the end, I suppose we both needed to retain an ounce of male dignity because we ended up parting with a smile. Just before saying goodbye, Lan Yu lay in my arms and listened to me as I spoke, just as he always had.

"Now that you've graduated, you have to learn to take care of yourself. If you get sick, go to the doctor, especially if you have a fever."

He squeezed my forearm, which was draped around his chest. I took it to mean *okay*.

"If you meet someone new, you have to be careful. I don't want to hear through the grapevine that you've caught some kind of disease!"

He clutched my forearm tighter.

"Even though we've agreed that we're not staying in touch, if you ever have a true emergency, come find me. Is that clear?"

He nodded.

Lan Yu asked me to leave first. It was better for me that way, too. Easier, somehow. I got up and started moving toward the front door, but slowed down as I got closer to it. Just as I was about to turn the doorknob, I turned to look at Lan Yu one last time. There he sat on the arm of the couch. He looked back at me, his face strange and unfamiliar, a tiny smile on his lips, but one that was forlorn, gutted. This is the last time I'll cross the threshold of this villa, I thought to myself, the last time I'll stand inside the house that Lan Yu and I had called home. Twisting the doorknob, I wanted to turn around and look at him one more time, but couldn't. I opened the door and stepped out, the image of Lan Yu's strange smile etched in my mind.

And that was how we broke up, as Lan Yu put it, for good.

Twenty

The heartache of losing Lan Yu was unlike any-thing I had ever known. However great the sorrow, though, reason told me that going back was not an option. I had played with fire long enough.

Were it not for my impending marriage to Lin Ping, I prob-ably would have wallowed in self-pity forever. Fortunately, the wedding itself helped assuage the pain of breaking up. It took place in the imposing and stately ballroom of the Grand Capital Hotel. Festive, dignified, and extravagant, it was every-thing a wedding should be. Seeing my mother's face brim over with happy, wrinkly smiles gave me a kind of satisfaction I had never experienced before.

Everybody knows that the best part of a wedding is the after-party. When the formal banquet was over and all the other guests had gone home, Lin Ping and I stuck around with our closest pals to laugh, drink, and have fun late into the night. Dutifully we performed all the traditional amusements a new husband and wife were expected to, including an array of mild humiliations imposed on us by our friends. First, we had to go from table to table, begging our guests to accept a toast even though we knew full well they would refuse until we answered an embarrassing question or performed some wild stunt. Next, we had to hold our hands behind our backs and try to gobble pieces of fruit and candy they dangled from strings in the air. Then, we were goaded into telling the whole story of how we met, went on our first date, and fell in love. And finally, they made us sing a traditional wedding song—"The New Couple Goes Home"—which, by the end of the night, had been turned by drunken party revelers into "The New Bed Gets Rode." I was in great spirits all night, not—or not only—because I had Lin Ping, but more importantly because I had finally gained something I had desperately longed for: the unconditional blessings of friends and family.

Legally speaking, the nuptial arrangement with Lin Ping was my first, but the truth is I was no stranger to married life. Lan Yu and I had no legal ties, but we had lived together just like any husband and wife. The life we shared was routine, even dull at times, but always fulfilling.

The day after the wedding, Lin Ping announced she wanted to quit her job as an interpreter. Work was irregular and didn't pay well, she complained. This didn't come as a surprise, since she had ended up rejecting her employer's offer for the three-month training in the United States. More vexing was her brilliant new idea of coming to work at my company. I was totally against the idea—hated it, in fact—but eventually caved in to her endless imploring and asked Liu Zheng to make the arrangements.

Lin Ping's decision to quit her job wasn't the only surprise that popped up after the wedding. Soon after moving into the apartment at Movement Village, I began to feel I was getting to know a completely different person. Everything, from the

207

food we ate to the household appliances, was a target for her fussiness. She insisted on nothing but designer products, and even the toilet paper she wiped her ass with had to be the most expensive on the shelf. In her assessment, "so-called Chinese designer brands" were garbage, and products from Hong Kong weren't much better. Only Japanese imports and things you would find in the department stores of New York's Fifth Avenue would satisfy her. Only things like that were truly "high end."

Nearly every day she went to the beauty salons of major hotels to get facials, manicures, and other treatments. Less than two weeks after the wedding, she hired a live-in maid because she didn't want her long, slender fingers and perfect nails to be marred by housework. I just stood on the sidelines, watching in amazement as she returned each day from her shopping trips. I wasn't bothered by her reckless spending habits per se. It's just that I couldn't comprehend how a typical girl from a poor family, someone who had once been a student and an ordinary worker, could burn through that much cash in such a short amount of time.

Nothing satisfied her. She wasn't happy with the Honda I'd bought her because she wanted a Mercedes-Benz. She didn't like the apartment we lived in and spoke incessantly of buying a house in the Northern Suburbs, an idea I vetoed again and again because, I said, I wanted to be closer to the city center. That was true, but an equally important reason was that I didn't want my marital home to be anywhere near Tivoli.

Despite Lin Ping's many shortcomings, however, the good always outweighed the bad. Every time she saddled me with a new demand, she would always turn around and do something so sweet, so loving, that it was impossible not to wrap my arms around her and forgive her for being such a pain in the ass.

One night after we'd had sex, she crawled into my arms, where I held her against my chest just like I had held Lan Yu a thousand times before. I looked into her dancing, whirling eyes and smiled.

"You know what you are?" I asked playfully. "You're a shrewd little she-wolf!"

Lin Ping laughed. "What does that make you, then?"

I closed my eyes and raised a single finger in the air as if about to say something important and philosophical. "I am the big, dumb sheep whose flesh the she-wolf has bitten!"

"Ha! Is that right?" she said, pinching my nose between her fingers. "Well, I'll tell you what you *really* are. What you really are is a *bad, bad* boy! A smart, romantic, and loving man—but also a sneaky and cunning *plaaaaaaayboy*!"

Oh dear, I thought. Where was this going?

"But that's fine with me," she continued, "because you're all mine now!"

Lin Ping squealed in my arms, looking wildly pleased with herself. Was she delighted by her own witty banter or by the fact that she had managed to snag me? Either way, we both knew her perception of me as a "playboy" wasn't entirely wrong.

Married life passed by quickly, and before long it had been six months since Lan Yu and I had broken up. Just as we had agreed, we had no contact with each another. But every time my cell phone rang, I wondered—with hope or fear, I wasn't sure—whether it was him. When we broke up, I was more than a little surprised by the calm, rational indifference he displayed. He was much more resolute than I had expected. At the same time, however, it was precisely his cold and tempered rationality that dissipated some of my worry over the breakup. It made me have faith that he was going to be all right.

I did everything I could to stop thinking about him and the private, intensely emotional world we once shared. And yet, every time I had sex with my wife, I thought only of him. My hands caressed her soft white skin, her thick, heavy thighs and breasts. She was so gorgeous, so loving, but none of her beauty provoked my desire, and when I closed my eyes, it was Lan Yu I saw. There were times when I almost managed to trick myself into believing it was him I was touching: dark and firm, a radiant sheath covering a strong back and two broad shoulders. Only then would I slowly start to get hard.

There were some things I wouldn't let myself think about: the touch of my tongue against his neck, the euphoric excitement he showed when I kissed him. These thoughts were off limits, outside the scope of the fantasy world I allowed myself to create during sex with my wife. I couldn't do those things with Lin Ping, and trying them would have caused nothing but disappointment and grief. She wasn't Lan Yu. She would never be Lan Yu.

I forced myself to have sex with her, but it was nearly impossible for me to come. Each time, I had to close my eyes and think about having sex with Lan Yu or, sometimes, with other men I had seen on the street that day, usually with Lin Ping on my arm. Only then was I able to climax. Pretty soon I started asking Lin Ping to let me fuck her on her hands and knees like I used to fuck Hao Mei. It worked at first, but in time even that wasn't enough. More and more, I found myself jerking off when she wasn't around, fantasizing about the men I wanted to be with. Finally, nine months after my wedding day,

I submitted to my relentless desire and hooked up with a guy. I had only met him a few times before we slept together. He was in his midtwenties and had been introduced to me by a friend in common. My memory of him is vague because we only had sex a handful of times, but I still remember his eyes, which radiated with intelligence. Sex with him was mind-blowingly good, in part, no doubt, because it had been so long since I'd been with a man.

The first time we had sex, I kept repeating something under my breath as I writhed on top of him, fucking him harder and harder while running my hands along his back. Lying in bed after we both came, he laughed and asked me if I had an ex-boyfriend named Lan Yu.

I knew it was only a matter of time before I broke down and contacted him. I had no real agenda, or so I told myself at the time. I just wanted to know how he was doing. I agonized for hours in my office before finally picking up the phone. I tried his cell first, but it was disconnected. Then I called Tivoli, but the phone just rang and rang. I had no choice but to call him at work. A woman answered the phone.

"City Nine!"

"May I speak with Lan Yu?"

"Who's calling?"

"A friend from college." I wasn't in the mood for an interrogation.

"He doesn't work here anymore," she said, as disinterested in the conversation as I was annoyed.

"What? Has he been transferred somewhere?" I asked, startled.

"He got fired."

"Why?"

"How the heck should I know!" she barked before slamming down the receiver.

When I got home that night I kept calling Tivoli, but no one answered. I called every five minutes until one in the morning, and still nothing.

The next day I asked Liu Zheng to go to China Telecom to see whether there had been any activity on either Lan Yu's cell phone or the landline at Tivoli. He could do that because both lines were paid for by the company. When he came back to the office he reported that neither number had been in use for over six months.

For the rest of the day I sat in my office agonizing over what to do. I recalled the strange smile Lan Yu had given me the day we said goodbye. Horrible scenarios flashed through my mind. Could he have done something stupid?

The following day I confessed to Liu Zheng that I was worried.

"Why don't I go over to City Nine and see if I can find out what happened?" he asked. Liu Zheng was a good friend, always eager to help.

"I'll go with you," I said, preparing for the worst.

Armed with a bogus letter of introduction requesting information for employment purposes, Liu Zheng and I showed up at the administrative offices of City Construction Number Nine. There we talked to two guys—a chubby, baby-faced security guard and a middle-aged cadre from human resources.

"So, here's the deal," began the cadre. He was in his midforties, short and muscular with an angular flattop and bulky military clothes. "Around five months ago, the company received a fax that brought to light certain . . . um . . . inappropriate activities. Bottom line: he was engaging in hooliganism."

I braced myself for whatever he was going to say next. But before he could continue, the younger, fat-faced security guard jumped in.

"Oh man!" he exclaimed, practically jumping up and down in his seat with excitement. "He seemed like a real good kid when he got here. A Huada graduate—real distinguished. Who would've guessed he was doing that!"

"Doing what?" I asked.

"Doing that kind of stuff!" the guard replied. He was a little slow.

"Male prostitution," the cadre said matter-of-factly. "He was a male prostitute."

Liu Zheng must have sensed I was about to fly off the handle when I heard this because he wisely intervened. "Can we take a look at the fax?" he asked calmly.

"Why, I believe I have it right here," the guard said as he reached into the drawer of the tiny wooden desk where he was seated. He pulled out a beige envelope, very nearly knocking over a glass jar full of tea leaves and hot water in the process. He was enjoying the excitement a little more than I cared for, but at least he was cooperating.

The message on the fax was computer generated, not hand-written as I had expected. It was almost completely faded, and all I could see were clusters of words punctuated with little black smudges: *Mr. Lan Yu . . . City Nine . . . public indecency . . . loitering in hotel lobbies . . . money . . . sexual services for men.* My head swam with words and I became vaguely aware of a lump in my throat. It grew bigger and bigger until I thought I was going to puke.

Finally, the beefy cadre with the flattop broke the silence.

"This stuff may not be true, you know. The kid never admitted to it, and frankly, it's hard to know what's what when you only have a fax."

"But when you look at the way he dressed and stuff," the security guard jumped in, "you gotta wonder where a guy like that—I mean, straight out of university and all—gets that kind of cash. You should have seen his watch! I heard it was real expensive."

I knew exactly the watch he was talking about. It was the Rolex I'd bought him when I was in London.

"So you guys fired him," Liu Zheng said flatly.

"We didn't fire him," said the cadre. "We let him resign. He wanted to. Fuck!" He gave an incredulous laugh. "Just think—a kid like that? A college kid, early twenties, going down that road? He was good at his job, too, hardworking and conscientious. He got along with everyone here. I'll tell you one thing: he may have been doing that kind of stuff off duty, but he never did it here." The cadre crossed his arms and looked at Liu Zheng and me righteously.

"If you guys want to hire him," he continued, "I guess I'd say give it a shot. After all, he is a graduate of a good university. But watch out for AIDS!"

"He has AIDS?" Liu Zheng and I exclaimed in unison.

"Everyone like him has AIDS," the cadre said cooly. "Our company doctor said so."

My head was a mess. My stomach was upset and I really did think I was going to vomit. Liu Zheng and I thanked the two guys and walked out.

"Whoever sent that fax is a real fucker!" Liu Zheng fumed as soon as we got outside. "It's not right!"

"Where could he have gone?" I asked in distress.

"He must have found another job," Liu Zheng replied.

"In any case, he wouldn't have left the construction industry, right?"

I was deeply alarmed by Lan Yu's disappearance. If he wasn't living at Tivoli, where was he? If he had encountered some hardship, why hadn't he come to me?

At the same time, though, the fax had been sent right around the time of my wedding. For all I know, he did try contacting me but had trouble getting in touch. My fear was that the hardship of breaking up would have been exacerbated by the humiliation of the fax, resulting in more pressure than he could bear. I hoped he hadn't done anything rash. I went home to Movement Village, and the questions churned in my head. My stomachache worsened, but I did my best to ignore it.

Lan Yu wasn't the only one that I wanted to find. I also had every intention of hunting down the person who had sent the fax.

But there was nothing I could do. No one in the gay circle knew Lan Yu, and the construction industry net was far too wide to search for him there. For the first time in my life, I felt overwhelmed by the sheer size of the capital. I didn't even have a phone number for his family, though I did have an address, so I took the extreme step of asking Liu Zheng to fly to far-off Xinjiang Province and seek out Lan Yu's father. When Liu Zheng called the following day, he told me that Lan Yu's dad hadn't spoken to his son in almost a year. Lan Yu, it seemed, had truly disappeared.

It's hard to describe the emotional state I was in during that period of time. In some respects, Lan Yu's disappearance wasn't as hard on me as our breakup, but that wasn't saying much. Wherever I went, an engulfing cloud of dread followed.

What I feared was not only the possibility that something had happened to Lan Yu but also the prospect of a lifetime of guilt for driving him to the desperate end I increasingly believed he had met. Up to that point in my life, I had always been a happy person. But those dark days saw me thrown into the deep hollows of depression.

Twenty-One

The demystification of married life was beginning to reveal more than just Lin Ping's single-minded attachment to luxury. I also learned she was a woman capable of climbing any social ladder put before her. Through me, she gained access to a world of powerful personages, including members of the Dai family, with whom she rapidly became closer than I had ever been. Each week she hiked with determination to their home for tea and conversation with Donald's wife Shu Mei, who I heard had an English name just as ambitious as her husband's. I didn't care what her name was. As Lin Ping's husband, I knew I would profit handsomely from my wife's budding friendship with them, for Donald would only be that much more likely to think of me when business opportunities arose. But even profit wasn't my main concern at that point. On most days what weighed heaviest on my mind was Lan Yu.

My wife's sudden appearance at my company—I had put her on as a human resource manager—radically limited my freedom. I hated it, but what was done was done and I was powerless to change the situation. Now that we were in an office environment together, the very qualities by which I had been so transfixed when we first met now appeared as little more than a veil of artifice. Routine contact regarding tedious work-related matters made her refined bearing and fashionable clothes lose their appeal. To make matters worse, our sex life was a travesty, at least as far as I was concerned.

One evening, Lin Ping and I were home watching television. "Did you hear that Wei Guo bought a villa in the Northern Suburbs?" she asked nonchalantly. "We should get one, too."

"Don't you like it here?" I asked, though I already knew the answer to the question. It was something we'd fought over repeatedly.

"What, *this* place?" she groaned. "Please, Handong! These apartment buildings are so common—public housing for the masses! Outside China, only poor people live in places like this."

"Well, the Northern Suburbs are too far from downtown," I said, trying to reason with her. "Besides, I hear there are always problems with the water and electricity being shut off out there."

"I suppose you would know," Lin Ping said evenly. "You already have a place there, don't you?" She looked up from the TV, a confrontational yet barely perceptible smile glued to her tightly clenched lips.

I had to think fast. "That's not mine," I said, the words coming out more defensively than I meant them to. I knew full well she was referring to Tivoli. "It's just a friend's house I was using for something." Man! I thought. How did she manage to find this stuff out?

Lin Ping didn't pursue her line of questioning, but just stared at me, utterly unable to comprehend why I had lied to her.

Another long, sweltering hot summer had passed. Each day I took walks outside to let the crisp fall air into my lungs. Autumn had always been my favorite season, and it was also Beijing's most beautiful time of year.

Lin Ping and I had only been married a year, but already I was beginning to wonder how long it was going to last. I was deeply conflicted. On the one hand, I couldn't deny that my wife was extremely good to me. Loving and considerate, she attended to each aspect of my daily life with unswerving devotion, even to the point of asking what I would be wearing each day. On the other hand, the relentless attention she poured on me could be suffocating. About this, however, there was nothing I could do. In addition to spending my money, meddling in my personal affairs was a marital right I couldn't deny her. Morality and law were on her side.

There were times I began to feel disgusted by Lin Ping, just as I had always ended up feeling disgusted by other women in the past. Things looked fine on the surface, but I knew we were living in two different worlds. Two people sleeping in the same bed, but cherishing entirely different dreams.

No matter how bad things got with Lin Ping, though, I couldn't bring myself to walk out on her. To begin with, her feelings for me hadn't changed so she was unlikely to agree to a divorce. But equally, if not more, important was the fact that she was very good to my mother.

My mother didn't want to live with us the way most parents of grown children did. She said she liked the freedom of living on her own. But nearly every weekend, Lin Ping dragged me to her house for a visit. To me this meant little more than the opportunity to indulge in excessive eating and sleeping for a couple of days. But Lin Ping would sit with my mother day and night, especially in the kitchen, where they would laugh and chat as if they had been mother and daughter by blood. It was moments like these that I understood and appreciated the joys of family life, even if I did little to directly participate. It was in moments like these that my marriage felt right.

Apart from the weekend visits, I sometimes went to my mother's house alone during the week just to escape the agonizing tedium of life with Lin Ping. One Thursday afternoon, I was sitting up in bed in my childhood room with a cup of tea. The warm afternoon sunshine filtered into the room as I pored over a thick stack of paperwork in my lap. I had just returned from a meeting at the Skysoar building that hadn't gone especially well. I thought I had been weak during negotiations. Now, reading the documents, I paused periodically to mentally kick myself in the butt over my performance.

The open bedroom door gave me an unobstructed view across the hallway straight into the dining room. I lifted my head from my paperwork and watched as my mother's short gray bob hovered over a thick wooden brush. She had registered for a senior-citizen art class and had fallen in love with traditional Chinese painting. Spread out across the dining-room table was an array of ink plates, brushes, and wide scrolls of paper.

"You and Lin Ping need to hurry up and have a baby!" she called out, apparently unaware that I was looking right at her. "What are you guys waiting for?"

"It's not that I don't want to!" I hollered from the bedroom. "It's that she's not doing it!"

"That's not what she told me," my mother replied, eyes still buried in her artwork. "She told me you're not trying!"

"Fine, believe her, then!" I returned to the data sheet in front of me. I didn't feel like talking about it. Lin Ping and I only had sex a few times a month at that point—and only when she was ovulating at that—but she still hadn't gotten pregnant.

"Have you guys been fighting?" I looked up and found her standing at the bedroom door, staring at me with a concerned look on her face. "I notice you've been coming over here a lot lately."

"We're fine," I said curtly.

"Okay, then!" she said, turning on her heel to return to her painting. A few minutes later she called out again. "By the way, did you hear Li Deshan's second daughter got a divorce?"

"I don't even know who that is, Ma," I said, getting up from bed, teacup in hand, and walking into the dining room. "But, hey, sounds good to me! You want me to get you a new daughter-in-law this weekend?"

Ma looked up in stern disapproval, but when she saw I was joking, she smiled. "Very funny," she said before growing serious again. "Listen, Little Dong. Lin Ping is good to you. She may not come from the best family, but she lets you get away with anything. I mean, when you were—you know, doing *that*—not only did she not cause a stink about it, she was actually really worried about you! That's why she came to talk to me about it. If she hadn't, you probably never would have come around!"

My heart pounded in my chest. "It was never anything to begin with," I said. "It was just the two of you making a big deal out of nothing."

"Well, we took care of it, didn't we?" she said, looking up at me with a knowing smile. "That little hooligan won't be bothering you again."

I nearly collapsed. Blood raced through my veins and my fingers clenched tightly around the cup in my hand.

"You're talking about the fax," I said, trying to stay calm.

"That was Lin Ping's idea!" my mother said. "If I had my

way, we would have gone and talked to that little hooligan face-to-face. I would have told him that if he ever spoke to you again, I was going to report him to the leadership where he worked."

I looked down at the cup in my hand and, with all my might, threw it against the wall. *Pow!* It exploded into pieces that fell to the floor. I grabbed my keys and stormed out the front door, ignoring the anguished sound of my mother's cries behind me.

Aimlessly, I drove through the city. It was already early evening when I arrived at One Two Three, where I had a few too many drinks before driving around aimlessly some more. Speeding through the desolate, almost rural outskirts of Beijing, I barely noticed the tall white birch trees as they bled into one another on the sides of the road. I looked at the sky and saw that the sun was setting. I changed the course of my direction and drove in the direction of the Northern Suburbs.

I hadn't been to Tivoli on a single occasion since getting married. Even when I figured out Lan Yu no longer lived there, I didn't have the guts to go inside. Besides, legally speaking, it wasn't even my property anymore. But I needed to see it. I needed to see the place where Lan Yu and I had lived in such happiness for so long.

The remote to the garage door was still in the glove compartment of my car. When Lan Yu and I had first moved into Tivoli, I designated the spot on the left for me, the one on the right for him. I pressed the button on the left and my side slowly rolled up and tucked itself inside the house. Then I pressed the button on the right. When I saw Lan Yu's white Lexus parked in the garage, a rush of adrenaline surged through me. Was he home? I jumped out of the car and rushed toward the door.

Entering the house, my nostrils were hit by a mild scent of mildew. It was the smell of a home lacking ventilation.

"Lan Yu!" I called out to the unsettling silence. The living room was just as neat and tidy as the day I'd left it, but a thin film of dust covered every inch of surface. On the table next to the couch sat the pack of cigarettes I had been smoking the day we broke up. Stepping into the kitchen, I suddenly remembered the can of soda Lan Yu had been drinking for breakfast. But now the kitchen table was empty, and it came as no surprise that he had cleared it before heading out to do whatever he did that day. When we were together, I rarely did any housekeeping and he managed most of the household affairs. He liked things to be very neat and tidy; everything had a proper place. I used to tease him for being so painstakingly clean, but he just laughed it off and said that was how people in his line of work were.

When I walked into the bedroom and saw the broad bed where we had made love so many times, my eyes filled with tears. I opened Lan Yu's closet, which was piled high with clothes. He and I were both particular about the clothes we wore—Lin Ping had wanted to pick out my clothes for me but I never let her—but Lan Yu had an additional layer of meticulousness. If he really loved an article of clothing, he would wear it again and again, barely taking it off long enough to wash it. And if he didn't like something, you couldn't pay him to wear it, however fancy or high-end it might have been.

I exited the bedroom and continued through the house, moving from room to room in an attempt to revisit each detail of the time when Lan Yu and I were together. His work studio, an ocean of books, papers, and blueprints, looked empty now. I looked at his cassette player—it doubled as a bookend—and recalled the time I came home one evening and heard those sad songs drifting softly into the living room. I left Lan Yu's

223

studio and made my way to the study. That, too, looked different somehow, though all the books were still in place. I rarely entered the study, but Lan Yu always spent a good amount of time there reading.

Nostalgically, I recalled one evening when Lan Yu had to make a phone call to another student in his program. The weightiness of the conversation struck me as comical, so I quietly snuck up behind him and yanked down his trousers. Flustered, he reached down to pull them back up with one hand while holding the phone in the other, all the while talking to his classmate and throwing annoyed looks in my direction. I thought the whole thing was hilarious, so I tried pulling off the rest of his clothes while kissing his neck and groping at his cock. At first, he tried pushing me off of him, but soon realized it was futile and gave in. There he stood in silent surrender as I gave him a blow job while he and his classmate debated the principle features of postmodern architecture.

After Lan Yu hung up the phone, he fell into a pretend fit of anger. Laughing and yelling, he threw me to the floor and covered me in kisses.

Tears welled up in my eyes. I couldn't go on with the memories.

As I was about to leave the study, I noticed a set of keys on the desk. These were the keys to Lan Yu's car. They were attached to a gold-plated key chain I had bought us on our trip to Hong Kong. For an additional thirty Hong Kong dollars, the jeweler had engraved two interlocking hearts with the letters *L & H* below them. I had long since lost mine, but Lan Yu not only kept his—he still used it. Until now.

The top drawer of the desk was half-open, so I pulled it open all the way and looked inside. All the house papers were there—property rights, insurance forms—as well as another set of keys, a cell phone, and a pager. Nervously, I fumbled through the drawer, certain I was going to find something—a letter, a note, anything from Lan Yu. Even, I thought with terror, a last goodbye to the world. But I found nothing.

I sat at the desk in despair, then went to the bedroom and lay on the bed. Muddled thoughts swirled in my exhausted mind:

Don't do this, Lan Yu . . . Please don't make me spend the rest of my life with this guilty conscience . . . Maybe I'm not some kind of noble and virtuous gentleman, but neither am I so cruel that the last vestiges of humanity have been wiped away from me . . . Come back, Lan Yu . . . Come back to me.

I must have fallen asleep, because the next thing I knew I was awakened by the brash sound of the telephone. It was Liu Zheng.

"Handong! Are you all right? Our Ma and Lin Ping have been looking everywhere for you! We've been going out of our minds with worry!"

I looked up at the ceiling and a wretched groan escaped my lungs. "Just tell them I'm not dead. Not yet, anyway." I closed my eyes and hung up the phone.

The following day I went back to my mother and wife as if nothing had happened. Trying to explain to them what Lan Yu meant to me was not an option. Nor could I point the finger at them for what they had done. All I could do was pretend, just as I'd always pretended. I even went so far as to tell my mother I'd thrown the cup, not because of the fax, but because I had been angry with Lin Ping about something.

I came down with a cold and fever in the weeks that followed. None of the medicine—first Chinese, then Western—that they heaped on me helped, and by the end of the month

I was convinced that whatever it was, it was going to be terminal. Lin Ping nursed me with a kind of stoic patience, and we both took great pains to avoid any fights.

One evening, my mother asked me if I knew a boy named Lan Yu and whether I owned a house in the Northern Suburbs. I told her she may as well stop questioning me because I probably wasn't going to live much longer anyway. This stunned the poor old woman into silence.

My cold persisted for two full months before finally going away. When it did, I started proceedings for a divorce.

Twenty-Two

"Lin Ping, let's just end this. This marriage is leaving us with too much suffering. We need to get a divorce." I was resolved to be as honest and straightforward as I possibly could.

"Has it really come to this, Handong?" she asked, tears welling up in her eyes. "Did I do something wrong? Have I treated you badly?"

"I just don't think we're happy together."

"But that's not true!" Lin Ping cried in distress. "I know exactly what's going on. You're just sick of me! But Handong, we've only been married a little over a year!" She looked at me pleadingly.

"Lin Ping, whatever you might think about it, we have to. We just have to." My resolve was firm and it showed in my words.

"You and I are adults, Handong. Getting married is not some kind of game. Don't you think you're being a little rash?"

"I've been thinking about this for a long time," I said flatly. "I just don't think we can live together anymore."

Thus ended the conversation. I knew I hadn't delivered the most eloquent case for a divorce, but I was just too tired for explanations.

In the weeks that followed, Lin Ping did everything she could to save our marriage. First, she relieved the maid of her cooking duties and began cooking herself—elaborate, multicourse dinners with soft, romantic music playing in the background. Under the glow of candlelight, she would take my hand across the table and look deep into my eyes. "I love you," she'd say as I sat on the other side of the table, feeling too weirdly uncomfortable to eat.

She took me to a concert where she snuggled up to me on the dance floor like she had done when we first met. The show she'd chosen was a cruel irony: a live performance of *The Butterfly Lovers*. A violin concerto penned in the 1950s, the story it told had much older folk roots. In the original legend, a fourth-century girl defies feudal morality by disguising herself as a boy and pursuing study. She falls in love with another student, a boy, but he remains ignorant of her love, and, besides, the pressures of family and society conspire to keep them apart. When the boy finally learns that his friend is really a girl, he declares his love for her, but circumstance continues to deny them happiness. In the end, the lovers die of heartache and are transformed into butterflies, able at last to join each other in eternal union.

Holding Lin Ping in my arms as we danced, I remembered something Lan Yu had once told me. He said the true historical basis of the legend was a passionate love affair between two real boys, not between a girl and a boy as depicted in *The Butterfly Lovers*. It was only that the legend had been distorted over time to have a heterosexual storyline.

"Ha!" I laughed at the time. "What a crock of shit!"

Lan Yu looked at me with his big, sorrowful eyes. "I believe it," he said.

Listening to the mournful cadence of the melody, I pictured Lan Yu's face as he told me this story, so sincere, so earnest. I thought about the butterfly lovers. The way they were forced to say goodbye to each other, the way their love was so powerful that they were able to defy death itself. My eyes filled with tears. Maybe I believed they were two boys, too. I raised a hand behind my wife's back to dry my eyes.

Four weeks later, I received a memo from my finance manager notifying me that my wife had transferred ¥300,000—the maximum amount she could authorize by herself—from the company account. She was acting fast, and I knew I had to do the same. When I got home that evening, I told her we weren't putting off the divorce any longer and that I was filing the paperwork the following day. After the inevitable fight that ensued, I sat up in bed reading the paper while she combed her hair at her vanity table.

"Handong," she started, "are you doing this because of a man named Lan Yu?" Her back was to me. I looked up and our eyes met in the mirror.

"What are you talking about?" I scoffed.

"Humph!" she grunted, shifting in her seat so I could no longer see her face in the mirror. "Ever since we started dating I've always known I had a rival, but never in a million years would I have imagined it was a man! How did I end up in this ridiculous position?" She was talking more to herself than to me.

Lin Ping put her hairbrush down and turned to face me. "Look," she said. "I care for you, okay? I don't mind that you have this . . . this . . . psychological disorder. I can forgive all that, and I'll do whatever I can to help you get over it. But to think that you actually want to divorce me!"

That was too much. "Save your speeches," I said. "Since when have you been so selfless? If you don't 'mind' this, it's because what you do 'mind' is my money. If I was some penniless bastard, you'd be out of here in a second!"

"Money!" she screamed, standing up from the table. "Everything is money to you! You think the whole goddamn world is after your money. So I've taken your money, but other than that, what else have you given me? What have you ever given to me as a man, as a husband? I've given you every ounce of love that I can, and that's all I ask in return. Can you give me that for once in your life? Can you?" Lin Ping seethed with anger. It was the first time I had ever seen her lose control in front of me.

"When have you ever cared about me or what I want?" she continued, tears streaming down her cheeks. "You can't even do the simplest things for me! When I asked you to go down south to visit my family with me, you said you didn't want to go because you weren't used to the weather. The *weather*! When we got married and my parents came all this way for the wedding, all I asked you to do was take one day of your precious time to show them around Beijing, and you wouldn't even make time for that! But me with your mom? I go to her house every weekend, I sit and talk with her, I take her out shopping . . ." She covered her face with her hands and sobbed.

"I love you, Handong," she said, gaining composure and staring at me defiantly. "No matter how many times you break my heart, I just keep hoping that a woman's love—*my* love— can move you, make you feel something, anything. But you? What sense of responsibility do you have to me, to this family?

Everything you want me to do, I do. I go out with you and your associates to your stupid social events. Do you think I actually enjoy them? I don't want your money, Handong, but what else is there for me to take from you? You don't even act like a normal man when it comes to our sex life! All I ask of you is to be a husband—nothing more, nothing less."

She broke down crying again. It was ages before she finally stopped. "Handong," she continued weakly, "if you would just love me, I wouldn't care how poor you were. I'd stay with you forever."

"But some of the things you've done have gone too far," I said somberly.

"So you admit it," she scoffed. "You hate me because of the fax. Well, that's nothing. You know what your mom wanted to do? She wanted your sister to go over to the Public Security office to have that little piece of shit arrested. Aidong was so angry she just about did it, too." Lin Ping's eyes burned into me. I looked away.

"How do you even have the nerve to sit here like this?" she continued. "If you're so convinced you've got justice on your side, why don't you look your mom in the eye and admit it? Why don't you confront her about the fax? Why don't you tell her and Aidong off for what they've done?"

"But it was your fault for telling Ma to begin with!" I yelled. "If you hadn't told her, she never would have known."

"Handong!" she screamed. "If you don't want to get caught doing something, then don't do it! I mean, how long did you think you could hide this? If you knew what you were doing was wrong, then why are we to blame for trying to help you?"

I had nothing more to say. There was nothing inside me but rage.

"I have done no wrong," Lin Ping said, raising her chin

righteously. "As your wife, I will do whatever it takes to protect my husband and family."

That was more than I could take. "What you did could make a man take his own life!" I screamed. "Don't you fucking get it?"

"Oh, don't make me sick!" she jeered. "What *man*? A grown man coming after you like that for absolutely no good reason—what kind of man would do *that*? Besides, people like that? What difference does it make if there's one less of *them* in the world?"

I wanted to smash her pretty face in, but didn't. I had never hit a woman before and wasn't about to start.

"Shut up. Just shut up. You got your ¥300,000. I'll give you two hundred more and it'll all be over."

Lin Ping turned to face me with a sudden steadiness in her voice. "And you're not afraid I'm going to tell people?"

I looked at her with daggers. "Do *not* underestimate me," I said icily. "Try it and you'll see who gets ruined in the end." I stormed out of the bedroom, slamming the door behind me to go sleep on the couch.

A long period of silence ensued on the other side of the bedroom door, then more crying. Finally, Lin Ping rushed out of the bedroom and into the living room.

"A million!" she screamed. "That's not too much for you!" She returned to the bedroom and slammed the door shut.

Thus went my first, short-lived marriage—down in flames. But just as Lan Yu had said: Where there's a loss, there's always a gain. Going through a charade of a marriage followed by a very real divorce made me confront something I'd never been able to, but which I had known all along. I finally admitted to myself that I was gay.

The news of my divorce shocked everyone I knew, but apart from Liu Zheng not a single person tried to talk me out of it. Not even my mother made any effort to interfere with my decision. Still, I could tell from the way she looked at me that she was in deep distress about recent events. "Further down the road," she assured me, "you'll find a more suitable woman." But I knew that no such woman existed.

A few months before the divorce, there was another guy I'd begun sleeping with. He had a different alma mater from me—I can't remember what it was—but he, too, had been a Chinese lit major. He now worked as a newspaper editor. He liked to tease me by saying I had somehow managed to graduate from one of China's top universities without actually learning anything. He was short, but very cute—one of those "cool" types who wore contact lenses because he didn't want to mar his handsome face with glasses. Four years younger than me, he seemed the perfect match in every way. We only got together a few times, but even in those fleeting moments we always had a great deal in common and never ran out of things to talk about. And yet, despite the mutual attraction, I always kept a certain distance. I wasn't ready for something new, and my emotions were too vulnerable from the chaos in my life. I told him a little bit about my relationship with Lan Yu. His advice? Let it go and move on.

The truth is, that guy was my only confidant, the one person in my life who knew anything about what I was going through. I knew he wanted to take things further after my divorce, but I told him there was an emptiness where my heart had been, an emptiness that wasn't going away and which nobody could fill. He was disappointed, angry even, but he finally said he understood. Eventually, we broke up, and I never made an effort to find another friend. The loneliness I felt during the final months of my marriage was at times unbearable, but isolating myself both emotionally and sexually was the path I chose.

At that juncture, my way of dealing with the pressures of life was to throw myself into work. If I was honest with myself, I had to admit my involvement in the joint-venture cosmetics factory wasn't working out. Operations management simply wasn't my strong point. I decided to let the factory go and focus on my real calling: trade and commerce. By chance, I stumbled across an excellent investment opportunity, but it was one that required a massive investment of capital. I began poking around to raise funds.

I became a drifter after the divorce, sleeping some nights at my mother's, other nights at my office, at Ephemeros, or at the long-term rental at Country Brothers. Most often, however, I slept at Tivoli. Legally speaking, it was no longer mine, but it was where my heart dwelled. It was Lan Yu's. It reminded me of him. Though I was unable to find him, I refused to believe he was truly gone, and each night before bed I looked toward the front door hoping that one day I would see him step over the threshold. I was waiting for a miracle.

Twenty-Three

Ever since I was a kid I had always hated Beijing's sweltering summers. Nature didn't care much what I thought, though, and the hot months were invariably the longest period of the year. By the time the summer after my divorce rolled around, Lan Yu and I had been apart for a year and nine months. It had been a late autumn day when I turned to look at him one last time before walking out the door, when I saw him sitting on the arm of the couch, eyes fixed on me but communicating nothing, and that strange, elusive smile dancing softly on his lips. How many late autumns would pass before I saw him again?

One afternoon, a friend of mine, a real estate developer, asked me to come to a construction industry expo. Held in the first week of June, it took place just days before the four-year anniversary of the events that had taken place at Tian'anmen Square. I wasn't especially interested in the business scheme my buddy wanted me to dive into, and I was also afraid that a construction industry event would remind me of Lan Yu, but

I agreed to go because I didn't want to cause a friend to lose face. When the event was over and I had fulfilled my duty, I stuck around for a while to check out the many displays dotting the floor of the exposition space. It was a mammoth event, and I was awestruck by the seemingly endless number of foreign and joint-venture enterprises that participated. I was no authority on the construction industry, but I had to admit the vendor displays were impressive to look at.

Scanning the room as if I'd been at a cocktail party, my gaze was suddenly detained by three men, a triptych of business suits standing before a vendor display. The one on the right was a foreigner—a white guy—and the other two looked Chinese. I couldn't see the one in the middle because his back was to me, but the one on the left was short, frumpy, middle-aged, and balding. When the one in the middle turned around slightly, my eyes nearly popped out of my head. Yes, it was Lan Yu! I was sure it was him! My heart leaped in my chest and for a moment it became difficult to breathe.

His dark blue suit hugged his tall, virile body. His hair, cropped short, looked nothing like the long, boyish haircut he used to have. He had lost some of the youthful innocence that once surrounded him like a halo, but the masculine allure he now exuded more than made up for it.

The three men were speaking, but I couldn't tell what language. I supposed it was English because the foreigner was not likely to speak Chinese. Lan Yu listened intently as the white guy spoke, and then turned to the middle-aged one. Was he interpreting? I was too far away to see my former lover's face clearly, let alone hear what he was saying. The only thing I knew was that nearly two years had passed and this charming man was just as gorgeous, radiant, and beautiful as ever. The only difference was that now his beauty was inflected by the relaxed charisma and distilled confidence of a grown man.

I moved closer to them, then lingered behind a display column so they wouldn't see me. The foreigner and the middle-aged guy left, leaving Lan Yu by himself. He went back to the display area of what must have been the company he worked for and stood behind a wooden podium. He took a sip of water from a plastic bottle he pulled out from inside the podium, then exchanged a few words with a Chinese girl—a coworker, I guessed—who stood beside him. He must have said something amusing because she gripped the podium with one hand and covered her mouth with the other to suppress her laughter. She recovered quickly from the joke, but her eyes lingered on Lan Yu's face for some time afterward. Did she have feelings for him? She picked up a folder and began to leaf through some documents.

Watching them from behind the faux-marble column, I recalled that Lan Yu had never been especially adept at interacting with girls. And yet, at that moment he looked so calm, so natural. I took it as sign of how much he had matured in the last twenty-one months, but I also wondered if perhaps, just maybe, he had developed an interest in girls. No sooner had the thought entered my mind than I dismissed it. Lan Yu knew who he was. We both knew.

A few minutes passed and the older guy came back. He waved his hands in the air authoritatively, then patted Lan Yu on the back. The way he touched Lan Yu somehow bothered me, as if he were encroaching on something that was mine. But before I had time to dwell on the injury, the two of them packed up their things and said goodbye to the girl, who stood there smiling as they walked off. Lan Yu was coming toward me. I stepped out from behind the column and our eyes met.

We froze. In some ways, nothing about him had changed:

he was just as beautiful as he'd always been. He stared at me in surprise, but this was quickly replaced by something else—what was it? A combination of pain and sadness—perhaps hatred, too. But in a flash this enigmatic expression was replaced by a vacant, emotionless look, a kind of nothingness. Finally, Lan Yu turned his eyes away from me and faced the middle-aged guy as if he hadn't seen me at all.

With no idea what to do, I remained rooted to the spot like an idiot. I needed time to pull myself together and figure out what to do. And yet there was no time. Here was the moment for which I'd waited for ages, but it wasn't going to wait around for me to seize it. After all the days and nights of longing, was I just going to let him go? I had to think fast.

I ran out of the building and into the parking lot, where I stuffed a handful of cash into my driver's hand and told him to take a cab back to the office. I sat behind the wheel, locking my eyes to the front of the building while waiting for Lan Yu and the other man to come outside. When they did, they got into an upscale Japanese car, black with tinted windows, and drove off. I followed, my mind a whirl of confusion. Where were they going? At first I had thought the middle-aged guy was Chinese, but now, looking at him more closely, I wasn't so sure. He looks like a fucking Jap! I thought angrily. What exactly was their relationship?

I followed them at a distance for twenty minutes before they stopped in front of Skytalk, a massive business complex housing a number of offices, mostly foreign companies doing business in China. Lowering myself in the driver's seat so as not to be spotted, I watched with anguished expectation as Lan Yu and the other man entered the building. By this time I no longer cared whether or not they were lovers. My only concern was not to lose track of Lan Yu's whereabouts. Besides, I told myself, this was a commercial space: the middle-aged guy was probably Lan Yu's boss. Once they were out of sight, I sat up straight in my seat, wondering how long I would have to wait for them to come back out.

At five o'clock, a flood of office workers began exiting the building. Beijing had no shortage of beautiful young women and men, and seeing so many of them concentrated in one place was quite a sight. Carefully, I examined each guy coming out of the building, but Lan Yu was nowhere to be seen. By the time he finally came into view, the hands of the clock had nearly crept to six. I was surprised to see that he had changed out of his suit and into a pair of jeans and a T-shirt. He was empty-handed—no bag, nothing—and was evidently in a rush as he walked hurriedly down the street. I trailed behind him in the car at a safe distance, thinking it was a good thing I was driving the black company Audi, which I knew he wouldn't recognize. He walked a few blocks, then came to a standstill at a bus stop: route 011. There he stood among the crowd of people staring vacantly into the distance, breaking his trance-like gaze only to look down at his watch now and then, apparently worried he was going to be late for something.

I watched him clandestinely from the car, my heart a jumbled mess of conflicting emotions—even I didn't know which one I felt the most. There he was, an ordinary kid who had tasted a lifestyle normally reserved for the Chinese elite. Through me, he had gained access to wealth and splendor beyond anything he could have imagined. He had a house, a car, and all the other things I'd left him with when our relationship had ended. And yet, at the end of the day, there he was standing at a bus stop, perfectly happy to—no, determined to—leave those things behind. It was as if he knew that the best way to get back at me for deserting him was to throw it all back in my face. He and he alone had the power to deprive me of the peace of mind I would have gained by seeing him accept all that I had given. I watched him standing there at the bus stop, an ordinary kid who'd come to Beijing like all the others. And yet, nothing about him was ordinary.

When the bus came, Lan Yu hopped on and I continued to follow. Half an hour later, he dismounted in front of a small residential complex—called Gala, I learned from the sign out front. When Lan Yu reached the main entrance, he paused to buy a few items from a vendor who had set up shop near the gate, as a steady stream of bicycles and pedestrians flowed past. He paid the vendor and I trailed behind him, still in my car, so that I could see which building he lived in. Straining my eyes, I peered through the tinted windshield, which suddenly seemed so dark that the world may as well have been steeped in tea. Eventually, I was able to read the number on the building: four.

I didn't have the guts to jump out of the car and follow him, but neither was I willing to turn around and go home. So I sat in my car watching the windows in his building light up one by one as the sun went down, wondering all the while which unit was his. At around eight, two men came out of the building. It was dark at that point, but I could see that one of them was Lan Yu. I was unable to make out the other guy's face clearly in the darkness, but I could tell he was wearing glasses. He looked a few years older than Lan Yu. Something about him reeked of the intellectual snob type. I gripped the steering wheel and my palms began to sweat.

The guy with the glasses unlocked his bicycle from the metal bicycle rack in front of the building. He and Lan Yu were standing close to each other, too close, and I even thought—

or had I imagined it?—that he reached out and squeezed Lan Yu's hand before jumping on his bicycle and riding off into the night. Lan Yu stood there for a while, watching him ride away until finally he disappeared, and then went back inside.

The following day I was a mess. No matter where I went or what I did, Lan Yu occupied my mind entirely. Shirtless, I stood in front of the mirror, shaving as I mentally walked through the reality of the situation. I yearned to see him, but I was too chicken. I kept thinking about the previous day, when we had made eye contact at the expo. What was it I saw in his eyes? Did he hate me? Was he disgusted by me? He seemed to be doing pretty well for himself. He had a job and also, apparently, a boyfriend. The words pulsed through my mind again and again: Leave him alone! He doesn't need you. I cut myself shaving. "Fuck!" I shouted at the mirror.

And yet, I reasoned, I have to see him—I need to see him! I stuck a tiny piece of toilet paper to my skin. Then I hatched a plan.

At five that evening, I drove back to Lan Yu's workplace at Skytalk. The instant he stepped out of the building, I slammed my foot on the accelerator and drove to his apartment complex, where I stood near the entrance of building number four until the sky was black and it was nearly nine. As I waited in the murky darkness, I thought back to that extraordinary night four years earlier when I sat on the side of the road waiting for Lan Yu to come back from Tian'anmen.

At last he came home. I fixed my eyes on him as he walked toward the entrance where I stood. Fumbling with a set of keys in his right hand, he held a small leather bag under his left arm. He approached the door and saw me in the darkness.

"Handong?"

I stayed planted on the ground, as silent as the moonlight illuminating his face.

"When did you get here?" he continued. "How did you know I lived here?"

"I got here a while ago," I said quietly. All this time I'd wanted nothing more than to talk to him, and here I was with nothing to say.

"Okay . . . so . . . can I help you with something?" The formal tone of his voice was off-putting, but at least he was speaking.

"No," I said awkwardly. "I just—I mean, I wanted to see you."

We stood in the dark. A neighbor exited the front door and he and Lan Yu greeted each other. "Hi, hi, have you eaten? Good, good." When the neighbor walked off, Lan Yu turned to face me, but an awkward silence ensued.

Finally he spoke. "Well, why don't you come in?" he said, smiling faintly. I had no idea if he really wanted me to come in or if he was just being polite, but I followed him inside and we made our way upstairs. When we reached the fourth floor, he stopped in front of apartment 419 and unlocked the door. I stepped inside and found myself in a small entry area, where I instinctively took off my shoes. Lan Yu handed me a pair of blue plastic slippers to wear, and I entered the living room. In one corner sat a blue table with chipped paint surrounded by a couple of chairs. In another corner was a couch. To my left and right were two doors, one shut, the other open and leading into a bedroom. At the far end of the living room was a small balcony. Clotheslines hung from the ceiling and a few empty flowerpots sat on the cement floor. Trying to look nonchalant, I peered through the door of the open bedroom: a double bed, two identical writing desks, a bookshelf, and a few empty boxes and suitcases piled up neatly in one corner. The room was small but tidy, and had a kind of Spartan dignity to it.

I wanted to just come out and ask Lan Yu why he wasn't living at Tivoli anymore, but decided to phrase the question indirectly. "You rent this place?"

"Yeah, but I only get these two rooms," he replied, waving his hand in a circle to indicate the living room and the bedroom on the right. "There's another guy in the other bedroom." He pointed toward the closed door on the left.

"He's not here?"

"The landlord says he's abroad or something. I'm not sure when he's coming back. Anyway, I was lucky to get this place."

We sat in the living room in silence. His movements were stilted and he repeatedly averted his eyes.

"Would you like something to drink?" He finally broke the silence.

"I'm okay, thanks."

He went into the kitchen and returned with two bottles of beer. "This is all I have right now," he said, giving me a real smile for the first time since seeing me downstairs. He opened one of the bottles, then hesitated. "Oh, right," he said. "You're probably driving. I guess you can't drink." He put the bottles on the table and walked into the bedroom. When he came back, he had an open pack of cigarettes in his hand.

"You smoke now?" I asked in disbelief as he handed me the pack. I had never seen him take so much as a puff.

Lan Yu gave me a sarcastic smile. "You know I'm not prone to addiction," he said. My heart sank. What was that supposed to mean?

The cigarettes were apparently someone else's. I put them

on the couch next to me. Lan Yu sat quietly in a chair a few feet away.

"So . . . you seem to be doing well," I said.

"I'm surviving," he replied. "What's new? How's business?" His tone was somewhat mechanical, like a bureaucrat asking questions from a list.

"Pretty good, thanks."

He sighed and looked out the window. "How's your—I mean, how's our Ma's health?" He turned from the window to look at me.

"She's great!" I answered, trying to sound chipper.

This kind of small talk continued until I told him I had to go. "Do you think—I mean, could I have your phone number?" I took a deep breath, not knowing what to expect.

Lan Yu went into the bedroom and produced a business card from one of the desk drawers. "Page me if you need anything." He placed the card in my hand.

We went downstairs, then stopped just inside the front door of the building. He looked like he wanted to say something. "Do you have a kid?" he asked.

"No." For some reason, I didn't want to tell him I had gotten a divorce. Awkwardly, I mumbled a goodbye and stepped into the night.

Twenty-Four

Lan Yu was alive! He was alive and had built a life for himself! The last two years of endless fear and anxiety had been a waste of time. I didn't have to dread the prospect of spending the rest of my days plagued by a guilty conscience any longer. The rediscovery of Lan Yu was my release. I could go back to the life I had before that nagging feeling of culpability had brought me to the brink of annihilation. Back to carefree decadence!

Lan Yu, on the other hand, had changed. The man I saw at the expo dwelled in the same physical body, but the boy I had once known was gone. There was a time when I would look into his eyes and understand what he was feeling: melancholy, a sense of infatuation, admiration. But now he withheld everything. The esteem in which he had held me was gone, replaced by cynicism, distrust. He was no longer mine.

I looked at the business card he had given me: *Yamato Building Materials Company, Lan Yu, Business Representative.* So it was a Japanese company, and the middle-aged man I

245

had seen him with was probably Japanese after all. I no longer cared either way. I gazed out my office window, twirling the card in my hand and wondering what to do next. Now that I knew he was alive, did I even need to call him? What did I expect to come of it? Questions like these swirled around in my mind, but before I could answer them I made up my mind to page him. Less than a minute passed and the phone on my desk rang.

"*Wei*?" Lan Yu hollered into the phone. "Did somebody page 2345566?" My eyes filled with tears. Lan Yu had dialed my office number nearly every day for four years, and here he was asking who had paged him! I felt betrayed.

"It's me, Chen Handong," I said, deliberately using my full name to create emotional distance. I guess I wanted to punish him for not recognizing my number.

"Oh . . . What's up?" he asked curtly.

"Nothing, I just—"

"I'm at work." He interrupted me. "If you want to talk, we can set up a time."

A long silence followed. I still wasn't sure why I had called him, or whether it was a good idea for us to see each other at all. Finally he spoke.

"Look, why don't you come over tonight?" An invitation, but not one that was extended with an especially warm voice.

"Okay, great," I said, pretending to be oblivious to the cold indifference he was showing me. I hung up the phone, telling myself that tonight would be the only time I'd see him.

The sun hadn't quite disappeared into the west when I knocked on Lan Yu's door. I stepped into the living room, where he treated me with the clinical politeness of a first-time visitor.

"Have you had dinner?" he asked.

"Yes, thanks." A small plate with a few cucumber slices was on the table, and I wondered if this had been his entire dinner. "Do you live here alone? I mean, apart from the roommate you told me about."

I was no longer nervous about talking with him, and consequently had no fear of how he might answer the question. I had one item on my agenda and one item only: to work up to saying my piece so I could do what I needed to do and leave. But if I was honest with myself, I had to admit I was also curious to know whether the guy I'd seen him with was his boyfriend.

Lan Yu hesitated. "Well . . . yes and no . . . There's someone who—he doesn't officially live here, but he's here a lot." It didn't escape me that he was just as honest and direct as ever.

"Well, I won't bother you again," I said. "I just wanted to see you so I'd know that you're okay. I've looked everywhere for you, Lan Yu. I was beginning to worry something might have happened." He sat at the table with the chipped paint in the corner of the living room, as far as possible from the couch where I was seated. He had no response to what I had said, so I continued.

"Lan Yu, I know that what I did was wrong. I owe you more than one man could ever give. I could spend the rest of my life trying and it would never be enough. So let's just say I owe you a lifetime. I'm divorced now, so if you need anything—I mean, apart from money—just contact me. Anytime."

He remained seated, quiet, eyes blank.

"Anyway . . . take care," I said, standing up from the couch.

I reached for the doorknob, but before I could touch it I felt a hand gripping my arm tightly. Turning around I found myself face-to-face with Lan Yu, who stood so close to me that I could hear his breathing and smell the familiar scent of his breath. This was the moment I had waited for, the fateful reunion I had mentally rehearsed each day for nearly two years. In my daydreams, our eyes would lock in a sublime union that no words could describe and felt as though we were peering into each other's souls. But what was actually happening was very different from that. Instead of looking into my eyes, Lan Yu fixed his stare to my shoulder and shoved his free hand into his pocket as if he didn't know what to do with it. I pulled him toward me and held him there in the dimly lit entrance hall. Wordlessly he began to cry, and pushed himself deeper into my chest, shoulders, even my armpits, until my upper body was wet with tears. He tried to stifle it, but his sobbing became heavier and heavier until he was biting my shoulder in grief-stricken agony. I had never seen him like this, not even when we broke up. So why was he like this now?!

I don't know how long the two of us stood there together in the doorway. There came a point when I tried wiping away his tears and slowly ungluing him from my body. But he wouldn't let go. A great deal of time passed before he finally peeled himself away and looked up at me with eyes that were as red as a rabbit's. I pressed my lips against his eyelids one by one to kiss the tears away. His eyelashes were wet and I could taste his brackish tears, but his lips were dry. I moved my lips to his cheek, my tongue periodically darting out of my mouth to touch his skin. He pulled away slightly to look at me intently, but I couldn't say what emotion I was seeing—was it pain or joy? I closed my eyes and kissed him again.

I pulled off his T-shirt and, for the first time in two long years, drank in his beautiful dark skin with my yearning eyes. I dove into his neck and chest and then slowly descended until I was on my knees and at eye level with his belt, which I unbuckled while gazing up at him submissively. We were still in the doorway of his apartment.

Lan Yu looked down at me in a way I had never seen before: controlling, dominant. It was the cold stare of contempt, the look of someone who intended to dominate. And for the first time in my life, I wanted to be the object of that domination. It was damaging to my self-respect, but it was precisely this humiliation that propelled me to further extremes of wanting to be degraded and even abused by him.

Yes, I thought. I'll be the bitch tonight. I was going to give him what I owed him.

Lan Yu entered my mouth and I sucked him with a sense of purpose. Submission, I believed, would repay him what I owed. I sucked longer than I had ever sucked before. I sucked until my knees hurt and my lips were numb, until my mind turned off and my motions were mechanical. It wasn't long before Lan Yu's breathing got heavier. I held on to his waist and looked up at him in surrender as he grabbed a fistful of hair. He pulled his cock out of my mouth and a warm shower of cum splattered against my lips.

As Lan Yu was coming down from the high of his orgasm, I went to the bathroom to clean up. When I came back I gathered my belongings and told him I was leaving. I wanted his last memory of me to be one of conquest, of him possessing me. But instead of applauding my exit as I had expected, he threw on his pants and looked at me in bewilderment.

"Why are you leaving?"

I leaned against the front door, trying to look detached. "Remember, I'm indebted to you forever. Anytime you need something, just come to me." I had completely avoided his question about why I was leaving.

Lan Yu's eyes filled with tears again. He threw himself into my arms, peeling off my clothes and kissing me with such intensity that I almost lost my balance and fell to the floor. He took me by the hand and led me into the bedroom, where he pushed me onto the bed. My head spun. He was on his knees now. I didn't want him to blow me, didn't need him to, but that's what he was doing. All I wanted was to say something. Something that needed to come out. Something I'd waited a lifetime to say. At the very moment I reached climax, I looked down at Lan Yu and cried out, "Don't leave me!" Tears streamed down my cheeks. "Don't ever leave me! I'm begging you!"

Listlessly we lay on the bed. I closed my eyes and felt we were in an ocean, rising and falling as wave after wave pushed us to the crest and carried us forward. Then it was calm, and the ocean became quiet. I heard the heavy sound of Lan Yu falling asleep. Then I fell with him.

The next day I sat in my office thinking again and again about what had happened the night before. My intention had been to offer recompense then disappear from his life forever. And yet, visions of him burned in my mind with a fiery intensity.

No longer afraid of seeming too direct, I picked up the phone and dialed his cell. He picked up and I asked him, more haltingly than I had expected, if he wanted to get together that night. He said he had plans.

"What plans?" I asked.

He hesitated. "Someone's coming over." The words were barely out of his mouth when I hung up.

Twenty-Five

For several weeks we had no contact. In the beginning I sat by the phone hoping he would call, but by the seventh day it finally sank in that he wasn't going to. By the end of the third week I broke down and called him to ask him to dinner. He accepted the invitation, but insisted it was *he* who was taking *me* to dinner. This, I figured, was his way of asserting his autonomy and financial independence. I insisted, however, and we argued briefly over who was taking whom to dinner until finally he laughed and said, "Fine, forget it! If you're not afraid of my cooking, why don't you just come over here?" I said yes.

When I stepped into his apartment and saw the crude collection of dishes spread out across the little blue table, I smiled. One thing was certain: he hadn't improved much in the cooking department.

After we greeted each other, Lan Yu returned to the kitchen and I went into his bedroom, more out of curiosity than anything else. One of the desks was piled high with books, mostly TOEFL and GRE study guides. On the other desk sat a tiny television and, next to that, a portable cassette player. I pressed the eject button and pulled out the tape, then slowly read the English words: *Classic Romantic Love Songs*. Lan Yu had never cottoned to English-language music, so I figured it must belong to the "someone" he had been talking about. Was the other desk that someone's, too?

When dinner was ready we sat down to eat. Lan Yu watched closely as I sampled the stir-fried green pepper he had made. "How is it?" he asked.

"Awful!" I joked with him.

"Don't eat it, then! Spit it out!" We both laughed, then fell silent for a while.

As usual, Lan Yu was the first to break the silence. "You must have thought I was a mess the last time you saw me," he laughed. "I have no idea what came over me. I must have looked pathetic breaking down and crying like that!"

"You're not the only one," I replied. "I was just as pathetic as you were!"

After dinner, our bodies came together and we made love. Really made love, not just me wanting to be his "whore" like the last time. Lan Yu climbed on top of me and straddled my waist, thighs open wide. With one hand on my chest, he used his other hand to reach back and guide me into him. The instant he put his hands on my thick chest muscles and began riding me in pleasure, I knew he was mine again.

Lan Yu and I had been together for four years before breaking up, so when it came to sex, we mixed as easily as milk and water. We knew everything about each other: what the other liked, how he liked it, where to touch and how. Nearly two years apart and sex with him was just as hot as before. Hotter, even.

The summer was as oppressively muggy as any other Beijing summer, and Lan Yu's tiny apartment could get excruciatingly hot. After we climaxed, Lan Yu went to the kitchen and grabbed a couple of cold beers. Plopping back down on the bed, he handed me one of the bottles and turned on the television: it was some American movie with cops and criminals beating the crap out of each other. Lan Yu had always liked war movies and action flicks—anything with blood, chaos, and pandemonium. I used to tease him by calling him lowbrow, but he would just laugh it off, insisting that I was just jealous of his refined taste. He was absorbed in the spectacle, but I wanted to talk.

"So how long have you been working at your new place, the Japanese company?" I asked.

"About a year," he replied, eyes glued to the TV set.

"How come you left City Nine?" I knew perfectly well the answer to this question.

"Isn't it better to work at a foreign company?" he replied. Mild Chinese curses—*shoot, darn it!*—flowed from the dubbed movie on the TV, out of synch with the lip movements of the English-speaking actors. It was evident that Lan Yu had no interest in discussing the past.

"It was because of the fax, wasn't it?" I asked.

Lan Yu turned his eyes from the TV set and looked at me in shock. "How did you know about that?"

"I looked everywhere for you, Lan Yu!" I exclaimed. "Including your old workplace! I was scared. I really thought something happened to you."

He scoffed and continued watching the stupid movie. "Why even bother?"

"Why didn't you come to me for help?" I persisted.

"And what good would that have done?" he snapped. "Look, Handong, it doesn't matter, okay? I was planning on leaving City Nine anyway." He wanted to end the conversation. "But if nothing else, I could have helped you find a new job."

He returned his attention to the movie, but the distressed look on his face told me he wasn't really watching. I needed to know more. I needed to know how he had survived after getting fired from his job.

"What did you do after you left?" I asked.

"Well, I got by, didn't I?" he retorted. "I didn't starve to death. Anyway, I don't want to talk about it, okay?" He was losing patience with the subject.

Lan Yu squinted in fixed concentration at the television. I didn't like seeing him upset and never had. I took the remote from his hand and clicked off the TV.

"My ex-wife did it," I said. "The fax. She did it."

Lan Yu looked at me in horror. "Are you fucking kidding me? What an evil bitch! How could you marry someone like that?"

There was nothing I could say. I certainly couldn't refute him.

After a few more minutes of angry cursing, Lan Yu calmed down. "Well, it's in the past now," he said. "As long as it wasn't you."

"How could it even cross your mind that it could have been me, Lan Yu? I was going crazy worrying about you! I looked in every corner of the city for you. I really thought—"

"Well, you were wrong," he interrupted me. "Sometimes things are horrible when they're happening, but you just have to clench your teeth and get through it." He turned the TV back on and looked at me. "Anyway, the fax wasn't nearly as hard for me as when we broke up."

I looked into Lan Yu's eyes. I knew them so well. They

were the eyes I had fallen in love with, those deeply troubled eyes that had ignited my desire innumerable times past.

Now, sitting there in the blue flicker of the TV set, his eyes penetrated me like a knife. Damp tufts of hair clung to his forehead, a sweaty reminder that we had had sex only a short while ago. The stiffness of his body told me he was still agitated from the conversation we had just had. He clenched his lips and squeezed the remote control so tightly I thought it might break. And yet he continued to stare at me. I kissed him until the tension in his body melted away and he at last locked his arms around my neck. We didn't have sex again, but stayed like that, kissing each other gently in front of the TV.

Lan Yu woke up early the following morning, grumbling about how strict his Japanese company was about punctuality. I wanted to offer him a ride to work, but didn't have the courage to say the words. Our relationship was different now— ambiguous, lacking in definition. Involvement in each other's daily lives belonged to the past, to the relationship we once had. Lan Yu seemed to want it this way.

After getting dressed we stepped out of his building and into the morning sunlight. When we reached the main gate of Gala, he rushed off to catch a bus, saying he'd be in touch. This, I knew, meant "don't call me, I'll call you." And I had no right to ask him for anything more. I had promised him my life.

When Lan Yu and I were together, especially during those precious moments when we made love, I felt so close to him that he sometimes seemed an extension of my own body. It was times like these I knew for sure that the person I was with was Lan Yu, that he was the same person I had known all this time. But most of the time there was only distance between us.

It was a strange and surprising feeling: for the first time in my life, I felt the pangs of unrequited love, the agony of wanting someone who was out of my reach.

I did everything I could to get over him. I slept with other men and even with other women. But Lan Yu was like a drug to me. When I couldn't get a fix, I craved him. When I got him, it was bliss. But when he was gone, the agony of the crash was unbearable.

In a sense I had Lan Yu back, but it was a narrow sense because our relationship was purely sexual. We rarely asked about each other's lives, and never uttered a word about the past. We spoke freely of sex, but emotions were off limits. I never did manage to find out what he had done between jobs at City Nine and Yamato. Lan Yu's reluctance to discuss it that night in front of the TV set made me drop the subject.

Each time I saw him, a long interval would pass before he'd pick up the phone and call me again. Gradually, however, he started contacting me more often. I, meanwhile, was growing accustomed to his lack of commitment. And yet, I sometimes couldn't help but wonder: Why did he keep coming back? Was there something about me that made him want me more than he wanted other men?

One Tuesday afternoon, I went to Skytalk to pick up Lan Yu after work. Exiting the parking lot, I suggested we go to Tivoli. The truth was, I didn't care much for being at Lan Yu's place. He made decent money at his job, but not enough to get out of the tiny, simple apartment he lived in.

"I don't want to go there," he replied bluntly.

"But it's your house."

"I don't want it."

"But I gave it to you."

"I don't want it!"

"There, you see? You do hate me."

"I do not hate you."

"Then why don't you want to go there?"

Lan Yu folded his arms in front of his chest and looked out the window. Then he laughed. "I guess it wasn't enough to buy my virginity with a thousand yuan," he said frostily. "Now you want to buy my love with a house, too."

I was so angry my hands shook. I slammed on the brakes. "Get out."

Lan Yu didn't waste any time mulling it over. He opened the door, jumped out of the car, and began walking down the street in the direction from which we'd just come.

It only took a few days for us to make up, but the incident made me begin to wonder if Lan Yu was right. Perhaps we were better off leaving things strictly at the level of sex. Words were dangerous. Anytime we used them, they only threatened the fragile simplicity of the casual relationship we had.

Twenty-Six

Two weeks after National Day I received a piece of news about as welcome as a kick in the teeth. Yang Youfu, the stubby, fat-faced cousin of my ex-girlfriend Hao Mei, had been arrested. There had been no warning signs. Before Liu Zheng walked into my office and told me the news, I never could have predicted he'd be grabbed.

My first instinct was to wash my hands clean of any ties we had, however minor they might have been. At the same time, I wasn't going to drop stones on a drowning man by going to the police with what I knew. I wasn't that callous, and besides, talking to the authorities would only be implicating myself in the case.

The night of the arrest, Liu Zheng and I stayed at the office longer than usual to discuss Yang Youfu's arrest and, more importantly, what might happen next. We needed to make an objective assessment of whether or not we were going to be affected. At first, Liu Zheng was brimming with ideas about how to divert the impending disaster. But by the time we poured our seventh shot glass of baijiu, helpful advice was turning into poison arrows. We had a fight, a big one.

"Handong," he said, "I gotta tell ya—and I'm speaking from the heart now—you're fucking up big time right now. It's just one mistake after another." He filled my glass. "If you don't come forward with information about Yang Youfu, you're only going to burn yourself in the end. I don't care if it seems callous. Whatever it takes to protect yourself, you do it."

"Yeah, I know," I said curtly. "Anyway, I've already helped the police as much as I can." That was bullshit and we both knew it. "I don't want to think about it anymore." I polished off another glass of liquor and plunked it down loudly on the table between us.

Liu Zheng looked at me in exasperation. "Well, if you don't want to think about this, Handong, what do you want to think about? Are you going to spend the rest of your life thinking about nothing but Lan Yu?" He looked at me fixedly.

"Look," he continued in a conciliatory tone. "I know he's not a bad kid, okay? But he's not exactly good for you either!"

"Excuse me," I retorted, "but I do recall you being the one who picked him up to begin with." I was becoming angry.

"Right," he said, "but I never imagined it would turn into something like this! I thought you were just messing around. How could I have possibly known you would end up taking the relationship seriously?" I stared at my glass in silence, and Liu Zheng saw his chance to dig in deeper.

"It was a mistake for you to leave Lin Ping," he said, taking a long drag on his cigarette. "Keep on like this and it's just going to get worse and worse, Handong." Red-gray ash sizzled and fell to the floor.

"Lin Ping was a fucking monster," I said.

"You're wrong, Handong," he said sternly. "That woman never did a thing to you. So she was a little scheming in the way she dealt with things. Who isn't these days? People aren't stupid anymore, Handong. They're going to catch on to things.

You know as well as I do that the whole fax thing wasn't her idea, it was our Ma's. And the money she transferred out of the company account? You divorced her, Handong—what was she supposed to do? You gave her no choice but to do it. Before this whole thing happened, she never did you wrong." He took a big mouthful of liquor, then looked at me as if waiting for a response. I didn't correct him by saying that Lin Ping was the true mastermind behind the fax.

"And don't forget," he persisted, "after the divorce was finalized, she never came after you for anything. She just went on with her life and let you go on with yours. Let's be clear about that, okay?"

I was growing sick of Liu Zheng's shrill housewife bitching. "If you think she's so great, why don't you go bang her yourself? I promise not to tell your wife."

Liu Zheng slammed his glass on the table. "I'm sick of your shit, Handong!" he yelled, his face purple with rage. "Let me make things clear for you, since you can't seem to figure it out on your own. You fucked everything up, but didn't have the balls to blame yourself or Lan Yu, so you saved all your venom for your wife. You know I'm right—if we weren't childhood friends, I would never say this to you!"

I stood up from my chair. "What the fuck do you know?" I shouted. "You're a fucking nobody! Who are you to come in here and throw accusations at me?" I knew I was going too far with this language, but I wasn't about to apologize.

"Right, Handong, I'm a nobody." Liu Zheng stood up and looked me in the eye. "Who else but a nobody would stick around in this shitty job for so long? You think I haven't paid my dues here? Well, let me tell you something: Putting up with the crap that goes on in this place, I've probably shaved five years off my life. If I was just muddling along, I'd have a lot less stress than I do now. I don't owe you shit, Handong, and I have no problem leaving this place. You want to fire me? Fucking fire me! China's a big country. Liu Zheng won't go hungry." He held his shot glass in the air as if to toast me, then dropped it on the table below. It didn't break, but the effect was jarring. He picked up his jacket and stormed out of the office.

I sat back down, utterly shell-shocked that someone I'd known for decades would turn against me in this way.

Whatever else had been said, we both knew the real issue was Lan Yu. There was nothing I'd been unwilling to sacrifice for him. I'd worried my mother to death. I'd sat idly by while my friends and associates gossiped about me. I'd insulted my closest friend and lost my wife. And yet, for all that, I was still alone, unable to hold on to the one person for whom it had all been done.

I slammed my fist against the wall. If Lan Yu didn't love me—if we truly weren't fated to be together—then it was all in vain, all this sorrow was for nothing. I calmed down somewhat and poured myself another drink. Maybe we really were better off apart.

I stayed in my office for the rest of the night, doing my best to process everything that had happened. At four in the morning, I finally fell asleep on the couch, swearing to myself that if Lan Yu didn't call me, we would never see each other again. I certainly wouldn't be calling him.

And yet, Lan Yu did call. The following Saturday he rang my cell phone—long since updated since the Big Boss days—and asked me to come to his house.

I was surprised. It was rare for him to invite me over on the weekend, so rare that I would joke sardonically that I was his "Tuesday lover," or perhaps one of the "discreet afternoon playmates" I had read about in the personal ads of American newspapers. But however surprised and even thrilled by the offer I might have been, it didn't matter anyway. I had to decline Lan Yu's invitation because I had a major dinner event that evening that I couldn't miss.

"Where's your dinner?" he asked. I told him it was at the Fangshan Hotel.

It was past ten when the banquet was over. I had drunk a lot that night, and my head felt heavy and dizzy as I stumbled back to the parking lot where the company driver was waiting for me. Just as I was about to get in the backseat, I heard a voice call my name. "Chen Handong!" I turned and found myself face-to-face with Lan Yu.

"What are you doing here?" I asked, surprised.

"I've been here all night," he replied. "I got here at seven."

It was a chilly late-October night and Lan Yu had waited outside for me for over three hours. What did it mean? I was completely thrown off guard by the idea that he cared for me that much. First he rejects me, now he's here. What kind of game was he playing?

I sent the driver off without me, and Lan Yu and I took a cab to his place at Gala. When I asked him why he had come looking for me at the Fangshan, he just smiled. I pressed him to answer the question and he laughed. "I guess I just had nothing better to do tonight!"

Waves of nausea hit me as the alcohol churned in my stomach and the smell of cheap cologne in the back of the taxi filled my nostrils. I didn't feel like talking—couldn't in fact—so I leaned my head against the window and shut my eyes.

"Have you been very busy lately?" a voice rang out of nowhere. I had almost forgotten where I was.

"Mmmm . . . ," I groaned, more asleep than awake. I looked

262

through the vertical bars separating us from the driver. I was looking for something to focus my eyes on to keep from vomiting.

He turned his head to look at me. "You okay?"

Slowly I rolled my head in his direction, then looked back out the window and squeezed out an "uh-huh." His gaze remained fixed on me, but he was quiet.

The taxi sped through the night, passing a seemingly endless number of intersections and traffic lights. It was close to eleven at that point, and the streets were empty except for the occasional cluster of late-night food vendors stationed along highway underpasses. I looked out the window at the throngs of weekend warriors slurping noodles from huge plastic bowls. Unrolling the window to get some air, I caught a few words from an argument taking place on the street. A skinny, red-faced guy with an impressively chiseled flattop and a girl with an even redder face and huge, clunky shoes were going at it.

"I never said that!" the guy threw up his hands and yelled.

"Bull!" the girl screamed back at him, hands on her hips, an angry look on her face.

Lan Yu's body morphed under the rapidly flashing lights, which transformed the inside of the car into a kaleidoscope of color. We were only arm's length from each other, and yet I couldn't see his face clearly. Was there something wrong with my vision, or was the distance between us greater than I had thought?

"I've been waiting for you to call," he said, pulling me out of my reverie. I turned to look at him and noted with surprise that I could finally see him clearly. His big, round eyes settled on my face, and he looked at me earnestly, as if trying to convince me that what he had just said was true. Clumsily, I reached out an arm to wrap it around him and pull him closer.

He laughed nervously and threw a glance at the rearview mirror, where we could see the taxi driver looking back at us with a wide-open stare.

"Who cares about him?" I whispered drunkenly into Lan Yu's ear. "None of his fuckin' business!" I pulled him closer, then collapsed onto his shoulder.

Don't overthink it, I told myself just before passing out. He came looking for you. He still wants you, and that's what counts.

Back in his apartment, Lan Yu made some hot tea to wake me up and shake me out of my languor. The shoddy little heater in his bedroom was hardly enough to keep us warm, so we shivered under the blankets. When I had more or less sobered up, I pulled him into my arms, hoping to trap our collective body heat between us.

"What the hell kind of way to live is this?" I complained. "Here it is, practically November, and they still haven't turned the heat on?"

"They don't turn it on till the fifteenth."

"That's bullshit," I replied grumpily. My temples throbbed in anticipation of the hangover that was coming.

"Aw . . . ," Lan Yu goaded me playfully. "Is the young master troubled by a draft?"

I laughed. No doubt about it: he had definitely become more skilled in the art of playful banter in the two years we'd been apart.

"Hey, you know I can't take the cold like you," I said, pressing my cheek against his lips in search of a kiss. "I still remember when you used to wear that thin white jacket in the wintertime. You must have been out of your mind!" I was recalling the day we had stood outside Country Brothers as light, fluffy snowflakes fell around us like feathers and I put my scarf around his neck. It was only the third time we had gotten together. A lifetime ago.

"What? When did I ever do that?" Lan Yu protested, as he pulled my arms tighter across his chest. "Oh, right! I remember that jacket. I used to wear it every time I saw you. It was the nicest thing I owned at the time." He laughed. "I used to go crazy before seeing you. I was like a girl meeting her suitor for the first time before the arranged marriage. Then you had that ex of yours bring me that other jacket from Hong Kong! I still can't believe you did that."

"So, what about now?" I asked. "Do you still feel like you're seeing your suitor for the first time?" I looked at his profile, wondering whether he still wore the bluish-gray jacket I'd asked Min to buy for him.

He stopped laughing. "No," he said. "I don't. It's not like that anymore."

"What's it like, then?"

Lan Yu stared ahead in silence, eyes fixed on the other side of the room. Then he turned to me with a teasing smile.

"Just messing around, right?" He freed himself from my gripping embrace and climbed on top of me. "Hey, Comrade Chen," he continued. "How about a little physical education? I want to see you work up a sweat!"

When Lan Yu and I kissed, nothing else mattered. The world disappeared and there was nothing but the mingling of our bodies. Right and wrong, truth and falsehood, the present moment and time without end—all these categories became meaningless. I needed him, needed his beautiful body. I could sculpt him like clay. I could bite him, even violate him. There was only us. He was mine.

But when we weren't together—that was when things became more complicated.

After making love we lay in bed quietly, just holding each another and basking in the postcoital glow. His breathing became steady, and before long he was fast asleep.

When we awoke the following morning, I asked him what he had on his agenda that day.

"Oh man," he said. "I have a ton of stuff to do today." And that was it.

I didn't ask for details. I was as busy as he was, and besides, I knew independence—cruel, secretive independence—was the basis of our relationship now.

I left Lan Yu's apartment and went back to my room at Country Brothers. That's where I was sleeping most nights at that point.

Lan Yu wasn't the only one with a lot to do that day. I needed to get started on the crisis management I would need to weather the storm I knew was coming in the wake of Yang Youfu's arrest. And yet, instead of doing this, I spent the day on the couch, watching TV and wondering where my life was going.

Twenty-Seven

Liu Zheng ended up staying at the company. I was glad, but not especially surprised. Monumental as our fight had been, quitting wasn't something Liu Zheng would do lightly. Nor was I about to fire him, because I didn't want to lose him as a friend. As for the argument itself, he only had one thing to say when he walked into the office a few days later: "Too much honesty is a form of stupidity."

Although I had patched things up with Liu Zheng, I was failing miserably at extricating myself from my relationship with Lan Yu. Each time he called, a rejection would form in the back of my mouth, but it always vanished before materializing on my lips. Then I would go see him.

One afternoon, I was on my cell phone at the little blue table in Lan Yu's living room. I needed to jot down a number, so Lan Yu told me to go to the bedroom and dig around in the desk for a pen. Fumbling through the top drawer, I came across a stack of photographs: It was the same guy I had seen squeezing Lan Yu's hand outside the building a few weeks earlier. He was more pretty than handsome, and his wire-rimmed glasses gave him a scholarly air. There was only one picture of the two of them together: two happy and handsome young men, sitting outdoors on two big rocks next to each other, broad smiles on their faces. I had come to hate the flippant, emotionally distant smirk Lan Yu always seemed to have on his face lately, but in all the years I'd known him this was the first time his true smile made me uneasy. More than uneasy. It was like my heart was being gutted with a knife.

One evening when we were at Gala, there was a knock at the front door. A utility worker had come to read the electricity meter and collect a payment. He and Lan Yu began to do bill calculations, so I stepped onto the balcony and lit a cigarette. The building facing us was barely a stone's throw away—so close that on the summer day when I had visited Lan Yu for the first time, I could hear the thumping sound of children racing around and shouting inside the other homes. But now it was silent. Just faint lights turning on and off and the mundane activities of tenants who'd forgotten to close their window curtains.

I was so absorbed in observing other people's lives that I didn't hear Lan Yu open the door and step out after the worker had left. He grabbed me from behind and I jumped, startled by his interruption of my trancelike musings. I struggled to turn around and face him so I could give him a playful slap on the cheek, but he held me tight, hooking his chin over my shoulder and pinning me to the spot. I felt his hot breath against the nape of my neck, then against my ear. Rapid, excited. Nearly all the curtains in the building opposite were shut by this time, but I still had a vague worry that someone would see us.

"You . . . here . . . just like this . . . it's so . . . ," he whispered, kissing the patch of skin he had exposed by pulling down the back of my shirt collar. "So damn . . ." His tongue darted around at the back of my ear.

"So damn *what?*" I asked with a laugh, throwing off his arms and turning to face him. Our lips touched, but before it could turn into a kiss he pulled away from me, apparently remembering he hadn't finished his sentence.

"So damn *sexy,*" he said, stressing the final word in English. He smiled sheepishly. Perhaps he was afraid I would think he was showing off.

"Quit making fun of me!" I laughed. "You know my English is shit." I combed my fingers through his hair and looked at him intently. I had something important to say.

"Lan Yu," I started. "I want things to be like they were before. I'm not seeing anyone else. I don't want to see anyone else. I just want it to be you and me." I was determined to give this thing the final push it needed to work.

"Give me a chance, Lan Yu," I persisted. "Give *us* a chance. My feelings for you are stronger than ever before. I'm serious," I said, and I meant it.

"*Serious?*" he scoffed, incredulous. "Since when is anything *serious* to you?" The excitement that had been in his eyes just moments earlier was gone, replaced by a cold and hostile indifference. Averting his eyes, he grabbed me by the hand and led me back inside. That was his way of ending the conversation.

"But I *am* serious!" I insisted, trailing behind him back into the apartment. "I'm not interested in women anymore, Lan Yu. I'm never going back to that life."

"You say that now," he said, "but things could change in the future. Besides, you don't live in a vacuum, remember? You have your mother to think of, your career . . ."

Your mother? I thought sadly. He no longer said "our Ma."

We entered the bedroom and Lan Yu jumped between the sheets. I stood at the foot of the bed with crossed arms, gazing down at him with an intentionally pouty look on my face.

"What?" he asked, scrunching his face up into a scowl and lifting his fists as if challenging me to a fight. Fine then! I thought. If he wanted to drop the subject and keep things simple and easy, I'd let him. For now, anyway.

"Don't be scared," I said, as I slowly walked around the bed like a tiger sizing up its prey. "I'm just going to give you a little kiss. Just a little hug and a kiss!" I jumped onto the bed and we both laughed. There was tension between us, but we were doing what we could to avoid an argument.

"Listen, Handong," Lan Yu said with sudden concentration. "Even if you *are* being real, I have someone now. He's good to me. We're happy together." He paused for a moment, then tugged at a button on my shirt as if he were thinking. "It's bad enough that I'm here with you. I don't want to do anything else to hurt him."

I couldn't believe what I was hearing. Here was Lan Yu lying in my arms, telling me about his devotion to another man—a man who had probably been in this very bed with him a dozen, two dozen, a hundred times. I hated it! I hated it with every fiber of my being. But it was no longer my place to question Lan Yu. Or his relationships with others.

"Is he the only guy you've been with these last two years?"

"God no," he replied. "There's been a bunch. Most were just a quick fuck, then *see ya later*! Pricks." He laughed.

"How did you meet him? I mean, your boyfriend."

"When you and I broke up, I started going back to Huada more often, even though I'd already graduated. I don't know why—I was probably lonely and missed the place. Anyway, one day I was sitting alone in this little gazebo they have—the Island, they call it. He came in and sat on the bench opposite me. I could tell he was watching me—he just stared at me for the longest time. Then he sat down next to me, gave me a cigarette, and told me I looked brokenhearted."

270

"Was he also a Huada graduate?"

"No, he had gone to a different school. But we had a lot in common. He gave me a lot of—" Lan Yu broke off his own sentence and looked up at the ceiling.

"You know," he continued, "when you and I were together, no matter how bad things got or how scary things were, as soon as I thought of you, I wasn't afraid anymore. It was only after we broke up that I realized that for people like us—I mean, it's just so fucking hard, you know?" He moved his eyes away from the ceiling and looked at me.

"At the time, I hated you for getting married. But I understand now. You've got a pretty good deal, Handong. You can be with men or women."

"You can get married too if you wanted!"

"No," he said firmly. "I can't."

I took Lan Yu's hand in mine. I didn't want to talk about it. I didn't want to talk about my marriage, and I certainly didn't want to talk about how great his boyfriend was. All I wanted was him. In that moment. The beautiful young man I was with.

So fuck it! I thought. If I can't have all of him, let me at least have this moment. I kissed him roughly on the lips. "Let's fuck," I said with a devilish grin. He smiled.

I got on top of him, then reached over to the desk next to the bed and grabbed my tie. Lan Yu gave me a puzzled look, but smiled when I lifted his arms and tied them to the steel bed frame. It was something I'd seen in a porn video.

Being tied up excited him. His lips parted in tortured expectation and he looked up at me in silent submission. There it was—that unconditional surrender I hadn't seen for so long. Instant hard-on.

"You'd better behave, little boy, or I'm going to have to discipline you," I said, trying to sound butch and authoritative.

I stripped the pillowcase off the pillow, then folded it in half and covered his eyes. With its floral design, it wasn't exactly the black leather blindfold I'd seen in the video, but it would do. After Lan Yu's eyes were covered, I kissed him roughly, then bit him from head to toe like a beast devouring its kill, leaving faint bite marks where my teeth had been. And finally, I dove into his cock like it was my last meal. I sucked greedily, hungrily. It was pleasure, but a strange kind of pleasure, a pleasure tainted by the sadness of knowing he wasn't really mine and never would be. For a moment I thought I was going to cry right there with his thick, pulsing dick lodged in the back of my throat.

I crawled back up to him and kissed him again, wondering if he could taste himself on my lips. I pulled the pillowcase away from his eyes and he looked at me with rapturous excitement. Soon enough, however, he saw there were in tears in my eyes. He looked surprised, but the next thing I knew there were tears in his, too.

"Turn around!" I barked like a military officer. I wasn't going to let a few tears get in the way of the hot scene we had going. I untied his wrists and turned him onto his side as he looked back at me with a wild expression: burning, desperate. His hands were free now, but he kept groping at the tie and bed frame, unwilling to be released from the bondage in which I'd placed him. I lay on my side next to him and slowly pushed inside, but things weren't going as planned because the only sensation I felt was a deep grief forming at the pit of my stomach. It was the agony of not being able to possess him entirely. When it was more than I could bear, I pulled out, turning Lan Yu to face me as I broke into uncontrollable sobs.

"Lan Yu, I can't take this anymore!" I heaved, tears streaming down my cheeks. I pulled him into my arms. "Marry me, Lan Yu! Why can't we . . . why? If I can marry a woman, why can't I marry you? I'll do anything . . . just tell me what you want me to do!" Frantically, I held him against my chest, then pulled away again to look him in the eye. "Men, women, I don't care anymore! I love *you*, Lan Yu! It's you that I love! I don't care if they say I'm sick, I don't care if people call me a hooligan. I love you!"

He trembled in my arms. I held him so close, so tight, his voice was barely audible.

"I don't want anything else," he said, choking with sobs. "I've never wanted anything else. I just want to be with you."

Forty-five minutes later, Lan Yu and I stepped out the front door of his apartment building and into the street, looking like nothing more than two ordinary friends. Even less than friends, I thought bitterly. Everything that had just transpired in his bedroom—none of it mattered now. We had nothing. No recognition from the outside world. None of the pressures keeping couples together, but all the ones keeping them apart. Walking down the street together, it was as if nothing had happened.

Twenty-Eight

When spring came the following year, I had a strange premonition that something bad was coming. Time revealed it wasn't my imagination. Everywhere I turned, spring flowers were blooming. But not for me.

The crisis began to take shape when my mother asked me to come home for one of her late-night talks, which were becoming more and more frequent. She wanted me to marry again, and without delay. With somber earnestness she told me about her life and my father's life, about their marriage, and about the hardship of life in general. Throughout her story, she paused periodically to stress the dangers of life without a woman.

"Handong," she said. "You can't go on with this lifestyle! It's reckless. You need to start taking responsibility for your life."

On and on she went while I stared at the floor in grumpy silence, cynically asking myself how a woman with a Republican Era high school education had suddenly become a philosopher. What she didn't openly state, of course, was her fear that I'd returned to my old "hobby," a hobby we both knew had not, in fact, been replaced by horse racing.

Before long, I learned that the censure wasn't coming from my mother alone. One weekend in March, I took the family to Beijing World Park to go for a stroll and enjoy the replicas of the Taj Mahal, Eiffel Tower, and other world marvels. My youngest sister, Jingdong, was married by then and had just become a mom like our other sister, so we were a big group. She spent most of the day keeping an eye on the baby, but I noticed her periodically looking at me in disgust. Later that night when I mentioned it to my mother, she said that Lin Ping had told Jingdong everything. It broke my heart to hear this. No longer was I the perfect big brother.

If my relationship with my family was in crisis, my professional life wasn't doing much better. The list of individuals tied to Yang Youfu's case grew in the wake of his arrest, culminating with the police striding into the office of an associate of mine, a bank director, and placing him under arrest. This bank director had been a miracle worker for me, a personal God of Wealth who'd given me major financial backing on more than one occasion. The threat of being dragged into the case was becoming real, so I decided to lie low for a while. I wanted to wait and see how things were going to unfold.

For some reason, the catastrophe crashing down around me made me start examining other aspects of my life. I began looking at my relationship with Lan Yu in a new light. I was in my midthirties at that point, ten years older than Lan Yu and well past the age when a man was expected to marry and have kids. I no longer had time for games, jealousy, or any of the bullshit that I had thrived on when I was younger. I no longer monitored Lan Yu's every move—who he talked to, where he went. None of this was my business anymore, and, in fact, I really didn't care what he did. All I wanted was to cherish each minute I had with him, for us to be happy in the short time fate had allotted us. I didn't know what Lan Yu needed from me, but I was going to do my best to give it to him.

One night later that month, Lan Yu and I were in bed enjoying the kind of quiet conversation that lovers all around the world have while lying in each other's arms after sex. At first we talked about nothing in particular, but soon the conversation shifted to heavier terrain. We began speaking of the journey of the human soul.

"Would you want to know me again in the next life?" I asked, pressing my lips against his sweaty forehead.

"No." His reply was blunter than I would have liked.

"So you're saying you regret knowing me in this life?"

"No," he explained. "I don't regret anything about this life. But I would never want to live this way again." He smiled faintly and I wondered what he meant.

An instant later, Lan Yu's pager beeped loudly on the night-stand next to us. He picked it up and glanced at it, but made no move to return the call. Instead, he reached farther across the nightstand to pick up a catalog. I stole a glance at the cover. It was a university brochure.

"Anyway," he said, flipping hastily through the pages, "whatever happens in this lifetime, I don't think MIT is going to be a part of it." He had told me about MIT. It was a prestigious engineering school in the United States.

"Well, that's okay!" I said cheerfully. "One day your son will go there."

"What son?" he laughed. "Since when am I having kids?"

His pager rang a second time, so I picked up his cell phone and handed it to him. Lan Yu got out of bed and threw on pants and a T-shirt.

"I'll be right back. I have to make a phone call," he said. There was something awkward about his manner. "I'll make it from downstairs, okay?"

A few minutes later he returned to the bedroom, moving as quickly and lightly as if he'd been floating in the air. There was a part of me that didn't want to ask what it was, but the part of me that did quickly won out.

"You look like you got some good news!" I said, trying to sound chipper.

"He got in!" Lan Yu exclaimed. "He got an acceptance letter! Twenty-four thousand a year. I can't believe it!"

"Twenty-four thousand *what*?" I asked.

"Twenty-four thousand dollars—a full fellowship! That's more than enough to live on. He's going to be able to do it!" Lan Yu jumped up and down like a kid. That's when I put two and two together and realized he was talking about his boyfriend. He had gotten into graduate school in the US.

"Humph!" I blurted out cynically. "At his age, what's the point?"

Lan Yu laughed. "He's not as old as you are. He's only twenty-eight!" This was an irritating comment, but I wasn't going to say anything nasty in return.

"Well, then you'd better get moving so you can go with him!"

"Easier said than done." Lan Yu sat back down on the bed and looked at me. "It's almost impossible to get funded with architecture. I have a huge stack of acceptance letters, but no money to do it." He scowled and looked lost in thought. "I'm thinking of taking the GRE again. My score was a measly 1980. I can't believe I didn't even break 2000!"

For the rest of the day, Lan Yu was moody and quiet. I thought this could only mean one thing: he was feeling down about the prospect of being separated from his boyfriend, even if it was only temporary.

A few weeks later, the bad news came. Because of my connections to the bank director who had been arrested, there was going to be an investigation into my company's financial records. First I panicked, then I braced myself for the worst. My world was about to collapse.

I rarely visited my mother during those weeks in April. She never smiled in those days, and I was unable to look her in the eye knowing she had lost all faith in me. I had failed her as a son. She was heartbroken.

Lan Yu called me a couple times a week to get together, but consciously or not I began avoiding his calls. When he did catch me on the phone, I usually found a way to turn him down. I still saw him now and then, but had to accept that our relationship simply wasn't enjoying the great renaissance I had hoped for. Either he was incapable of loving me, or he didn't want to. Even if I had wanted to see him, though, it would have been hard, since most of my time was spent doing what I could to halt, or at least mitigate, the approaching catastrophe.

On one of the rare occasions when we were together, we lay in bed after a long session of lovemaking. I'd put him on his stomach with two pillows under him so his ass was up in the air and fucked him that way, slapping his ass until he came. I collapsed next to him, a sweaty, sticky mess.

"Hey, do you still have your old passport?" I asked before we'd even come down from the high.

"Huh?" he replied, still out of breath and apparently thrown off by the randomness of the question. "Why?"

"It's probably expired," I said. "Give it to me and I'll get you a new one. You're going to need a new reason for going abroad, but I should be able to get you a new passport within a week." Leaning over the edge of the bed, I reached down to the floor and opened my briefcase. From there I pulled out an envelope with two pieces of neatly folded paper inside. "Here," I said, handing the envelope to Lan Yu. "These are bank guarantees. One for a bank in China, one in the United States. You said you have acceptance letters, right? Just take this with you when you apply for your visa and they'll give it to you."

Incredulous, Lan Yu opened up the envelope and looked inside. "They won't automatically give you a visa just because you have these." He had done his homework.

"I know, but listen. I have a friend, a woman, who handles visas for the Ministry of Economy. She's tight with the Chinese secretary at the US embassy and is on good terms with two of the visa officers there, too. After you get your new passport, she'll take you there and you'll get the visa."

"You think that'll work?" he asked doubtfully.

"I know it'll work," I reassured him. "Just get the visa, go to the United States, and worry about what to do next once you get there. I opened a bank account there with $50,000. If you get in a jam, use that money and pay me back later."

Lan Yu stared at the piece of paper in his hand, silently fingering the corners and biting his bottom lip. I figured he must have been so moved by my kindness that he was unable to speak, but suddenly and unexpectedly he looked up at me with a cold smile.

"You don't have to do this, Handong. I mean, it's obvious the way you've been avoiding me lately. If you're sick of me, just say so. It's like you're in this big hurry to ship me off." He folded the papers back up and handed them to me. "Hold on to your money. Sooner or later I'll get to America on my own." He stood up from the bed to get dressed. I got up, too, and threw on a shirt, but dug around in the pocket of my trousers before putting them on.

"Here," I said. "This is her card." I handed him the thick rectangular paper. "When you have your passport, call her. I've already talked to her. She says she wants to help." Lan Yu looked at the card skeptically, visibly reluctant to take it.

"This is your chance, Lan Yu!" I pressed. "Don't you want to be with your boyfriend in America?" He looked up at me and I continued, "If you don't want to do this, you may as well take the bank guarantees and throw them in the trash. And you can burn your acceptance letters while you're at it."

Lan Yu continued looking at me in silence, still not taking the business card. Why don't you fucking say something? I felt as if a fire were burning in my belly.

"Anyway," I said, picking up my wallet and keys, "time to say goodbye. And don't come looking for me, either. There are plenty of guys out there who are a better fuck than I am."

He looked devastated. I hadn't seen him look like that in ages. But I couldn't, wouldn't, feel sorry for him. The only thing I felt was anger. I slammed my keys back down on the desk.

"You know what, Lan Yu? Ever since we met seven years ago and I gave you that thousand yuan, you've seen me as nothing but a bank account. That's all I've ever been to you. Do you even remember what our first fight was about? Money! Must be pretty humiliating for you, huh?" I tossed the business card of my associate at the Ministry of Economy to the floor. "But if you think that's humiliating for *you*, what about me? Imagine how I must feel knowing that in your eyes, my only role in this relationship has been to dish out a couple of fucking bills. Now, that's humiliating!"

I stormed out of the bedroom, through the living room, and toward the front door, yelling as I went. "I'm not sleeping here tonight! I'm sick of your fucking heater being broken all the time. I've been freezing my ass off!" I reached the front door, then turned around abruptly. "Are you going to walk me out or not?"

Lan Yu turned his back to me. "You know the way out."

He was right. I knew the way out.

This time it's really over. Each day, that's what I told myself.

Unlike the first time we had broken up, for some reason this time wasn't especially hard for me. By that point, my heart had been broken so many times there was nothing left for me to feel. This, I imagined, was how Lan Yu must have felt three years earlier when I had left him for Lin Ping.

He called me a few times in the weeks that followed. Each time he asked if I wanted to meet for a drink, and each time I said I was too busy. "Besides," I lied, "I'm trying to quit drinking."

They say the human body can't feel pain in two places at the same time. It must be the same with emotional pain, because if there was any sadness in my heart after things ended with Lan Yu, it didn't stay there long. Less than four weeks later, one misery was replaced by another when the police walked into my office and put me in handcuffs.

There's not much to say about the case. Just that on the day of my arrest, two plainclothes cops came into my office, showed me a warrant for my arrest, then made me sign something. I reached out my hands, and the next thing I knew I was cuffed.

It's funny when I think about it now. I know myself well.

Under normal circumstances, if something like that happened I'd be thrown into a panic. But for some reason, I was so calm, so composed, at peace even, as though nothing had been transpiring at all. Perhaps it was because I unconsciously suspected it was coming all along. The charges were big, the dangers acute, and I had done everything I could to rally support and protect myself. But when the ax came down, I found that everyone I had considered a friend wasn't. I can't say I blame them. They were only trying to protect themselves.

The list of offenses I was charged with was long: bribery, smuggling, illegal pooling of funds, on and on it went. It was during those days that I learned that if you really want to nab someone, it's not that hard to come up with a reason.

I knew in my heart that whatever I had done, it was no worse than what everyone else was doing. My only disadvantage was that I lacked the right connections at the right time to bail me out. Nor did I have the backstabbing nature I would have needed to save my own ass. Maybe I'm not ruthless enough, I thought, as the warden gripped my elbow and walked me to my cell. All those years in business, and I was just as naive as the day I'd started.

Twenty-Nine

They locked me up in a local jail cell, where they made me write a confession of what had happened. I was terrified at first. I could have received the death penalty and I knew it. But from fear there emerged some good, too, for it was precisely this confrontation with mortality that caused me to start reflecting on the person I had been for most of my thirty-four years.

I knew I had done some awful things. Again and again I told myself that if I was sentenced to death, it would be nothing more than payback for all the shitty things I had done. In that respect, I was resigned to fate.

But in other respects, I was anything but resigned. It made me angry knowing there were people out there who weren't just lawbreakers, but were truly evil. And yet, those same people were moving around freely on the other side of the prison wall, living large like fat, blood-filled ticks. Most days I tried not to think much about them, filling my mind only with the two people in my life who mattered most: my mother and Lan

Yu. Especially my mother. Each day I wondered how my death would affect her, what it would mean to her.

Lan Yu, I didn't worry about as much. I knew he'd be fine. With him it was just a feeling of sadness and regret. He was the one true love I had had in this lifetime, yet he never fully understood it. Nor had he ever said, not even once, that he loved me, too.

Needless to say, prison life didn't leave me much time to agonize over whether I was gay or straight. Questions like these were irrelevant in the face of death. Prison taught me that the only thing of real importance is what's on the inside: what one gives and takes on the emotional level.

After about a week of this kind of reflection, I finally received some good news from my lawyer. A typical power struggle had erupted among high-ranking government buffoons, creating a deadlock that was likely to draw the case out for some time. To me, the news couldn't have been more welcome. I sighed a breath of relief knowing that, at a minimum, I wasn't going to be executed right away. But still, I knew it wasn't over yet.

There's an old saying: "When the city gate catches fire, even the fish in the moat get burned." I knew in my heart that I was an innocent bystander, a small fish caught in a big fire. But I still got burned.

At first, they wouldn't let me see anyone except my lawyer. But he was useless anyway. Whether he was impotent in the face of the arbitrary decision-making processes of administrative authorities, or just didn't give a crap, I couldn't say. But during my second week in jail, a miracle happened: they let me see Liu Zheng.

My childhood friend walked into the preliminary hearing and sat down at the table across from me. To my astonishment, the two officers who had escorted him into the room turned around and walked out, leaving us to talk alone. The company, I knew, would have had to drop a lot of cash for him to be able to speak with me in private.

I don't know precisely how, but Liu Zheng had detailed information about what was going on. It turned out that not only the company assets but even my personal ones had been frozen. An audit was underway and, for the time being, the company had effectively ceased operations. All the members of upper management—those kowtowing old myrmidons once so eager to follow whatever directive I gave them—had disappeared into their various new positions like monkeys scattering when the biggest tree in the jungle falls. I knew Liu Zheng would have had to rally friends, family, and associates to pool the money required to get me out of there. He assured me he was working every angle, every connection to get me out.

"How's Ma?" I asked when we were done discussing my case.

"She's holding up," he said reassuringly. "Don't worry, Handong. She'll be fine."

"Please, Zheng," I pleaded, reaching across the table to grab him by the hand. "You're like a brother to me. You've got to check in on her to make sure she's okay." I let go of his hand then wrung my own hands together. The shame I felt when I thought of my mother was unbearable. First, I'd failed to give her the one thing she wanted most in life—to see her son married with a child—and now I had wound up in jail.

Liu Zheng sat up straight in his seat and faced me squarely. "Listen, Handong. Don't worry about our Ma. You know she's like a real mother to me. No matter what happens to you, I'll always be her son. I've visited her almost every day since you got arrested. If anything happens to you, I'm going to take care of her, and when the time comes, I'll be the one who sees her off to the end."

My eyes filled with tears. "Thanks, Zheng!"

Liu Zheng. He was a true friend. And yet, I only realized it because of Lan Yu. I thought back to the time he convinced me not to fire Liu Zheng. "You businessmen don't know a thing about friendship," he had said. Perhaps this was beginning to change; if so, it was something that Lan Yu had taught me.

Liu Zheng and I sat in silence for a few moments, then his eyebrows lifted as if he'd remembered something. "Oh, right!" he said. "Lan Yu wanted me to give this to you." He pulled a thin sand-colored piece of paper from his pocket. The instant I unfolded it, I recognized Lan Yu's handwriting. A lump formed in my throat.

We're doing everything we can to get you out of there, Handong. You have to have faith! I don't care how long it takes. You're getting out of there and I'm going to be right here waiting for you. You owe me a lifetime, remember? Don't go back on your word. You're getting out of there! Until then—take care of yourself, Handong, take such good care! Yu.

When I saw that he had written his name simply as *Yu*, heavy tears rolled down my cheeks. In all the years we had known each other, neither of us had ever used this intimate, shortened form of his name. What did it mean that he was using it now?

"How does he know what happened?" I folded the note, wiping my eyes with the back of my hand.

"He called me because he couldn't get in touch with you and he was worried. He's real upset, Handong. He's waiting outside right now. They wouldn't let him in with me. The agreement with the prosecutor was that I would see you alone."

"What?" I raised my voice in shock. "He's here now? Listen, Zheng. Lan Yu and I are finished! You need to help him go abroad!"

Liu Zheng nodded his head understandingly, but said nothing in reply. Instead, he spoke of my ex-wife. "Lin Ping's been calling, too, Handong. She's worried. She's been asking me if there's anything she can do to help."

"Please, let's not talk about her." Mention of those dark days only made me feel worse.

Liu Zheng cast me a feeble smile. "I know she had her bad side, but she never meant any harm." He had always been good at defending her.

The three months I spent in that cold little cell were difficult. One can imagine what it was like: no trial, no legal process, just a lone man thrown unceremoniously into a prison cell. And on the day I was released, they pulled me out of my cell just as they had thrown me in: without any rhyme or reason.

Stepping back into the world with Liu Zheng on one side, my lawyer on the other, I enjoyed the feeling of warm rays of sunshine hitting my face. A broad grin appeared on my face when I saw Lan Yu in the distance leaning against his car. Arms folded and legs crossed at the ankles, he reeled me in with his strong and gentle smile. As always at the end of the summer, he was darker and thinner than usual, but to me that only gave him an additional layer of sexiness. He scrutinized me as I walked toward him as if not yet convinced that I was real. We didn't say a word as I got in the car. No hugs, no tears—this wasn't an option for us in public—but I felt his gaze cling to me as I opened the door and got inside.

Lan Yu and I sat in the backseat and Liu Zheng drove, the

passenger seat next to him empty. I took a deep breath and looked out the window. I'm free, I thought. I was free and alive and returning to the city, to that seething metropolis I knew so well. As these thoughts churned in my mind, I suddenly felt the warm touch of Lan Yu's hand against my own. The motion was slow at first, halting, as if he wasn't sure what my reaction would be. That's when I squeezed back and his grip became firmer. I looked down at our hands, the hands of two men binding themselves together, and then into his eyes, where I saw a mixture of steady resolve and boundless tenderness. I pressed my hand deeper into his, so hard it hurt, but neither of us let go. The pain reminded me that I was alive, alive and with the man I loved.

Liu Zheng drove straight to my mother's house, where my mother and sisters were waiting. Lan Yu said he would wait in the car. As I walked toward the house, my mother came running out the front door, throwing her hands into the air before clutching frantically at my shoulders. She fell against my chest with a heavy wailing that hung in the courtyard.

I held her, patting her on the back while trying to keep myself together.

"C'mon, Ma!" I said. "It's nothing. What are you crying for? Aren't you glad I'm home?"

All my efforts at consolation were to no avail. On and on my mother cried with no end in sight until I began thinking I myself was going to cry. Finally, my sisters intervened by prying her off of me and, eventually, coaxing a smile from her face.

When all the excitement and fuss started to wind down, my mind returned to Lan Yu, who was still waiting in the car for me. It was an awful feeling. There I was emerging from a major crisis and I couldn't have the two people in my life I cared about most—my mother and Lan Yu—with me at the same time. I gave my mother a final hug and invented some pressing task I had to take care of at the office. Then Liu Zheng and I went back to the car.

"That was fast!" Lan Yu exclaimed as we got back in the car. "Is our Ma okay?" He's saying "our Ma" again!

"She's fine," I said. "It took her a while, but she's fine." Lan Yu's worried expression turned into a smile.

"So, where to?" Liu Zheng asked, glancing back at us through the rearview mirror. "I'll take you guys wherever you want to go."

"Are you guys hungry? Why don't we grab a bite to eat?" Lan Yu suggested. "My treat!"

"Sure," Liu Zheng said. "But it's my treat, not yours—to celebrate Handong's safe return!"

"We can eat," I said, "but I don't want to go out. And whatever we do, I'm taking a shower first!" I hadn't had a decent bite of food in months, but I didn't feel like being at a restaurant.

"Let's go to my place, then," Liu Zheng offered.

It was a real men's night at Liu Zheng's that evening. I took a quick shower, and within half an hour, heavy clouds of smoke filled the living room and our ears rang with the sound of shot glasses clinking together. Also filling the air was an endless stream of cursing, not from Lan Yu, but from Liu Zheng and me. I was first to get drunk, but Liu Zheng followed quickly. Lan Yu drank very little. He mostly just sat quietly, looking supremely contented as Liu Zheng and I bitched and moaned about everything that was wrong with the world.

"Liu Zheng!" I roared, holding my glass high while trying to focus my bleary eyes. "To you, buddy! I'm gonna make it up to you! We've been through thick and thin, but I'll tell you one thing, I'm gonna make it up to you!"

Liu Zheng and I never spoke of it directly, but Lan Yu later told me that my childhood friend had spent ¥3 million securing my release—his entire life savings. He had risked everything—his livelihood, his family—to bail me out. This, I felt, was his way of returning the debt of gratitude I had earned by not firing him five years earlier.

"Let's not speak of the past," Liu Zheng said. "You're back now and that's what counts!" He lifted his glass to mine.

I turned to Lan Yu. He was his usual laconic self, but was genuinely pleased by the drunken banter happening around him.

"And you!" I hollered, raising my glass with a smile. "Thank you so much for your note! I couldn't have survived another minute in that hellhole!"

Lan Yu beamed. "Drink!" he shouted, raising his glass to mine.

It took many months, but at last there was a desirable outcome to my case. They threw out all charges against me because of a lack of evidence. Still, the audit they had performed brought to light other discrepancies, such as tax evasion, and I was hit with a series of heavy fines. It wasn't going to be easy, but one way or another I would recover.

There was some good that came out of the bad. Returning from the brink of ruin brought a new kind of clarity to my life. The excesses of my past now seemed empty, dissolute. I decided to start living a little more simply, a little more sincerely, in a way that was a little more real.

Thirty

After the impromptu celebration at Liu Zheng's place, all three of us fell asleep in our respective chairs—two of us passed out drunk—until early morning, when the virgin rays of sunlight burst into the room and coaxed us out of slumber. Liu Zheng stumbled off to join his wife in their bed, and Lan Yu and I took a cab back to Gala, where we jumped immediately into his. Lan Yu sat up against the headboard; legs open in the shape of a *V*, he patted the open space between them to invite me to sit. I nestled against his broad chest and he held me tightly in his arms, kissing the back of my neck. It was rare for him to hold me that way, the exact opposite of the pattern we'd established through innumerable hours of cuddle time. He leaned forward to look at my profile, kissing my cheek now and then. I loved the feeling of his arms around me as much as I loved my newly restored freedom.

"Do I look any different?" I asked, turning my head slightly so he could see me better.

"Not really. A little thinner."

"I was sure you had forgotten about me." I tugged at his arm, tightening it around my chest.

"Are you kidding me? Never!" He nuzzled his nose against my ear. "I was worried you wouldn't be able to take it, that you might even . . . ," his voice trailed off, then he continued. "Believe me, I know what those confessions are like. When they got the fax at my work, every single manager in the company pulled me aside to 'talk,' then security made me write a statement. It was such bullshit. When my coworkers found out about it, they started getting on board with the inquisition, too. So I knew exactly what you were going through. And I was worried about you."

Quietly, I listened to him speak. Lan Yu had never been much of a talker, and he wasn't always good at expressing himself. But I always understood what he meant.

"All right, mister, time's up!" I pulled myself out of his arms to swap positions with him. I wanted to take him in my arms and hold him as I'd done so many times before. I wrapped my arms around the front of his torso and scrutinized his profile, noting all the things about him that had changed since we met. The childlike innocence he once had was completely gone now, permanently replaced by a deepening maturity that was just beginning to dig into the length of his brow. In the past, when he had looked at me it was with anxiety, suspicion. But he now possessed a kind of relaxed and easygoing self-confidence. I squeezed him tightly. He seemed even thinner than the day before, when I'd seen him waiting for me outside the jailhouse. I wondered if being with me somehow made him unhappy.

I stretched my neck forward to press my lips against whatever part of his face I could find. Eyebrows, nose, then lips. He returned my kiss by pushing his tongue into my mouth, inviting me to push back deeper. Pulling back slightly, I studied his profile while combing my fingers through his hair. There was something I needed to ask him.

"In the note you wrote me, why did you sign your name *Yu*?"

He smiled, but didn't answer the question. So I tried another one.

"So, if I'm going to repay you . . . I mean . . . how do you think I should do it?" More silence.

"Tell me!" I said, squeezing my arms around his chest as tightly as I could.

He turned and looked at me cunningly. "I guess you'll just have to figure it out on your own!"

I looked at him closely. Why didn't he tell me he loved me? I had nothing to go on but intuition. I knew he loved me, and I had once thought that knowing it without having heard him say it was more romantic and exciting than a million sweet words. But knowing it was no longer enough. I wanted to hear it.

"I want you so badly," I whispered into his ear as I enveloped him in my embrace. "We're going to be together forever, okay?"

"What about when we're old?"

"As long as you still want me."

He laughed, and it hurt. I was trying to be sincere, and he was laughing at me.

Lan Yu could see I was bothered by his flippant response. He turned to me and rubbed his nose against mine.

"You're like a drug," he said matter-of-factly. "I know I shouldn't go near you. I know you could ruin me. But I can't stay away."

Upon hearing this, I realized it wasn't just me who'd thought of him as a drug. He thought the same of me!

"So you *are* prone to addiction!" I laughed. "And how do

293

you intend to manage this problem, young man?" I wanted to take the same light tone as him. It would be easier that way.

"I guess one day I'll just have to quit!"

"And when will that be?" I held my breath, praying he wasn't suggesting we should break up.

"Oh, I don't know. When you get married again, or find someone else." His tone of voice remained cavalier.

I closed my eyes. How could I put my feelings for Lan Yu into words? He still distrusted me because of what I had done in the past, and yet there he was, forgetting the past so he could be with me. I opened my eyes again.

"So, are you going to go abroad this year?" I wanted to change the subject.

"Ugh," he lamented. "It's hopeless!"

"Has your boyfriend gone yet?"

"He left a month ago."

"Did you guys break up?"

Silence.

"He knows everything about us, doesn't he?"

"He doesn't know a thing," Lan Yu replied. "I never told him about you." That surprised me. It was hard to believe he'd never said a word about a relationship that had lasted as long as ours. But there was more.

"I've never told anyone about us," he continued.

"Why not?"

Lan Yu turned to look me in the eye. "It's ours, Handong. It doesn't belong to anybody else."

The words hit me hard. I had known Lan Yu for seven years at that point. I always knew he was a sensitive person, the kind of person who values feelings more than anything else. But it was only in that moment that I realized just how strong his feelings for me really were. Maybe I didn't need to hear him say he loved me. Maybe this was his way of saying it. When evening came around, Lan Yu and I made love for the first time in over three months. Whatever else could be said of him, he had always greatly enjoyed the pleasures of sex. I did, too, but on that night—our first real night together since my release—a nagging caution tugged at my heart. I was deathly afraid—afraid of losing myself, afraid of falling so deep that our bodies and souls became one.

I barely slept a wink that night. Lan Yu, on the other hand, slept heavily. Lying in bed drenched in pools of moonlight, I held him in my arms, thinking about the strange and unlikely path my life had taken. I thought about my mother, my career, the days I had spent behind bars. I took in Lan Yu's beautiful face with my eyes and made a vow to myself: unless there came a day when he grew tired of this life—tired of me, tired of being with another man—I was going to stay with him forever.

The following morning, the sun rose in the east, and Lan Yu and I began our respective days. I dropped him off at work, then drove to my office to commence the long and arduous process of mopping up the shitstorm created by jail time. I essentially had to start my career over from scratch. A herculean task, but an exciting one, too, since it represented the new start on life I desired.

Arriving at my office, the first thing I did was call the front desk of Country Brothers. It was time to rid myself of my secret little room there, that house of pleasure that time and again had opened onto a seemingly endless horizon of new adventures. I also made arrangements to sell my apartments at Movement Village and Ephemeros, though this idea had more to do with needing fast cash than wanting to turn over a new leaf. Apart from the occasional visit to my mother's house, I stayed with Lan Yu each night, joking that I was a down-and-out drifter who had found shelter at Camp Gala. I never went to Tivoli, nor did I mention it to Lan Yu.

The Japanese company Lan Yu worked for was exacting, and he spent long hours at work each day. He often grumbled about how vile foreign bosses were. He said if he had his way, he'd wipe the Japanese off the face of the earth.

"What are you, some kind of radical nationalist?" I feigned shock.

"Damn right!" he beamed with pride.

Lan Yu was good at his job. One evening after work, he burst through the apartment door shouting that his boss had given him a raise. I gave him a big hug and told him we were going out to dinner that night—on him! He laughed when I threatened to order lots of pricey dishes.

Lan Yu rarely talked about the past and talked even less about the future. He said he didn't believe in the future. I didn't know exactly what that meant, but it didn't matter. We were happy in the moment, in the present. That was enough for me.

One late afternoon, I went to Skytalk to pick Lan Yu up after work. I wanted to surprise him, so I parked at a distance so he wouldn't be able to see me when he walked out. At ten past five, he stepped out of the building, chatting spiritedly with a strikingly attractive girl. They waved goodbye as she hopped on her bicycle and rode off.

When Lan Yu saw me, he waved excitedly. He dashed to the car, opened the passenger door, and jumped in.

"Look at you," I teased. "Reeling in the babes, huh?"

"Hey, she's the one who's after me!" he said, clearly pleased with himself.

"I bet she is!" I said breathlessly. "Why don't you go for it?"

It would be hard to describe the look on Lan Yu's face when he heard this. Somewhere between disbelief and disgust.

"Well, that would be unfair to her, wouldn't it?" he said coldly.

"Come on, I was only joking," I said, realizing the stupidity of what I had said. "I thought maybe you were into her!" I was trying to find a way out.

"Well, I'm not," he said, throwing his bag into the back seat. "And I'm not getting married, either. Don't you get it, Handong?" He turned to me austerely. "I just don't understand why so many people like us get married. It doesn't make sense. And it's wrong."

I laughed sheepishly. We both knew who he was talking about.

Thirty-One

Living with Lan Yu in his little apartment at Gala represented a strange reversal of the dynamic we had shared for most of our relationship. In the past, he had always been financially dependent on me. But now, except for when we went out to eat, Lan Yu covered nearly all our expenses. Money became a taboo subject for us, the proverbial elephant in the room. It was an awkward arrangement for both of us, but this was how it had to be. It often occurs to me today that we could have been much happier if our relationship had not been so intimately tied up from the start with that peculiar thing called money.

One evening, when we were staying in for dinner—we had both started learning some basic cooking at that point—Lan Yu told me his landlord wasn't going to continue renting to him the following year.

"Is he raising the rent?" I asked.

"No," he replied. "He says the guy in the other bedroom is coming back."

I wanted to be optimistic for him. "That's okay! We'll just look for a new place for you."

"Apartments are hard to come by these days," Lan Yu replied. He was standing over the burner in the kitchen making a dish of egg fried rice. It reminded me of the joke I'd made so long ago about using his sweat as cooking salt. That was only the second time we had met.

I took a deep breath. I was about to say something I'd been thinking of for a while. "What about us going back to Tivoli together?"

He lifted the wok by its handle and shook it, but didn't say a word. I tried looking busy by grabbing something from the refrigerator, but my real objective was to catch a glimpse of his expression from the corner of my eye. I recalled that grotesque day a year earlier when I threw him out of the car for accusing me of trying to buy his love with a house.

"Listen," I continued. "If you really don't care about that house, is it okay with you if I sell it? I mean, god knows I could use the cash right now." Lan Yu stared down at the wok. Still he said nothing.

A few moments later, he switched the burner off and faced me. "I sold it," he said flatly.

"What?" I shrieked. I was speechless.

Lan Yu smiled and turned back to his cooking. "You said you were giving it to me, didn't you? Have you changed your mind?"

"No, it's just—I mean, when did you sell it? *How* did you sell it? To whom? And for how much?" I had a million questions.

"I sold it to some real estate guy from Shenzhen," he said. "Three hundred eighty thousand US dollars." I was floored.

"Listen, Handong." He crossed the kitchen to where I was standing and wrapped his arms around my neck, then kissed my nose. "You're the one who told me to sell it if I didn't want it. You see? I *do* listen to you."

"And I guess this means you really love me, too," I said sardonically.

"Correct!" He smiled, pressing his lips to mine and running his hand under my shirt to gently rub my stomach.

I could tell from the way Lan Yu kissed me that he wanted a quickie before we sat down for his fried rice. I wasn't in the mood. I was still thinking about the $380,000 he'd acquired from selling the house. I didn't ask him what he had done with the money, but there was so much mystery surrounding the sale that it was bound to stay on my mind for a while.

Money! Lin Ping had said it: I placed too much value on money. The truth was, I had mixed feelings about Lan Yu selling the house, and couldn't make heads or tails of what it meant. On the one hand, it was gratifying to know he had truly accepted something from me. But on the other hand, I couldn't help but wonder: Did selling Tivoli mean he had forgiven my mistakes, or that he no longer loved me? I couldn't say for sure, but I did know that he had finally taken something from me, and this, I felt, made us even. No longer did I have to tiptoe around him because of the many blunders I had made. At last, the guilt could go away.

Thirty-Two

One evening in late September when Lan Yu and I were at home having dinner, I asked him if he wanted to go to Mount Wutai for a couple of nights over National Day. I wasn't a Buddhist, but I liked the idea of getting out of town to decompress after the spate of bad luck I'd been having. The sacred Buddhist mountain area was about four hundred kilometers from Beijing.

"I was just meaning to talk to you about that," Lan Yu said as he took a bite of the braised pork belly we had managed to conjure up. "I'm going to go visit my dad." There was excitement in his voice.

"What?" I asked in surprise. "Why? You haven't been back to Xinjiang in years!"

"I know," he replied. "Not once since coming to Beijing. But I should at least go for a visit, right?"

"Well, if you ask me, I don't see why you *should* do anything. And besides, what's the point? You've been away, what—seven years now? In all this time your dad hasn't so much as returned a phone call from you. What kind of father is that?"

"I know, but the poor old guy doesn't even have time to take care of himself, let alone worry about me." Lan Yu stood up and went to the kitchen to refill the rice bowl.

"Okay, but then why waste your time worrying about him?"

Lan Yu didn't answer. He was standing in the kitchen so it was possible he hadn't heard me, but I couldn't be sure. So I kept talking. "You really are incapable of holding a grudge, aren't you?"

"Ha!" he laughed as he returned to the table and sat down. "If I was the kind of person who held grudges, I would have dumped you long ago!" The words stung. His comment made me lose my appetite, but I didn't want to show it.

"Anyway," he continued, "they called me yesterday to say he just went into the hospital. He has an intestinal sarcoma and they have to perform the surgery right away. What can I do? He's my dad!" Lan Yu gave a bighearted smile.

"And you, my boy, are a dutiful son," I said with just a bit of humor. "How are you getting there, anyway?"

"Train, of course."

"Lan Yu!" I said. "You make decent money now. Why don't you fly? It takes over two days by train. Flying only takes a few hours!"

"I may not be a student anymore, but I'm not exactly rich either," he said, taking a swig of beer. I lit a smoke and stared at him from across the table, telling myself not to debate him on the issue. The only thing I couldn't understand was why he still hadn't told me what he had done with the money he made from selling Tivoli. And yet, I was resolved not to ask. It was up to him to tell me or not.

The following morning, I took Lan Yu to Beijing Railway Station, where he hopped on a long-distance train to the far West to go see his father. At first, I was disappointed we wouldn't be going to Mount Wutai together. At the same time, though, I didn't mind having a few days to unwind at my mother's house. I wasn't especially fond of Lan Yu's place and only slept there to be with him. He knew that.

Since my release from jail, my mother hadn't said a word about my personal life. Whatever she may have thought on the inside, she was clearly doing her best to avoid the subject. That's why I was a little surprised when, on the third day of my visit, she asked me in a somewhat offhanded manner if I was planning on moving back in with her for good.

"No," I said. "Just visiting."

"Are you living at a place called Gala now?"

"Huh?" I was stunned—how did she know? Sharing any details about my life with Lan Yu was out of the question, so I just grunted a muffled "uh-huh."

"I see," she said. "All right then." All right then? What does that mean? Was this her way of giving tacit approval? What was going on in her mind?

A few days later I discovered just how fragile my mother's emotional state was. My sisters had come home for the family gathering our mother planned each year, their husbands in tow with big crates of fruit and kids with lollipops in their mouths. It was a festive day, but the difficulties of recent months also left me drifting with a malaise that followed me wherever I went. Equally frustrating, Jingdong's seven-year-old boy darted around the house, jumping on anything with a flat surface, and Aidong's baby girl cried for hours, making it impossible for me to get the peace and quiet I'd been craving. Still, there was something about having three generations under one roof that brought me joy.

As all this pandemonium was going on, my mother

abruptly burst into tears. It came out of nowhere, an explosion of emotion, leaving my sisters no choice but to take her into the kitchen to console her while their husbands remained in the living room with kids in their laps and puzzled looks on their faces. When the commotion was over and things had settled down, I pulled my sisters aside and asked them why mom was crying.

"Why do you *think* she's crying, Handong?" they snapped in unison.

The episode made me think about everything that had happened. The fax. The divorce. Prison. How much sadness and heartbreak had I made my mother endure? Had I been a selfish son? And if so, was there anything I could do to make up for it? The questions churned in my head, but I didn't have any answers.

A week later, Lan Yu returned to Beijing. He had already told me on the phone that his father's operation had gone well, adding that, although they were still waiting for a few tests, the doctor said things were looking good. Just before hanging up, I had asked him if he wanted me to pick him up at the railway station.

"If I had a magic button, I'd push it so I could you see right now!" he had replied. That made me smile.

Lan Yu's beaming face peered out from an open window as the train pulled into the station. "Handong!" he called, reaching out an arm and waving. When the train stopped, he jumped out of the carriage door and we practically hugged each other right then and there on the platform. I wouldn't have even cared if we got strange looks from the people in the station, so intoxicated was I by the warm, embracing love he radiated. But despite all this excitement, we didn't say much as we exited the station and hailed a cab.

"You must be exhausted," I said, squeezing his knee in the back of the cab and looking at him with rapt attention. I wanted to show him that I was interested in how his trip had gone.

"Oh man," he sighed, gently resting his hand on mine. "Am I glad not to be in a hospital! When I got off the bus in my hometown after transferring at Ürümqi, I went straight to the clinic where my dad was. I didn't even go to the house the whole time I was there. I just sat by his sickbed twenty-four hours a day. I even ate and slept there!"

"How did it go with her? I mean, with your dad's wife?" I asked.

"You won't believe this, but the day I got there, my ten-year-old half sister got sick—acute appendicitis—and had to go to the hospital. So my dad's wife drove her there."

"Wow, weird coincidence!" I squeezed his hand, and my eyes settled unconsciously on the taxi driver's ID perched on the dashboard. *Wu Meimei.* Female taxi drivers were rare in those days.

"I know!" Lan Yu sighed. "You know, for the first time since that woman entered our lives, I actually felt a bit sorry for her. I mean, you should have seen her, running back and forth between the pediatrics department and my dad's hospital room. When I left, she wouldn't stop thanking me for being there."

I put a sour look on my face. "Saying one nice thing to you doesn't change all the horrible things she's done in the past."

Lan Yu let go of my hand and looked out the window. "I suppose I'm just not as heartless as you are." I sighed, turning my head to look out my own window. Had I really not changed at all since the day he'd met me?

When we entered the apartment, Lan Yu flung his bag on the floor and jumped right on top of the bed. "Home!" he shouted, looking at me with a smile. "And look at this: a cute-as-hell guy right here waiting for me!"

"Ah-ha!" I said, pouncing on top of him. "You see how lucky you are?" We rolled around in each other's arms, kissing and chatting vivaciously about everything that had transpired in the previous week.

Before long, though, Lan Yu fell quiet. He looked up at the ceiling with a kind of meditative calm, seemingly lost in thought about his visit with his father.

"It's nice to have a home," he finally said, wistfully. "You know, this whole time in Beijing I always thought my real home was at my dad's house. But now I know it's been here all along."

I smiled and joked with him. "I think you've been lying to me this whole time. I bet you don't even really have a dad over there!"

Lan Yu offered me his gentle smile, the one I knew so well. It was the one that told me he'd humor me, but that he himself wasn't in the mood to joke around.

"You know," he continued, a distant look on his face, "my dad actually reached out from the bed to hug me. Then he started crying. He didn't even do that when my mom died!"

Lan Yu pulled his eyes away from the ceiling and looked at me. "You know what else? He apologized to me. He said he knew he hurt me. You know what I told him, though? I told him the only one who deserves an apology is my mom, because she was the one he hurt the most. He didn't have much to say to that." Lan Yu paused and a wave of sadness poured over him. "Why won't he own up to what he did?"

"Because he doesn't think he owes her anything," I said. "How can you even think of him as family, Lan Yu? It doesn't make sense."

"I know, you're right," he said. "Well, it doesn't matter

now. I don't have a family anymore." He paused. "You're my family now."

I couldn't tell if he was joking or serious. Gently, I kissed his lips, then turned him around so I could hold him from behind. Squeezing him tightly I whispered in his ear, "If I'm your family now, then you'd better be a good boy and stay with me. Don't go flying away all the time!"

"Hey, watch it now," he laughed, struggling to pull himself out of my arms. "I think I'm the one who's supposed to be saying that to *you*!" He freed himself from my embrace, then pinned my arms to the bed and kissed my neck. There was more that I wanted to say—so much more. But by then he was already attacking me with kisses and, before long, unzipping the fly of my trousers.

In the early years of our relationship, the sparks between Lan Yu and me when we saw each other after one of my business trips were like those of a newlywed couple on their honeymoon. That's how I felt when he returned to Beijing after his visit to Xinjiang Province. Had we really returned to the romantic excitement of a blossoming love, or was I just moved by his saying that I was his only real family? It didn't matter. All that mattered was that there was something about him that still ignited my desire.

Frantically, we rolled on the bed—so frantically that we nearly fell to the floor. That gave me an idea. Taking Lan Yu by the hand, I got off the bed and pulled him with me. We were standing face-to-face now. I kissed him, then used my hand to push his head downward. He lowered himself to his knees and blew me for a few minutes. Then, joining him on the floor, I pushed his face up against the side of the mattress. In all our time together we had never had sex this way. I lifted my cock to enter him.

Lan Yu looked back at me mournfully and motioned toward

the bed as if trying to tell me he wanted to get back on it. But I held him in place. "Don't move," I said. That's how I wanted to come. And I'd make Lan Yu come that way, too.

I wanted Lan Yu to know the nostalgia I felt. Nostalgia for the way things used to be, the way he used to be. Before everything changed, he was attentive, deferential: I always looked good in his eyes. As we made love that evening, I imagined that the man I was kissing, touching, holding, making love to, was the Lan Yu I had loved in the past, the Lan Yu I would never let go of again.

I wanted him to know these things. But the words wouldn't come out.

Thirty-Three

The six-day workweek was being phased out as the new two-day weekend calendar gradually went into effect. One Sunday morning on a two-day weekend, I was deep in sleep when I felt the vague sensation of two hands gliding up and down the length of my body. Alternating between upper and lower halves, they paused periodically to jerk at my dick and tug at my balls. That little brat! I thought, suppressing a smile and feigning sleep to see what would happen next.

The little brat—Lan Yu, of course—kissed my chest, then twisted one nipple between his thumb and forefinger while gently biting at the other. Then he abruptly pulled away. I could tell by the roaming vibrations of his warm breath against my skin that he was moving downward. When I felt the flicker of his tongue against my still-flaccid cock, I couldn't take it anymore.

"What are you doing?" I burst out laughing as he jumped on top of me.

"It just occurred to me, I've never given you a proper inspection!" he said.

"Inspection of *what?*" I laughed. "I'm not one of your building designs, you know."

"I was just thinking it's weird how our dicks are basically the same size when soft, but yours is a little bigger when hard."

"Excuse me, but mine is bigger soft, too!"

"No it isn't!"

"If you don't believe me, go get a ruler."

To my amusement and surprise, Lan Yu actually got up from bed to go look for a ruler. But by the time he came back, I had already changed the rules of the game.

"Hey!" he protested, pointing at my erection with an injured expression on his face. "That doesn't count—that's cheating!"

Jumping up from bed, I threw two pillows against the headboard, then pushed Lan Yu back gently so he would sit upright. I loved the way it made the skin and muscle of his stomach bunch up into sexy little folds.

"If mine's too hard, then let me measure yours!" I laughed. "But not with that." I grabbed the ruler from his hand and threw it onto the floor.

Lan Yu's eyes widened. "What are you going to measure it with?"

"Mouth ruler," I said nonchalantly. He laughed. That sweet, beautiful laugh. The laugh that was part of what made me fall in love with him.

My lips trekked the length of his body, kissing every spot along the way until I arrived at his waist. Lan Yu entered my mouth, pushing into the back of my throat and making me reel with that familiar intoxication. I was so in love! Nothing could release me from the viselike grip he held me in, body and soul.

With Lan Yu's cock still in my mouth, I looked up at him, consumed by the desire to make him mine. I reached up and gripped his chin. "Do you love me?" I asked, as his swollen dick slipped out from between my lips. He said nothing in reply, so I tightened my grasp. Frowning and twisting his head from side to side, he pried the offending fingers away. He knew I was waiting for an answer, he knew the words I wanted to hear. I knew something too—that he wasn't going to say it. My eyes filled with tears. I moved up higher until we were face-to-face and drilled my eyes into his. My stare excited him, yet he remained quiet.

I repeated the question. "Do you love me?" He nodded vigorously and I couldn't bear it anymore.

"Say it!" I shouted. "I want to hear you say it!"

Silence. Cruel, agonizing silence.

"I love you, Lan Yu! *I love you!* Don't you fucking get it?" I grabbed his chin again, utterly defeated by his refusal to say what I so desperately needed to hear. Gently, he pushed my hand away and smiled.

Fuck! It was times like these that I hated his smile. Ever since we had gotten back together, it was precisely that smile, so detached, so indifferent, that made me completely unable to gauge his feelings for me. I knew he wouldn't say he loved me if it wasn't true. But it is true, I told myself again and again. So why did I have to force it out of him?

I fell into his arms and we held each other, kissing feverishly until I made my way back to his cock, which I again took into my mouth. Just as he was about to climax, he called out my name:

"Handong!"

I held his cock tightly in my mouth, and he moaned loudly as a surge of warm liquid filled the back of my throat. It was the first time I had ever let someone come in my mouth, let alone swallowed.

Lan Yu was appalled that I had swallowed his cum. "What did you do that for?" he asked in horror.

"Why not?" I replied. "It's good for you. Full of nutrients." I scooped the excess off his belly with a finger and moved it toward his lips.

"Ack!" he cried, shaking his head wildly to dodge it. But he wasn't fast enough, and before he knew it, I smeared a fat, drippy glob of his own semen onto his upper lip. He scowled.

"It tastes like . . . *milk*," he said, as the white mustache dribbled onto his lower lip. "Milk mixed with . . . I don't know . . . fish soup?" We both laughed.

I crawled back up to him and gave him a sloppy, wet kiss on the lips. Then we jumped up from bed, racing to the bathroom to see who could get into the shower first.

The mantra I told myself in those days was: Things with Lan Yu are good. They're comfortable. Don't overthink it. But the reality was that even if I'd wanted to overthink it, I wouldn't have been able to. The monumental task of rebuilding my career left me little time to think about anything else.

Truth be told, things in that arena weren't going as well as I'd been hoping. In business, getting ahead usually meant one of two things: kissing ass or screwing the people around you. I wasn't good at either.

One Monday morning, I had barely stepped into the office when I got a phone call. It was the last person I had expected to hear from: my ex-wife.

"Lin Ping!" I hollered into the phone. "What's going on? How ya doin'?" I didn't think this woman could be calling with good intentions, but I received her call with courtesy anyway. There was no need to make her lose face.

"Just fine, doing good!" she exclaimed. "Hey, listen, Handong. I want to ask you something. I've got two hospitals—one in Shanghai, one in Guangzhou—that want to import $8 million worth of medical equipment. They've already allocated funds for it. They just need someone with business connections outside China to get it done. Are you interested?"

I couldn't believe my ears. "Look at you!" I said with a laugh. "You're in business now? I'm impressed!"

"Yes I am, and I'm damn serious about it, too," she replied before explaining the ins and outs of the deal. Little did I know that in just two years she had worked her way up the ladder at a major company called Double Ace. I even learned she was tight with some of my associates. I had to admit, I was impressed by her new business persona.

"So, what made you think of me for this?" I asked when we were done talking shop. "I thought you hated me!" If she was going to be so direct in her way of speaking, I reasoned, then I would be too.

Lin Ping hesitated for a moment. "Well, just because we didn't make it as a couple doesn't mean we have to be enemies. Besides, Handong, this deal could be a coup for both of us."

She was right. The medical equipment deal turned out to be a huge success. Everyone benefited, including Lin Ping's colleagues at Double Ace and the leadership of the two hospitals. I made a small fortune as well. But the person who made the most money from the deal was Lin Ping herself.

Seeing this sharp, savvy, and sophisticated side of my ex-wife made me wonder for the first time since our divorce whether it was true what Liu Zheng had said. Maybe leaving Lin Ping had been a mistake after all.

Thirty-Four

The New Year was right around the corner, and even if I'd wanted to weasel out of it, there was nothing I could do. The last night of the year would have to be spent at my mother's house.

Back when Lan Yu and I were still together—really together—I had always spent New Year's Eve at my mother's house until the clock struck midnight. Then I would rush back to Tivoli to be with him. So when the last day of the lunar calendar came I figured I would do the same. But when I spoke with Lan Yu about it, I found out that he had other plans.

"You don't need to come back at midnight," he said. He was sitting up in bed. "I'm going out with friends. We're renting a hotel room!" He set the newspaper he'd been reading down in his lap.

"Are you kidding me?" I whined as I walked into the bathroom. "What do you want to hang out with those people for?"

I knew exactly who he was talking about. In the two years we had been apart, he had met a group of real jerks in the gay circle. I thought they were nothing but trouble and didn't like it one bit.

"No, it'll be fun! I can't wait." His voice was barely audible over the splashing sound of my piss hitting the water.

I flushed, and then stood in the doorway of the bathroom to watch Lan Yu as he continued reading in bed. He loved the adventure stories found in the trashy tabloids cluttering Beijing's many news kiosks. I figured he just needed something easy to think about after a hard day's work.

"Hey, Handong!" he called out without looking up at me. He held the paper close to his face and squinted. Then he looked straight at me.

"Why do you think the imperialist aggressors were able to completely annihilate the waterborne forces of the Beiyang Fleet during the Qing dynasty? I mean, I know the Chinese navy had poor equipment in the nineteenth century, and they definitely had bad leadership, but still! Just take military officer Deng Shichang, for example. You know how he—"

"What are you asking me for?" I interrupted as I turned off the bathroom light. "Go ask Li Hongzhang, field commander of the Qing navy, or how about the Empress Dowager Cixi herself?" I jumped into bed.

Lan Yu didn't seem to be listening. "Huh?" He lifted his head from the paper and looked at me.

"It's late," I said, pulling a blanket over my head and rubbing my feet against his. "Get some sleep."

On New Year's Eve I drove to my mother's house as always. Fireworks had been banned in Beijing for several years at that point, and an eerie silence hung in the air as my car wheeled into her neighborhood.

I stepped into the house, shouting out greetings to family members old and young. Then I switched off my cell phone and told my mother that if anyone called, I wasn't there. I had one goal and one goal only: to get as much peace and quiet as I could. I'd even conjured up the naive fantasy of getting to bed early despite the inevitable racket I knew I'd have to contend with. Sure enough, the house was soon buzzing with the harsh bleat of the television, the endless sounds of kids running through the house screaming, and the relentless *tap-tap-tap* of mahjong tiles clicking together. Still, I managed to fall asleep by eleven.

The following morning, I woke up at six and headed back to Gala. Lan Yu wasn't home yet, so I sat on the bed for a while, staring abjectly into space and wondering what he was doing. Just as I was about to give up and leave, I heard a key turn in the front door.

Lan Yu stood in the doorway, struggling to shut the door behind him without dropping the plastic shopping bags dangling precariously from one finger. "Hey!" he said with a big smile. "What are you doing here? Why didn't you call me?" The festive mood of the previous night clung to him as tightly as the black wool cap on his head.

"What did you do last night?" he continued, seemingly unable to detect the funk I was in. "Didn't you go to our Ma's house? I called your cell a million times but you didn't pick up." He put the bags down and walked toward me to give me a hug.

The icy winter air clung to his hair and clothes, and for a moment he was completely enshrouded in the heavy clouds of smog that always seemed to blanket Beijing on winter mornings. His cheeks were bright red from the steady lash of freezing winds, and a clear, thin crust had formed under his nostrils. He looked at me in happy excitement, as cheerful as a kid on New Year's Day, which is exactly what he was.

"I've been here, waiting for you all night," I lied, smiling faintly.

Lan Yu blinked with heavy eyes. Was it the wind that had produced those tears, or was he moved by what I had said? I never got an answer, but the next thing I knew, he threw himself into my arms and kissed me.

"Hey, be careful!" I laughed in a loud whisper. "The door is open. I don't want the neighbors to see!"

It was getting harder and harder for me to know what was going on inside Lan Yu's head. Each time our relationship entered a new crisis, he would turn around and surprise me with another expression of intimacy. Was he for real or just playing games? Often I didn't know the answer to this question, but on that one cold winter morning, at least, I felt that he cared about me.

Now that Lan Yu was home, we curled up in bed together and fell asleep. When we awoke, it was past noon and our stomachs were growling. Lan Yu wanted to go out and get something to eat, but I protested on the grounds that no decent restaurant would be open on New Year's Day. Besides, I added, it was cold out and I had a bit of a headache. We stayed in bed and cuddled for a while.

"Hey, speaking of cold," I said, "when are you going to move out of this place? It's freezing in here! They barely turn the heater on, and look—you can actually see your breath when you talk." Maybe I was spoiled, but I wasn't exaggerating. It was the middle of winter and his heater was falling to pieces.

"Oh, it's not so bad," he said, snuggling against my chest. "Besides, this is nothing compared to my old place. I was renting this little apartment behind Huada—you never saw it. There was a radiator in the bedroom, but it was a real piece of garbage. I'd be wearing a down jacket indoors *and* be wrapped up in a blanket and I was still freezing! That was right after graduation."

Right after graduation, I thought. That meant "after we broke up."

"So you moved out of there as soon as you could, right?"

"No," he smiled. "The rent was so cheap I couldn't bring myself to leave. It was during the time when I didn't have a job and rent was only ninety-five yuan a month."

When I didn't have a job, I thought. That meant "when I got fired because of the fax." He was using a lot of euphemisms that day.

"Oh, right," he continued, evidently remembering something. "The guy who lives in the other room is coming back at the end of March. But guess what? I found a new place! It's over in Fang Village. The only problem is it's really far from work. For me at least. For you, it's pretty close. Just a few minutes from your office."

"Fang Village? That *is* far from your work!" I said. "It's at least a forty minute drive! How did you find it?"

"Through a friend. You don't know him."

When Lan Yu and I first got back together, I didn't give two shits whom he spent time with. But as time went by, I developed a strong distaste for these mystery "friends."

"You can't just say everyone you know is a *friend*, Lan Yu," I said grumpily. "You need to be careful about who you associate with. There are people out there who would sell you down the river, then turn around and ask you to help them count the money!"

Lan Yu laughed and raised his eyes to look at me. "Well, friends are more reliable than lovers, aren't they?"

That was a shitty thing to say. I looked away to show him I was hurt, but Lan Yu had already gotten out of bed and was making his way toward the kitchen. "You should try to buy an apartment!" I called after him.

"You've got to be joking!" he hollered back. "Who's going to pay for it—you? By the way, what do you want to eat? There's some stuff in the fridge. I'll make us something."

"Great!" I yelled, trying to conceal the confused jumble of emotions I felt. Had he just asked me for money? He knew things were different now, both financially and between us. And besides, I had already given him everything I could. What more did he want?

I shut myself up in Lan Yu's apartment for several days after New Year's Eve, hiding from the world and pretty much doing nothing. He did everything he could to cheer me up, but I just couldn't drive away the clouds of darkness hanging over my head.

I had known Lan Yu for eight years at this point. He was completely different from the person I'd first met. It seemed like a lifetime ago. More and more, I found myself lost in daydreams, remembering what he was like on that day so long ago when I first saw him at the Imperial, trailing behind Liu Zheng and looking like a stray puppy. Earnest, shy, submissive—everything about him was transparent in those days. He was different now. Grown-up, yes, but glib, sarcastic, full of insinuations and half-truths. I never knew what he was thinking. He was much less conservative in his lifestyle now, too—in sexual behavior, at least, or so it seemed from the fragments of information he'd given me. A vague foreboding told me that we were going to break up again. But for real this time—forever.

A few days after New Year's, Wei Guo dragged me off to Ming Palace to play cards. I hadn't been there in years.

Some guy named Zhou Wen was going to be meeting us there. I had met him once or twice in the past, but didn't know him well. From what Wei Guo had told me, he had a pretty incredible story.

Zhou Wen was in his midforties and part of the generation of urban youth that got sent to the countryside to live and work during the Cultural Revolution. But Zhou Wen got lucky. He had an uncle who was some kind of local government big shot, so instead of being sent down, he got placed on a municipal Communist Party Committee doing who knows what. When the National College Entrance Examination was reinstated in 1977, he got into Muda University the very first year. After arriving in Beijing from his small town in Hebei Province, however, he saw that the world was a big place and came to feel he should have set his sights on a more prestigious university. After just one semester at Muda, he quietly slipped back to his hometown and took the college exam all over again, but this time using a fake name. The outcome of the illicit strategy was that he got into Tianda University. When Muda found out, they notified the National Education Committee. At that point the charade was up. Tianda had no choice but to kick Zhou Wen out in the middle of his second year.

After that, everything went to shit. Zhou Wen's girlfriend dumped him when she found out he had been kicked out of school. He was deeply in love with her, so he went back to his hometown and tried to kill himself. But that didn't work out either, so he spent the next two years feeling sorry for himself and trying to figure out what to do next. Then his uncle pulled some strings and got him into graduate school at the Trade Institute.

After starting graduate school and immersing himself in the study of money, Zhou Wen became weirdly obsessed with old coins. This "hobby of the kings" was an interest that the budding numismatist happened to share with Donald Dai—they had met at some business conference—so the finance guru became Zhou Wen's personal mentor and de facto academic advisor while the hatchling worked on his PhD. When Zhou Wen finally finished his dissertation, he was assigned to some government post, then became Donald's personal secretary. Two years ago, Zhou Wen entered the business world and became the vice director of China's largest government-operated company, Light of the Orient. By the time he walked into the Ming that evening with a black leather bag full of cash and smokes under his arm, he was already a real powerhouse.

My depression had gone from bad to worse over the last few days, so although I beat the guys at several rounds of cards, I wasn't really in the mood to hang out. Under the pretext of going to the bathroom, I snuck off to a side room, where I sunk into a huge brown leather couch and tried to watch TV.

"What's wrong, Handong?" Zhou Wen came into the room and handed me a cigarette. "How come you disappeared?"

"Oh, it's nothing," I lied. "I'm just not playing well today. Things have been real busy since the end of last year. I've been pulling too many overnighters lately, so . . ." My perfunctory excuses weren't very convincing.

Zhou Wen smiled, but it was a weird smile. A smile that told me he suspected I wasn't telling him the whole story, or, perhaps, that he himself wanted to let me in on a secret. Instead, however, he changed the subject. "Hey! I hear you're having trouble with some imported car parts."

"Man!" I laughed. "Brother Wen has sharp ears!" I looked at his middle-aged face, nearly ten years older than my own. Calling him "brother" instead of "uncle" was more or less a form of flattery, but I needed his help if I was going to get my career back to what it used to be.

"Listen," I continued plaintively. "I really need your help

with this stuff. You know things haven't been going well for me lately. This whole car deal has only been making things worse." Zhou Wen knew everyone. He could make things happen, so I spilled my guts to him.

"All right," he said. "I'll ask around for you, but I can't guarantee anything will come of it." *I'll ask around.* I knew what this meant. It meant he would pull some strings and make the car deal work.

"Thanks, Brother Wen," I said. "It's been a hell of a year."

"No worries," he said. "If Tripitaka Master Xuanzang and his disciples can make it through the Flaming Mountains unscathed, so can you!" Apparently, I wasn't the only one who liked to reference *Journey to the West*.

"Oh, hey, I meant to tell you," Zhou Wen continued, leaning forward and taking a heavy drag off his cigarette. "Wei Guo and I are heading over to my place in a bit to pick a few things up. Why don't you come with us? You know, hang out for a while?" He patted me on the back. Something about the way he touched me was as strange as his smile.

Zhou Wen owned an enormous house—a mansion, really—in Pixie Hamlet, a little neighborhood about a half hour southeast of Beijing proper. It was beautiful there. Lots of trees and fresh air. By the time we arrived it was already dark out.

As the three of us pulled into the driveway, the front lights of the house came on and two girls came rushing out to greet us. When we got out of the car, they ambushed Zhou Wen, giggling and whispering to each other.

"Whoa!" I whispered, leaning my head toward Wei Guo. "These chicks are something else. Fucking Amazons! They're taller than me!" Wei Guo didn't say a thing. He just smiled, casting me a somewhat cryptic look.

The five of us walked inside, and Zhou Wen led us to the

living room. The men sat on the couch while the girls hovered over us with attentive looks on their faces.

"Care for a drink?" one of the girls asked, smiling down at me before turning around to shake her ass in my face. She turned to me again, bending over in a slutty tease that thrust her heavily made-up face into the lamplight. That's when I got a better look at her and discovered that "she" wasn't a she at all. I was more than a little surprised, but kept my cool until she went to the kitchen to get my drink. Then I turned to Zhou Wen.

"Damn!" I said. "Brother Wen sure as hell knows how to have a good time!" He laughed.

For the rest of the night, the little siren stuck by my side, chatting animatedly, pouring me drinks, and cooing a series of flirtations into my ear. At two in the morning, I stood up to say good-night. Zhou Wen pulled me into the hallway.

"Handong," he whispered. "If you like what you see, you're welcome to . . ."

"Oh, I couldn't possibly—it would be far too much of an imposition," I protested. Zhou Wen was asking if I wanted to take the little slut home with me, and the answer was no. But despite my effort to politely decline, Zhou Wen wouldn't take no for an answer. It looked like I would be leaving his place with some overnight company.

The Bamboo Garden Hotel wasn't quite four stars, but the amenities were decent and the service wasn't bad, either. There I booked a long-term suite not unlike the one I had previously kept at Country Brothers. In the weeks that followed, I would stay there often, and would also return frequently to my mother's home to stay with her. Eventually, I ended up booking another room at Country Brothers, as well.

Stepping into the room at Bamboo Garden with the little tramp in tow, I decided I may as well get used to the place. If Lan Yu really did move out of his apartment, I wouldn't be too put out by the transition.

Thirty-Five

It wasn't quite spring when Lan Yu moved into his new apartment in Fang Village. The snowfall of recent weeks had frozen into thick layers of ice, and I wondered how he'd managed to get his belongings from one place to the other. I couldn't have known, since he moved without telling me. The day he moved, I found out he was gone by knocking on his old apartment door at Gala, then calling his cell phone in confusion.

It was already past nine when we got home from dinner later that night. I slipped off my burgundy Cole Haans and stepped tepidly across the threshold of his new place. I was amazed at how tidy it was, given that he had just moved in. His new apartment was even smaller than the last one, but it was much newer, giving everything a clean and orderly veneer.

Lan Yu collapsed on the bed, exhausted. I lay next to him on my side, propping myself up on one elbow and looking at him intently while he gazed at the ceiling.

"You should have seen this place, it was a mess," he sighed, lifting his head off the pillow and looking around the room with a weary air of pride. "Now that it's somewhat in order, you can just stay here every night so you can go straight to work in the morning. It's so close to your office!"

I looked at him with a smile, but it was a forced one. I had only half heard what he said because I was still brooding over being excluded from his move. I unbuttoned his shirt and planted a few halfhearted kisses on his chest while he ran his fingers through my hair.

"We'll see," I said. "The traffic can get pretty hairy around here."

Lan Yu went quiet and pulled his hands away from me, folding them behind his head like a pillow.

"If the traffic is so bad, then why did you come here? Just looking for a quick fuck? Just want to 'get some'?" I remembered the time so long ago when I'd used those words with him. He obviously remembered it, too.

"Would you mind not talking to me like that?" I retorted as I got out of bed and faced him. "You know, Lan Yu, I think those whores you've been hanging out with have been rubbing off on you."

"Well, you would know, wouldn't you?" he fired back, rising from the bed so that he was upright on his knees. "You're the biggest whore of all!"

I looked at him in disbelief, then rage. With a single blow, I slammed my fist into his chest, sending him spiraling off the bed and onto the floor. He didn't skip a beat. He jumped up and without a moment's hesitation took a swing at my face. He missed. We struggled on the bed, then fell to the floor.

In all the years I had known Lan Yu, this was the first time we'd ever had a physical fight. I was taller, but he wasn't one bit lacking in strength.

In the end, neither of us got hurt, and neither of us won the fight. We ended up back on the bed, both of us out of breath and feeling a little stupid.

"Well, that was good exercise!" he said with a laugh.

"You want some more?" I rolled on top of him.

"Sure," he said, putting a hand down the front of my pants and squeezing my dick. "But this time, I want some *real* exercise."

I laughed, but in my heart I knew he was losing me.

Not long after the fight with Lan Yu, I had to stop by Lin Ping's work unit to handle some paperwork for the medical equipment deal we were collaborating on. I had misgivings about seeing her face-to-face, but my hesitation melted away the moment I entered her office. There she was, walking toward me with a smile, her long, slender arms extended for a quick but cordial hug. I hadn't seen her in over two years. She was exactly the same gorgeous woman she had always been.

When lunchtime came around, I asked her if she would join me for a bite to eat. She wavered momentarily, but quickly smiled. "Sure," she said, reminding me of the first time I'd asked her on a date nearly four years earlier.

We went to Old Peking, a restaurant specializing in traditional Beijing dishes. After stopping at the buffet-style counter, we sat at one of the many red lacquered antique-style tables lining the walls. We continued talking about business matters for a while, but pretty soon the conversation turned personal.

"So, I hear you're getting married!" I said cheerfully.

"Yep!" she replied, visibly happy. "Spring next year!"

"That's wonderful. Congratulations."

"Well, I'm keeping my fingers crossed!" She laughed, then looked at me thoughtfully. "You know, for a long time I thought I would never get married again. But I think I'm ready now. I've learned a lesson, you know? I've learned that dating and marriage are two different things. You can't jump lightly from one to the other." She paused pensively. "Especially if you're a woman."

I looked down at the cup of tea in front of me and smiled sheepishly. "I know," I said. "And you're right. I take full responsibility for what happened."

I liked the fact that we weren't afraid to talk about the past. But apparently there wasn't much more to say, because for the next few moments we just sat there, looking at each other in silence until she averted her eyes and her cheeks flushed red.

"Don't look at me that way," she said. "Why do you think I was stupid enough to marry you to begin with?" She laughed.

"Oh, really?" I joked. "Then don't go through with the wedding next spring. Just marry me again instead!"

"*No way!*" she cried in English, laughing loudly.

As we were saying goodbye, Lin Ping gripped my elbow and told me that if I ever got married again, she hoped I would let her know so she could congratulate me. I said I would probably stay a bachelor forever. "Besides," I added, "your fiancé and I both know we could never do better than you!" She seemed to want to say something in response to this, but must have changed her mind because she just smiled and walked away.

It had been six months since my release from jail. Half a year since the day I vowed to myself that unless Lan Yu left me, I was going to stay with him forever. Half a year. It felt like half a century.

After lunch with Lin Ping, I walked back to my car in the crisp, almost spring air, my mind whirling with contradictory thoughts and emotions. Does the vow still mean anything to me? Again and again I rolled the question over in my mind.

On my way back to the office, I drove past Huada University. Passing the south gate, I was struck by the thunderous sound of loudspeakers blaring trite slogans. *"Graduates!"* boomed a disembodied voice. *"Go out and give fifty years of hard work to the motherland!"* When Lan Yu and I had first started dating, I always told him I hated going to Huada to pick him up or drop him off. I couldn't stand the tired, artificial orthodoxy of the university environment. Now, however, there was something bittersweet about what I saw all around me. It reminded me of him.

I forced myself to stop thinking about it. I was tired of constantly worrying about my relationship with Lan Yu and our future together, if we even had one. All I wanted was to let nature take its course.

Thirty-Six

As promised, Zhou Wen helped me resolve the hapless affair with the imported car parts. Because of this, I guess you could say we became friends. True, he pocketed more than a few taels of silver from me, but I knew money wasn't the only reason he had helped.

To thank Zhou Wen for everything he had done, I invited him to dinner at the Grand Capital, the very place Lin Ping and I had gotten married. By the time the appetizers hit the table, we were already talking about the little hussies he kept at his place in Pixie Hamlet.

"So, how about Annie? Not bad, eh?" Zhou Wen asked, lifting a thick piece of seaweed to his lips. Annie—that was the name of the one I had slept with at Bamboo Garden.

"Not bad, not bad at all!" I replied. "That little number sure had all the right moves."

The truth was that Annie—this was his chosen name, of course—wasn't exactly my type. In fact, I had only slept with him because I didn't want to offend Zhou Wen. Still, I was curious to know more about his interest in boys who dressed like girls.

"So, when did Brother Wen start to get into this sort of thing?"

"Oh man, years ago," he said with a laugh. "At first it was just something new and different, almost like a novelty. But now, you know what? I've been doing it for so long that I'm practically over it!"

"Ha!" I laughed. "Not doing it for you anymore, huh?"

Zhou Wen took another bite of seaweed and laughed so hard that green specks flew out of his mouth and hit the table. Then he put down his chopsticks and looked at me somberly.

"So, tell me, Handong. How did you get into this stuff?"

"Oh—well!" I fumbled. "That was a long time ago, you know. I was just messing around, really." I paused, desperate to think of something to say. "If you don't mind me asking, how did Brother Chen know?"

"Fuck!" he chortled loudly. "Who can hide this sort of thing?" He leaned into me and whispered, "I heard you even got a house to keep him in, just like a real concubine. Now, that's doing it right! Not just messing around like me and Annie."

Zhou Wen leaned back into his chair and stared at me through two blinking eyes as if waiting for a response. My gut instinct was to deny everything, but for some reason I didn't. Instead, I mumbled a vague affirmation which, Zhou Wen and I both knew, meant yes.

"So it's serious, huh? I mean, the relationship." He stared at me gravely. The conversation was entering uncomfortable territory. I gave an awkward chuckle.

"Well, let me tell you something," he continued. "It's not worth it, okay? A man only gets so many chances in this lifetime to get serious in a relationship. And when he does, he damn well better be sure there's a future in it. It has to lead to some bigger picture. Family. Kids." He lit a cigarette. "But you

331

know what? With this kind of thing, there is no bigger picture. This is it! You can't even tell people about it without ruining yourself."

The conversation was getting to be too much. The last thing I wanted was to lose face in front of Zhou Wen by getting gushy over a guy. So I distorted the facts to make things look the way I wanted.

"I know, Brother Wen. You're right. It's not worth it. But no matter what I do, I just can't get rid of him!"

He nodded sympathetically, then laughed. "The problem with you is you're too goddamn nice. A real fuckin' Buddha!" He laughed again, but only for an instant before leaning into me as if he wanted to say something momentous.

"He's really devoted to you, isn't he?" he asked in a gentle voice. "I mean, he can't stay away from you, right?"

I was on the verge of caving in. I wanted to tell Zhou Wen the truth, not so much because I trusted him, but because the more I thought about Lan Yu, the more frustrated I felt. I needed to get it off my chest or I was going to explode. I looked at Zhou Wen in distress and took a deep breath.

"I don't know what to do, Brother Wen! He just won't stop playing games with me. I mean, one day he wants me and the next he's indifferent. All I want is to know what he's thinking. Is that too much to ask? It's getting to the point where I can't take it anymore."

Zhou Wen nodded his head in understanding. "Look," he said in a voice as empathetic as it was stern. "That's his trick, okay? He chases after you one day, then rejects you the next. He's playing hard to get and that's exactly how he holds on to you." He took a deep drag on his cigarette and a chunk of gray ash fell onto the mustard-yellow tablecloth. "Damn," he continued as if speaking to himself, "that guy sure knows what he's doing."

My talk with Zhou Wen was a real eye-opener. He was an expert when it came to reading between the lines, and I trusted what he said. He really nailed it, I thought, as we said goodbye that night. Lan Yu sure knows what he's doing!

A few days later, Annie called my cell phone. At first I was confused because I hadn't given him the number, but quickly realized that Zhou Wen must have given it to him.

I had mixed feelings about seeing Annie again. To begin with, there was no question that I had only taken him home because it would have caused Zhou Wen to lose face not to. True, he turned out to be a great lay and had a hot little body, but for some reason I just didn't feel like getting together again. At the end of the day, I knew he was fine for a one-night stand, but for anything beyond that, he just wasn't my type.

What I wanted didn't matter though. Annie, I figured, had called me because Zhou Wen wanted him to, and he was determined to fulfill the assignment. So I agreed to meet him that night at Bamboo Garden. All I asked was that he come dressed as a boy—not wear a bra and nylons and all that. No offense, I said. It was just a turnoff.

When Annie walked into the hotel room, it was a total transformation. Wearing a jacket, wing tips, and a neatly ironed button-down shirt tucked into pleated trousers, he looked every bit the pretty, delicate boy. He was still very feminine, but without the exaggerated affectations from the first time I'd met him. I had the impression that he had no real preference for dressing as a boy or a girl, that it was mostly a matter of what the client wanted.

Annie was adept at reading other people's body language. He lived, it seemed, entirely for the purpose of satisfying others' desires. And yet, when I asked him if Zhou Wen had told him to call me, he said no, that he had called because he himself had wanted to. He also added that he wasn't staying at Zhou Wen's house anymore. That's when I learned that "Brother Wen" had some weird thing about the number three. "He likes everything in threes," Annie explained patiently. Thus, when it came to lovers—male or female—he never kept anyone around for more than three months. Apparently, Annie's three were up.

Annie was naked from the waist up as he told me this. The unblemished white skin of his face, so encrusted with makeup the first time I saw him, was smooth, almost matte, under the dim yellow light pulsing softly above the mirrored headboard. I sat up in bed, watching as he lovingly carved slices of roasted lamb from the room service I'd ordered and placed them directly in my mouth. There was such an earnestness in everything he did, not only in his eyes, but also in his body language, perpetually oriented toward my every need. Annie told me that he had never been sexually attracted to men when he was growing up, that he didn't even know that sex between men was possible. But from the moment he discovered that it was, he wanted men and men only.

Swallowing the last piece of lamb, I shifted my body so I could lie flat on the bed. I motioned with my hand for Annie to come closer, then gently pushed him downward toward my cock, which had become stiff the moment he said "sex between men." I already knew from the first time we were together that Annie was an extremely talented cocksucker. When we were together, he cared about one thing and one thing only: getting me off. He sucked my dick for a full half hour before suddenly stopping and standing upright on the bed. Gazing at me seductively, he peeled off his socks with one hand while putting his other hand against the wall for balance. Everything about him was calm, relaxed, and professional as he pushed down his trousers, grinning mischievously. That's when I noticed he had violated my instructions. Despite the masculine exterior, he was still wearing women's panties. "Naughty girl!" I chastised him, as he lowered himself to straddle my waist as if riding a seesaw. He loved it.

Annie guided my cock inside him with expert precision. With one hand he reached back to cup my balls while the other arm rose to the back of his head like he was some kind of pinup girl. He loved this position, but it didn't last long because I quickly jumped up and threw him on his back. With a single hand I held his ankles together high above his torso while my other hand stroked his dick and played with his balls.

Some guys who fuck boys like Annie like to pretend they don't have male parts, but not me. I wanted to see him get off.

Whether getting fucked in the mouth or ass, penetration alone wasn't enough to make Annie come. He continued stroking his dick as I nailed him—this, apparently, was the only thing that could make him climax. When he did, I beamed with satisfaction knowing that even a veteran hooker like Annie came when I got ahold of him.

Soon after, Annie was in the shower. I closed my eyes and listened to the water splashing, recalling with relief that Zhou Wen had assured me he was clean.

I was conflicted about whether or not to hold on to Annie. On the one hand, he was young, beautiful, and hot in bed. Only a monk, and a highly disciplined one at that, could have resisted him. On the other hand, there was something about his enthusiasm that didn't quite ring true. He was skilled at what he did, but at the end of the day it was an act, a performance, a job.

Annie didn't sleep at Bamboo Garden that night, saying he would rather take a cab home with the money I'd given him. Switching off the light to go to sleep, it crossed my mind that despite his shortcomings, I would probably be better off with Annie than with Lan Yu. At least Annie wouldn't require much effort.

I had never wanted a life that required much effort.

Thirty-Seven

One afternoon while I was at the office, Lan Yu called out of the blue to invite me to his home that evening. I didn't even have to think about it. I told him the traffic was cruddy and I wasn't coming.

"It takes ten minutes to get here, Handong!" he said, annoyed. "So if you don't want to come, just say so. But don't start coming up with excuses."

"Fine, I'm coming," I said. I didn't say it out loud, but I knew perfectly well that I was being the unreasonable one.

"Forget it," he said coldly. "I won't be here."

I wondered why I had rejected him. It's not like I had anything better to do that night. Virtually all my evenings at that point were spent either at the office or at Bamboo Garden or at my mother's place. The real reason I didn't want to see him, I knew, was that I couldn't bear confronting the empty shell of a relationship that Lan Yu and I had become.

It killed me. The cold, indifferent tone of his voice. The snide, apathetic smirk that always seemed to linger at the corners of his mouth. The cutting remarks. Especially anytime I tried talking about us, about our relationship.

What Zhou Wen had said was right: the point of two people being together is to find happiness. But Lan Yu and I had nothing. No bond of marriage, no consideration of property, profits, children, or social opinion. It's one thing to have nothing in the world but the happiness you feel. But when you have nothing and you're not happy to begin with, then what's the point?

That night, I went to One Two Three, where some Polish exchange student with passable Mandarin chatted me up as I knocked back a few drinks. It was nearly midnight when I stumbled back into the street, my compass set on Fang Village despite Lan Yu's explicit instructions not to go there. I had drunk far too much to be driving and was more than a little buzzed upon my arrival. I knocked on two or three apartment doors before realizing I wasn't even in the right building. Then I went back outside and walked in circles, muttering incoherently until I located the correct building. By the time I finally found his apartment door I was tired of looking, so I just twisted the knob. It was open.

"Who's there?" Lan Yu's voice called out from the bedroom. It was dark in the front entrance.

"It's me," I said, noticing a cluster of empty beer bottles standing erect on the living room table. It was the same little table with the chipped blue paint from Lan Yu's old living room. He had brought it with him in the move from Gala to Fang.

Lan Yu came out of the bedroom, dragging his feet and looking drowsy, but just as fully dressed as if he had still been at work.

"You're still awake?" I asked.

"What time is it?" His eyes swept the wall in search of a clock before he gave on up the idea. He must have remembered that, like most of his belongings, it wasn't unpacked yet.

"What are you doing here at this hour?" he asked.

"What's wrong with that?" I answered him with a question. "Can't I come over?"

He looked at me with a sort of neutral gaze. He didn't seem particularly upset that I was there, but nor was he happy to see me. Wordlessly, he turned around and went back into the bedroom. I grabbed a chair from the blue table and followed.

His bedroom was a mess, and we had to navigate a sea of books and dirty clothes to get to the bed. Lan Yu sat up against the headboard, staring at me with a clinical eye, while I sat on the chair near the foot of the bed, trying my best to avoid eye contact. I lit a cigarette and stared at the wall. It was too quiet in that little room, so quiet that the only noise I could hear was the sound of two people breathing and the aggravating buzz of the ceiling light. I wanted Lan Yu to say something, but he must have wanted the same thing from me, because the minutes ticked away and neither of us said a word. Finally I spoke.

"So, I guess you don't want me here. You've pretty much had enough of me, huh?" I asked, still staring at the wall. A thick rope of cigarette ash fell to the floor, so I reached under the bed to pull out the ashtray he had always kept there for me. I turned to look at him. I wanted to see his expression so I could understand what he was thinking, but his face was hidden under dark shadows, barely visible in the dimness of the light. He remained silent, so I kept talking.

"Look, Lan Yu. If you have a problem with me or if you're just sick of this or whatever, I wish you would open your mouth and say so."

More silence. I'd long since learned to expect silence from him, but that didn't mean I liked it.

"Fine," I said. I was starting to get pissed. "I suppose you've got it all planned out, right? Just keep playing games with me till you get on the plane, then *see ya later*! Is that it?" I smashed the cigarette butt angrily into the ashtray. His silence made me seethe with rage.

"Goddamn it, fucking say something, Lan Yu!" I shouted as I stood up from the chair. "I mean, look at the way you're behaving. Quit acting like the entire fucking world revolves around you, like it owes you something!"

"The way *I'm* behaving?" he scoffed. "What about you?"

Maybe it was only because I was drunk, but when Lan Yu finally opened his mouth it made me laugh. A cynical laugh. "Me?" I asked sardonically. "I'm just a big whore, remember?"

Lan Yu didn't think it was funny. His big, sad eyes looked like black holes carved out with a knife. He lowered his head.

"Listen, Lan Yu," I continued, sitting down again. "Ever since my divorce—since we got back together—all I've wanted is to be with you. To *really* be with you. Especially since I got out of jail. I even made a vow to myself—" I faltered, unable to tell him the promise I'd made.

"If you don't believe me, just look at what my life has become! I've trampled on my parents' wishes. I've insulted my friends. I've lost face in every possible way I can." I laughed darkly and shook my head in disbelief. "I must have been on some weird fucking drugs to do all that!"

This made Lan Yu snap. "What the hell do you want from me, Handong?" His voice seethed with anger.

The battle was beginning to wear me out. I barely had the energy to speak, but somehow managed to assemble my forces and look him in the eye.

"Nothing," I said resolutely. "You should just know that I'm done with your games. It's over."

I stood up from the chair and stalked toward the front door. I was about to turn the knob when I heard his voice. "Chen Handong."

Still clutching the doorknob, I turned around halfway and found Lan Yu standing in the bedroom doorway. His eyes flashed with anger, but it was an anger infused with sadness. We looked at each other as best we could in the darkness that enshrouded the room.

"It's just that—you made up that stupid excuse not to come here!" There was a distinct tone of anger in his voice, but I didn't mind. What mattered was that his voice lacked the sarcastic aloofness of recent weeks and there was no trace of that infuriating smirk. He looked worried, frustrated, like an anxiety-ridden kid. It had been ages since I'd seen him like that.

"Right," I said calmly, letting go of the door handle to fully face him. "Because you didn't want me here."

He cocked his head and looked at me with a kind of tortured smile. He wanted so desperately to say something. What was it? What was that thing he wanted to say so badly, but couldn't, or wouldn't? For a moment I really believed that whatever it was, he was finally about to say it, but instead he just looked at me with tears in his eyes.

"Why did I move so far away?" he said, more to himself than to me, shaking his head and looking up at the ceiling to suppress the tears. "This guy I know, he said he could help me find a place over by Blackstone Bridge 'cause . . . 'cause I know how much you hate traffic and how hard it is to get here and how you'd rather sleep at your office and—" He looked at me helplessly. "Do you know how long it takes me to get to work now?"

There was nothing I could say at this point. We stood in the darkness staring at each other until I had the sudden urge to pull him into my arms and hold him. Lan Yu leaned against my chest, arms hanging lifelessly at his sides. We stood like that for a long time until he pulled his head back and looked up at me numbly. I released him from my embrace and went back to the bedroom, where I lay on the bed fully clothed. He followed. There we remained, two heartbroken men, for god knows how long till at last we fell asleep.

The following day I wanted to put aside the problems of the previous night so I went to Lan Yu's office to surprise him when he got off work. Sure enough, he was astonished to find me standing outside the main entrance to Skytalk, leaning up against the metal railing with my arms folded and a warm smile on my face. His shock quickly melted away, though, and was replaced by a radiant smile that made me wonder how it was that after nearly ten years of knowing him, this man still held such an intense power over me.

It was nearly ten by the time we finished dinner and got back to Lan Yu's place. He busied himself with apartment stuff—putting his room in order, throwing clothes in the washing machine—and I had to make a phone call. My client and I entered into a protracted session of haggling over some details, and the conversation soon turned into a bit of an argument. When the washing machine switched cycles, it suddenly became so loud that I had trouble hearing my client, so I raised a hand to cover my ear. Lan Yu stood on the sidelines, watching me try to talk in the droning hum of the washing machine and laughing at what he apparently thought was a highly comedic scene.

After Lan Yu was done cleaning and I had finished my call, I took a shower and jumped into bed. Lan Yu sat up next to me watching TV.

"It's almost eleven," I mumbled as I pulled the bedsheet over my head. "Let's go to sleep. I'll drive you to work tomorrow." I turned onto my side with my back against him and closed my eyes.

Lan Yu snuggled up behind me, kissing my upper back and the nape of my neck. I knew from the way he was touching me that he wanted to make love. "Handong . . . ," he purred into my ear, rolling me over onto my back and crawling on top of me.

"Nnnnnnnn . . . ," I groaned. "I don't feel like it."

He stopped what he was doing and looked down at me. "It's been two weeks! You must have blue balls by now."

"C'mon, stop it," I said, gently pushing him away.

Lan Yu had no way of knowing I had fooled around with Annie just a few nights earlier. And yet, he must have sensed something, because he rolled off me and returned to his side of the bed. A long silence ensued.

"Is there someone else, Handong?" his voice finally broke the silence. I stayed put with my back against him.

"Yes," I answered quietly.

"Fuck," he scoffed and looked up at the ceiling. "I knew it! A man or a woman?"

"A man, of course," I said, jumping up and pouncing onto him. "Surname Lan, given name Yu!"

I took him into my arms, laughing and kissing his face. Lan Yu exploded in laughter, allowing me to believe for one blissful moment that everything was all right.

I didn't want to lie to Lan Yu. But at the same time there were some things I just couldn't explain. Annie was one of them.

I peeled off Lan Yu's clothes, then laid him on his stomach spread eagle so I could feast on him with my eyes. I gazed at his profile—somberly earnest but distant, and steeped in a cautious restraint I hadn't seen in a long while. It didn't matter how many times I looked at Lan Yu, I was always struck by his face, so beautiful with its high arched nose and full red lips. Looking at him now, it was impossible not to notice how he had changed. The youthfulness of his face, gone; his body, thinner than when we first met. But still so pure, so handsome. He still had those broad shoulders and those thick, strong arms. I collapsed on top of him, digging my nails into his skin and kissing him behind his ear.

"You see what you do to me?" I exclaimed, almost in tears. "I'm lost in you!"

Hooking his ankles around my calves, Lan Yu pushed his ass up into my groin. I would have done anything for him. Nothing we had gone through mattered. The years of hurt, the sorrow. I was going to keep him by my side forever.

Since the day we met, Lan Yu and I had been together and apart so many times. We really were like the butterfly lovers, doing whatever we could to stay together despite the odds. I knew him so well. What excited him, what got him off. I knew his limits and how to control them.

When we made love I rarely let him come in my hand and even less in my mouth. Often, I didn't even let him come when I fucked him. My pleasure was the pleasure of control: controlling him, controlling myself. I reveled in Lan Yu's pleasure, but it was mine to give, drop by drop, until he exploded in ecstasy. What got me off was torturing him, not just with pleasure, but with the promise of ever-greater horizons of pleasure to come. Sex with Lan Yu meant denying him release until he showed me he was ready. When I entered him, his deep moan intoxicated me, and together we went to a place of bliss.

"I'm in heaven!" I would cry out loud. I looked into his eyes and saw excitement, expectation. There was never a moment when he wasn't immersed in the euphoria of the present. I'll do anything for you, I thought. None of the sacrifices I'd made mattered. I was going to keep him forever. He was mine!

That night I held Lan Yu in my arms and pondered the mysteries of makeup sex, nature's superglue for lovers. Everything was back to normal. We could forget the fight we'd had the night before when I showed up drunk on his doorstep. We were good again.

"You fucked me so long before coming!" Lan Yu laughed.

"And what's wrong with that?" I countered playfully. "Don't you want a man with a little endurance?"

He turned onto his side and pressed his back up against my chest. "Yeah," he said. "I'd love a little endurance. Endurance for more than two days before breaking up with me!" He laughed.

I propped myself up on an elbow and peered over his shoulder. I wanted to catch a glimpse of his eyes, which I hoped would tell me why he had just made this flippant remark. But his eyes were closed.

"You know, they say it's hard for people like us to stay together," he said out of nowhere.

Pulling the blanket up tightly around us, I kissed the nape of his neck. "It's been almost ten years," I said. "Well, on and off," I added. "You don't think that's a long time?"

Lan Yu turned around to face me, wrapping his arms around my neck and kissing me deeply. "I want more!" he said, resting his forehead against mine.

Then let's do it, I thought.

After my reconciliation with Lan Yu, Annie continued calling me periodically. After the second time we slept together, I was even beginning to think that the little fairy might be able to move this mere mortal's heart. But by the third time I saw him, it was becoming clear that he just wasn't doing it for me. Annie sensed it, too. The last time we got together he bitched endlessly that there wasn't one good man on the planet. Then he stopped calling.

Thirty-Eight

My mother's sixty-third birthday was on the twelfth day of the sixth lunar month. Everyone forgot about it, including me. Aidong and her husband were always swamped with summer orders that time of year—they ran a flower distribution company—and Jingdong had recently moved to Australia with her husband and daughter. On the morning of my mother's birthday, the old lady called to ask me to visit her in the evening, but it was only when I got there that Auntie Xiao, my mother's maid, pulled me into the hallway to remind me in a hushed and somewhat flustered voice what day it was. Auntie Xiao wasn't my real aunt, we just called her that.

It was too late to go back in time and wish my mother a happy birthday, so I gave myself a mood adjustment and tried to think creatively about last-minute ways to do something nice for her. I walked into the kitchen and grabbed her by both hands. "Let's go out to dinner!" I said excitedly. Any restaurant, I knew, would have a little birthday routine for elderly folks that they could do. But my mother wasn't having it.

"Oh, it's okay, Little Dong!" she exclaimed. "Auntie Xiao is making *sau mein!*" Sau mein, longevity noodles, were a birthday tradition for old people. More than enough to make my mother happy on her birthday.

"Well, where's Aidong then?" I asked in a huff. "I'm going to call her and tell her to get her butt over here!" I picked up the clunky beige rotary telephone my mother kept on the table next to the couch.

"Don't!" my mother screeched, rushing toward me to grab the phone out of my hands. "She's busy today! I already talked to her!"

"What on earth can be so important that she has to miss your sixty-third birthday?" I protested. "Don't worry, Ma. I'll just give her a quick call." It was just the opportunity I needed to show her I'd remembered her special day.

"Chen Handong, you listen to your mother," she said in a stern voice. "Aidong is so busy right now she doesn't even have time for her own kids, let alone me. Besides, she already stopped by yesterday with the loveliest presents. You have to see what she brought!"

I hung up the phone, fighting the urge to lower my head in shame. I knew my mother hadn't mentioned Aidong's gifts to make me feel bad, but I felt like an ass for showing up empty-handed.

"Anyway," she continued. "As long as you're here, I'm happy. You know the door is always open for you." She trailed behind me as I crossed the kitchen carrying a heavy pot of water she had asked me to place on the stove. "And don't wait for me to pick up the phone and call before you come over here," she continued. "You and Lin Ping used to visit every weekend, remember?" I placed the pot of water on the burner, and Auntie Xiao took over.

"And if you don't want to come alone, there's always room for two."

If I had still been holding the pot of water, I would have dropped it. Did she just say what I think she said? Astonished, I turned to look at her, but she was already at the kitchen sink with her back to me, calmly washing a bowl of dried black mushrooms, seemingly oblivious to the vortex of emotions into which her words had thrown me.

My professional life wasn't improving and was, in fact, deteriorating with each passing day. Upticks happened here and there, and money flowed periodically into my bank account, but it was nowhere near the great bounce back for which I had hoped. Apart from nights when I had business-related social engagements that kept me away, I stayed with Lan Yu at Fang Village, where our life had become routine to say the least. Each day after work I came home, took a shower, then napped until he got off work. Then we would either go out to eat or make something simple at home. After several months of living together in this way, we settled into a routine that was not so much happy as it was practical. The comfortable monotony of our day-to-day existence left us with some much-needed peace of mind.

One warm and beautiful Sunday afternoon, Lan Yu jumped into my arms, giddy with excitement. He said he wanted to go outside and enjoy the sunshine. I felt like crap because I hadn't slept well the night before, but agreed—"As long as you drive," I had said—and asked him where he wanted to go.

"Heaven!" he shouted. He wanted to be in a place that was outdoors but isolated, a place where we could be alone, where we could actually express our affection for each other. A place where we could, for once in our lives, be like any other couple.

Until that day, I had never thought such a place existed.

"Watch out!" he threatened with a laugh. "I'm going to hold your hand in public!"

We got into the car and drove toward the Western Hills. Lan Yu was so excited about our getaway that he practically bounced up and down in his seat as he drove. Turning to look at me, he laughed when he saw I couldn't stop yawning. "Come on, wake up!" he said cheerfully, placing his hand on the back of my neck and giving it a gentle squeeze.

"I'm an old man, leave me alone!" I joked. "I need you to wake me up. Sing a song or something."

"A song!" he exclaimed. "What do you want to sing?" He stared at the road in fixed concentration, evidently trying to come up with something. Then his eyes lit up and he took a deep breath.

"*March on! March on! Our troops march toward the sun! On the motherland's soil we step, on the motherland's soil we run!*"

Lan Yu didn't have to tell me what he was singing. It was "The March of the Chinese People's Liberation Army," a military anthem that had been around in various forms since the 1930s. I took the next line.

"*The hope of our people is on our backs, an invincible force are we!*"

I held Lan Yu's hand tightly against my knee. The car rolled forward and we began to sing in unison.

"*March on! March on! Our troops march toward the sun! To the victory of the revolution, and the entire nation's liberation!*"

We fell into peals of laughter. Never had a song felt so good.

We parked and walked into a secluded area of the Western Hills, hoping to avoid the judgmental eyes of the very Chinese masses we had been extolling in song just moments earlier.

We stumbled upon a beautiful clearing with shady trees and a cool, gentle wind. I sat up against a tree and Lan Yu lay down with his head resting in my lap. He looked up at the sky, his countenance betraying that he was lost in a faraway dreamworld.

"I don't know why," he began, "but the sky has always seemed so much bluer here in Beijing. Bluer than it ever was in my hometown."

I smiled down at him. "I'll bet the sky is even bluer in America. No wonder you want to go there: you're a blue sky yourself!" It was true. Lan meant *blue* and Yu meant *sky*.

He smiled and looked up at me. "You probably think the moon is fuller in America, too, don't you?" His voice floated upward like birdsong.

"Hey!" I said, craning my neck down to kiss his nose. "You're the one who's always bitching and moaning about how you want to go there!" I laughed.

"What do you mean, bitching and moaning? If I ever left Beijing, it would only be because I had no choice."

"What do you mean, no choice?"

He paused, gazing at the trees overhead. Then he returned his eyes to mine. "Listen, Handong. I would never leave Beijing unless you broke up with me. But if you did, I would leave forever. I would never come back." His tone of voice was dead serious. I looked up at the trees, where I saw two little red birds flutter downward and land on a branch.

"Anyway," he continued, "I was just thinking about that. Why don't we go there together? Just you and me. What do you think?"

I looked back down at him. "I like visiting the US, but I don't want to live there." Lan Yu became quiet, but raised himself slightly so that he was now snuggled up against my chest.

"Speaking of which," I continued, "did you get everything worked out with your schools?"

"I got two fellowships, but not from very good universities."

"So, are you going to take one of them?" I asked, trying to conceal my sudden alarm.

Lan Yu returned his gaze to the blue sky overhead. "I never called that friend of yours about the visa," he said. "Anyway, who cares? I like Beijing!"

In the distance we heard the jarring sound of human voices. "Someone's coming!" I panicked. "Get up!"

Lan Yu kept his head firmly in my lap. "What are you so afraid of?" he asked. "Let them come. Whoever it is, they won't stand a chance with me!"

"What if it's two people?" I asked.

"Don't I have you here with me?"

"And if it's three?"

"Three of *them* aren't necessarily stronger than the two of *us*." He laughed.

"Well, what if it's a whole bunch of people?"

"So we get our heads cracked open!" he said. "I'll fight them to the death if I have to!" Smiling, I recalled what Zhang Jie had told me about Lan Yu's fight with Yonghong: *That little guy of yours is tough as nails.*

"Okay, tough guy," I said, my eyes fixed on his smiling face. "Huada would be proud to call you a graduate!"

I looked at the sky reflected in his eyes: deep, dark, almost black. I admired him so much. He possessed a kind of bravery I would never have. When I looked at his face, I saw not just a handsome young man but the breathtaking power of youth itself.

Lan Yu sat up and I pulled him into my arms. There we sat, our lips pressed together with the fervent madness of a first-time kiss. In nearly a decade of knowing him, it was only the second time we had ever shared a kiss outdoors. But now, instead of darkness, we were surrounded by radiant sunlight, blue skies, and the beautiful, rolling hills around us.

Thirty-Nine

Autumn! Once again the stunning, golden autumn of Beijing had arrived. The air was cool and dry, and the sky peeking through the tree branches was exceptionally blue. It was as if the sky was trying to tell the world that something had changed—or was about to. Leaves fluttered and fell to the ash-colored streets below. The roads were usually so broad and barren, but in autumn they always came alive with a thick carpet of color.

Early one morning—*that* morning—I woke up in Lan Yu's little apartment in Fang Village to a spray of sunshine bursting through the bedroom window. I moaned softly, loving the warmth on my face, the way it made up for the failure of the endlessly incompetent heater in the corner to dispel the cold of the night before. A few minutes later, Lan Yu woke up and we languished in bed for a while before getting up for work. I had an early meeting to get to and Lan Yu had a deadline to make. He jumped out of bed and threw on his favorite white shirt, the one he'd worn that day at Tian'anmen, then washed his hands and face. It was time for us to commence our separate, equally busy lives.

Just before stepping out the door, Lan Yu leaned up against me to give me a kiss goodbye. Gently pinching the lapel of my suit jacket between his fingers, he held my tie with his other hand and pulled me toward him. I was feeling rushed, so I planted a perfunctory kiss on his nose and asked him if he needed a ride to work.

"I'm going to take a cab," he replied, "but can you pick me up when I get off?"

"Of course!" I grabbed my briefcase. "See you at five!"

I made it to my meeting on time, but kicked myself for forgetting my cell. It didn't matter anyway. The negotiations went well, and I was going to make a killing from the deal.

Driving back to my office, I started planning a trip to Europe. The list of countries floated through my mind: Germany, the Netherlands, Denmark—including, of course, a visit to Tivoli Gardens. I smiled thinking about how much Lan Yu would enjoy seeing the historic buildings of Northern Europe that he had thus far seen only in pictures.

I stopped at a red light and closed my eyes. I, Chen Handong, will recover from this mess! Success was imminent. I felt it.

But in an instant, everything changed.

I entered my office and a grave-looking Liu Zheng grabbed my arm. "Sit down, Handong." He pushed down on my shoulders to make me sit on the sofa.

"What is it?" I asked. "You're acting weird."

"I need you to brace yourself, Handong. I mean, emotionally . . . ," he stammered.

"What the hell are you talking about, Liu Zheng?" I thought something had happened to my mother.

"It's Lan Yu," he said. "Something happened."

My mouth fell open. I didn't understand what he meant.

"The taxi he was in, it crashed into a truck. He was—I mean, it happened right there on the spot."

A hand gripped my elbow and led me outside to the street, where someone put me in a car and took me to a hospital. My mind went numb and it felt as though I were falling through clouds. I looked up and the skyline fused heaven and earth in a vast swath of blue and gray.

When we arrived at the hospital, someone in a white coat took me to a room where beds covered with white sheets lined the walls. We stopped before one of them and someone, I don't know who, lifted the sheet.

There I saw a face: red, blue, black. My knees swayed and I lowered myself to the ground—it was Lan Yu. I reached up and grasped his shoulders, the shoulders I had touched so many times. But they were stiff now, cold. My eyes dug into him; he had seen my eyes a thousand times, but could no longer return their gaze. I looked at the high bridge of his nose, his red lips, his dark brown eyes, eyes I had lost myself in countless times. And suddenly, I laughed! It didn't matter that his face was covered with a thick coating of black and red blood. It was Lan Yu! I didn't need to see him clearly to know it. I held him with all the strength that I had.

Someone tried to pull me away. I struggled to free myself, then collapsed on top of the man lying before me. A sound came out of my mouth. It was a cry of anguish, of two invisible hands squeezing my throat.

"Calm down, Handong!" Someone grabbed my arm as if to pull me away and my head surged with anger.

Get off me! the words swirled in my mind.

Someone, something, pulled at me harder, pulled me away from him.

Fuck you! You want to laugh? Laugh! But I won't leave him! He needs me! He's safe in my arms!

I tugged at Lan Yu's arm, pulled him toward me, wanted to feel his body melt into mine.

Because he's not dead! He told me to pick him up, he told me to kiss him goodbye! He never does that! He was trying to tell me something, but I didn't hear him! I didn't give him a good kiss goodbye! How could I have been so stupid?

I kissed the twisted, red-and-black flesh before me, and my own face became smeared with blood. I gave him a final kiss. A good kiss this time. The right kiss this time.

I don't know how long it took, but a powerful force finally pulled me away. They led me out of the room, I don't know where to. I wanted to stay with him, but I couldn't. I was powerless.

Forty

No longer did I love autumn in Beijing. When I awoke on the floor of my office the morning after Lan Yu's death, the capital looked just as cold and bleak as if a mighty zephyr had come and blown the entire world away. I sat at the window for three hours. Only then did the whole thing become so cruelly real.

I went to Lan Yu's apartment, and it filled me with terror. Everything was just as it had been left. A glass of water he had been drinking sat half-full on the kitchen table. I didn't dare touch it. I couldn't even look at it.

I entered the bedroom, where the reminders of Lan Yu's life surrounded me in silent torment. All those things—why didn't their owner come back? I remembered telling Lan Yu not to bother making the bed, that there wasn't time. He just laughed and said he couldn't stand my sloppiness. Sure enough, there was the bed with the blanket pulled up neat and tight. At the foot of the bed was a neatly folded stack of clothes, the items he had been wearing the previous day. I picked up his shirt and held it against my chest. The warmth of his body was gone, but his scent clung to it, just as real as if he had been in the room with me. I collapsed on the bed, burying my face in the shirt. That's when I heard a voice, a wailing sound unlike anything I had ever heard, not even when I was at the morgue. It was the sound of a man in grief, a soul torn apart by the agony of loss. It was my own voice. Absolute. Irreversible.

I fell apart in the weeks that followed. I couldn't bring myself to sleep in the bed that Lan Yu and I had once shared, but nor did I want to be at my mother's. Even less did I want to be at a hotel. So I slept at my office each night.

Three days after I stopped eating the hallucinations began. They were mostly auditory—again and again I heard Lan Yu calling my name—but there were visual ones, too. Believing he was in the room with me, I opened doors and pulled back curtains to find him. My mind was on the verge of collapse. I had entered the world of the living dead.

It was only a matter of time before my mother noticed that my visits had stopped. She called and insisted that I come over.

I parked the car outside and walked in through the front door, spitting out a cursory hello as I made my way to my room. I didn't want my mother to see the pathetic state I was in, and didn't feel like talking anyway. What would we have talked about?

I lay on my bed, half-asleep or perhaps half-dead, completely unaware of how much time had passed. I vaguely heard the sound of my mother pushing the door open and stepping inside, but only when she sat next to me on the bed did I fully realize that she was there. I kept my eyes closed, pretending to be asleep. She touched my arm like she did when I was a child, and I heard her breathing: rapid and shallow. I opened one eye and saw her twist my shirtsleeve between her fingers as if she wanted to say something.

"Little Dong," she said. "I know this is hard for you, but we can't bring back the dead." She cried softly as she spoke. My eyes filled with tears.

"Little Zheng told me everything," she continued. "I want you to know that if that boy hadn't died, I wouldn't try to stop you from being together."

Heavy tears poured out of my eyes onto the pillow. It's too late, I thought angrily. Why didn't you say that when he was alive?

Two weeks later, Liu Zheng pointed out the obvious: that I needed to call Lan Yu's father to tell him that his son was dead. I dug around in my desk for a while before finding the number, which Lan Yu had given me before his trip back to Xinjiang. When I told the old man the news, the only thing I heard on the other end of the line was the deep howl of a father in pain.

A few days later, though, Lan Yu's dad called me back. I didn't even realize that he had my number.

"Did my son say anything before he died?" his voice creaked.

"No. It was so sudden. He never had a chance to say any final words."

Lan Yu's father hesitated. "I mean, did he leave anything?"

"Some clothes, books, that sort of thing. If there's anything you want, I can mail it to you." I thought maybe he wanted a keepsake to remember his son.

"What I mean is, well . . . " He wanted to say something.

In an instant I understood. He wanted money.

I knew Lan Yu still had the $380,000 from when he sold

the house, but I had never asked him where he put it. There was no trace of it in his apartment—no bank deposit slip, nothing. All I found was a savings account with a couple thousand yuan in it. I told the old man that his son hadn't left anything behind.

Later that day, I mentioned the phone call to Liu Zheng.

"Did you know that Lan Yu sold Tivoli?" I asked.

"Of course."

"It's odd . . . I have no idea what he did with the money. His dad called asking about it. I mean, what a horrible father! A time like this, right after his son dies, and all he cares about is whether he can get some cash out of it! But anyway, it doesn't even matter because I don't know what Lan Yu did with the money."

Liu Zheng looked at me in shock. "He didn't tell you?" he asked.

"Tell me what?"

"He used it to get you out of jail, Handong."

"What?" I was stunned. "Why didn't you tell me?"

"He didn't want me to say anything. He said he wanted to tell you himself. Listen, Handong, that first week you were in jail, we thought you were going to be executed, and for all we knew you already were! Lan Yu called me every day to find out whether I had heard any news or found somebody with the right connections to get you out. Finally, our Ma was able to get in touch with some guy your dad knew, but the bastard said he wanted ¥10 million to pull the strings to get you out. We managed to come up with it, but it wasn't easy!"

"¥10 million? You told me it was ¥1 million!"

"Lan Yu told you it was a million, but it was ten. Between me and our Ma we had seven, but we were still three million short. Our Ma asked everyone she knew for a loan, but no one would do it. Even your sisters said they didn't have anything. At first, Lin Ping said she wanted to help, but when push came to shove she started saying she couldn't come up with it." Liu Zheng paused and appeared thoughtful. "Anyway, I guess I don't blame them. For all they knew, they'd never see the money again." He looked at me as if waiting for a response. When he didn't get one, he continued.

"Lan Yu was desperate to come up with the money. He called me in tears, saying that never in his life had he thought money was so important. We talked for a long time, then he remembered the house. It was his idea, Handong. He knew it was in his name and that he was free to sell it, so he asked me to help. I sold it in a week. Everything—the furniture, even the car! We sold the entire lot for $380,000. When we converted it to yuan, it was exactly the ¥3 million we needed. We sold that place way below market value, but under the circumstances we weren't exactly in a position to haggle. After we had the full ¥10 million, we transferred it to your dad's contact, and that was it. You got out." Liu Zheng sat next to me and gently touched my shoulder.

"Handong," he continued. "It's no secret that I didn't like Lan Yu at first. You knew that. But after what he did for you, I really came to admire him. I mean, it's like he became a friend, you know? And if you and him had—I mean, if you and him had that kind of relationship—then he really stepped up and played the part, didn't he? If I had been in your shoes, I don't know if my own wife would have done that for me!" He gave a gentle laugh.

"Then why did he hide it from me?" I cried, tears streaming down my cheeks.

"He just said he wanted to surprise you with it one day. I thought he would have told you by now. Either him, or our Ma."

"Ma knew?"

"Of course she knew! The day you got out of jail, when we went to her house and Lan Yu was waiting in the car, what do you think she was doing while you were in your bedroom? She was standing at the window, watching Lan Yu in the car outside."

Forty-One

It's been three years since Lan Yu died. I live in Canada now, in West Vancouver, where I bought a house and live with my new wife and our daughter. My mother lives with us, too.

I never did find Lan Yu's courage. The courage I would have needed to face—really face—my gay identity. But even if I had, it wouldn't have mattered anyway since my heart died long ago. As for my young wife, I treat her well and do my best to take care of her, but I'll never be able to love her. Not like I loved Lan Yu.

My wife is a devout Christian and often tries to share the gospel with me. I just laugh it off. I've always been an atheist, and besides, I know God thinks homosexuals like me aren't worthy of his glory. But about six months ago, something happened that I'll never forget.

It was Christmas Eve and my wife dragged me off to church as usual. Standing there, surrounded by congregants and the solemn sound of hymns rising in the air, I suddenly felt that there must be more to this life than the material world. For the first time it seemed to me that after we die, there must be a heaven and there must be a hell. I heard the pastor's long, tedious sermon, but had only one thing on my mind: Where is Lan Yu now?

He must be in heaven, I thought, because when he was in this world he never harmed a living soul. He was so good, so decent, so kind to everyone around him. His only crime was that he loved someone he wasn't supposed to. The world thought his love was ludicrous, sick, degenerate. But I knew it was pure, innocent, eternal.

And me? I won't make it to heaven. Not because I loved another man, but because of the suffering I caused him. Lan Yu is dead now. I can't change that. I can't undo what I've done. All I can do is spend the rest of my life wondering whether his death was a punishment for him, or for me.

All around me, the congregants lowered their heads in prayer as the pastor continued eulogizing the universal love of the heavenly Father. I couldn't hear him clearly, but it didn't matter anyway. I closed my eyes . . .

God, I ask only for one thing, and I beg you to grant it. Wherever you have sent Lan Yu, please let me go there when I leave this world. If he is in heaven, let us be there together, able at last to openly share the love we had for each other in this world. There, I will repay him all that I owe. I will reverse the sorrow that I caused him in this lifetime.

If he is in hell, let me go there, too. Let me stand behind him and place my hands firmly on his shoulders. There, we will suffer hell's torture and fiery torment together. I will have no regrets, and feel no resentment.

A melody rose from the pews, stirring me out of my reverie. Amid the sound of singing churchgoers, my wife turned to look at me, her face frozen in stunned silence when she saw the tears streaming down my cheeks.

It's all warm blue sunshine here in Vancouver. In early autumn there's no trace of the chilly fall winds that howl through the streets of China's northern capital. Even the leaves stay green—just a few golden, dying ones that flutter through the air and land on the lawn outside.

I am sitting in the front yard, my back to the house, watching the horizon as the sun sets on another dying day, thinking with wonder how the end of the day here brings a new one to the other side of the world. I hear the happy, laughing sound of my mother, wife, and daughter behind me. I look at the sky, where the faint rouge of the setting sun lingers on the edge of space and time. Sweet, radiant, beautiful.

Postscript to the Revised Tohan Taiwan Edition*

Bei Tong
Translated by Scott E. Myers

I shot my first roll of film in 1994 in the United States. When I finished the roll, I rushed uptown to a drugstore near Columbia University to have it developed, thinking about how I was going to send the pictures back to my family in China. They were anxiously awaiting my news, and I wanted to tell them that everything here was fine. I pulled the pictures out of the envelope and flipped through them one by one.

"Great shots!" a voice behind me creaked.

I turned my head and saw a person in their seventies speaking to me with a smile.

This is how I met Bob and his wife, Jan. They were the first

*This postscript was originally published in the 2002 Tohan Taiwan version of the novel.

friends I made in America. Bob was a World War II veteran who had served in MacArthur's military command center and fought against the Japanese while stationed in the Philippines. He enjoyed befriending students from Asia, especially young people from mainland China, Taiwan, and South Korea. He didn't like Japanese people. He said the world was changing too quickly, that yesterday's enemies were today's friends, and that yesterday's friends were the adversaries of today.

Bob and Jan had long ago sold their big house in New Jersey and moved into an apartment in New York City's Upper West Side. They had two sons and two grandsons who, one could easily tell, were their greatest riches and source of pride.

For Bob's eightieth birthday, his sons planned a series of surprises. First, the older son arrived from Ohio with his family in tow. Then Bob's seventy-seven-year-old brother arrived from out of state for the party his nephews had planned.

A few months later the family celebrated Jan's eightieth birthday even more grandly than her husband's. The entire affair was organized single-handedly by their younger son, Christopher. Jan's eyes filled with tears as she described the details, and before long she became so choked up that she couldn't speak. I was surprised to discover that in a money-driven capitalist society there existed strong family sentiment after all.

Once when we were chatting, I casually mentioned to Bob and Jan that a friend of mine never went to the hospital, not even if they had a fever, because they couldn't afford health insurance. A few days later Bob and Jan mailed me a check for $300 with a note telling me to give it to my friend. In their letter they wrote that the money had come from an organization devoted to helping people in need.

By 1996 life was getting better and better. Bob and Jan called to convey their good wishes, then told me with great excitement that they had gotten a computer for their home. They also invited me to their place for dinner.

"Chris helped us get it and showed us how to use it!" Jan enthused. She was elated.

I knew their son Chris was a computer engineer and that he, too, lived in New York. Bob and Jan hadn't had him until they were in their forties. Each summer, Chris would take his parents to Acadia National Park to vacation and escape the summer heat.

"Jan's already a computer maniac!" Bob laughed.

After dinner, Bob and Jan grabbed a stack of photos and showed me pictures of their sons and grandsons. "This is David and his wife. They just moved to Louisiana. And this is their son Matthew. He studies at UC Berkeley. He's only seventeen and is so smart!"

"This is Chris, he visits us a lot. He's not married, he's gay." Jan raised her head and smiled, and her face beamed with happiness and pride.

I looked at the picture and saw a mature, gentle-looking, handsome man in black.

After a period of good luck, the days of autumn 1998 were the grayest I'd had since coming to the United States. I had no idea where my life was headed. I had tried everything I could, and for the rest, resigned myself to fate. I immersed myself in the world of the Internet: playing chess, chatting online, surfing porn sites.

After reading all the pornographic stories that were out there, I cursed: FXXX! What the hell is this? I knew I could write something better.

And so I threw myself furiously into writing, then posted my writing online. Some readers said they liked it, so I wrote more, and gradually lost track of where I was. Had I created a story or stepped into one? Was this a dream or was it the real world? Was all of this taking place in the bone-chilling cold of early winter in Beijing, or in the late autumn rain of New York? The only thing that was clear to me was that I had profoundly learned the meaning of these five words: forgetting to eat and sleep.

There were people on the Internet who asked, "Is this a true story?" I told them I didn't know how to answer the question. When they pressed me for an answer, I said, "It's pure fiction."

Some people said it was the most moving story they had read in recent years. Others said that the author was probably writing with one hand while masturbating with the other.

Having nearly drowned in the tidal wave of praise and vitriol that followed, I made a vow to myself: I would never write another novel.

It now seems to me that 1998 was the dark night before the sunrise. By the second half of 1999, my eyes had been greeted not only by the rising dawn but by a bright sunlight that shone on all things.

There are still people on the Internet who ask, "Are you Handong? Are you Lan Yu?" I tell them that I'm not Handong. Even less am I Lan Yu.

"Then why does your email address have the name *Lan Yu* in it?"

"Because I like this name, just like you do. Because the story is going to be published as a book with the title *Lan Yu*."

Yesterday I called Bob and Jan to tell them that my novel is going to be published. They offered their congratulations.

"We can't read Chinese, but please send us a copy when it comes out!"

"Of course!" I replied.

From Identity to Social Protest:
The Cultural Politics of Beijing Comrades

Petrus Liu

Owing in no small part to the commercial success of its film adaptation as *Lan Yu*, *Beijing Comrades* is one of the most iconic texts of 1990s China that influenced and, one could say, defined an entire generation. Like other landmarks in the history of modern Chinese queer writing, *Beijing Comrades* encapsulates the worldviews, memories, and angst of a community in the making, bearing dense emotional freight and witness to the changing tides of history.[1] While many of its salient characteristics can be traced back to the specific tradition of writing same-sex desire in Chinese, *Beijing Comrades* also parts company with other queer texts in significant ways: as the current translation of the original text, Tohan version, unpublished chapters, and other fragments show, the novel is a living text, a dynamically evolving dialogue in the making of global gay history. To the extent that the Internet made it possible for the author not only to publish the novel but also to incorporate netizens' feedback with complete anonymity, *Beijing Comrades* can be characterized as an "authorless" text, a vortex of signifiers emanating from different circles across two decades. This aggregated text stands in contrast to queer works that are thematically transgressive but socially legitimated under the strong "aura" (in the Benjaminian sense) of a single author, such as Pai Hsien-yung's *Crystal Boys* and Chu T'ien-wen's *Notes of a Desolate Man*. The suppression of *Beijing Comrades*'s authorial identity—the fact that its author's ambiguous gender identity and sexual orientation did not prevent gay men's enthusiastic reception of the text—raises interesting questions for the cultural politics of gay identity and identification. Indeed, the rise of "cyber literature" (for which there now exist writing contests and professional associations in China) has fundamentally altered the ways that queer people in China articulate their subterranean desires and organize their lives.[2] All of this makes the analysis of *Beijing Comrades* a critical task for understanding global queer cultures.

Queer literature is always a site of identification and a form of social protest. Regardless of their literary merit, queer texts are important cultural artifacts bearing the indelible imprints of a collective struggle for recognition, enfranchisement, and community. Just as each queer text signals a different way of projecting our cathected desires, each offers a different tactic of intervention that must be historicized. A queer text could, for example, combat the stereotypical conflation of AIDS and homosexuality by disarticulating same-sex desire from other forms of sexual stigma, or a text could offer a model of thinking that encourages gay men and women to stand in solidarity with all victims of normative conceptions of sexuality. One could seek acceptance on the basis of the commonality of gay and straight people ("don't ask, don't tell"; "we are just like you except for what we do in the bedroom"), or one could defend alternative configurations of kinship and desire on the basis of diversity ("we're here, we're queer, get used to it"). As an erotic text that does show what gay people do in the bedroom, *Beijing Comrades* embodies and enables a historical resistance to heteronormative assimilation. Bei Tong's straightforward depictions of gay sex are powerfully liberating: no shame, no euphemisms, no apologies. Although the author's effort to officially publish the text in book form in mainland China has not been successful, the circulation of the cyber novel preserves the author's daring style. Scott E. Myers's marvelous translation captures the richness and intensity of *Beijing Comrades*'s sexual vocabulary, putting to rest, once and for all, the myth that gay sex remains an unspeakable topic in the PRC's "traditional" culture.

But in addition to the intricately detailed and candid descriptions of gay sex, what exactly explains the historical influence and success of *Beijing Comrades*? This text follows the emotional roller-coaster ride of the on-off relationship between Handong, an arrogant, wealthy businessman born to high-ranking communist cadres, and Lan Yu, an innocent and hardworking sixteen-year-old student who falls for Handong, not because of, but in spite of the latter's money. The novel portrays love and money as diametrically opposed goals in life, symbolized by Lan Yu's unwavering devotion and Handong's worldly mercantilism. The novel romanticizes the conceptual dichotomy between love and money, presenting Lan Yu as the embodiment of values and emotions found in our "natural" state of being prior to, or at least untainted by, the complications of economics. The drama centers on Handong's struggles between his desire for Lan Yu and his recognition that he cannot "live in a vacuum" without considering his family and career (203). Toward the end of the novel, Handong concludes that "happiness" alone cannot sustain a viable relationship, which is unable to escape factors such as the "bond of marriage" and the "consideration of property, profits, children, or social opinion" (338). For Handong, therefore, a relationship is always also an economic arrangement. Handong leaves Lan Yu again and again for different reasons: his intimacy issues after he and Lan Yu get too close, boredom with a monogamous relationship, social and family pressures to get married, the intervention of medical experts, a plot hatched by Handong's wife and mother to ruin Lan Yu's reputation, and Handong's bouts of internalized homophobia. Circumstances, however, keep bringing Handong back to Lan Yu, who remains loyal. After Handong goes to prison for "bribery, smuggling, [and] illegal pooling of funds" (282), his family and his ex-wife Lin Ping declare him a lost cause, but Lan Yu comes to his rescue by paying an obscenely large sum of money to someone who can pull strings to help Handong.

By constructing Lan Yu as a figure of true love who, despite his background as an impoverished migrant, remains utterly uninterested in monetary gain, the novel appeals to contemporary Beijing gay men's prevalent fear of being associated with or, worse still, mistaken for "money boys."[3] In this sense, Lan Yu is a modern version of Du Shiniang, the well-known prostitute figure in classical Chinese literature who turns out to be not only a pure-hearted person but also an unexpected reservoir of rainy-day funds.

Written in the period of intense neoliberalization in China that brought about, among other things, the birth of a "pink economy" sustained by trendy gay bars, bathhouses, and restaurants, *Beijing Comrades* articulates a cultural fantasy about the separability of love and money in human relations.

The centrality of this fantasy also explains a strange inversion of the fortunes of the humanities in the story. The novel begins by telling readers that Handong majored in Chinese literature in college. This seemingly trivial detail accrues a new layer of significance in the first meeting between the lovers, when Handong tries to make small talk by praising Lan Yu for picking a major that will "make a lot of money," unlike "humanities majors" like himself who are, when in college, "chronically broke" (19). However, the three principal characters who are financially dependent on Handong all have very "practical" skills: Liu Zheng (Handong's old classmate and loyal employee), a physicist by training; Lan Yu, an architecture major; and Lin Ping, an English interpreter with a degree from the fictitious Fifth International Studies University (which could be a stand-in for Beijing International Studies University). As depicted by the novel, a person's chosen subject of study has no bearing on his or her economic standing. The source of Handong's fortune is instead a combination of family connections and shrewd capitalist investments. Lan Yu never once acknowledges Handong's literary training; instead, he repeatedly addresses Handong in the collective: "you businessmen" (123). The novel's emphasis on the disconnect between access to economic resources and the interiority of a person (suggested by various majors and interests) helps to characterize Handong and, by extension, China's postsocialist economic boom as a mirage without substance. Hence, Handong's business crumbles as fast as it begins. By the time Handong ends up in prison, the novel's anticapitalist discourse is finally complete: love perseveres, while money is only ephemeral.

We never find out exactly why Handong goes to prison, only that he has made some enemies in the business world.

However, we may explain the sudden collapse of Handong's business as a representation of the volatility of material wealth in the service of the novel's critique of the postsocialist economy. With Lan Yu's sudden car accident resulting in his death,[4] the novel's ending may serve to highlight the fragility of life and the anguish suffered because of missed opportunities. Bei Tong succeeds in bringing a sense of closure: after Lan Yu's passing, Handong decides to enter a second heterosexual marriage and lead a peaceful life, now living in Vancouver at an emotional distance from his "Beijing story." Both his daughter and second wife remain nameless. Contrasted with the finely detailed sex scenes, scintillating conversations, and textured emotions in the preceding chapters, the blurriness of the story post–Lan Yu succeeds in creating a clear shift in narrative tempo. Clearly, the novel's center of interest remains in Beijing.

The development of Handong's materialism and the vicissitudes of his economic fortune have allegorical dimensions which inspire critic David L. Eng to characterize the film adaptation of this novel as a melodrama of neoliberalism that "places the emergence of homosexual subjectivity ... squarely within . . . a gendered developmentalism."[5] While the novel's anticapitalist themes place it in the context of postreform China, the storyline has an abstract quality that suggests that it could have happened anywhere. The decision to keep the story unanchored appears to be deliberate in comparison to Pai Hsien-yung's *Crystal Boys*, which memorializes certain venues like the New Park in the popular imaginary.[6] By contrast, while Bei Tong's work provokes thinking on the mutual entanglement of modern gay subjectivity and postsocialist development in China, the novel does not produce a distinctive narrative about Beijing. References to Beijing's unique colloquialism (*zan ma*, "our Ma"), political events (Tian'an-men), fictive venues (Lan Yu as a student at "Huada"), and urban problems (traffic, inflation, corruption, income dispar-ity, real estate development, and the influx of migrant work-ers) are incidental to the plot. Many chapters begin with a comment on Beijing's inclement weather, though the primary purpose of these details is not to ground the text in locality but to create a journal-like quality, which, together with the two confessions that conclude the novel (a legal one after Han-dong's arrest and a Christian one after the loss of Lan Yu), place *Beijing Comrades* in a family of first-person confessional gay writing in modern Chinese literature.[7]

The radical generalizability of the novel's setting elevates one of the novel's most unique contributions: its rejection of identity narratives. Whereas both the novel and its film adaptation represent a consolidated, self-affirmative social identity, *Beijing Comrades* never congeals into a predictable coming-out narrative. Unlike *The Wedding Banquet* and other influential queer works from the 1990s, *Beijing Com-rades* is not a melodramatic story centered on a closeted gay man who eventually comes to accept his identity. Polyam-orous in practice, Handong does not believe in labels such as gay and bisexual. The tale concludes with Handong's decision to marry another woman, on the conviction that he will "never . . . find Lan Yu's courage to . . . face . . . [his] gay identity" (364). The word "courage" seems improperly attributed to Lan Yu, for Lan Yu never develops a self-con-scious gay identity. In fact, neither Lan Yu nor Handong defines their relationship in terms of sexual orientation. If Lan Yu never struggles with his sexuality, it is not due to a precocious degree of self-awareness or unparalleled courage that Handong never finds in himself; rather, it is because homosexuality simply appears to be a nonissue for Lan Yu. At the beginning of their sexual relationship, Lan Yu is only sixteen and just arriving from China's northwest. If Handong does not consider himself gay at this point though he has had sex with men, Lan Yu is an even less qualified candidate for the term. Whereas Handong has given the matter some thought, Lan Yu's positive responses to Handong's sexual advances seem to be more of a natural reaction than the expression of a carefully chosen identity. The fact that Lan Yu "always greatly enjoy[s] the pleasures of sex" (295) with Handong can hardly be described as a politically progressive act embodying the "courage to be gay." Rather, Lan Yu's embrace of their relationship can be explained as the result of an absence of identity, a romanticized innocence untainted by the descriptive powers of social categories. Similarly, Lan Yu never develops an identity as a top or a bottom, unlike the drummer Huang Jian. We learn that Lan Yu prefers hand jobs and oral sex to both positions but usually bottoms because it pleases Handong, or sometimes just "to get it over with" (74). By contrast, the act of penetrating the less powerful partner (in terms of age, gender, or status) furnishes an important kernel of Handong's identity: for Handong, the "sexual pleasure" is only "part of it; the real high [is Lan Yu's] unswerving commitment to endure" the pain of anal penetration to please him (56).

Lan Yu's inexperience thus makes him a role model of nonidentity, whereas Handong stands as an example of a failed gay identity. *Beijing Comrades* is therefore a significantly different kind of identity narrative. The resistance to identity politics is perhaps the most remarkable aspect of this text and sets it apart from other examples of late-1990s queer sinophone literature. In *Beijing Comrades*, we encounter an intriguing moment in the history of modern Chinese gay writing that disrupts a unilinear movement toward identity politics.

But although *Beijing Comrades* does not promote positive gay images, easy identification, or catharsis, it is still a richly complex work that captures the zeitgeist of 1990s China in paradoxical ways. Instead of positive or negative gay characters, it offers a complex cultural fantasy of the separability of human connectedness (gay or straight) from economic entanglements. At the same time, the novel also undermines that very fantasy by showing economic developments' deterministic and even devastating effects on the ways in which human beings love and relate to each other. For the provocative questions it asks about the relationship between gay identity and social constraints, *Beijing Comrades* is a refreshing work that covers uncharted territory in Chinese queer writing.

Notes

1. *Beijing Comrades* (*Lan Yu*) emerged during the height of the *tongzhi wenxue* (queer writing) movement of the 1990s, which significantly broadened the cultural archive of gay references in popular culture. In addition to the literary counterparts discussed in this essay, significant cinematic works that prepared the viewers for the success of *Lan Yu*, the film adaptation of the novel, include *The Wedding Banquet* (1993), *Farewell My Concubine* (1993), *Boys?* (1996), *East Palace, West Palace* (1996), *A Queer Story* (1997), and *Happy Together* (1997).
2. For a study of the interactions between new digital media, censorship, and literary production in China, see Hockx 2015.
3. On the prevalence of such perceptions, see Rofel 2010.
4. Versions of this text may vary. Myers treats the epilogue as a final chapter in the current forty-one-chapter translation, with Lan Yu's death in chapter thirty-nine.
5. Eng 2010, 470.

6. See Martin 2003 for a lucid analysis of Pai's New Park in the geography of desire.
7. See Liu 2015 for the development of first-person confessional narratives in modern Chinese queer literature.

Bibliography

Eng, David L. 2010. "The Queer Space of China." *positions* 18 (2): 459–87.

Hockx, Michel. 2015. *Internet Literature in China*. New York: Columbia University Press.

Liu, Petrus. 2015. *Queer Marxism in Two Chinas*. Durham, NC: Duke University Press.

Martin, Fran. 2003. *Situating Sexualities*. Hong Kong: Hong Kong University Press.

Rofel, Lisa. 2010. "The Traffic in Money Boys." *positions* 18 (2): 425–58.

Translator's Acknowledgments

A number of people assisted me in the realization of this project. I am grateful to my literary agent, Jayapriya Vasudevan, who enthusiastically embraced *Beijing Comrades* after I sent it to her to read. I am also grateful to Jennifer Baumgardner at the Feminist Press for her support of the book. In particular I would like to thank my editor, Lauren Hook, for her patience, guidance, and meticulous work on the manuscript, and Kait Heacock for her excellent publicity work. Special thanks are due to Dr. John Balcom, my graduate adviser at the Monterey Institute of International Studies, who was tremendously supportive when I decided to translate the novel for my master's thesis. I am also indebted to Marcus Hu of Strand Releasing and to Zhang Yongning, producer of the film *Lan Yu*, who helped put me in direct contact with Bei Tong when I approached them for help in locating her.

Additionally, a number of individuals shared their ideas, insights, support, and, in many cases, friendship. Clarence Coo, Cui Zi'en, Yali Dai, Fan Popo, Angela L. Gibson, Ted Gideonse, Ziqin Hu, Ivo, Henry Lien, Ma Xiufeng, Vestal McIntyre, Ng Yi-Sheng, Michelle Kathleen O'Kane, Rakesh Satyal, Mikkel Sonne, and Xiaogang Wei: thank you. Thanks also to my parents and brothers for their love and support over the years. Petrus Liu wrote the afterword to this book, and it is that much more enriched because of it.

Most of all I am grateful to Bei Tong, who had the passion, vision, and drive to write this novel; who enthusiastically supported my desire to publish it in English translation; and who patiently answered the many questions I had along the way. Though we have not met face-to-face, we shared many months of correspondence and I have come to regard her as a friend.

The contemporary poet Mu Cao has written of the "cry of a hundred Lan Yus." It is to those Lan Yus, numbering not in hundreds but in millions, that this book is dedicated.

The Feminist Press is a nonprofit educational organization founded to amplify feminist voices. FP publishes classic and new writing from around the world, creates cutting-edge programs, and elevates silenced and marginalized voices in order to support personal transformation and social justice for all people.

See our complete list of books at
feministpress.org

THE FEMINIST PRESS
AT THE CITY UNIVERSITY OF NEW YORK
FEMINISTPRESS.ORG

31192020938880